Praise for

# GINNA GRAY

"One of the most consistently excellent
writers in the genre today."
—*Romantic Times BOOKclub*

"*Pale Moon Rising* is resplendent with
larger-than-life characters and situations.
An entertaining read."
—4****, *Romantic Times BOOKclub*

"Gray manages to keep the pace moving quickly
while also conveying the minutiae of police work in
convincing detail—no mean feat! The characters
are wonderful, especially Casey and her partner."
—*Romantic Times BOOKclub* on *Fatal Flaw*

"This page-turner from a seasoned romance novelist
boils down to deliciously wicked brain candy."
—*Publishers Weekly* on *The Prodigical Daughter*

# GINNA GRAY

# the TROPHY Wife

MIRA

**MIRA**

ISBN 0-7783-2290-4

THE TROPHY WIFE

www.MIRABooks.com

Printed in U.S.A.

To Brad:
My husband, my love, my best friend.

# *One*

She needed a miracle. Fast.

Elizabeth Stanton sat at the desk in the study of her Houston home, a gray stone mansion nestled among huge oak and pine trees in exclusive River Oaks, the "old money" section of town.

Her father, grandfather and all the previous generations of Stanton men as far back as the early 1800s had worked at the mahogany desk.

At five foot four and one hundred and six pounds, Elizabeth was dwarfed by the massive piece of furniture, and the well-worn leather chair seemed to swallow her.

Had she been aware of such things she would have thought the image appropriate: at that moment she felt small and helpless, with no place to turn.

Elizabeth gazed at the financial report that her banker had given her less than an hour before, as though if she stared at the figures long enough they would somehow miraculously change.

After a time she sighed and lowered her head, cupping her forehead with her hand. She had to face it. She was broke. Or as good as. What in God's name was she going to do?

"Damn you, Edward Culpepper. Damn you to hell," she railed through clenched teeth.

At her wit's end, Elizabeth shot to her feet so abruptly the chair rolled back and crashed into the mahogany credenza. At any other time she would have been concerned about possible damage to the family heirloom, but she was so agitated she barely noticed.

She paced the Oriental rug, but after a few aimless circuits of the paneled room she came to a halt in front of the French doors that led out to the side terrace. With her arms crossed over her midriff, she absently massaged her elbows through the sleeves of her teal satin blouse and stared out over the side lawn.

There was nothing much to see at that time of year. A couple of weeks ago, in late October, a "Texas-blue norther" had blown in, and within the space of an hour the temperature had plummeted from a muggy ninety-six to just above freezing. Since then the region had been blasted by one cold front after another.

Outside the French doors, gusting winds tore at the trees, sending showers of oak leaves and pine needles dancing across the lawn. Near freezing temperatures had turned the grass the color of straw. The azalea beds, laid out in fanciful shapes of butterflies and rainbows, were now dormant, the plants stripped down to bare sticks. So were the crepe myrtle and oleander bushes that formed the hedge around the property.

A hard freeze was expected that night, and Dooley Baines, their gardener-handyman, was fighting the wind to cover the tender plants.

Dooley and his wife Gladys, the cook-housekeeper, had worked at the Houston house ever since Elizabeth could remember. Their entire married life they had lived in the three-bedroom apartment above the garage, had raised their two children there and, with the help of Elizabeth's father, had put them both through college. The couple fully expected to continue at their jobs as long as they were able.

Elizabeth watched Dooley, his back bent from years of stoop work, tending his beloved garden, blessedly unaware that his employer, and his secure world, were teetering on the brink of ruin.

Elizabeth's Houston property, and that of most of her neighbors, covered several acres. Over the top of the hedge she could glimpse the slate roof of the Whittingtons' home through the stripped tree branches.

Mimi Whittington was her closest friend, one of only a handful of people on whom Elizabeth knew she could count to stand by her through good times and bad.

And these were definitely bad times.

As though Elizabeth's thoughts had somehow conjured her up, at that moment Mimi stepped through the gap in the hedgerow between their houses and headed for the side terrace.

That gap was the only flaw in Dooley's otherwise picture-perfect garden and the bane of the poor man's existence. Years of her and Mimi squeezing through the hedge had created the hole and worn a trail through the grass. Dooley had fussed and scolded, but in the end he had given up and shaped the gap into a narrow arch and laid a path of stepping-stones from the opening to the side terrace to accommodate the daily foot traffic that occurred whenever Elizabeth was in Houston.

Watching Mimi, Elizabeth had to smile. Her friend scurried along the path in stiletto heels, clutching her ankle-length sable coat tight at her neck. How typical of Mimi to wear fur for an afternoon visit.

Beneath the coat Elizabeth caught glimpses of skintight black leggings and a big shirt in a wild print of purple, gold and black. Her friend's blond hair was being whipped every which way by the wind.

Mimi called to Dooley and waved. Then she looked toward the house and saw Elizabeth standing at the study doors and grinned and waggled her fingers at her.

Elizabeth opened the door when Mimi reached the terrace, and her friend burst into the study on a gust of frigid wind and a cloud of Chanel perfume.

"Laudy, Laudy, Miss Claudie! It's getting' cold out there," she exclaimed in her syrupy East Texas drawl, giving an exaggerated shiver. "I nearly froze my arse off just runnin' over here. I swear to goodness, there's nothin' between us and the North Pole but a barbed-wire fence."

She slipped out of her sable coat, tossed it over the back of one of the fireside chairs as casually as she would have an old rag and fluffed her short platinum hair with both hands, the rows of gold bangles around both wrists clanking. "I declare, that wind destroyed my do. And I went to Mr. André this morning after dance hour. If he could see me now the poor man would have a hissy fit."

Elizabeth stifled a grin and the urge to ask how he would know that Mimi's coiffure was mussed? Currently she wore her hair in one of those spiky, "artfully messy" dos. With Mimi, one never knew from week to week what style she would be sporting or what color her hair would be.

"By the way, don't think that just because you missed dance hour this morning because of business that you don't have to make it up. I'm gonna work you into the ground tomorrow morning."

Elizabeth rolled her eyes. "I figured as much. You old slave driver," she added in feigned annoyance.

For the past twenty-three years, ever since Elizabeth was nine years old, Mimi had given her dance lessons in the attic studio in her home that her late husband had built for her. Mimi liked to give the impression of being languid and spoiled and that was most people's opinion of her. Few knew about those vigorous early-morning dance sessions, which had become a fitness workout for both of them.

"Gotta keep the bod in shape, and dance is a lot more fun than a gym," her friend insisted.

Shivering, Mimi held out both hands to the cheery blaze dancing in the fireplace. Her acrylic nails were long and painted crimson, and every finger, including her thumbs, was adorned with a ring. From her ears hung long, linear diamond earrings that almost brushed the tops of her shoulders and swung and sparkled at the slightest movement of her head.

"Mmm, that feels divine," Mimi purred, turning to warm her backside. She rubbed her rear end with both hands and fixed Elizabeth with a look. "So? How did the meeting with Walter and John go? Please, please, *please* tell me John has found a way to recoup your money and throw that two-timin' snake in the grass in jail where he belongs."

The other woman's ire on her behalf brought a feeble smile to Elizabeth's lips. Though Mimi was ten years her senior, the two of them had been friends almost from the moment they met.

Mimi claimed that they had been friends in previous lives and were destined to be friends forever.

Whatever the reason, most people in their social set were baffled by their friendship. They were about as different as any two women could be.

Elizabeth was quiet and reserved by nature.

Brash, outrageous, flamboyant, unpredictable—those were but a few of the words that people used to describe her

*Ginna Gray*

friend, and Mimi would be the first to admit that she was all of those things and more. A free spirit with a heart of gold, a somewhat bawdy sense of humor and the means to do just exactly as she pleased. She thumbed her nose at convention, and if you didn't like it, tough.

When Horace met her she'd been competing in ballroom dancing competitions and occasionally working as a Las Vegas showgirl.

"The only assets I had were a pretty face and a knockout body," her friend freely admitted with no apology. "So I put them to good use in a place where I could make the most money and not betray my principles or make my dearly departed mama ashamed of me. Dance competitions and the Vegas stage beat dancing in a sleazy strip joint or flipping burgers."

When fifty-two year old Horace Whittington married nineteen-year-old Mimi, to no one's surprise she had been labeled a gold digger by Houston society.

On the surface the match had appeared to be the same old story, a pathetic older man attempting to regain his youth by marrying a young, mercenary female with dollar signs in her eyes.

What few people had realized at the time was that Mimi truly loved her Horace—whom she called "Big Daddy"—with every fiber of her being. And why not? Horace Whittington had been a thoroughly nice man, good natured, honest, loyal and generous with those whom he loved.

He'd also been a handsome devil. Horace had kept himself fit, and at six feet tall, with his shock of silver hair, twinkling blue eyes and tanned craggy face, he'd looked like the Hollywood version of the successful westerner.

There were many in Houston society who would like to snub Mimi, but they didn't dare. The Whittington family was too influential.

"Now that Big Daddy's gone, some of the old biddies would like nothing better than to revoke my membership in the River Oaks Country Club," Mimi had told Elizabeth a short time after Horace's death. "But they don't dare. Not as long as I've got Big Daddy's money.

"You know how the 'committee junkies' are always throwing some hoity-toity ball or other kind of fund-raiser for their current pet charity. Big Daddy used to call them the 'Cause of the Month' events. The Whittington Foundation contributes more than a million dollars every year at those shindigs. The blue bloods may not want me, but they sure as heck want the Whittington money, and they're willing to grit their perfect capped teeth and put up with me to get it.

"Personally, I don't care didly whether I belong to the country club or not. I only keep my membership because I know it irritates the you-know-what out of them to have to rub elbows with a nobody from nowhere."

Elizabeth gently chided her friend for such remarks, but in truth the assessment was not far off the mark.

However, no matter how anyone felt about Mimi personally, eventually even her harshest critics had been forced to admit that the Whittington marriage was a happy one. Horace and his Mimi had been inseparable throughout their twenty-one-year marriage.

For months after his death of a sudden heart attack less than a year ago, Mimi had been inconsolable. That was the only time that Elizabeth had ever known her to cry, and it had broken her heart to see her scrappy friend so despondent.

After a while, though, she had picked herself up and gotten back into the game of life with all the gusto and flair that was uniquely Mimi.

"Big Daddy would not want me to grieve forever," she had proclaimed in her syrupy drawl. "Why, if that man looked down from heaven and saw me weepin' and wailin' and carryin' on, he'd wrangle a pass from St. Pete himself and come down to earth and personally kick my incredibly cute butt up over my shoulders."

And he would have, too, Elizabeth thought. If there was one thing that Horace had wanted above all else, it was for his Mimi to be happy. The same couldn't be said for Elizabeth's marriage.

Other than her attorney, John Fossbinder, and her banker, Walter Monroe, who had also been serving as her financial adviser for the past year, Mimi was the only person who knew the full story of Elizabeth's ex-husband's desertion. Most people in their set assumed that Edward had developed a roving eye and Elizabeth had kicked him out and quietly sought a divorce.

The bare bones of the story was accurate, but the full depth of Edward's betrayal had not yet leaked out. Still, Elizabeth knew it was only a matter of time. You couldn't keep a scandal like the one her ex had created quiet forever. Neither could she keep from selling off family heirlooms and jewelry to keep up with expenses and preserve the appearance that the Stanton fortune was still intact.

Elizabeth gave her friend a helpless look and shook her head. Mimi knew that she had just returned from a meeting with her banker and her attorney. For hours the three of them had discussed her situation and what, if anything, could be done to salvage the Stanton fortune.

"I wish I could tell you that things are looking up, but I can't. Over the past year John has exhausted every avenue that might be even remotely available to me, with no luck. Apparently I have no legal recourse. According to John, what Edward did was unethical, even bordering on criminal. But he was clever. It seems there are no charges that I can bring that will stick. And no way to reclaim my money."

"Unethical, my patootie!" Mimi scoffed. "That bastard robbed you and your aunt blind. The records prove that practically from the day your father died and you inherited his two-thirds of the estate, Edward began siphoning off money from the Stanton holdings. And his sticky fingers were in the till right up until the day that he took off with his little chippie for parts unknown. If that's not a crime, I don't know what is! You ask me, that spineless worm should be tarred and feathered and locked up in the cross-bar hotel for life!"

"I don't know that he's spineless, necessarily." Elizabeth gave her friend a wry look. "He had the guts to rob me of most of my family's money and get away with it. Then run off with my lifelong enemy."

Mimi snorted. "Sugar, that doesn't take strength or character. That just shows what a low-life, cheating thief he is. And you ask me, any man who'd choose Natalie over you has no taste a'tall."

Mimi's vehemence brought another wan smile to Elizabeth's lips. Her friend always carefully avoided any mention of Edward's mistress unless Elizabeth introduced the woman's name into their conversation. She knew that Mimi's silence took extreme willpower; Mimi boiled with anger on her behalf and desperately needed to vent.

"How Edward could so much as look at that woman is beyond me," she railed on. "Natalie Brussard may have money and looks, but she is one nasty piece of work."

"She is that," Elizabeth agreed.

Ever since they had been children, Natalie had harbored an almost pathological envy of Elizabeth. For her part, Elizabeth had never understood why. Natalie's family was wealthy and socially prominent. Growing up, she had enjoyed the same privileges as Elizabeth, attended the same private schools, belonged to the same clubs.

In their senior year of high school, to Elizabeth's embarrassment and Natalie's fury, Elizabeth had been voted most beautiful. The accolade was a meaningless, teenage thing that Elizabeth had dismissed as unimportant, but in hindsight she realized that it was at that point that Natalie's envy had turned to hatred. Why, Elizabeth couldn't fathom. With her dark hair and black eyes, Natalie was a beautiful woman, in a sultry, femme fatale sort of way.

Yet throughout their lives she had always wanted anything Elizabeth had, whether it was a piece of clothing, a car, a part in a school play, whatever. Ever since their early teens Natalie had practically made a career out of trying to steal Elizabeth's boyfriends. With Edward, she'd finally succeeded.

The pain of Edward's desertion and cheating had paralyzed Elizabeth at first, but that blow had been minuscule compared to the shock she received when she filed for divorce and discovered the depth of his perfidy. With the exception of the family farm and the Houston house, her husband had stripped almost bare every asset, every account, every Stanton investment, and transferred the money to a secret Swiss account.

"You mean there's *nothing* John can do? Nothing at all?" Mimi asked, bringing Elizabeth back to the present.

"Apparently not."

"Damn." Mimi sank down on the leather hassock in front of one of the fireside chairs and let out a long sigh. "If that's what he told you it must be true. John's a real barracuda when it comes to looking after his clients' interests. If there was a way, he would've found it."

Elizabeth strolled back to the French doors and resumed her absent contemplation of the scene beyond the panes. With his old peacoat buttoned up to his throat and his stocking cap pulled down low over his ears, Dooley pounded stakes into the ground to secure the tarps over the plants. Over her shoulder, Elizabeth murmured, "The toughest thing is going to be explaining all this to Aunt Talitha."

"You haven't *told* her?"

Elizabeth winced and shook her head. "Just that our investments are down. What else could I do, Mimi? She is eighty years old. This house and Mimosa Landing have been home to her all her life, just as they've been mine. I'm afraid she'll have a heart attack if I tell her how bad things truly are."

"Don't sell her short. Talitha's a tough old bird."

Elizabeth sighed. "The mistake Aunt Talitha and I made was giving Edward full power of attorney over everything but Mimosa Landing and this house. Now that's all we have left."

"Oh, sugar, you *didn't!* When you told me you'd turned everything over to Edward I thought you'd meant he was advising you on your investment portfolio."

"At the time it seemed like the thing to do," Elizabeth explained, watching Dooley work. "I trusted Edward. Why wouldn't I? He was my husband. His parents and mine had been friends for years, and I'd known him all of my life. I had no training or experience in business or finance, but Edward had both. Plus a law degree. It seemed logical that he should take over." Elizabeth shook her head. "He took over, all right."

"Oh, sugar. I do wish you had come to Big Daddy for advice after your papa died. He would've told you the same thing he always told me.

"'Mimi, darlin',' he used to say. 'When I kick the bucket and you've got all my money, you can bet your sweet cheeks that the scallywags will be after it. Just you remember one thing and you'll be okay. Never let anyone else sign the checks.'

"And I haven't," Mimi declared. "Anytime my money

leaves my possession, I'm going to know who it went to and why."

"Yes, well, that's a lesson I've learned the hard way." Elizabeth turned from the French doors and started pacing the room again. "If only Ian had lived," she murmured. "If he had, Edward wouldn't have gotten his hands on the Stanton money and none of this would have happened."

All of his life, Elizabeth's younger brother, Ian, had been groomed to take over management of the family's fortune. No one, including Elizabeth, had seen any need for her to study finance or business in college since Ian would be steward of the family fortune for her generation. The possibility that he would be killed in a head-on collision with a drunk driver at age twenty had never occurred to any of them.

"C'mon, sugar. You don't really believe that, do you? A snake is a snake, whether you find it in the garden or the parlor. Edward may not have gotten away with as much if Ian had lived, but you can bet he'd've found a way to make off with some of your money. *And* he would've cheated. If not with Natalie, with someone else. Because that's what he is, a snooty, pretentious, low-life, untrustworthy son of a bitch."

Elizabeth sighed. "You're right. And wallowing in what-ifs isn't going to help me, either. What is, is, and I'm going to have to find a way to deal with it."

A heavy silence followed as both women pondered the situation. The only sounds were the crackle and pop of the fire, the whistle of the wind under the eaves of the big house and the muffled *thump, thump, thump* of Dooley's hammer.

"Sugar, I hate to see you so worried," Mimi said after a while. "Why don't you let me loan you the money you need to tide you over. You know I've got plenty."

Elizabeth sat down on the hassock facing Mimi and took her friend's hands in hers, her gaze warm and full of appreciation. "Mimi, we've been over this before. You're a dear to offer, but I can't accept. First of all, loaning or borrowing money from a friend is never a good idea.

"*That's* a lesson I learned from my papa. And second, it wouldn't do any good. I've been tiding myself over from month to month by selling off valuables, mostly jewelry. Just last month I sold my great-grandmother Ida's diamond necklace."

"Oh, no. Sugar, you didn't! Not the Stanton diamonds."

Elizabeth nodded. "I had to. But it's like putting a Band-Aid on a sucking chest wound."

"Oh, dear. Are your finances *that* bad? I thought you were just having a cash-flow problem. I had no idea the situation was critical. I mean, the Stanton fortune was so huge!"

"Let me put it this way. At present, my outgoing is more—much more—than my income. The few investments that Edward so kindly left me don't earn enough to cover payroll and expenses every month."

"Oh, sugar," Mimi murmured, squeezing Elizabeth's hands. "I'm so sorry."

"The crazy thing is, technically Aunt Talitha and I are not without assets. I still have this place and Mimosa Landing. For now, at least. For the past four years straight the farm has been operating in the red. One year the crop was poor because of the drought and the next the hurricane wiped us out. Then the grasshoppers came.

"I wasn't too worried until this year, after I'd found out that Edward had stolen almost all of my family's fortune.

"And wouldn't you know, this year's farm expenses have been the highest yet. Our farm equipment is old. One of our harvesters had been on its last legs for years, and we had at least one tractor that was good for nothing but scrap metal.

"Truman managed to keep the harvester patched together and running until this spring, but it's on its last leg. We had no choice but to purchase a new tractor and a new harvester, to the tune of well over a hundred and fifty thousand dollars. And that's a conservative estimate. I had to put up fifty acres of land as collateral before the bank would loan me the money to buy the machinery. It was land that wasn't originally part of Mimosa Landing, but even so, losing any patch of land will be wrenching."

"How close are you to that happening?"

"Too close. A big payment on the note is due next month, and I don't have it."

"Can you scrape enough together to pay the interest? I'm sure Walter would cut you some slack if you could do that."

Elizabeth shook her head. "I don't even know where I'm going to get the money to put in next spring's crop. Or make payroll next week."

"Oh, dear. So…what are you going to do?"

Elizabeth sighed. "I guess I'll have to sell this house. I should be able to get a few million for it. I don't know how long that will last, though. Most people don't realize how much it costs to operate a farm these days. Especially an enormous place like Mimosa Landing."

"Sell this house? You can't do that! Why, I wouldn't know what to do without you here to talk to once in a while!"

"I know. I'll miss you, too, but I don't have much choice. I'm certainly not going to sell the farm. Not so much as one acre. Not as long as I have breath in my body."

The farm had been in Elizabeth's family for almost two hundred years. Each succeeding generation had added to the family's fortune, and over the years their base of wealth had expanded into many areas, but it was the old homestead that Elizabeth valued above all else, as had all of the Stantons before her.

Mimosa Landing was her heritage, her birthright. Generation after generation of Stantons had poured their blood, sweat and tears into that land, and she could not let them down. No matter what other losses she had to endure, she had to hold on to Mimosa Landing.

"Okay, Miss Scarlett," Mimi teased. "I understand how you feel about that farm. But there has to be some way to fix things without selling this house. If you do that, word that you're broke will spread like wildfire."

"I don't care about that. The loss of the money and the lifestyle that comes with it don't matter that much to me. I can do without those things. But I can't bear the thought of losing Mimosa Landing. I can't. I *won't!*"

Elizabeth bit her lower lip, her eyes conveying her fear. "I'll miss seeing you, too, Mimi. You have to know that."

Her gaze swept the elegant, walnut-paneled room. The furniture in the mansion had been passed down through the years, with almost every generation putting their personal mark on the place. Many things, like old Asa's desk, were older than the house itself.

The mansion was big and sturdy and at the same time elegant. For business reasons, ever since her great-grandfather'd had the place built in the early twentieth century her family had divided their time between their Houston home and Mimosa Landing. The estate meant almost as much to Elizabeth as did the farm. "My great-grandfather had this place built when River Oaks was a new neighborhood. It's going to break my heart to sell it.

"But what concerns me even more is what will happen to Dooley and Gladys. They're not old enough to retire, nor do they want to, but I can't be certain that new owners will keep them on, especially given their ages."

"Oh, dear. I hadn't thought of that. I can't imagine this place without Gladys and Dooley."

"I know. They've lived in the apartment over the garage nearly all their adult lives. They consider it their own. I can't bear the thought of them being kicked out."

"Mmm, me neither," Mimi agreed. "Gladys loves this house. She's more protective of the place and all the antiques than you are. And the grounds here are Dooley's pride and joy. It would break his heart if he couldn't putter around with his plants or tinker with something around the place every day. Oh, dear. This is bad."

"And I don't know what to do to fix things. If I don't sell this house I won't be able to meet payroll, or pay taxes."

A knock interrupted their conversation. The door opened and the housekeeper stuck her head inside the room. "Pardon me, Miss Elizabeth, but there's someone here to see you."

"Who is it, Gladys?"

The older woman sniffed and folded her arms beneath her ample bosom. "I've never seen him before," she said with undisguised suspicion.

Gladys prided herself on knowing every member of Houston society by sight, their family tree and every scrap of gossip ever uttered about them. "I asked if you were expecting him and he said no, but that it was important that he speak with you. He says his name is Max Riordan."

"Oooh, yum," Mimi purred.

"Maxwell Riordan?"

"Yes, ma'am. Here's his card," Gladys said, stalking into the room. Everything about the older woman spelled *disapproval,* from her pursed lips and stiff posture to the way her sensible, rubber-soled shoes squeaked on the wood floor. Gladys and Dooley were every bit as protective of Elizabeth as they were of the River Oaks estate. "He doesn't look like a flimflam man, but if you want me to send him away, I will," the housekeeper volunteered.

And she would, too, Elizabeth thought, tempted. She glanced at the card. The visitor was, indeed, Maxwell Riordan.

"No, I'll see him. Show Mr. Riordan into the front parlor, Gladys, and tell him I'll be there shortly. Oh, and bring in a tray of coffee, please."

"Yes, ma'am."

"What on earth does Maxwell Riordan want to see me about?" Elizabeth wondered aloud as the door closed behind the housekeeper.

"That's what *I'd* like to know." Mimi gave Elizabeth a sly look. "What's going on between you and that good-looking hunk? Is there something you haven't told me?"

"Don't be ridiculous. I barely know the man."

Elizabeth had met Maxwell Riordan about a year ago, and a few times since then they'd run into each other at various functions, but they were more acquaintances than friends.

He was someone who was considered to be on the fringes of Houston society, someone who was invited to fund-raisers because of his money, but who wasn't truly part of the social scene.

Elizabeth's conversations with the man had consisted of little more than a greeting and a few words of polite chitchat before moving on. He certainly wasn't someone she would expect to drop by her house for a social visit.

"And I wouldn't call him good-looking," Elizabeth added. "*Dangerous*-looking is more like it."

"Sugar, don't you get it? That's what makes him so gorgeous and sexy. Max Riordan may be a bit rough around the edges, but he's all man." She gave an exaggerated shiver and rubbed her hands up and down her arms. "I declare, just thinkin' about the man gives me goose bumps."

"Mimi Whittington, behave yourself. I swear, since Horace died you've had sex on the brain."

"Maybe so, but I'm not the only one who thinks that man is delicious. I went to a fashion-show luncheon at the club last week and the gals at my table—Trudy, Delia, Blair, Madison, Becca, all of them—were practically drooling over him. There was a lot of speculation about what it would be like to have Max Riordan as a lover."

"Oh, really?" Elizabeth raised an eyebrow. "They'd go to bed with him yet they're not willing to let him join the country club, even though he lives in River Oaks?"

"Isn't that a hoot!" Mimi replied, laughing.

Elizabeth rolled her eyes. "If that's all those girls have to talk about, they have entirely too much time on their hands."

Elizabeth was fairly certain that the speculation had merely been idle talk. The friends whom Mimi mentioned were all basically nice women, but other than golf and tennis, "doing lunch" and attending committee meetings for their various charities, they had little of substance to occupy their lives. Elizabeth was grateful that she had Mimosa Landing to run. The farm took up most of her time.

"Oh, you know how they are," Mimi replied with a wave of her be-ringed hand. "If you can believe the gossips, Max is filthy rich, but he's learning that it takes more than money to be accepted by this hoity-toity bunch. We both know that the only reason I got into the country club was because Big Daddy had money, clout *and* the proper pedigree. And, of course, having your family's support helped a lot, too.

"Unfortunately for Max, no one seems to know anything about him or his family, or where he got his money. There's a rumor that he's spent some time in the Middle East and South America," Mimi confided. "Brud Paine hinted that he may have gotten his start importing drugs."

Elizabeth's eyes widened. "Really?"

"Mmm. But I don't know if there's any truth to that.

You know how jealous Brud is of any man who catches the ladies' eyes. One thing is certain, though. Max doesn't have the polish or sophistication of someone born to money.

"Being an outsider myself, I know what that's like. Lord knows, it took me a year to learn which fork to use and what a finger bowl was for. In addition, you know how the old families around here feel about the nouveau riche."

Elizabeth nodded. She did not believe in class distinction, as did some of her contemporaries. Her great-great-great-grandfather Asa Stanton and his wife had lived in a two-room log cabin with a packed dirt floor when they first homesteaded along the Brazos River. Elizabeth's parents and grandparents had stressed to her and her brother that they were never to forget their family's humble beginnings and to never, *never* look down on someone else because of theirs.

Both Elizabeth's grandfather and her parents had stressed to her and her brother that the lifestyle they had was not an irrevocable birthright but a gift that they enjoyed because of the hard work of every previous generation of Stantons. Her grandfather also stressed that she and Ian owed future generations the same.

"Always remember two things, and you'll be all right in this old world and the next," her father had advised them as children. "The first is, privilege carries with it responsibilities. The second is, never judge a man by his pocketbook, but by his actions."

Elizabeth tried to live by those two tenets. She had voted for Max Riordan's acceptance into the River Oaks Country Club when his name had been submitted to the general membership, but she had to admit that she had not been particularly upset when one of the other members had blackballed him.

Elizabeth could not put her finger on what it was about him

that bothered her, though she could truthfully say it had nothing to do with his family history or the newness of his wealth. Whenever she was around the man, something made her… well…not nervous, exactly, but a bit on edge.

She sighed and stood up. "I guess I'd better go see what he wants. Are you coming?"

Mimi lounged back, elbows bent, her forearms resting on the seat of the leather easy chair behind her, and shook her head. "No, I'll wait here. He came to see you. He might not appreciate me horning in. But when he leaves hurry back and tell me what he said."

With her hand on the doorknob, Elizabeth paused and gave her friend a droll look. "Oh, right. As if you're not going to listen in at the parlor door."

"Who, me?" Widening her brown eyes, Mimi placed her hand on her bosom and blinked, the picture of innocence. "Now, would I do that?"

Chuckling, Elizabeth turned to leave. "Just do me a favor and don't make any noise, okay?"

# *Two*

Max stood at the window with his back to the room, staring out at the Stanton estate. This place made a statement, he thought. A quiet, tasteful, but strong statement—the owners had money, lots of it.

More than that, though, the house and grounds oozed class. And permanence.

And a long family history. Roots that went deep. Like the enormous oaks that dotted the grounds. The trees had probably been there for hundreds of years. Their girths were more than two or three men could span with linked hands.

This, Max thought, was exactly what he'd been striving for all of his life. The sense of having made it, the serenity and belonging that this place exuded.

In the beginning he had believed that those things would come to him through achieving wealth, and he had set his sights on building a massive fortune. He'd reached that goal years ago. Still, that elusive something he yearned for remained just out of his grasp.

Turning away from the window, Max scanned the parlor,

drinking in the quiet elegance and timelessness that was evident everywhere he looked.

He had paid an interior designer a small fortune to decorate his penthouse. Most people thought the place was beautiful, but to Max it had that "showroom" look and feel, as though no one lived there.

In a way, he supposed he didn't, really. The condo, less than a mile from here, was little more than a way station for him, a place to sleep, shower and shave and store the majority of his clothes. He was seldom there for more than a few days at a time.

Whereas this place, for all its grandness, felt like a home. Everything was perfect, right down to the tiniest detail, from the antique furniture, to the Oriental rug, the brocade draperies at the tall windows, the sixteen-foot ceilings rimmed with intricate molding, the crystal candy dish on the coffee table and the knickknacks scattered around. Yet there was not a trace of that sterile feel his condo had.

He heard the *tap-tap* of high heels on the marble floor of the foyer and turned to see Elizabeth Stanton enter the room.

"Mr. Riordan, I'm sorry I kept you waiting," she said with a polite smile.

"No problem." Max gave her a quick, unapologetic once-over as she walked toward him.

Even at home on a blustery autumn afternoon she had a look of elegance about her. Just as he'd expected.

Her shiny, bluish-green blouse exactly matched her eyes and looked terrific with the brown tweed trousers. Simple gold earrings and a gold watch with a brown leather band were her only jewelry.

"Won't you sit down?" she offered, gesturing toward the sofa.

Those times when he'd run into Elizabeth at parties or

other formal occasions she'd worn her hair in some fancy updo, but today the thick mane swung loose around her shoulders. The style was casual, but even he could see that her hair had been expertly cut. It swung forward like a shiny, mahogany silk curtain as she sat down in one of the Queen Anne chairs flanking the fireplace, then swung back when she straightened, every hair settling back into place perfectly.

The sour-faced housekeeper stomped into the room carrying a tray containing a china pot and two matching cups and saucers. She plopped the tray down on the coffee table and straightened, giving him a sharp look before turning to her employer. "Will there be anything else, Miss Elizabeth?"

"No, that's all, Gladys. Thank you."

The older woman sniffed and shot him another look. "If you need me, just call," she said, somehow managing to make the statement sound like a warning.

"I will."

Max watched the old prune stomp out of the room with her back ramrod stiff and close the door behind her with a sharp snap.

"How do you take your coffee, Mr. Riordan?"

"Black."

Elizabeth poured the steaming brew and handed it to him, then poured herself a cup and added a dollop of cream. Settling back in the chair, she took a sip, watching him over the rim. "I must say, I was surprised when Gladys told me you were here and that you needed to speak to me. I can't imagine about what."

"I'll get straight to the point, then." Max didn't believe in shilly-shallying around. Small talk or skirting around an issue was a waste of time and a colossal bore, two things he could not tolerate. When action needed to be taken or something needed to be said, his instinct was to cut to the chase and be done with it. Belatedly, though, it occurred to him that Elizabeth might be put off by his abrupt manner, so he tacked on, "That is, if that's all right with you."

"Please do."

"I'm here because I know about your financial situation."

Until that instant she'd been the picture of graciousness, even though there had been a flicker of unease in her eyes, but at his words she stiffened. Her dainty little chin went up a notch and her expression turned cool.

Leaning forward, she placed her cup and saucer on the coffee table, her movements controlled and careful. She straightened and folded her hands together in her lap. Her greenish-blue eyes sparkled at him like ice on a frosty morning. She looked every inch the patrician lady. "May I ask just how you happen to come by that information? It's supposed to be confidential."

"I'm on the board of directors of your bank."

"Really? Since when?" she asked, her tone clearly revealing that she didn't believe him.

"I've held the position for almost a year. When your ex-husband took off, I was asked to fill his seat on the board. Since I'm a major shareholder in the bank, it wasn't that unusual an occurrence. At the time a notice was sent out to all the bank customers announcing my appointment."

"Oh. I see. I...I must have overlooked it."

Or didn't bother to read it, Max thought. But then, who could blame her? She'd had a lot on her plate during the past year.

"I'm not one of those people who accepts a position on a board and just collects a fat check and sleeps through the meetings," Max continued. "I'm a businessman. I have a vested interest in the financial health of the bank, and I keep close tabs on all my investments. I periodically review all the major accounts."

He paused to take a sip of coffee, then leveled a steady look on her. "Imagine my surprise when I discovered that your account balances were hitting rock bottom. The bank's records show that Edward Culpepper regularly withdrew large sums from all your accounts. Once I'd made that discovery I checked with our investment manager and found out that your stock portfolio has been stripped to bare bones. You're as good as broke."

Though her expression remained neutral, he watched the uneasiness in her eyes deepen.

After a moment of tense silence, she sighed and murmured, "I see. I suppose it was foolish of me, but I'd hoped that I would have more time before my financial situation became common knowledge."

"It hasn't yet, don't worry. No one at the bank knows but Walter Monroe and me."

"I suppose you came to inform me that the bank is going to foreclose on the land that I put up as collateral on the loan I took out last spring?"

Her expression remained cool and composed, but Max could see the fear and desperation in those expressive eyes of hers.

"Not at all," he assured her.

Though she didn't move a muscle other than to blink several times, her relief was almost palpable. After his assurance had completely soaked in, she looked at him with puzzlement. "I don't understand. If you're not here to foreclose on my land, then why are you here?"

"Actually, I came to offer you a possible solution to your situation."

"Really? Why would you do that? You barely know me."

"True. However, I'm not here to make a philanthropic gesture," he said in his usual gruff way. "What I'm offering is a deal that will take care of both of our problems."

He downed the last half of his coffee in one swallow and returned the cup to the tray, then leaned back against the brocade sofa, slung one arm out along the top and fixed her with an unwavering stare.

"I believe that a marriage between us would be mutually beneficial."

For the first time since he'd known her, her poise slipped. Her eyes widened and her jaw dropped. For a moment she was so stunned she could only gape at him. "Wh-what did you just say?" she finally managed in an incredulous voice.

"I know I've shocked you, but if you'll just think about it for a minute I'm sure you'll see the advantages."

"Mr. Riordan, I can't possibly…"

He raised his hand to stop her. "Just hear me out before you say anything, okay?"

After hesitating, she consented with a dazed nod, and Max continued.

"For my part, the old monied families of Houston represent a deep well of potential investment resources that I have been trying to tap into for years, with little success. They're a tight group that doesn't easily accept newcomers. I need your social contacts and the benefit of the unimpeachable social position you hold to get my foot in the door.

"In addition," he went on matter-of-factly, "I'll admit that I've reached the stage in life where I want a home and a permanent partner. I like women and making love to them," he added, as though discussing the weather. "But I don't have the time or the patience for the ritual mating dance that men and women put themselves through—the dating, the wooing, the whole courtship thing. You ask me, it's all a waste of time. I'm a good judge of character and I know what kind of woman I like. From my observance of you, I've come to the conclusion that you would be the perfect wife for me."

He also admired the dignity with which she'd weathered Edward Culpepper's desertion and all the gossip and tittle-tattle that had come afterward, but he saw no reason to bring up such a painful subject. Equally as important, she seemed to him to be a rather distant, self-sufficient woman who would make few demands on his time.

"On the other hand, there are obvious advantages to you. First of all, I will bail you out of your current financial crisis. I am aware that your farm has failed to show a profit for four straight years. I propose to set up a trust large enough to insure that you never lose your farm. I believe you call it Mimosa Grove, or something like that, right?"

"Mimosa Landing," she murmured.

"Right. Anyway, with your permission, I'll also rebuild the Stanton investment portfolio."

Stiffening, Elizabeth blurted out, "Oh, no. I will never again give anyone else control over my family's holdings."

"Nor would I expect you to." He gave her a long, steady look. "I know all about Edward's sneaky maneuvering and misuse of power of attorney. That was your mistake. Never give anyone, and I mean anyone, full power of attorney."

"I know that now."

Noting the bitter edge to her voice, for once Max reined in his urge to ream her out for being so foolish. "What I propose is that I act strictly in an advisory capacity.

"Everything that is yours will remain in your name. Therefore, of necessity, you will have to review and sign every document that in any way alters your holdings. I will merely act as your adviser. I, of course, will keep you and your attorney fully informed on every deal I propose. However, I assure you, the final decision on anything involving Stanton money or holdings will be yours.

"There will, of course, be a prenuptial agreement outlining all the particulars, but that, in a nutshell, is the deal I'm proposing. I'm sure that if you give yourself time to really think about it you'll agree that the marriage would be advantageous to us both." Having stated his case, Max waited for her reply.

Elizabeth stared at him, flabbergasted. She could barely believe that she'd heard him correctly. This man, whom she barely knew, marches into her home and proposes marriage as though it was one of his business deals. Calm as you please, he suggests that they spend the rest of their lives together—intimately—and acts as though the idea was perfectly reasonable and logical? Was he insane?

Apparently not. There he sat, without the least sign of nervousness, watching her in that steady way he had, waiting for a reply.

Maxwell Riordan was an impressive man in any setting. Elizabeth could see why women found him appealing, though he was not truly handsome. His features were too rough hewn and craggy for classic good looks. However, he exuded strength and male vitality. He was the kind of man who would stand out in a roomful of men.

She guessed his height at an inch or two over six feet. He had the broad shoulders and the muscular physique of a man who was, at least at some point in his life, accustomed to hard physical labor. His large, callused hands bore out that assumption.

Though olive-skinned with hair as black as a raven's wing, he had azure-blue eyes that seemed to pierce right through you. A scar bisected his right eyebrow and angled across the bridge of his nose and left cheek. His nose had been broken at least once.

She couldn't fault the way he spoke or dressed. His grammar was correct, although his speech was a bit too gruff and direct for politeness. His clothing was obviously custom-made and tasteful. Yet, for all that, he lacked polish, and there was a definite aura of toughness about the man.

For her taste, he was simply too much—too aggressive, too dangerous, too…too rawly male.

"I see," she finally managed to say. "I must say, Mr. Riordan, you have taken me by surprise. I was curious as to what brought you to see me, but I certainly did not expect this."

"Pardon me if I came across as abrupt. That seems to be a failing of mine, or so people tell me. However, for years I've made my living—and a fortune—by seeing the possibilities and making things happen. As I said before, I don't have the time or the patience for courtship. You captured my attention the first time we met, and since then I've observed you closely."

A tiny shiver rippled down Elizabeth's spine at that revelation. The idea that he'd been watching her all this time was unnerving.

"I've also done a little checking. I know that you were faithful to your ex-husband, that you are liked and admired by all your peers, with the possible exception of Natalie Brussard, that is. I know that you are said to be honest, sweet-tempered and gracious. I also know that your domestic staff at both of your homes—housekeepers, gardeners, farmhands—have all been with you for years. That alone speaks volumes."

"A little checking? It sounds to me as though you've had me investigated," Elizabeth replied with an indignant edge to her voice.

Max shrugged. "I'm a careful man. But don't worry, everything I learned about you was positive. That's one of the things that make me certain that we are suited."

"Really?" Beginning to recover from her initial shock,

Elizabeth stiffened her spine and sat a bit taller. "Let me see if I have this straight. What you're proposing is that I marry you for your money, and you marry me for my social position and contacts. Oh, and for a permanent bed partner. Is that right?"

Not in the least put off by her tone, Max shrugged again. "That about sums it up."

Elizabeth didn't know whether to be amused or indignant. "I see. I'm curious. If I were to agree to this, just how long would you expect such a marriage to last?"

"'Till death do us part.' Isn't that how the vow goes? However, if you'd like we can put a stipulation in our prenuptial agreement that we will review our situation at the end of five years. That should be adequate time for us to know whether or not we can rub along together. And by then I hope to have your investment portfolio healthy again and I should have made inroads into Houston society.

"At that point, if either of us wants out, we'll go our separate ways with no hard feelings. You'll have your trust for the farm and the income from your trust and I will have gained the investors that I want."

"If you have so much money that you can afford to do what you're proposing, why do you need more?" Elizabeth asked.

"It isn't about the money," Max replied. "It stopped being about the money after I made my first couple of million. It's about the game. Putting together deals and making them come to fruition gets into your blood. The profit you make for yourself and others is secondary."

"I see," she murmured, although she didn't. Each generation of her family had worked hard and increased their wealth out of a sense of responsibility to future generations, but Max seemed driven. A workaholic who was addicted to wheeling and dealing.

"I must say, Mr. Riordan, I've received more romantic proposals." Her old friend Wyatt Lassiter, for one, had been proposing to her on an average of once a week for months now.

"Sorry. I'm not the romantic type."

"Ah, but you see, there's the rub. I am. I'm sorry, but—"

"Call me Max," he insisted.

"Very well…Max. I'm afraid I could not possibly marry for the reasons you're proposing."

He gave her another of those long looks he was so good at. It felt as if those intense blue eyes were searing a hole straight into her soul. "I take it you married Edward Culpepper for love?"

"Yes. Yes I did."

"Hmm. Evidently that's not the magic ingredient for success, is it?"

The question hit her like a slap, but she held on to her composure. Barely. "I guess not. Still…marrying for money seems so…so crass."

"Crass? It seems honest, open and mutually beneficial to me. Let me remind you that it has only been in the past hundred years or so that people have married for what they call love.

"For centuries down through time, marriages were arranged for many reasons other than love. Financial or political gain, family alliances, companionship, security, progeny, et cetera. And the practice still thrives in certain parts of the world. Many of those were and are successful unions. If you marry with realistic expectations, you have a good chance for satisfaction with the union, I'd say."

"Satisfaction? What about happiness?"

Max shrugged. "That, too. I expect we'll grow attached to each other as time goes by."

"And if we don't?"

"Then we'll treat each other with mutual respect. One thing I can promise you—I'll never be unfaithful. With me you'll never have to endure the humiliation that Edward put you through. I keep my word."

Max reached into the inside pocket of his suit coat and withdrew a business card and a pen. Scribbling something on the back of the card, he said, "My business numbers are on this card. On the back I'm writing the number of my private line at my office. It rings straight through to my desk. Only a handful of people have it. I'm also giving you my home number and my private cell phone number." He handed the card to her across the top of the coffee table. "Take a few days and think over everything we've discussed, then telephone me with your answer."

I can give you my answer now, Elizabeth thought.

However, she forced a weak smile to her lips and heard herself saying, "Very well."

"Promise me that you'll take your time and really think over all I've said," he repeated, as though he'd read her thoughts.

"I will. I promise." Elizabeth stood up to signal the end of their conversation, leaving Max no choice but to do the same.

"Good. I'll look forward to hearing from you soon."

So cold and unemotional, Elizabeth thought as she walked with him to the front door. To Maxwell Riordan marriage was just another business deal.

When he'd gone Elizabeth closed the door and with a sigh leaned back against the thick mahogany panel and closed her eyes. She felt oddly shaken. What a brash, unpredictable man. When Gladys had announced him, she had been surprised and puzzled as to why he wanted to speak to her, but the last thing she had expected was a marriage proposal.

The double doors that led into the dining room slid open and Mimi burst out into the foyer, giving Elizabeth a start. She had been so stunned by Max's proposal she'd forgotten that her friend was still there and had, in all probability, listened in at the parlor door.

Mimi's wild-eyed look and the first words out of her mouth confirmed that she had, indeed, been eavesdropping.

"Omigod! Marriage! He actually proposed *marriage!* I just about peed my pants when he dropped that bomb! It was all I could do not to march into the room and tell him off. The nerve of that man."

Giving her friend a wry look, Elizabeth pushed away from the door. "Why, Mimi, I thought you said he was a hunk," she tossed over her shoulder as she strolled past the other woman.

Mimi followed, her stiletto heels hammering out an angry staccato, first on the marble of the foyer, then on the hardwood floor of the parlor. "Yes, I said he was a hunk. Because he is. But that doesn't mean I think you should *marry* him!

"Anyway…who the devil does he think he is? The very idea, suggesting that you marry him for his money? And worse, admitting that he only wants to marry you for your social position. And for a convenient lay. I should've walked in and boxed his jaws just for that remark alone.

"Is the man blind or just plain stupid? Doesn't he realize what a smart, sweet and terrific, not to mention beautiful, woman he'd be getting if he were ever lucky enough—God forbid—to get you to the altar?"

"You have to admit, he was honest." Elizabeth sat down in the chair she had vacated just moments before and picked up the coffeepot again. "Would you like some coffee? I can have Gladys bring in another cup."

"No, I don't want any coffee," Mimi snapped. She began

to pace back and forth in front of the fireplace. "I want to know what you're going to do."

"I'm going to do just what I promised that I would do. Give the offer a lot of thought, then call Max with my decision." Elizabeth added her customary dollop of cream to her coffee, stirred it and gave her friend a smile before she took a sip.

Mimi stopped pacing and gaped at Elizabeth. "Surely you're not actually considering saying yes?"

"Why not? Max is rich, he's attractive—in a rough sort of way—and he's willing to bail me out of my financial fix. Sounds like a perfect solution to me. You yourself said that you and the girls at the club have been drooling over him. And you have to admit, he has made a generous offer. I'm not likely to get a deal like that anywhere else."

"Offer! Deal!" Fairly crackling now with outrage, Mimi stood over Elizabeth with her fists planted on her hips. "Have you lost your freakin' mind! We're talking marriage here. Not a corporate merger! How can you even *think* about accepting such a ridiculous proposal?"

Wound tight as a spring, she started pacing again, gesturing wildly with both hands. "The man's practically a stranger, for God's sake! I've heard him described as a wheeler-dealer, an entrepreneur and an investment mogul, but no one seems to know exactly what it is he does. For all we know, he really *could* be a drug dealer or…or…a gangster! He could even be a serial killer. Or…or a hit man for the mob."

Elizabeth laughed. "Honestly, Mimi. What a vivid imagination you have."

It was the first time in months Elizabeth had experienced genuine amusement. The lighthearted sensation that wafted through her was a welcome release from the constant worry that had weighed her down for so long. Thanks to Maxwell

Riordan, she felt as though an iron weight had been lifted from her chest.

Her amusement, however, had the opposite effect on Mimi. Scowling, she stopped in her tracks and snapped, "Dammit, Elizabeth! This is no laughing matter!"

Deciding that she'd teased her friend long enough, Elizabeth relented. "Relax. Of course I'm not going to accept Max's proposal. I was just pulling your leg a little."

Mimi gave her a dubious look. Deciding she was telling the truth, she sank down onto the sofa, kicked off her high heels, stretched her long dancer's legs out across the cushions and, with a dramatic sigh, leaned her head back against the padded arm. "Well, *that's* a relief."

"Mmm." Elizabeth tapped the edge of the card that Max had given her against her pursed lips. "Although, Max did provide me with an answer to my dilemma."

"Oh? What's that?"

"I hadn't thought of marriage as a solution to my problems, but it's really not a bad idea."

As though she'd been shot from a cannon, Mimi popped back up to a sitting position and swung her feet to the floor. "What? Elizabeth Victoria Stanton! I'm shocked."

Elizabeth shrugged. "As Max pointed out, people do marry for all sorts of reasons. He was also right about Edward and me. I was in love with him, and he swore that he loved me, too. Yet he betrayed me, robbed me blind and broke my heart. Maybe I would be better off marrying for practical reasons."

"Oh, sugar, don't say that."

"Why not? It seems to me that if you're honest about everything from the beginning and you both go into the marriage with your eyes wide open, not expecting any more than a loyal helpmate, well then, what would be the harm?"

"The harm would be that you're not being fair to yourself.

What if later on you did meet someone and fall in love? You'd be trapped in a loveless marriage."

Elizabeth shook her head. "That's not going to happen. To tell you the truth, despite what I said to Max about being a romantic, I've lost all faith in love. I had already decided that I would never marry again. That I'd never again trust anyone with my heart—*or* my inheritance.

"However, it's beginning to look as though marrying a rich man is about the only option open to me if I'm going to have any hope of hanging on to Mimosa Landing."

"There *has* to be another way," Mimi said in almost a desperate voice. "There must be *something* else you can do."

"If you can think of something, I'm open to suggestions." She watched her friend's mouth open and close several times as she groped in vain to come up with an alternative. Elizabeth returned her coffee cup and saucer to the table and straightened, fixing Mimi with a wry look. "You see? There is no other way."

"I guess you're right," Mimi replied with a defeated sigh.

"If I have to marry for money to save Mimosa Landing, I prefer that my groom at least be someone I know."

"Do you have someone in mind? Someone besides Max Riordan, that is?"

"Actually, I do. As you know, Wyatt Lassiter has been begging me to marry him."

Mimi groaned.

"What?" Elizabeth demanded. "What's wrong with Wyatt?"

"You mean besides being a pompous ass? And an arrogant, spoiled little rich boy who lives on Mama's and Daddy's money?"

"That's not true. Wyatt has a job," Elizabeth defended.

"Oh, sure, he's *supposed* to be a practicing attorney with

Fossbinder, Lassiter and Drummond, but I doubt that he spends ten hours a week at the law firm. If his daddy wasn't a partner he wouldn't even be on the payroll. I swear, sugar, you have the most abominable taste in men. First Edward, now Wyatt."

"I didn't say that I was attracted to Wyatt," Elizabeth insisted. "I simply think he would be a safe choice for a husband. We're friends. I've known him almost all of my life."

"You'd known Edward all of your life, too. Remember?"

"That's not fair. Where Edward was concerned I was blinded by a foolish, young girl's love. Wyatt knows that I don't feel that way about him. I've made that perfectly clear on numerous occasions, but he claims that he doesn't care. He says that he loves me enough for both of us. He's confident that, given time, I will return his love."

"He would be," Mimi said with a disdainful sniff. "With his ego, he can't imagine that any woman wouldn't swoon at his feet."

"Wyatt is cocky and self-absorbed, but there are worse traits. I know that all of this sounds selfish and one-sided, but if he'll have me, and bail me out of debt, I'll be a good wife to Wyatt. I swear I will."

Mimi knew her well, and Elizabeth could see that her friend had recognized and accepted the determination in her voice. She looked at Elizabeth, her blue eyes limpid with sadness. "I know you will, sugar," she said in an uncharacteristically subdued voice. "I know you will."

# *Three*

"Mr. Lassiter is here to see you, Miss Elizabeth," Gladys announced from the parlor doorway.

Elizabeth's nerves tightened, but she squared her shoulders and drew a deep breath. She'd thought long and hard about her situation for almost a week, and she'd made her decision. This was no time for second thoughts.

"Show him in, please, Gladys."

Gladys nodded, and seconds later Elizabeth's old friend, Wyatt Lassiter, came striding into the parlor.

"Elizabeth, sweetheart, I was delighted to get your message. Although, I was going to take a chance that you hadn't returned to Mimosa Landing yet and drop by today, anyway." He held both of his hands out to her, and when she gripped them he pulled her to him and kissed her cheek. "You look gorgeous, as always," he said, stepping back to survey her from head to toe.

"Thank you." Elizabeth pulled her hands free, experiencing a vague uneasiness that Wyatt's nearness had generated not one iota of reaction in her. Not attraction, not revulsion, not contentment. Nothing.

"Won't you sit down?" She gestured toward one of the sofas sitting at right angles to the fireplace.

In that fussy way he had, Wyatt carefully hitched up his pant legs and sat down, then straightened the creases in the material just so. Elizabeth sat down in her favorite of the two Queen Anne chairs that flanked the hearth. "Ah, here's Gladys with our coffee," she said, grateful for the small interruption.

The older woman fussed with the tray and exchanged a few polite words with Wyatt. Elizabeth used the lull to give her guest a curious once-over. Why wasn't she attracted to him?

He was nice-looking, in an aristocratic sort of way. He was considered quite a catch among their social set.

Though thirty-nine and quite the ladies' man, Wyatt had never been married. His blond hair was going a bit thin on top, but expert styling hid that for the most part. Just as good tailoring helped to disguise that, like his father, Henry, he was getting a bit fleshy with age, especially around the midsection. Despite those physical flaws, he was still an attractive man. An attractive, very wealthy man.

Maybe she'd never been attracted to Wyatt because he was ten years her senior, and until recently, she had not thought of him as a contemporary. Or maybe she had simply known him too long to think of him in romantic terms. Long familiarity had certainly dulled the romance in her marriage to Edward.

What did it matter? If Wyatt never aroused so much as a flicker of passion in her, so what? That part of her marriage to Edward hadn't been all that exciting, either. She and Wyatt had a lot in common and they were old friends. She was confident that they could get along well as husband and wife.

*Who are you trying to convince, the rest of the world or*

yourself? a little voice in her head prodded, but Elizabeth pushed it aside.

She and Wyatt would have to sign a prenuptial agreement, of course. Max Riordan had the right idea there.

Elizabeth poured the coffee, taking her time about the simple task, but when Gladys left and they were comfortably settled she knew she could stall no longer.

"I know you're wondering what it is that I want to talk to you about."

Wyatt took a sip of coffee, then gave her one of his most charming smiles. "I'm happy for any excuse to see you."

"Thank you." Elizabeth stared down at the shiny surface of her coffee, as though she would find courage there. Finally she drew a deep breath and looked up, straight into Wyatt's hazel eyes. "I was wondering if you still want to marry me?"

His face lit up. "Of course I do." He put the cup and saucer down on the coffee table and sat forward on the sofa, his expression eager. "Does this mean that you've decided to accept my proposal?"

"Possibly."

"Oh, sweetheart, you've just made me the happiest man on earth." Wyatt started to stand up, but she stopped him with a raised hand.

"Wait. Don't say anything yet. Before I say yes, there is something I have to tell you."

He sat back, an amused smile on his face. "All right. But whatever it is, it won't make any difference, I assure you."

"Hear me out before you commit yourself. Okay?"

"All right."

"First of all, I want you to know that I'm fond of you, but I'm not in love with you. I know I've told you that before, but I want to be certain that you understand that."

"I'm not worried. Love will come later. As I said before, I love you enough for both of us."

"I also have to be honest with you about…about my financial situation."

For the first time since he walked into the room, Wyatt's expression turned somber. "What do you mean?"

"It isn't common knowledge yet, although I'm certain it will be before long, but I've recently discovered that, over a period of years, Edward systematically raided all the Stanton holdings and transferred the money to his private Swiss account."

"*What?* Why that sorry…" Wyatt clenched his jaw, and his face worked with anger. "I shouldn't be surprised, I suppose. I never did like the man, especially after he stole you right out from under my nose the way he did."

"Pardon?" Confused and diverted by the statement, Elizabeth gaped at him. "What do you mean, he 'stole' me?"

"Sweetheart, I picked you out as the future Mrs. Wyatt Lassiter years ago, when you were just a little girl. Why do you think I've stayed single so long? I was waiting for you to grow up so that I could court you. Before I had a chance, you were engaged to Edward. Believe me, I was furious. Then last year I was equally delighted when he ran out on you. Although, of course, I regretted that he'd hurt you," he hurried to amend. "But I had no idea that he'd robbed you as well. The bastard."

Blinking, Elizabeth stared at him, at a loss for words. Was she supposed to be flattered that he had singled her out from all the females he knew? Like cutting a cow from the herd? Without any consideration for her feelings on the matter?

Wyatt stood up and started pacing the room. "How much damage did Edward do?"

"A lot," Elizabeth said, watching for his reaction. "Except

for this house and Mimosa Landing, the Stanton fortune is all but wiped out."

Stopping short, Wyatt stared at her. She could almost swear that he had turned pale. "Good Lord. *That* much? Surely you've consulted with John. What's being done to re-coup your money?"

"At the moment, nothing. John tried, but Edward was too clever. Apparently there is no legal recourse open to me."

Wyatt looked as though he'd taken a blow to the solar plexus. It was the first time she'd ever seen him rattled. He raked his fingers through his hair, unconsciously mussing his careful do.

"I see. Well that, uh…that changes the picture quite a bit, doesn't it?"

"I suppose it does," Elizabeth replied. Her gaze followed his restless pacing back and forth across the room. In deep thought, he frowned and pounded one fist into the palm of his other hand. It was not the reaction she had hoped he would have. An uneasy sensation began to niggle at her. "From the way you're taking this, I have to assume that my financial situation nullifies your proposal."

He winced at that. Sitting down at the end of the sofa, as close to her as he could get, he leaned forward and took one of her hands in his. "Elizabeth, sweetheart, you have to know that I'm crazy about you. And that I'd give almost anything if I could make you my wife."

Elizabeth cocked one eyebrow. "I think I hear a 'but' coming."

Wyatt sighed and gave her a regretful look. "Please understand. I have to think of my family. I'm expected to marry well. Every Lassiter is, male or female. That means I must marry someone with impeccable breeding, social posi-tion…and wealth. You, of course, meet the first two criteria with flying colors. No family in Texas is more respected than the Stantons. However, my family would never tolerate me marrying someone who would not bring additional wealth to the Lassiter holdings."

"I see." Elizabeth withdrew her hand from his. "Then it appears that we have nothing left to discuss."

"Well…not necessarily. Let's look at all our options before we give up. You could probably get a couple of million for this place, although I was planning on making this our home. On the other hand, Mimosa Landing is a virtual gold mine. Large parcels of land like that along the Brazos River are in short supply in today's world. If you'd be willing to sign over the farm to me, say…as sort of a dowry, I think I could convince my family to accept a marriage between us."

An ironic little smile tipped up the corners of Elizabeth's mouth. "Really? How generous of them. However, that's not going to happen."

"But, sweetheart, it's the perfect solution."

"For you, maybe. I'm sorry, Wyatt. I've already lost most of my assets by turning control of them over to someone else. That's a mistake I won't make again."

He sat back with an affronted expression. "Are you saying that you don't trust me? I am *not* Edward Culpepper, you know."

"True. But that land has been in my family for more than a hundred and eighty years. Stantons have poured their lives into that farm. I have no intention of relinquishing ownership or control of so much as an acre of the place. Whatever it takes, whatever I have to do, Mimosa Landing will remain in Stanton hands."

Wyatt's mouth compressed into a grim line. "Really, Elizabeth. I credited you with more common sense than this. You're romanticizing that farm. It's just land. Not some sort of shrine to your ancestors. If your finances are in the deplorable shape that you say, you have to be practical."

Elizabeth cocked her head to one side and studied him for a long moment. Why hadn't she seen it before? He wanted Mimosa Landing. And he was willing to marry her to get it.

"You're right," she agreed finally. "Practicality is called for in this situation. I must do what I have to do."

Wyatt looked relieved. "Good. When I tell my dad that you'll be signing over Mimosa Landing to me, I'm sure he'll have no problem with the marriage." He reached across the space between them and patted her knee. "I knew that I could count on you to be sensible."

"No, you misunderstand me. You and I won't be getting married."

"But you just said—"

"I said I would be practical. And I will. But on my own terms."

"Elizabeth. Sweetheart, listen to me…"

Wyatt did his best to get her to change her mind. He cajoled and reasoned and pleaded. Several times he came close to losing his temper. Through it all Elizabeth calmly but adamantly stuck to her refusal.

As she listened to Wyatt it occurred to her that even had she not already made up her mind, his condescending tone would have driven her to refuse him. She'd never noticed before, but he spoke to her as though she were a not-too-bright child in need of his guidance.

Finally, tired of the endless discussion, she stood up and announced, "I'm sorry, Wyatt, but you'll have to excuse me. I have some calls to make."

"Very well. Perhaps it would be best if I left you to think things over," he arrogantly told her while she saw him to the door. "I'm certain that when you're thinking clearly you'll change your mind."

Elizabeth merely smiled. Closing the door behind him, she leaned her forehead against the thick mahogany panel and sighed. Oddly, she felt almost weak with relief.

Straightening, she returned to the parlor, deep in thought, and through one of the tall windows she watched Wyatt climb into his Mercedes and drive away down the long drive.

The nerve of the man. Did he really think she was so dim-witted that she would *give* him Mimosa Landing? Not on your life.

Although…she supposed she couldn't truly take offense. After all, her reason for accepting Wyatt's proposal had been financial. She couldn't very well fault him for having the same motive.

Except that he claimed to love her.

Elizabeth sighed again. No matter. She knew what she had to do.

She marched from the parlor and down the long central hallway to the study. Sitting at the desk, she picked up the telephone and punched Mimi's number on the speed dial. Her friend answered on the first ring.

"Hi, sugar. What's up?"

"You sound groggy. I hope I didn't wake you." Most days Mimi retired to her boudoir after lunch for a short beauty nap.

"No, I was just lyin' here readin' a fashion magazine. Tiffany's has an ad in *Glamour* showin' a gorgeous diamond pin. Sweetie, if I'm lyin' I'm dyin', it'll make you drool. I was thinkin' about flyin' up to New York for the weekend to have a look at it. Brooches are gonna be very big this season. I thought maybe you'd like to go with me. We could take in a play and do some serious shoppin'. What do you think?"

"Sorry, I can't."

"If it's the cost, the trip will be my treat."

"No, it's not that. Well…not entirely. Listen, Mimi, I need a favor."

"Sugar, you know you can count on me."

"I have a couple of questions for you," Elizabeth said.

"Shoot."

"First of all, is your offer of a loan still good?"

"You betcha. Whatever you need."

"Good. My second question is, do you know of a really good private detective?"

She could sense the instant change in Mimi's demeanor. She could almost picture her friend languidly lying on the brocade chaise in her bedroom, then jerking to attention, swinging her long legs over the side and sitting forward, her ears perked up like a bird dog on point.

"Who're you havin' investigated?"

"Max Riordan. I'm thinking about accepting his proposal."

"*What?* You can't be serious! You don't know anything about the man."

"That's why I want to borrow money to hire a private detective. I want to check him out before I make my final decision."

"We need to talk about this. Give me ten minutes to throw some clothes on and I'll be right over."

In slightly over five minutes, Mimi burst into the study through the French doors, her hair standing on end and wearing not a speck of makeup, which spoke volumes about the depth of her concern.

"Now, what is this about Maxwell? You can't marry a man we know nothing about."

Elizabeth made an ironic little sound and shrugged her shoulders. "I'm beginning to wonder if we ever really *know* anyone."

She told her friend about her meeting with Wyatt and his disappointing reaction.

"You have to admit, if I'm going to marry for reasons other than love, all things considered, Max Riordan's proposition is looking better and better. At least a marriage between us would be mutually beneficial. I wouldn't be made to feel like some simpering damsel in distress in need of rescuing."

"Well…put that way, Max's offer *is* more appealing than Wyatt's. But I hate to even think about you in a loveless marriage. I mean, sweetie, let's face it. Men are difficult enough to live with when you adore them. God forbid you should be tied to one you don't give two hoots and a holler about."

"If you can think of a better solution, I'm all ears."

Mimi grimaced. "Damn. I wish I could."

It took the investigator Elizabeth hired, a retired HPD detective by the name of Donald Summers, barely a week to conduct a thorough background report on Max.

In his late fifties, Mr. Summers was a big man with salt-and-pepper hair, a broad, lined face and gentle eyes. Though his size was intimidating, he inspired trust with his solid, steady manner.

Mr. Summers and one of his old police buddies had set up their own investigative agency after retiring from the force, and they had a reputation for being thorough, honest and discreet.

According to Mimi, their agency had done work for several people she knew, mostly gathering evidence in divorce cases, or doing preemployment background checks.

"This turned out to be an easy job," Mr. Summers related, while both he and Elizabeth scanned copies of his typed report. "Your Mr. Riordan's life is pretty much an open book. One that reads like the American success story.

"He conducts his business in a straightforward manner—no dummy companies, no under-the-table deals, no shady business of any kind that I could find. And believe me, I dug deep, but there was nothing to find.

"Among the people with whom he does business he has a reputation as a straight shooter. Apparently he's short on tact and patience, drives a hard bargain and he's demanding, but he's also fair.

"His fortune, as you can see by the numbers listed on page four, is enormous. It consists of stocks, real estate, oil leases, outright ownership of several businesses and factories, plus he owns a large chunk of a pharmaceutical company, a quarter interest in a shipping line and several other ventures. They're all listed in the report. He's an extremely wealthy, self-made man with a sterling reputation and a first-rate credit history. All the bankers and businessmen who know him seem to regard him with awe. They all agree that when it comes to business and finance he's a genius.

"As for his personal background, it's strictly blue-collar. Mr. Riordan had what I guess you could call a nomadic kind of haphazard childhood. His father was an oil-field worker, what's known in the oil business as a tool-pusher. His mother was always a homemaker. The old man worked on oil rigs all over the world and dragged his wife and son along with him.

"Except for a four-year hitch in the Marine Corp, from his mid-teens through his mid-twenties, Max himself spent his summers in the oil fields working as a roustabout. He used that money, along with some scholarships, to put himself through college. State schools. He earned double degrees from Texas Tech in petroleum engineering and finance. Throughout his college years he was on the dean's list. He also earned a master's in business from Stanford.

"His father died about ten years ago. He's on excellent terms with his mother and supports her in a very comfortable style. She lives in one of those plush, high-toned assisted living communities for wealthy seniors. Her name is Iona Belle Riordan. She has never remarried."

Mr. Summers closed his copy of the report. "All in all, I'd say he's a decent guy. I'd trust him. In fact, I wouldn't mind getting some stock tips from him. I hope this report tells you what you wanted to know."

"Yes. Yes, it has. Thank you, Mr. Summers."

After showing the detective out, Elizabeth marched into the study, found Max's business card and dialed his private number before she could change her mind. He answered on the first ring.

"Yeah," he barked.

Elizabeth jumped at his harsh tone and almost hung up. She was shaking, she realized. Annoyed with herself, she squared her shoulders. "Max. This is Elizabeth Stanton. I've…I've thought over everything we talked about and…and I've decided to accept your proposal."

There was a moment of silence. Then, his voice softening fractionally, Max said, "I'll be right there."

"You'll be right where?"

Sitting in front of Max's massive desk, Troy Ellerbee, his right-hand man, scowled at him as he hung up the telephone and stood up. "You can't leave. Have you forgotten? We have a meeting with Dewitt Scarborough and his attorney coming up in—" Troy shot back his shirt cuff and glanced at his wristwatch "—two hours and forty-four minutes."

"On my way out I'll get Carly to reschedule the meeting. This is more important," Max replied absently. He went into his adjoining private bathroom to check his appearance in the mirror. Troy followed. After rebuttoning his shirt collar, Max cinched up his tie and ran a comb through his hair.

"What do you mean, more important?" Troy demanded from the doorway. "What could be more important than the Scarborough deal? We've been working on old man Scarborough for more than a year to sell us that land."

Brushing past his assistant, Max returned to his office and retrieved his overcoat from the closet and slipped into it.

"Dammit, Max, are you listening to me? If you reschedule at the last minute, old man Scarborough may back out of the deal. You know what a curmudgeon he is. For Pete's sake! What is so important that you'd risk that?"

"I'm getting married."

"That's no reason to—" Troy stopped short, his eyes widening. "What? What did you just say?"

"I said, I'm getting married." Oblivious to his assistant's agitation, Max patted the pockets of his overcoat. Where the devil had he put that ring? Frowning, he thought for a moment, then snapped his fingers. Right. The safe.

He marched across to the other side of the office, opened out the hinged oil painting that hid the safe and proceeded to twirl the combination dial. Again, Troy followed right on his heels.

"You're getting married? Since when? And to whom? When did this happen? I didn't even know you were seeing anyone."

Max pulled the black velvet jeweler's box from the safe and placed it in the inside pocket of his suit coat. Next, he removed a folded legal document, stuffed it into the same pocket, then closed and locked the safe and returned the oil painting to its usual position. "I'm marrying Elizabeth Stanton. Tonight, I hope. If her schedule permits."

"*Elizabeth Stanton!* Good grief, man! Have you lost your mind?"

"Why are you so shocked? You're the one who told me that the only way I was going to break into Houston society and tap into the old monied investors was to marry a trophy wife. One of their own. Someone with a mile-long pedigree. Elizabeth fits those prerequisites to a tee."

"Good Lord, man, I never thought you'd take me seriously. I was only kidding around!"

"I know that. But the more I thought about it the more I realized it was an excellent idea. These people are a tight group, particularly the decedents of the original Texas 'Three Hundred,' who came here with Stephen F. Austin. They tend to close ranks against newcomers. Having Elizabeth as my wife will open doors—and hopefully some deep coffers for me."

"But marriage? Damn, Max. How long do you think the marriage will last once she realizes that you married her for her contacts?"

"She already knows that. I laid it all out for her."

Troy looked dumbfounded. "And she's okay with that?"

"Why wouldn't she be?" Max headed for the door. "Our marriage will be a mutually beneficial arrangement. Thanks to her ex-husband, Elizabeth is in financial trouble. She's marrying me for my money and I'm marrying her for her social position and contacts. We're both going into this with our eyes wide open.

"Now, if you'll excuse me, I have to go meet with her and work out the last-minute arrangements."

At the door Max paused and looked back at Troy, who stood staring after him with his mouth agape. "Stand by, will you? I may need you to act as best man."

"Sure. Right. Whatever you say," Troy mumbled.

\* \* \*

Elizabeth had not expected Max to drop everything and come over. She replaced the receiver and looked around in a panic. It wouldn't take him long to get there. His office in Greenway Plaza wasn't far from River Oaks.

She went in search of Gladys and told her that she was expecting Mr. Riordan momentarily, then hurried upstairs to powder her nose and gather her composure.

Fifteen minutes later when she came back downstairs Max was in the parlor, standing in front of the fireplace, staring at the oil painting over the mantelpiece. He glanced over his shoulder at her as she entered the room and nodded toward the painting. "One of your family?"

"Yes. That's my great-great-grandmother, Ida Stanton."

"Those are beautiful jewels she's wearing."

"Thank you." Elizabeth looked up at the painting in wistful silence. Ida had sat for the portrait wearing a formal evening gown of dark wine silk trimmed in ecru lace in the mid-nineteenth-century Victorian style. In her ears and around her neck were the exquisite gold-and-diamond earrings and necklace that had become known as the Stanton Diamonds.

"My great-great-great-grandfather, Asa Stanton, had the set made for his wife, Camille, for their twenty-fifth anniversary. She gave them to their son Jonathon to give to his bride, Ida O'Keefe, on their wedding day. They've been passed down from generation to generation ever since."

"So they're family heirlooms. I look forward to seeing them on you someday."

"Yes…well, I'm afraid that's not going to happen. I had to sell the set last spring in order to meet payroll and purchase a new harvester for Mimosa Landing."

Max raised his eyebrows at that, but to Elizabeth's vast relief he didn't question her decision. Parting with the Stanton diamonds had been wrenching enough without rehashing the matter.

"Won't you have a seat," she invited, gesturing toward the sofa. She sat down in her favorite chair and folded her hands together in her lap. "I really didn't expect you to drop everything and rush right over."

"No problem. I'd like to get this done as quickly as possible. The next few weeks are going to be very busy for me. On the chance that you would accept my proposal, I had my attorney draw up a prenuptial agreement over a week ago." He pulled the legal document from his pocket and handed it to her. "If you can contact your attorney and have him okay the agreement today, we could sign it and fly to Las Vegas and be married tonight."

Stunned, Elizabeth looked from Max to the document she held in her hand, then back to Max. She blinked several times, at a loss for words. The man was like a steamroller. No small talk, no finesse, no subtlety. Just wham-bam, here's the deal, let's get on with it.

"You must be joking," she managed finally to say in an appalled voice. "Las Vegas? There is no way I will take my vows in some sleazy marriage mill in Las Vegas. I would never do anything so…so tacky."

"I hope you're not thinking of staging one of those ritzy society weddings that take a year to arrange," Max countered. "Because it isn't going to happen. I don't have the time or the patience for all that hoopla."

"No, of course I'm not considering a formal wedding. Under the circumstances, that wouldn't be appropriate, either. However, if we're going to do this, I insist that we do it with some degree of decorum. I think we should have a small, tasteful ceremony, either here or at Mimosa Landing, with our families and closest friend as witnesses.

"Believe me, when word of our marriage gets out, there is going to be plenty of gossip without adding fuel to the fire by doing something so tasteless as getting married in Vegas."

"Hmm. I suppose you're right. But I don't want to drag this out. How long will it take to put together the kind of ceremony you're suggesting?"

"Well, first we'd have to get together with our attorneys and work out the prenuptial agreement. Then we have to get blood tests and a license. Make arrangements with my minister to perform the ceremony. Call the people we want to attend and invite them. Arrange for the flowers and a small buffet. Oh, yes, and we'll need to buy rings."

"Oh, yeah. I almost forgot." Max reached into the inside pocket of his coat and withdrew a small jeweler's box. "I picked this up last week. The jeweler at Tiffany's assured me it was your size." He tossed the box to her, and Elizabeth caught it reflexively.

"What...?"

"It's an engagement ring. Go ahead. Open it."

"An engagement ring?" Elizabeth's chin tilted up at a haughty angle. "Were you so certain that I'd say yes?"

Max shrugged. "I find it pays to approach every transaction with a positive attitude. Anyway, the jeweler said I had thirty days to return it."

"I see." Looking down at the box, Elizabeth snapped it open and sucked in a sharp breath. "Oh, my word." Nestled in the blue velvet was a magnificent, glittering solitaire diamond ring. The stone was large, but the elegant simplicity of the gold Tiffany-style setting kept it from being ostentatious. Elizabeth hadn't given any thought to rings, but even if she had, she would not have expected Max to present her with an engagement ring. Their marriage didn't seem to warrant one.

However, she had to admit, if she had picked out the ring

herself she could not have found one more perfectly suited to her taste. It was so lovely she could only stare at it, speechless.

"It's just two carats," Max said when the awkward silence stretched out. "I looked at bigger stones, but they seemed gaudy to me. But if you don't like it you can exchange it for a bigger diamond or a different ring, if you want."

"Oh, no. No. It's beautiful. Absolutely perfect." She put the ring on her finger and looked up at Max with a hesitant smile. "Thank you."

She halfway expected him to respond with a token kiss on the cheek or at the very least a tender word or two. But Max merely replied, "No problem."

For heaven's sake, she thought. They'd just gotten engaged. He'd presented her with an absurdly expensive ring. Within a few days they were going to be married and spend the rest of their lives together. And all he had to say was "no problem." Did the man even *have* a softer side?

"I'll also have my attorney set up the Mimosa Landing trust." Max pulled out his PDA and punched a few buttons with the stylus. "Let's see, this is Monday. We should be able to get all that done by the end of the week. Which means we could get married on Saturday. How does that work for you?"

"You mean this *coming* Saturday?" Elizabeth said in a squeaky voice.

"Yes. I don't see any reason to delay, do you?"

"Well…no. I suppose not. I just…didn't expect things to move quite so rapidly."

"Fine, then. Saturday it is. If it's all right with you, we'll fly to New York for a short honeymoon. I have some business there that I need to take care of next week, anyway.

"Now, why don't you give your attorney a buzz and see if he can see us this afternoon. If he can, tell him to meet us at my office in Greenway Plaza as soon as possible. I've already put my attorney on notice. He's waiting to hear from me.

"As soon as we get the prenup hammered out and signed, you and I will go get the blood tests and get the ball rolling."

# *Four*

There hours later, sitting in Max's plush Greenway Plaza office, Elizabeth felt as though she were being swept along by a force over which she had no control.

Her lips twitched in a sardonic smile. A force by the name of Maxwell Riordan.

She wouldn't necessarily describe Max as domineering. He did frequently ask for her opinion or preference and her wishes seemed to matter to him. However, he was a decisive, forceful, take-charge kind of man. He exuded authority and strength. Watching him in operation was awe-inspiring.

When she'd called John and explained that she and Max were getting married, her attorney had been appalled. John Fossbinder was no fool; he knew exactly why she was marrying Max without her having to tell him. He heartily disapproved and had tried to talk her out of going ahead with the plan.

Listening to her end of the conversation, Max had figured out what was going on and took the receiver out of her hand before she could comply. In less than a minute her attorney had agreed to meet them at Max's office.

When Elizabeth and Max arrived there, John was waiting for them along with Max's attorney, Harry Ackerman.

Mr. Ackerman, a pleasant man of about fifty, wore thick wire-rimmed glasses that gave him an owlish look. It took only a moment for Elizabeth to peg him as one of those men so intent on his job that he gave no thought to such mundane things as grooming. Consequently he appeared perpetually disheveled.

His stained tie sat askew, the tips of his shirt collar curled up and his glasses were in such dire need of cleaning Elizabeth was amazed that he could see through them at all. At some point he had run his fingers through his thinning hair and the sparse strands stuck straight up in the front.

His wife probably picked out his clothes, Elizabeth thought. And tied his ties and sent him out into the world each morning looking tidy, and that was the last thought he gave to his appearance.

In stark contrast, her attorney looked as though he'd just stepped out of GQ magazine.

Tall and lean, with every silver hair in place, John Fossbinder looked every inch the sophisticated, learned gentleman that he was in his Brooks Brothers suit, crisp white shirt and tasteful silk paisley tie.

As soon as the introductions were made and they were seated, John turned to Elizabeth with a worried expression. "Elizabeth, are you sure you want to do this? You know almost nothing about this man."

"Actually, John, I know a great deal. I'm not stupid. I've had Mr. Riordan thoroughly checked out. I assure you, there is nothing at all objectionable in his past."

"You had me investigated?"

She smiled, experiencing a minor sense of victory at Max's

disconcerted frown. "Yes. As a matter of fact, I did. Turnabout is fair play, you know."

Max's laser-blue stare held hers for a long moment. Then one corner of his mouth quirked. "Touché."

After that they got down to business.

It soon became apparent why Max had Harry Ackerman on exclusive retainer. Despite his untidy appearance, the man was a brilliant attorney who easily held his own with John Fossbinder, who was considered one of Houston's top attorneys.

Elizabeth felt that the agreement that Mr. Ackerman had drawn up was more than generous, and she suspected that John thought so as well, though you'd never know it by his serious expression as he read through the document. She was prepared to sign the thing as written, but John felt duty-bound to score some points for his client. Therefore, for a tedious hour and a half the two attorneys went over the prenuptial line by line.

Finally they reached a mutual agreement on every point and Harry announced, "Well, that about does it. To summarize in layman's terms, the main points are as follows. Article I—prior to the marriage, Max will set up a trust fund in the amount agreed to by both parties. Said trust will be solely for the operation of Mimosa Landing. Elizabeth will be executrix of the fund. The trust and all its proceeds will belong solely to her or her heirs in perpetuity.

"Article II—the two of you agree to remain married for a minimum of five years. If, after that time, either of you wants out of the marriage for any reason whatsoever, you will part. Amicably, we all hope.

"If you do eventually part, as previously stated, the trust will remain in Elizabeth's hands. In addition, Max will give Elizabeth a settlement equivalent to twenty percent of his net worth at the time. He also agrees to make no claims on the Stanton holdings.

"Article III—the one and only reason for dissolving the marriage before the five years are up would be infidelity committed by either party. If Max is the offender, the terms of the prenuptial will stand exactly as if the marriage had been of a five-year duration."

"That won't happen," Max inserted. He looked across the table at Elizabeth. "I honor my contracts and commitments."

Harry cleared his throat. "Yes…well…to continue. If Elizabeth is the offending party the same would be true, with the exception that Max would not give her a cash settlement."

Harry gathered the pages and tapped them against the table top. "I think that covers everything."

"Not quite," John said. "What if there are children resulting from this marriage? Who would get custody?"

"Hmm," Harry mused. "I suppose now is the best time to address that question. Ms. Stanton, what are your thoughts on the matter?"

The question had taken Elizabeth by surprise. She had not considered that she and Max might have children. Or that he might want them.

"To be honest, I don't think that will ever be a problem. My marriage to Edward produced no children, even though I desperately wanted a family," she said, struggling to hold on to her poise. The admission of such an intensely personal failure humiliated her, but she was determined to be open and honest with Max. She didn't want him to accuse her of hiding anything.

Drawing a deep breath, she forced herself to explain. "Several years ago I underwent a battery of tests to find out if there was a problem. They turned up no reason for infertility. Nevertheless, I never conceived. The doctors finally told me that it was doubtful that I ever would."

She looked directly at Max then. "If that makes a difference and you want to withdraw your offer, I'll understand."

Max mulled over the matter. "To tell you the truth, I haven't considered that possibility," he said finally. "I'll be honest also. Having offspring has never been a high priority for me. It's not a negative, mind you. I always just assumed that when the time was right I'd marry and have a family, but doing so isn't a burning passion of mine.

"However, if you and I should have children, then subsequently parted, it seems logical to me, given my hectic work schedule, that they remain with you. Of course, I would expect flexible visitation."

Once again, Elizabeth was amazed at how reasonable and generous Max was being. Even though the possibility of having a child was almost nonexistent, she nevertheless experienced a sense of relief that if that miracle did occur, there would be no bitter custody battle.

"Is that agreeable with you, Ms. Stanton?" Harry asked. "If so, we will include that proviso in the prenuptial."

"Yes. Yes, that's fine."

"Well, then, we're done. I'll have the revised version drawn up and ready for you both to sign tomorrow."

They all filed out of Max's office, but in the reception area, when Max stopped to talk to his secretary, John nudged Elizabeth to one side. "Elizabeth, I think you're making a terrible mistake," he murmured. "Give yourself some time, my dear. We'll come up with a solution eventually."

"I don't *have* time, John. You and I have tried for the past year to find a way out of this financial nightmare with no luck. Now the wolf is at the door. I simply can't stall any longer."

She patted his arm. "I know you're worried about me, and I appreciate that, but I'll be fine. Really. Just do me a favor, and keep all this to yourself, okay?"

John drew himself up to his full height, affronted that she could so much as entertain the notion that he would do otherwise. "Of course. Attorney-client privilege is sacrosanct." He relented quickly, however, and gave her one last worried look. "So…you're comfortable with this arrangement?"

"Yes."

That, of course, was not absolutely true. She was nervous and apprehensive, but she dared not reveal that to John.

"Are you ready?" Max asked, cupping her elbow.

Before she could reply, a door on the other side of the reception room opened and a familiar-looking man strode out. It took her a few seconds to remember where she had seen him before. He had accompanied Max to a few charity events. As she recalled, his name was Trent…or was it Troy? Something like that. And he was Max's right-hand man.

"Max! Thank God you're here." The man nodded to Elizabeth. "I'm sorry to interrupt, Ms. Stanton, but this is urgent."

"That's all right," she replied, but he had already switched his attention back to Max.

"I called your cell phone and got no answer. I was just coming to see if Carly knew how to get in touch with you. We have to talk."

"Not now, Troy. I'm going to take Elizabeth home."

"Dammit, Max, listen to me. Old man Scarborough is on his way over. He wouldn't agree to reschedule our meeting. He said if you weren't here by the time he arrived, the deal was off."

"Damn," Max muttered. "Do you think he meant it?"

"Absolutely."

Elizabeth put her hand on Max's arm. "Please, don't worry about me. I'm sure John will drive me home."

"Certainly," her attorney chimed in. "It will be my pleasure."

Max cocked an eyebrow at Elizabeth. "Are you sure?"

"Yes, of course. Go ahead and take care of your business. I'll be fine."

"All right. I'll call you tomorrow and we'll go get our blood tests."

Elizabeth nodded and took John's arm. Watching them walk out together, Max frowned. He didn't like leaving her alone with the attorney. The man had made no bones of his disapproval. Max knew that Fossbinder would try to talk her out of marrying him, but he'd just have to take the risk. He couldn't brush off a multimillion dollar deal that he and Troy had been putting together for months.

"So…you're going through with this insanity," Troy said the moment he and Max were alone in the conference room.

"If by that you mean I'm going to marry Elizabeth, then the answer is yes. We just hammered out our prenuptial."

"Well, at least you had sense enough to do that." In an agitated move, Troy raked his hand through his dark brown hair. "Dammit, Max. I know I said that what you needed was a trophy wife, but I was just kidding around. Honest. I didn't think you'd take me seriously."

"Let it go, Troy. We've been through this already. I know what I'm doing," Max said, giving his friend a reassuring smile. "Look, if it makes you feel any better, one of the reasons that I chose Elizabeth is because I find her attractive. She not only meets all my requirements, she's reported to be sweet-tempered and she's easy on the eyes, as well. She's perfect."

Well…almost perfect, he added to himself.

Restless, Max walked over to the outer glass wall of the conference room and looked down at the sprawling city, eighteen floors below. The sun was setting in a glorious kaleidoscope, turning the clouds various shades of orange, red, pink and purple. The air itself had taken on the dusty purple of twilight that occurs just before darkness falls. Rush-hour traffic was beginning to clog the freeway as workers began their daily exodus to the suburbs. Streetlights were beginning to blink on. So were car headlights. Through the gloaming, the lines of traffic resembled strings of diamonds going one way and rubies the other.

The thought reminded Max of the diamond ring he'd given Elizabeth...and her disconcerting confession.

The deep pang of disappointment he'd experienced when she revealed that she probably could not have children had taken him by surprise.

Not that he hadn't been truthful with her. Until recently, settling down with a wife had been one of those things he'd thought about only in an abstract sort of way; something he'd get around to someday when the time was right. Only since meeting Elizabeth had he given serious thought to marriage. Until now, the idea of having children had not even been on his radar screen.

So why now, all of a sudden, did thoughts of a future devoid of children make him feel so hollow inside? Curious.

To Elizabeth, the rest of the week seemed to speed by in accelerated motion, like watching an old-time silent movie. Before she knew it, Saturday afternoon arrived.

Dressed in her robe, she sat at her dressing table in her bedroom at Mimosa Landing, staring at her reflection in the mirror. In just a short while she would become Mrs. Maxwell Riordan.

The thought sent a flutter through her stomach. She closed her eyes and breathed deeply.

"You know, sugar, you can still change your mind."

Elizabeth's eyes popped open. Her gaze fixed on Mimi's reflection in her dressing-table mirror. Her friend stood just inside her bedroom with her back to the closed door.

"You don't even have to see him," Mimi went on. "You

just say the word and I'll go down there and shoo everybody off the property."

Elizabeth shook her head. "No. No, don't do that."

Mimi tipped her head to one side and studied Elizabeth's pale reflection. "You're determined to go through with this?"

"Yes."

"Nothing I can say will change your mind?"

"No."

"Then what're you doing sitting there in your bathrobe? Everyone is here and Aunt Talitha is beginning to fret. The service is supposed to start in ten minutes."

"Oh, dear! Is it that late?"

"I'm afraid so. If you're going through with this cocka-mamy arrangement, it's time to get dressed and get this show on the road," her friend declared. "C'mon, sugar. I'll help you."

In a daze, Elizabeth followed Mimi's instructions while her friend helped her dress in the champagne-colored silk suit that Martha, her housekeeper at Mimosa Landing, had laid out earlier.

Ever since she had returned to Mimosa Landing two days ago, the house had been a beehive of activity. All that morning the florist had bustled about downstairs decorating the front parlor and dining room, and the caterer had taken over Martha's kitchen, much to the housekeeper's distress. Luckily Gladys and Dooley arrived early so Martha had the couple to commiserate with and help calm her down.

"Have Quinton and Camille arrived? Or called?" Elizabeth asked as she stepped into her pumps.

"Not that I know of." Mimi straightened the collar of Elizabeth's suit coat and plucked a loose hair off the shoulder. "Were you expecting them?"

"Not really. I called them both several times but I always

got their answering machines. They're probably out of the country."

Elizabeth had assured Max that theirs would be a small wedding, and that was exactly what they were having. The staff from both of her households, her great-aunt, Talitha Stanton, Mimi, John Fossbinder and his wife, Marie, her banker, Walter Monroe, and his wife, Anna, were Elizabeth's only guests.

Other than her great-aunt, Elizabeth's only other living relatives were her second cousins, Camille Moseby Holt Edwards Kincaid Lawrence and Camille's brother, Quinton Moseby. Elizabeth was surprised that neither had responded to her calls. Especially Camille. She usually jumped at any opportunity to spend time at Mimosa Landing.

She had felt obligated to invite her cousins to the wedding, but it was just as well that Camille wasn't attending, Elizabeth thought as she put on pearl teardrop earrings.

She'd always gotten along well with Quinton, but his sister was a different story. Elizabeth was generally mild-tempered, but whenever she was around Camille she felt like a cat whose fur has just been stroked the wrong way.

Not that she hadn't tried. For Aunt Talitha's sake, she'd done all she could to maintain the family connection, distant as it was.

Elizabeth would have liked for Quinton to be there for her wedding, but she was relieved that she would not have to contend with Camille's constant complaints and innuendos. She was under enough strain as it was.

Max's guest list had consisted of his mother, Iona Riordan, his assistant, Troy Ellerbee, Harry Ackerman and his wife, his secretary, Carly Womack, and a few others on his office staff.

Elizabeth had met Max's mother just moments ago. When Aunt Talitha had learned that Iona had yet to meet Elizabeth, she had insisted that Max's mother come upstairs with her so that she could introduce them.

A bright, cheery little woman, Iona seemed to bubble over with happiness that her bachelor son and only child was finally getting married.

She was about Elizabeth's height of five foot four, but thirty or so pounds heavier. She reminded Elizabeth of a plump little bluebird in her blue silk suit and matching pillbox hat. During their short conversation Elizabeth learned that Iona didn't see much of her son. That bit of information made her wonder if Max and his mother were on as good of terms as Detective Summers seemed to believe. In her family, they kept their beloved old ones with them.

"There, you're all ready," Mimi pronounced, stepping back to survey Elizabeth. She caught her breath. "Oh, sugar. You look so beautiful," she said with awe.

"Here now, cut that out, Mimi, or you'll have us all bawling," Aunt Talitha scolded from the doorway.

"You're absolutely right," Mimi agreed. "Let's get this show on the road. Do you have everything? Something old, something new, something borrowed, something blue?"

The abrupt laugh that burst from Elizabeth bordered on hysteria. "Under the circumstances, I hardly think I need to bother with that tradition."

"Nonsense. Of course you do," her great-aunt declared. "Just because this is your second marriage doesn't mean that you have to forgo the traditions."

She stepped inside the room and closed the door behind her. "I came back up here to see what was taking so long," the old lady said. "And to tell you that Quinton just called. He's been in Greece, visiting his sister and her husband, and he just got back this morning. He said to tell you that he's sorry he's missing your wedding."

Great-aunt Talitha walked to the center of the room slowly, looking as majestic as a queen. As always, though she relied on a cane for support, she held her back ramrod straight and her head high. A tall, slender woman, she exuded a sort of old-fashion gentility that was in short supply these days.

At eighty, Elizabeth's aunt still had the thick hair typical of all the Stanton women, though it had long ago turned from a rich brown to gray. For the past ten years or so, the old lady had worn her abundant tresses braided, the thick plaits wound into a coronet on top of her head like a silver crown. The style only served to reinforce her regal look.

The dear old soul was the only close family that Elizabeth had, and she loved her dearly. Not wanting to upset her aunt, she had not revealed to her the full extent of Edward's perfidy or the circumstances of her arrangement with Max. As far as Aunt Talitha was concerned, this marriage was a love match.

"Well? What're you just standing there for?" Aunt Talitha demanded, thumping the floor with her cane. "Get cracking."

At once, Mimi drawled, "Don't you worry, Aunt Talitha, darlin'. I've got it covered. Her suit is new. And those are your mama's pearl earrings, aren't they? I thought so," she said at Elizabeth's nod. "So that's your something old. And I brought just the thing to cover the last two."

Mimi pulled a lacy confection out of her purse and dangled it from one finger. "Here you go—this is your something borrowed and it's blue."

"What *is* that?" Elizabeth asked, looking askance at the object that Mimi twirled around her forefinger.

"It's the blue garter that I wore when Big Daddy and I got hitched. We had a wonderful marriage, so I'm hoping that it'll bring you good luck this time around."

"Oh, Mimi, I don't th—"

"Perfect. That's a splendid idea, Mimi. Well?" Aunt Talitha thumped her cane against the floor again. "What are you standing there lollygagging for? Get on with it, girl. Put the thing on and let's go. That delicious young man of yours is downstairs waiting, and he's beginning to get restless."

"Why, Aunt Talitha. I do believe you've got the hots for Elizabeth's intended," Mimi teased.

"Humph. Just because I'm eighty and a maiden lady doesn't mean I don't know a real man when I see one. Anyway, I always did have a weakness for dangerous men. If I was fifty years younger I just might steal him away from Elizabeth." She got a faraway look in her eyes and added with a wistful sigh, "In a way, he reminds me of my Martin."

Elizabeth and Mimi exchanged a quick look but said nothing. They both knew the story of Great-Aunt Talitha's one true love. When she'd been eighteen she and Martin Delany had been engaged to be married. All the plans had been made and the invitations mailed when, just ten days before the wedding, Martin had been killed in action in the Korean War.

He had gone out on what was supposed to have been his last maneuver before shipping out to return home. He and his platoon had walked into a trap and been caught in a crossfire that cost them heavy casualties.

Aunt Talitha, never completely recovering from the loss of her beloved Martin, had remained single.

"There. All ready. And here's your bouquet," Mimi announced, handing Elizabeth the nosegay of cream-and-pink rosebuds and baby's breath.

"Oh, my dearest girl," Aunt Talitha murmured. Her patrician features softened and her faded blue eyes misted over as she inspected her great-niece. "You look so beautiful. So very beautiful." She leaned in and pressed her papery cheek to Elizabeth's. The familiar scents of lilac perfume and lily of the valley sachet that her aunt kept in her lingerie drawer enveloped Elizabeth. "Be happy, my precious," she whispered. "You deserve only the best."

The old lady sniffed and dabbed her eyes with a lace-trimmed hankie, then straightened her spine. "Now then, give me a minute to get downstairs in the elevator. As soon as I'm seated I'll signal the pianist to start the wedding march and you and Mimi come down."

The ceremony went off without a hitch. The parlor furniture had been moved to the perimeter of the room and the guests were seated in the rows of folding chairs that had been set up. Reverend Harvey, Max and his friend Troy waited in front of the fireplace as she followed Mimi into the room.

If Max was impressed with her appearance it did not show. His harsh face wore its usual stern expression. Not by so much as a flicker of an eyelash did he reveal what he was thinking.

Elizabeth went through the ceremony in such a daze that she had to be prompted twice to respond. It seemed as though suddenly she had a ring on her finger and Reverend Harvey was pronouncing them husband and wife.

Reverend Harvey's, "You may kiss the bride" were the first words that truly registered with Elizabeth.

She darted a horrified look at the minister, then at Max. Her eyes widened, and she experienced a moment of panic as Max pulled her into his arms and lowered his mouth to hers.

Elizabeth expected a token buzz on the lips to comply with tradition, but there was nothing perfunctory or quick about the kiss. It was hot and sensual and thorough, and lasted so long that a few of their guests began to chuckle, then clap. When Max at last raised his head and ended the embrace, Elizabeth felt light-headed and had to clutch his arm to keep from staggering.

If he was at all affected by the kiss it did not show. As Reverend Harvey announced "Ladies and gentlemen, may I present Mr. and Mrs. Maxwell Patrick Riordan," Max turned with a smile to accept the congratulations and good wishes of the guests who crowded around them.

When the well-wishes were done, everyone went into the dining room, where the caterers had set up a sumptuous buffet. For the next hour or so, Elizabeth, her untouched plate in hand, circulated among their guests and somehow managed to make small talk, though she could not have told you what she had discussed or with whom.

All too soon Max sought her out and murmured, "We'd better be leaving soon. I don't want us to be too late arriving in New York."

The knot in the pit of Elizabeth's stomach twisted tighter, but she gave him a wan smile. "All right. I'll run upstairs and change into something more suitable for traveling. Dooley has already put my cases in your car. I won't be long."

Max walked with her to the foot of the stairs. He watched her climb the steps, his expression pensive.

Damn, but she had great legs, he thought. It occurred to him that in the past whenever he'd been around her she'd worn an evening gown or slacks or one of those long skirts with high-heeled dress boots. This was the first time he'd gotten a look at her legs, and they were terrific.

"Do you have any idea just how lucky you are?"

Max turned at the drawled question and saw Mimi Whittington standing in the archway between the parlor and the foyer. With a hand on one hip and a champagne glass in the other, she strolled toward him with languid steps. Stopping at the foot of the stairs, she took a sip of bubbly and cocked one eyebrow at him. "Well? Do you?"

Max glanced up the stairs, but Elizabeth had already disappeared down the hallway. "You're right. I am lucky. She's a nice-looking woman."

"That's not what I meant. Although, she's a damned sight more that *nice*-looking. What's the matter with your eyes? She's downright gorgeous. And her soul is just as beautiful. She's also smart and sweet and she's got a heart as big as Texas."

"Is that right?" Max wondered where this conversation was leading. He did not have to wait long to find out.

Mimi looked him up and down. "I don't know you very well, but my first impression is that you're a fairly decent guy."

"Thanks," Max replied with a twisted grin. "I like to think so."

"See to it that you don't prove me wrong." She poked his chest with one long, red-enameled fingernail. "Because I'm warning you, big fella, you make her unhappy…and I'll hurt you. That's a promise."

Before Max could reply, the woman turned and sauntered back into the parlor and rejoined the other guests.

Had anyone else made that threat he would have thought it a joke. Or at least an exaggeration. But the look in Mimi Whittington's eyes told him she was dead serious.

Max shook his head. How, he wondered, had those two women become best friends? He could not think of any two people who were more opposite if he tried. Elizabeth was refined and elegant and Mimi was flashy and flamboyant. At times even bawdy. Never in a million years would he ever have suspected that they could be friends, yet they were.

"I'm ready," Elizabeth said from above him in a not-quite-steady voice.

"Good." Turning back to the stairs, Max watched her descend the steps. She had changed into a pencil-slim brown suede skirt, brown knee-high boots with three-inch heels, a brown turtleneck sweater with a butterfly brooch pinned to the collar and a tweed jacket in earthy autumn tones. As always, she looked perfect.

Max took her hand as she descended the last two steps. "You look nice."

A look of surprise flickered over Elizabeth's face. "Thank you," she murmured politely, but Max did not miss the wariness in her eyes.

What was that for? he wondered, frowning. Didn't she believe him?

Taking Elizabeth's elbow he shot her a hopeful look. "You know, we could sneak out now while no one is looking and miss all the hoopla."

She looked at him aghast, as though he'd just uttered a heresy against God and country. "What? Absolutely not. That would be impolite. I'd never do that to our guests. Besides, Aunt Talitha and Mimi would be crushed."

"Somehow I knew you'd say that," he replied in a resigned tone, and nudged her toward the parlor. "C'mon, let's get this over with and be on our way."

They worked their way around the room and said their goodbyes. While giving her aunt and Mimi a farewell hug and kiss, Elizabeth clung to the women, fighting back an almost irresistible urge to run upstairs and lock herself in her room.

She could stall only so long, however, and finally Max put his arm around her waist and murmured, "It's time to go, Elizabeth."

Their guests had gathered on the front veranda and lawn, and when she and Max came out of the house they were peppered with rice all the way to his black BMW.

In the excitement Elizabeth didn't notice that they were not alone in the car until Max had driven halfway down the mile-long drive and Troy Ellerbee spoke up from the back seat.

"Thank goodness that's over," Max's assistant said, and Elizabeth jumped as though she'd been shot.

She twisted around and gaped at the man seated directly behind her. "Wh-what are you doing here?"

"Oh, I forgot to tell you," Max answered for him. "Troy is going with us."

Looking away from Troy Ellerbee's cold stare, Elizabeth focused her gaze on her new husband. "Going with us? You mean as far as Houston?"

"No, he's going with us to New York. I told you, I have an important meeting there on Monday. I need Troy with me."

Elizabeth glanced at Troy and found that he was watching her with a smug expression. She straightened around in her seat and stared ahead. "Oh. I see," she replied, although she didn't. She didn't *see* at all. What kind of man took his assistant with him on his honeymoon?

The answer came to her immediately. A husband who, as Mimi would say, didn't give two hoots and a holler about his bride, that's who.

Throughout the drive to Houston International Airport, and the long flight to New York aboard Max's private jet, her new husband didn't say a dozen words to her.

When they boarded the sleek plane, he introduced her to the pilot, a man by the name of Tom Givens, then gave her a speedy tour of the plane's interior, pointing out the bedroom and adjoining bath at the rear of the plane, the salon and bar and the cockpit. The whole while Elizabeth had the feeling that Max was impatient to get back to work.

"Well, that's it," he said finally. "You've seen everything but the luggage bay. Make yourself comfortable. We'll be taking off any minute now."

He and Troy sat down at a small table and resumed their business discussion as though she weren't there.

Feeling like a third wheel, Elizabeth made her way to the front of the salon and buckled herself into one of the easy chairs. By that point Max and Troy were so immersed in their talk that she doubted either man remembered she was there, or were aware of the jet streaking down the runway and lifting off the ground.

She might as well not be there, Elizabeth thought, growing peevish. Throughout the flight she idly flipped through several financial magazines, which seemed to be the only reading material on the plane, not absorbing a word.

It was insulting, she fumed in silence. So theirs wasn't a love match. So what? And truth be told, she wasn't looking forward to the night to come. But you'd think the man would at least show some interest in the woman he was about to bed.

With the time-zone change it was almost midnight when they checked in at the Ritz-Carlton Hotel. The bell captain, the concierge and the desk clerk recognized all of them. Ever polite, each addressed Elizabeth first, calling her Ms. Stanton, before welcoming Max and Troy.

Max let the mistake go until they reached the front desk. There he explained that, as of that afternoon, Elizabeth was now Mrs. Riordan. At once the well-trained staff showered her and Max with effusive good wishes.

"The suite your secretary booked is ready, sir," the desk clerk informed Max. "Oh, and before I forget, you have several messages."

As the clerk handed over the stack of slips, Elizabeth experienced a moment of panic. Surely Troy wasn't going to share the suite with them. The night ahead was going to be awkward enough without that.

Max shuffled through the message slips, then almost as an afterthought he looked up and added, "Did you have a smaller suite available on the same floor for Mr. Ellerbee?"

Elizabeth closed her eyes, almost faint with relief.

"Yes, sir." If the clerk thought it peculiar that Max had brought his business associate with him on his honeymoon, he had the exquisite good manners and training to keep his expression deadpan.

When they stepped off the elevator on their floor, Troy nudged Max and said, "You probably ought to give Mr. Aramoto a call back right away. He left three messages for me to remind you."

"Yeah, will do. I've got four messages from him myself."

In silence, her insides aquiver, Elizabeth walked beside the men down the wide hallway. At the door to their suite, they all stopped.

"I'll see you in the morning, boss," Troy said to Max. For the first time since they'd left Mimosa Landing that afternoon, he looked directly at Elizabeth.

"Good night, Mrs. Riordan." His tone was polite, his expression noncommittal and his blue eyes were cold as a glacier lake.

"Please, call me Elizabeth," she requested.

"Yeah, do that," Max absently interjected. Still sorting through the message slips, he seemed oblivious to his assistant's frosty attitude. "You'll be seeing a lot of each other in the future. No sense standing on formality."

"All right. Good night, Elizabeth," Troy murmured, then turned and headed down the hallway.

Watching him go, Elizabeth wondered what it was about her that he disliked so.

Max unlocked the door to their suite and motioned for her to precede him, but when she started to step through the doorway he said, "Whoops. I almost forgot."

"Oh! Max! What are you doing?" Elizabeth squealed as he swooped her up in his arms.

"Carrying you over the threshold. Isn't that what bridegrooms are supposed to do?" He stepped into the room and kicked the door shut behind them.

In that dizzying moment a flood of sensations cascaded through Elizabeth. She became intensely aware of several things all at once—Max's heat, the hardness of his chest against the side of her body, the strength of the arms that held her, the breadth of his shoulders. The manly scent of him.

He hefted her experimentally and frowned. "Good grief, woman, don't you eat? You can't weigh a hundred pounds soaking wet."

Flustered, Elizabeth could feel embarrassed heat rising up over her chest and neck and flooding her face. She had never been this close to him before. He carried her as easily as he would a child.

"I most certainly do. I weigh a hundred and six. And it isn't polite to comment on a lady's weight."

"Is that right?" He walked to the center of the lavish sitting room, his intense gaze zeroing in on her for the first time that day.

Unable to look away from those mesmerizing blue eyes, Elizabeth caught her breath. The change in him was stunning. It was as though he'd punched a button and switched gears. In an instant his demeanor changed from that of a tough, distant businessman to that of a sensuous and seductive lover.

Elizabeth shivered. Her heart began to pound. Like a banked fire being stirred to life, sensual heat began to burn in the depths of his blue eyes.

"You, uh…you can put me down now," she said, still unable to look away.

"Hmm. When I'm ready," he murmured. His gaze dropped to her lips and lingered there. His eyelids lowered drowsily and his head began an angled descent.

The telephone rang and Elizabeth jumped within Max's embrace.

"Dammit," he spat. He glared at the telephone as though debating whether to answer it or rip the thing out of the wall. When a knock sounded on the door he cursed again, but this time he lowered Elizabeth to her feet. "That's probably the bellman with our luggage. Why don't you get the door while I answer the phone. It'll be Mr. Aramoto calling again."

Struggling to regain her composure, she hurried to the door and instructed the bellman to put their cases in the bedroom. Max was still embroiled in conversation with whomever was on the telephone when the man left. Once again, he seemed unaware of her presence.

Not anxious to attract his attention, Elizabeth escaped into the bedroom. After unpacking both her and Max's cases, she took her nightclothes, a long midnight-blue, silk-and-lace nightgown and matching peignoir, and went into the bathroom. Twenty minutes later, standing in front of the bathroom door, she closed her eyes, placed her palm flat over her midriff and commanded herself to be calm. It wasn't as though she was a virgin. She and Max were married now, and sex was part of marriage. It wasn't a death sentence or anything like that, so don't be such a ninny, she scolded herself in silence.

Opening her eyes, Elizabeth drew a deep breath, opened the door and stepped through it, only to come to a halt three steps inside the bedroom. It was empty.

She went to the double doors leading into the sitting room and opened them a crack. She could see Max pacing back and forth across the room, still talking on the telephone. At some point he had taken off his suit coat and tie, unbuttoned the top three buttons on his shirt and rolled up his shirtsleeves, exposing a mat of black curls on his chest and a liberal sprinkling of short dark hairs on his forearms. He looked sleek and powerful…and dangerous. Like a prowling leopard, she thought uneasily.

Other than an occasional word or curse, Elizabeth could not make out what Max was saying, but he appeared to be arguing with the person on the other end of the line. As he paced he gestured with his free hand and periodically raked his fingers through his jet-black hair.

Elizabeth quietly closed the door. She took off her negligee, tossed it over the chaise lounge in the corner and climbed into bed, leaning back against the mound of pillows piled against the headboard. Lacing her fingers together on top of the covers at her waist, she looked around the sumptuous room.

After a while she picked up one of the magazines on the bedside table and flipped through the pages without interest. Tossing the periodical aside, she sighed. She laced her fingers together again and twiddled her thumbs.

She glanced at the clock on the bedside table. She'd been in bed for more than an hour. Though she'd been anticipating this night with dread, minute by minute her nervousness gave way to irritation. To come in a poor second to a business deal on your wedding night was insulting.

Tossing back the covers, she climbed out of bed and marched to the double doors again. This time she jerked both doors open, making no effort at silence. She stood in the doorway with her hands on her hips and glared daggers at Max.

The pointed reminder that he had a bride waiting in the next room had no effect. Max's focus was solely on the conversation.

With a huff, Elizabeth banged the doors shut. Spinning around, she marched back to the bed, tossed aside the extra pillows and lay down, pulling the covers up to her chin. "To heck with him," she muttered to herself, squirming into a comfortable position in the bed. "Let him cuddle up with a business contract."

The slam of the doors broke Max's concentration for an instant. He glanced over his shoulder toward the bedroom, then checked his wristwatch and grimaced. He hadn't realized that he'd been on the telephone so long.

He did his best to speed up the discussion, but, as usual, Mr. Aramoto was antsy about the latest venture into which he'd entered with Max. Never mind that Max had made the man millions in the past. Mr. Aramoto was notoriously reluctant to part with a dime and always needed to be coddled and reassured every step of the way through any deal. Another twenty minutes passed before Max succeeded in reassuring the man and was able to end the conversation.

Returning the receiver to its cradle, Max glanced at the closed bedroom doors. "Good going, Riordan," he muttered to himself. "Great way to start off your marriage."

He checked his wristwatch again, and again he grimaced. He couldn't blame her if she was angry. He was the first to admit that he wasn't the most sensitive guy in the world, but even he knew that ignoring your bride on your wedding night wasn't a bright idea.

Turning out the sitting room lights on the way, he headed for the bedroom. At the doors, pausing to brace himself to face a barrage of female fury, he drew a deep breath, then went inside.

Instead of a vitriolic tirade or frosty glares, he was met with silence. The only light burning was the lamp on his side of the king-size bed. Elizabeth lay on her side, facing the center of the bed and him, the covers up to her chin, sound asleep.

Standing beside the bed, Max studied her and thought about what Mimi had said to him after the ceremony. The woman was brash and bold, and he'd be damned if he could understand the friendship between her and Elizabeth, but he had a gut feeling that she was right.

He *was* lucky. Elizabeth had not only the connections and pedigree that he needed in a wife, she was a damned fine-looking woman.

That was a bonus. Or then again, maybe not. He would not have picked her had he not found her physically attractive, no matter how much he wanted to tap into Houston's "old money." There were other attractive women among Houston society. He could just as easily have chosen to marry one of them, but there was something about Elizabeth that had drawn him from the first moment they met.

Max slipped the gold cuff links out of the cuffs of his shirt and placed them on the bedside table. A wry smile twisted one corner of his mouth. He remembered how disappointed he'd been at the time to learn that she was married. Especially so when he'd found out that she was married to Edward Culpepper.

Max did not like the man. Edward was, and he supposed still is, a pompous stuffed shirt. Worse, Max had no respect for the man. Nor did he trust him. By running off with Natalie Brussard and Elizabeth's money, Edward had validated Max's low opinion of him.

Looking at Elizabeth with her face scrubbed clean of makeup and soft with slumber, it was easy to believe that her soul was as sweet as the rest of her. She looked like a beautiful angel.

Edward Culpepper, Max decided, was an idiot.

With her eyes closed, her long lashes lay like crescent-shaped fans against her high cheekbones. Her unpainted lips were slightly parted. They were soft and full, and damned inviting. So was all of that shining mahogany-brown hair that lay spread out on her pillow.

He pulled his shirt from the waistband of his trousers, stripped the garment off and tossed it onto a nearby chair. Still watching her, he took off his shoes and socks, then unbuckled his belt and stepped out of his trousers and tossed them on the chair as well.

It was their wedding night. He would be justified in waking her and consummating their vows, he told himself. If she was as sweet-natured as everyone claimed, she probably wouldn't even object.

Standing beside the bed, clad in only a pair of black briefs, Max debated. She looked so small. And so peaceful. It had been a long and tense week. Between the hurried planning, the anxiety of the last few days, the wedding and jet lag, she was probably beat.

Hooking his thumbs beneath the waistband of his briefs, Max stripped them off and climbed into bed beside her. Propped up on one elbow, he looked down and studied her from this new angle. Damn. Everything about her was dainty and ultra-feminine, even the curve of her cheek and her straight little nose. With a resigned sigh, he leaned over and kissed her forehead.

"Good night, Elizabeth," he murmured.

# *Five*

Twenty blocks away, a silver Lexus climbed the dimly lit ramp of a deserted parking garage. A few bare bulbs cast pools of light here and there onto the concrete floor. The only sounds were the hum of the car engine and the crunchy hiss of the tires.

The Lexus exited the ramp on the third level. Following instructions, the driver guided the car to the center of the floor and stopped near the elevator. The driver put the gearshift in Park, but left the engine running. Just in case.

Lowering the side window, the driver looked around and shivered. On the sunniest of days parking garages were not cheerful places, but at one in the morning there was something creepy about the cavernous space.

It had stormed earlier, and moisture seemed to ooze from every pore of the concrete structure. The air was heavy with the dank smells of gasoline and motor oil and rain.

Growing more nervous by the second, the driver shifted on the leather seat and peered through the gloom. Damn, this place was spooky. And quiet. Too quiet.

Perhaps agreeing to meet here wasn't such a good idea.

There was no reason why they couldn't have carried out this business in more congenial and civilized surroundings. Somewhere more public. Like say…over drinks at a high-end club. In this town no one paid attention to the people around them. New Yorkers had minding their own business down to an art form.

Below, on the street, a horn honked, and the driver jumped. Damn! Didn't people ever sleep in this town?

The minutes ticked by with agonizing slowness. The driver was beginning to think the man wasn't going to show, when from below came the unmistakable purr of a well-tuned car slowly gliding up the ramp.

Reaching the third level, the black sedan crept out onto the floor and came to a stop. The dark tint of the vehicle's windows made it impossible to see inside, but the driver of the Lexus knew that the new arrival was checking out the place, making certain he wasn't being followed or led into a trap.

Somehow the man's extreme caution made the situation all the more scary. Watching the other car cruise slowly around the perimeter of the garage, the Lexus driver shivered again.

There was an almost palpable aura of menace surrounding the black vehicle. Maybe it was the color. Or the dark-tinted windows. Or the eerie slowness with which it circled the garage before approaching. Whatever, the mere sight of the vehicle caused the hairs on the Lexus driver's nape to stand on end.

The sedan made a complete circuit of the third level of the garage before coming to a halt beside the smaller car. The dark-tinted front window on the passenger side silently glided down halfway. "You got something for me?" came the chilling monotone.

"Are you Angelo?"

"Yeah."

. The driver climbed from the Lexus and reached for the handle of the sedan's passenger door but was brought to a halt by the blinding beam of a flashlight to the eyes. "Hold it right there. And keep your hands where I can see them."

"Now, see here—"

"Trust me. It's better for both of us if you don't see my face. Just hand me the instructions, nice and slow."

"Very well. You'll find everything you need in here," the Lexus driver said, shoving a black briefcase through the open window. "In there is a photo of the target, addresses of and directions to both the Houston house and the farm, plus the keys and alarm codes for both places and a telephone number that you can use to contact me, should that be necessary. The briefcase also contains half of your fee. You'll get the other half when you finish the job."

Holding the tiny flashlight in his mouth, the man inside the sedan opened the briefcase and counted the stack of one-thousand-dollar bills, then aimed the beam of light on the photograph. "Hmm. She's a beautiful woman. You sure you want her killed?" he mumbled around the flashlight in his emotionless voice.

"Quite sure."

The Lexus driver sensed rather than saw the hit man shrug his shoulders. "It's your money."

"Are you going to have a problem killing a woman?"

"No," he replied in that same flat tone. "Although it seems a shame to whack a looker like this. I just may have myself some fun with her first. Sample the goods, so to speak."

"That won't be necessary. I want her dead, not humiliated."

The flashlight beam hit the Lexus driver full in the face again. The voice of the shadowy figure behind the light dropped to a more threatening pitch. "I'll do the job you're paying me to do. That's all you got any say about."

A slightly sick feeling knotted the driver's stomach at what was probably in store for Elizabeth, but any second thoughts or pangs of conscience were firmly tamped down. "How long do you estimate this will take?"

"It takes as long as it takes."

"I'd like it taken care of as soon as possible."

"Get in line. I have two other jobs to do first for Mr. Voltura. And the big boss, he don't like to be kept waiting."

"But you don't understand. She's here. In New York. If you do her in the next few days you won't have to fly to Houston."

"Here? Where's she staying?"

"At the Ritz-Carlton. She just got married, so she and her husband are registered as Mr. and Mrs. Max Riordan. If you do the job right away, you won't have to go to Texas."

There was a heavy silence as the man mulled that over. "I tell you what. I'll give you two days. If I can catch her alone during that time I'll whack her. If I don't, well then, you'll just have to wait your turn. I'll let you know how I do."

"What's your best estimate of how long it'll take?"

"If I miss her here and have to fly to Houston, then maybe…oh, I don't know. Maybe a month. Six weeks. A word of advice, though. Don't get antsy and start calling me every half hour. I don't take well to being rushed. I do a thorough job and guarantee that nothing will be traced back to you *or* me."

The dark-tinted window glided up, ending the discussion, and the sedan glided away. Within seconds the car's taillights disappeared down the exit ramp, leaving the Lexus driver standing in the middle of the deserted garage, chilled to the bone.

"Well, you've done it," the driver murmured to no one in particular. The words seemed as loud as cannon fire in the vast space. There was no turning back now.

Elizabeth Victoria Stanton Riordan was as good as dead.

# *Six*

Snuggling deeper under the blankets, Elizabeth smiled. She stretched, luxuriating in the warmth along her back and the cloudlike softness of the mattress beneath her. Her heavy eyelids lifted partway. She blinked, then blinked again and stared across the unfamiliar room. Her smile collapsed into a frown.

Where in the world...?

Then it all came flooding back.

She tensed, still as a stone. Turning her head with extreme caution, she looked over her shoulder. Max lay on his back beside her, asleep. Oh, Lord, the warmth she had been enjoying had come from him!

The covers were pushed down to his hips, leaving him barely decent. Elizabeth's wary gaze traced over the mat of hair on his chest, then followed the narrow line of dark hairs downward to where they swirled around his navel, then went lower still to disappear beneath the edge of the sheet, which barely covered his privates. One of his arms lay across his flat belly, the other was flung over his head. She stared at that tuft of dark hair in his armpit.

Elizabeth swallowed. He appeared to be naked. Oh, God.

As carefully as possible, she scooted to the edge of the bed, checking over her shoulder every few seconds. Inch by inch, she eased herself into a sitting position, swung her legs to the floor and stood up.

Quiet as a mouse, she gathered her clothing and tiptoed into the bathroom. Once inside, she leaned back against the closed door and released the breath she'd been holding. Whew. She'd made it.

Elizabeth was no innocent. She knew and accepted that the marriage would be consummated, probably sometime soon, but she'd rather the deed not be done in the harsh light of early morning.

Moving quickly, she stripped off her nightgown, gathered up her shampoo and shower gel, climbed into the luxurious glassed-in stall and turned on the multiple showerheads. Water sprayed her from two large rain showerheads in the ceiling and from numerous sprayers on three of the side walls. Elizabeth poured a dollop of shampoo into her palm and vigorously massaged the suds through her hair. By the time Max woke up she intended to be showered and dressed.

After washing her hair and body, she stood with her face turned up to the overhead spray, her eyes closed, relishing the soft shower of water running over her skin.

The shower door opened and Elizabeth let out a squeal, her eyes flying opened. She darted a look over her shoulder just as Max, stark naked, stepped inside the stall.

Instinctively, she hunched her upper body forward and crossed her arms over her breasts. "*Ma-aax!* What are you doing? I'm taking a shower."

"I know." His big hands settled on either side of her waist as he moved up close behind her. "I thought I'd join you."

He edged closer still, his hands sliding over her wet skin

to splay over her quivering belly. Exerting slight but insistent pressure, he pulled her back against his burgeoning man-
hood. Lowering his head, Max began to nibble on the tender
skin just below her right ear. "Mmm, you taste good," he murmured, running the tip of his tongue over the swirls in her ear.
"And you smell delicious."

Elizabeth sucked in a sharp breath. "But, Max, I haven't…
I don't…I mean…"

He chuckled, and she could feel his grin against her neck.
"What's the matter, sweetheart? Haven't you ever showered
with a man before?"

"No! O-of course…not."

"Not even with Edward?"

"Who? Oh! Uh, no. He…we…"

"Then he's an even bigger idiot than I thought. *And* a
stuffed shirt."

"That's true, but— Oh! Wha-what are you doing?"

"Furthering your education. Ssh," he instructed as his
hands slid upward over her slippery skin and cupped her
breasts. "Just relax and enjoy."

While his thumbs rubbed back and forth over her button-
hard nipples, he nipped her ear, then slid his open mouth
down her neck, across her shoulder, back up the other side.
His hot breath skated over her wet skin, leaving a path of
goose bumps in its wake.

"But, Max, this isn't…" She caught her breath, then a
sound, somewhere between a sigh of pleasure and a groan,
rolled from her throat as his roaming right hand slid downward. His fingers winnowed through the triangle of feminine curls, then slipped between her satiny thighs. "We…we
barely…know each other."

"Can you think of a better way to get acquainted?" he
countered with a note of laughter in his voice. All the while

his fingers explored with a gentle sensuality that drove her crazy.

Elizabeth tried to think, but her brain seemed to be short-circuited. All she could do was feel.

She groaned again when his fingers found that sensitive nub that he'd been seeking. Whatever protest had been on the tip of her tongue was instantly forgotten. Like a wilting flower on a stem, Elizabeth's head lolled back against Max's chest. She could barely stand. Her breathing became heavy. Her eyes closed, her lips parted. Her whole body seemed to hum.

Max's hands roamed leisurely over her, as though he were a blind man, committing her shape to memory. "Damn, you have a beautiful body," he whispered in her ear. "I thought you might be skinny, no more than you weigh, but you're gorgeous. And perfectly proportioned."

"Skinny? *Skinny?*" Elizabeth retorted, latching on to outrage to momentarily subdue the embarrassment and sensual fire that threatened to consume her. "I'll...I'll have you know—"

"Take it easy, sweetheart. Don't get your panties in a wad," Max drawled. "That was supposed to be a compliment."

Chuckling, he reached around her for the tube of shower gel. "And just to show you what a sport I am, I'll wash your back."

"I've...I've already showered. I was about to step out of the stall when you...uh..." She waved her hand in a vague gesture.

"Barged in on you?" he finished for her, unabashed. "In that case, you can wash me." He gave the gel back to her and turned around. "You can start with my back."

"Wa-wash you?" Elizabeth turned around, then stood stock still with the tube of gel in her hand. She stared, dumbstruck, at his broad-shouldered, muscular back and the tight-est buns she'd ever seen. His arms were muscular as well. So were his long legs. Both were sprinkled with short, dark hair that lay plastered to his skin by the shower sprays.

Max glanced over his shoulder with a knowing smile. "What're you waiting for? C'mon, squeeze some gel into your hands and lather up."

Except for the trembling that came from deep within her, Elizabeth didn't move. She stared, dry-mouthed, at Max's magnificent male body. Finally, unsure of how to extricate herself from the embarrassing situation and still retain a shred of dignity, Elizabeth complied and squeezed a blob of gel into her hand.

When she had a mound of thick lather in her palms, she hesitated, staring at the expanse of bare skin, just inches from her nose. Rivulets of water streamed down Max's back. His skin was several shades darker than hers and had an olive undertone, but it had a rosy glow from the warm spray. A dark mole near his right shoulder blade was the only blemish on that rippling expanse of golden skin.

Dear God, he was gorgeous, Elizabeth thought helplessly.

Sucking in a deep breath, she gathered her courage and placed her lathered palms flat against his spine. Slowly she ran her hands over his back and shoulders in a circular motion.

"Mmm, that feels good," Max praised. "Now lower."

He stood with his arms out to each side, his feet braced wide. Like some potentate waiting for his handmaiden to do his bidding, Elizabeth told herself, trying her best to whip up some indignation.

The effort failed miserably.

Staring at those tight buns, she felt a wave of heat wash over her from her toes all the way to her hairline. When she cupped her hands over the firm flesh she almost went weak in the knees. Hesitantly, her sudsy hands traveled over his slick skin, swirling, massaging, squeezing. They traveled over the hard mounds of his buttocks, the sides of his narrow hips.

Emboldened by the sounds of pleasure he made, she reached around him. Her fingertips danced over the points of his hip bones, the hollow just beneath them, edged lower...

Losing her nerve, Elizabeth snatched her hands back and retreated.

To cover her embarrassment, she quickly bent her knees and began to work her way down his legs, front and back, all the way to his toes.

"Hmm. Nice." Taking her by surprise, Max turned, reached down and grasped her elbows, bringing her to her feet. "Almost done," he said in a raspy whisper. His azure gaze burned into her. "Now wash my front."

"Your front? Oh, but I could'n—"

"Just do it." He took her hands and placed them on his chest. "Wash me, Elizabeth."

Confused, aroused beyond all rational thought, Elizabeth stared up at him, unable to speak. Max's tough face was flushed with passion, tightly held in check. His blue eyes had darkened almost to navy and burned with desire. She swallowed hard.

Hesitant and unsure of herself, she placed her hands flat against him. Almost of their own accord, her fingers threaded through the mat of hair on his chest. Max sucked in a sharp breath when her fingertips grazed the tiny nipples buried in the thatch. Instantly, Elizabeth jerked her hands away.

"Don't stop." His voice was harsh, almost guttural. Grasping her wrists, he pulled her hands back into contact with his body.

Trembling so hard she was afraid her knees would give

way, Elizabeth washed hard pectorals, bulging biceps, hairy underarms. Her gaze still held by his hypnotic blue stare, she ran her hands over his ribs, his diaphragm, her fingers swirling around his belly button, dancing over his hip bones, caressing every inch of him except for that most intimate part.

"Touch me," Max ground out. Taking her hands in his, he placed them on his aroused member. He groaned and gritted his teeth as her slender fingers closed delicately around him.

Elizabeth's eyes closed, only to snap open again when he growled, "Look at me."

Again her gaze was caught by his, and as her fingers gently washed and caressed him, the very air between them seemed to pulse and shimmer, like heat waves rising off the desert floor.

Elizabeth felt as though she were melting from the inside out, her body on fire with an intense longing that she'd never experienced before.

All at once, as though unable to tolerate the exquisite torment a moment longer, Max removed her hands from his body. "Time to rinse," he announced, and supporting her with one arm around her waist, he turned to allow the shower spray to hit him.

Mounds of lather sluiced down their bodies and disappeared down the drain. When the water ran clear again Max turned Elizabeth to face him. "You set me on fire," he whispered. "Did you know that?"

Incapable of speech, she shook her head.

"I've wanted to do this from the first time that I met you. I can't tell you how disappointed I was when I learned you were married."

Putting his hands on either side of her waist, Max lifted her above his head, as easily as he would a child.

Instinctively, Elizabeth clutched his shoulders for balance.

"Put your legs around me," Max ordered in the same sensual whisper, and she obeyed as he turned and pressed her back against the inner tile wall of the shower stall.

Holding her gaze, he lowered her, letting her slide slowly down the slippery tile. "Oh!" She sucked in a sharp breath and her eyes widened when she felt his sex nudge that most sensitive part of her. The part that burned and throbbed with need. Unknowingly, she dug her fingernails into Max's flesh.

He continued to let her slide down the wall, entering her with excruciating slowness. All the while his gaze remained locked with hers. Elizabeth could feel herself stretching, his rigid shaft filling her until at last she was seated to the hilt.

For a moment neither of them moved or spoke. Breathing hard, they simply stared at each other, locked in the most intimate of embraces. Finally Max leaned forward and kissed her tenderly. "Hello, wife," he whispered against her lips.

Then he began to move. Slowly at first, but with each thrust of his hips the rhythm grew stronger, faster, more insistent.

Elizabeth was so completely out of her depth all she could do was curl her arms around Max's neck, bury her face against the top of his shoulder and hold on. Their mating was the most unconventional, most erotic, most intensely pleasurable experience of her life. She'd had no idea that sex could be like this. So wild and free. So acutely pleasurable. So perfect.

Awash with so many sensations, Elizabeth felt as though she might explode from sensory overload. All at the same time, she was aware of the slick, cold tiles at her back, the warm spray of water coming from several directions, the heat and hardness of Max's body, the hairiness of his chest abrading her nipples, the satiny friction of their slippery skin sliding together.

Vaguely, Elizabeth heard the sounds of water spraying, their labored breathing, her pulse thundering in her ear. Mostly though, she was so caught up in the ever-building pleasure that conscious thought or reason was beyond her. A prisoner of her own desire, she could do nothing but experience the heavenly sensations roaring through her slender body.

Max was in no better shape. With single-minded purpose, he drove into her again and again, following that age-old instinct to mate. To seek the ultimate physical pleasure. His hands cupped her bottom and a small guttural sound tore from his throat, punctuating each thrust of his hips.

The feelings pounding through Elizabeth were so blissful, they were almost pain. The pleasure was too intense to last, yet their bodies kept striving, and striving, driving for that pinnacle that beckoned.

The end, when it came for Elizabeth, exceeded anything she'd ever experienced. She could not have stopped the keening cry that escaped her throat had she been aware of it. The exquisite pleasure pierced her to her very soul.

Her climax seemed to trigger Max's, and he pressed hard into her, a low growling sound rumbling from him.

They collapsed against each other, wrung out, used up, too exhausted to move. Arms and legs still wrapped around Max, Elizabeth was limp as a cooked noodle.

He leaned heavily against her, pressing her back to the cool tiles. His ragged breathing rasped in her ear.

"Are you all right?" he managed to say after a while.

"I—I think so," she whispered back, not moving.

With care, Max eased back and looked at her. He smoothed a strand of wet hair off her face. "You sure?"

As the pleasure faded to memory, embarrassment began to seep back in. Elizabeth could feel it gathering heat and rising up over her chest and neck. She ducked her head. "Yes. You…you can put me down now."

Max complied, but when her feet touched the shower floor she was so wobbly her knees would have buckled if he hadn't kept his arm around her.

"Here, let me help you wash again," Max offered, and before she could refuse or object he washed first her, then himself, thoroughly. He did the chore so casually and efficiently, as they rinsed off Elizabeth wondered how many other women he'd showered with before her. The sobering thought brought her back to earth with a thump.

Glad to escape the intimacy of the glassed-in stall, Elizabeth stepped out and grabbed a towel from the warming rack and made quick work of drying her body, all the while keeping her gaze averted from Max. When done, she slipped into one of the thick terry-cloth robes that the hotel provided and tied the sash tightly around her waist.

While Max followed suit, she picked up a large round brush and the hair dryer and began to style her hair, with perhaps more vigor than normal. The sound of the dryer produced a barrier that shielded her from conversation, for which she was profoundly grateful.

Shaken by her response to Max's lovemaking, she wanted nothing more at that moment than to escape somewhere by herself and think.

As though the powers that be were listening to her thoughts, at that moment the telephone rang.

"I'll get it in the sitting room," Max said, raising his voice to be heard over the dryer's blast and gesturing as he strode out of the bathroom.

Elizabeth hurried to finish styling her hair. When she turned off the dryer she peeked out of the bathroom door. There was no sign of Max, though she could hear the murmur of his voice coming from the next room. Taking advantage of his absence, she slipped out of the enveloping bathrobe and donned her panties and bra and the long skirt and sweater she had chosen earlier.

Feeling more confident and a bit calmer now that she was clothed, she sat down at the dressing table in the bedroom. She had just started applying her makeup when Max returned.

"That was Troy," he informed her. "He'll be here in ten minutes or so. We need to go over our strategy before we leave for the two o'clock meeting with our client."

"I see," Elizabeth said, still not looking directly at him. She could not, however, avoid seeing his reflection in the dressing table mirror.

Without one iota of self-consciousness, he took off the robe and tossed it on a chair. Elizabeth told herself to look away, but she could not drag her gaze from his reflection. She caught her breath at the sight of him striding naked across the room. He pulled a clean pair of jockey shorts from the dresser and stepped into them.

Elizabeth closed her eyes and shivered. Lord, he was an impressive male specimen. The man could have posed for a Michelangelo sculpture.

But it was more than just his physique that was so mesmerizing, she realized. With every move that Max made—the way he walked and gestured, his posture and bearing, the way he spoke—he exuded an aura of self-confidence and command.

"I know this isn't much of a honeymoon, but this deal is important," Max said. Oblivious to her scrutiny, he pulled on his trousers. "I'll do my best to wrap the meeting up early enough to take you to dinner tonight. And if you'd like, I'll see if the concierge can get us tickets for a play. How's that?"

"That would be nice. Thank you."

He looked up at her ultra-polite tone. "You sure you don't mind me leaving you on your own?" Before she could answer he picked up his wallet from the dresser and pulled out a plastic card. "Here's my credit card. Use it to go shopping."

"Max, I don't need your credit card. And don't worry about me, okay? I'm a big girl. I can entertain myself."

He didn't know it, but he was handing her a lifeline. She needed time to herself to think, something she couldn't seem to do when he was around. It was as though he gave off a highly charged magnetic field that interfered with her thought processes. He was just so…so dynamic and forceful. Whenever he was near her she felt edgy and her body seemed to hum in the most unnerving way.

"Anyway, I'd rather go to the Metropolitan Museum. They have a new exhibit there that I haven't seen. And I may give my cousin Quinton a call and see if he'll meet me for lunch."

"I didn't know you had any cousins. I thought your mother and father were both only children."

"They were. Quinton and Camille Lawrence are my second cousins. Their grandmother was Mariah Stanton. She and Great-aunt Talitha were twins and my grandfather's sisters. Although being late-in-life babies, they were closer to my father's age than to Grandpa Pierce's.

"I never knew Aunt Mariah personally. She and her husband were killed years ago in an avalanche while skiing in Switzerland."

"I see." Max walked up behind Elizabeth, looking into the dressing table mirror while buttoning his shirt. She felt his body heat all across her back and gave an involuntary shiver. "So how did that branch of the family end up here in New

York? It's a long way from an 1800s plantation on the Brazos River in Texas to Manhattan. Both in distance, culture and lifestyle. Even as recently as fifty years ago."

"Yes. You're right. Mariah and her husband had only one child, a son named Colin. He inherited what was left of her inheritance, which included a lovely five-story brownstone in New York. That branch of the family has called it home ever since."

Leaning in toward the mirror, Elizabeth applied a touch of pale brown eyeshadow to her eyelids and blended it outward. "These days Quinton lives alone in the brownstone most of the time, but he loves to travel, so he's gone a lot. Camille moves in and out periodically, usually between husbands or during prolonged separations."

Max chuckled. "How many husbands has she had?"

"Four. As for separations, I've lost count. Camille is a volatile person." She slanted Max another dry look. "As you can probably tell, she and I don't get along all that well. Quinton and I, on the other hand, are great pals."

"In that case, I think you should give him a call. And take the card, anyway, in case you change your mind about shopping," he insisted, and stuffed the credit card in her purse.

Elizabeth made good her escape before Troy showed up. In the cab on the way to the museum she debated about calling her cousin. She wasn't in the mood for company, but it seemed incredibly sad to be all alone on her honeymoon. In the end she placed the call.

Though he had returned home just the day before, Quinton was packing to leave on another trip and couldn't go museum-hopping with her, but they made arrangements to meet for lunch at a charming little bistro that he recommended.

The talk of food made Elizabeth realize that she hadn't eaten anything solid since the wedding buffet the day before, if you counted the few bites she'd had as eating. She stopped at one of her favorite cafés for breakfast, then, despite the freezing temperature, she walked the rest of the way to the museum.

For the next few hours Elizabeth roamed around the various exhibits. Museum-browsing was one of her favorite things to do, but by the time she left she could not have told you what she had just seen.

No matter how much she tried, she could not get Max and the sizzling sex they had shared out of her mind.

What was it about him that had produced such a reaction? she wondered. She had never behaved so…so wantonly with anyone in her entire life. And with a man who was almost a stranger, for God's sake.

She had entered into the marriage expecting to endure their sexual encounters much as a Victorian lady would, to grit her teeth and bear it as a wifely duty. Instead, Max had merely to touch her and all sense of decorum and propriety went flying right out of her head.

She didn't understand it. Sex with Edward had been pleasant enough. At least in the beginning of their marriage. But at no time had their lovemaking rocked her world. The physical part of their marriage had been something she could take or leave.

She arrived at the restaurant before Quinton, which was typical. She'd never known her cousin to be on time in his life. Seated at one of the fireside tables, Elizabeth was sipping hot tea and looking over the menu when he rushed in, full of apologies and oozing charm, which was also typical.

"Hi, doll. So sorry I'm late. The traffic was hellish. I hate driving in the city. Then I had the devil's own time finding a parking place." Quinton grabbed both her hands and bent over and kissed her forehead. His hands were icy and he smelled of expensive cologne and the cold crispness of the New York winter. "You look fantastic."

"Thank you," Elizabeth replied with a warm smile. Looking up into brown eyes that held a perpetual devilish twinkle, she was suddenly glad that she had called him. If anyone could lift her spirits it was Quinton.

Her cousin was always good-natured and courtly and he had the knack of knowing exactly how to make even the homeliest of females feel as though he found her fascinating. With his blond hair, brown eyes and well-defined features, he was an attractive man. Elizabeth had often wondered how he'd reached the age of forty without marrying. Women were crazy about him and he never lacked for female companionship. A single, heterosexual male, he was the darling of society matrons.

Even as he sat down opposite her, other women in the restaurant were casting covert glances his way. A natty dresser, Quinton wore a camel-colored sweater, jeans and black suede blazer, striking just the right note of casual elegance.

"So…" he began, casting her a teasing look while he shook out his napkin. "What the hell are you doing having lunch with me when you just got married yesterday? Is this new husband of yours stupid? I was hoping he'd be an improvement over Edward."

"Max had an important business meeting that couldn't be delayed. And I thought that you liked Edward."

"I thought he was a jerk. But I love you, so I made nice whenever I was around him. You ask me, he did you a favor by running off with Natalie Brussard." Quinton's mouth twisted with distaste. "I don't like to speak ill of women, mind you, but that one's been around the block a few too many times for my taste."

Elizabeth laughed. "Thanks. I needed that."

"Anytime. I'm glad to be of service. But let's forget about Natalie and your jerk of an ex-husband. I want to hear about the new man in your life. I gotta tell you, sweetheart, this meeting he's attending, it must have been damned important to let it interrupt a honeymoon with a gorgeous creature like you. What kind of business is he in?"

Elizabeth toyed with her water glass. "Max is in investments. Finance. That sort of thing," she replied vaguely. "He puts together deals and investors."

The waiter came and took their orders. When he left, Quinton grinned at her. "So tell me, is he rich?"

"*Quinton!* What a thing to ask."

"Well? Is he?" he returned, not one whit abashed.

"You're terrible," she mumbled, and looked down at the menu, trying to ignore him and at the same time bite back a grin. Both efforts failed miserably.

"I know," he agreed cheerfully, and when she looked up he waggled his eyebrows at her. "But you love me, anyway, don'tcha. Now, answer my question."

Elizabeth laughed. "Yes. He's filthy rich."

"Hey! Way to go, cuz!" He clinked his water glass against hers then raised it in a salute. "May your life be full of happiness, love and hot sex and your bank account full of dough."

"I'll drink to that," she said, clinking her teacup to his glass. "So, how is Camille?" she asked, mainly to be polite.

"Ah well, you know my sister," Quinton said. "I just returned from visiting her and Leon. They've been married three years, and the bloom is definitely off the rose. She was making noises about divorcing him the whole time I was there."

"Oh, dear. How does Leon feel about that?"

"He doesn't have a clue, poor devil. He worships at her feet, which is probably why she's bored with him."

"So do you really think she'll divorce him?"

"Trust me, sweetie. I expect her to come swooping down on me any day now with enough suitcases to fill the basement. One thing I'll say for my sister, though. Every man she has married has been richer than the last. She'll get a healthy alimony out of Leon."

Throughout lunch their easy banter continued. It was as though it had been days, rather than months, since they'd last been together. Usually Elizabeth saw Quinton only three or four times a year, whenever she and Mimi came to New York for the fashion shows, or occasionally when he came to Texas to visit, yet he was one of her closest friends and confidants.

She had told Quinton about Edward's theft of her assets, not in any great detail, but enough for him to know that she was in financial trouble. She was tempted to confide how her marriage to Max had come about, but something held her back. It seemed somehow disloyal to Max to reveal something so private to anyone other than Mimi.

After lunch Elizabeth walked a block and a half with Quinton to where he'd parked his car. The minuscule back seat of his sports car was overflowing with suitcases. He was leaving immediately to drive down to Miami Beach to visit friends.

The wind was raw and biting, dank with the feel and smell of coming snow. Shivering, Elizabeth huddled deeper in her mink-trimmed long swing coat, and when they stopped beside his little fireball of a car, she stood on first one foot then the other, trying to ward off the penetrating cold.

"Well, cuz, it was great seeing you again," Quinton said. Giving her a warm smile, he reached out and smoothed a strand of hair off her face and tucked it behind her ear. "All kidding aside, sweetie, I do hope you have a long and happy life with your Max. And you tell him for me that if he doesn't treat you right, I'll personally come to Houston and kick his ass."

Elizabeth chuckled. She had a sudden vivid mental picture of her lean, elegant cousin and her husband butting heads. In any sort of physical confrontation Max could and would wipe up the floor with Quinton.

"I'll tell him," she agreed. They hugged and Quinton climbed into his car. Waving goodbye, Elizabeth watched him drive away.

She was glad she'd made an effort to see Quinton. With his easy charm and "don't take life too seriously" attitude he had a way of keeping her grounded while at the same time cheering her up.

Another blast of wind cut through her. She shivered and raised the fur-lined hood on her coat and stepped off the curb, raising her hand to flag down a cab. "Taxi!"

"Hey, watch out!"

The shouted warning came from behind Elizabeth. Instinctively she turned around partway toward the voice.

In the space of a heartbeat, though the scene seemed to play out in ultra-slow motion, she saw a car bearing down on her and the cold face of the driver, while from her left an elderly woman, her face twisted in a desperate expression, reached for her with both hands. "Wha—"

Everything seemed to happen at once. Several more shouts went up. The woman grabbed hold of Elizabeth's coat and did her best to snatch her back out of harm's way, but she wasn't quite quick enough. There was a sickening thud as the sedan hit Elizabeth a grazing blow, and pain exploded in her right hip.

The next thing she knew, she was lying in the street, partially on top of the old woman who had saved her, and other people were crowding all around.

"Did you see that? That guy ran her down on purpose!"

"Yeah. He took dead aim, right at her."

"Somebody call the cops."

"Anybody get a license number?"

"I did!"

"Here comes a cop."

"What's going on here? Police. Stand clear. Outta the way."

Elizabeth found herself looking up into the concerned face of a young uniformed police officer. "You okay, lady?"

"Ye-yes. Thanks to this lady. You saved my life," she said to the older woman. "I'll never be able to thank you enough." Elizabeth disentangled herself from the woman's grip and tried to stand up, only to cry out in pain.

The officer squatted down beside her. "Are you hurt?"

"Of course she's hurt," the old woman snapped, climbing to her feet with the help of some bystanders. "She was hit by a car. It's a miracle she wasn't killed."

*"Sí,"* a Hispanic man in the crowd agreed. "It was no accident, either. The man, he tried to run her down."

"You sure about that?" the cop asked.

*"Sí,* I'm sure."

"Me, too," another man agreed. "He was just sitting there with his car engine idling. The cab driver behind him was honking his horn for him to move—"

"That was me," said the man who took down the plate number. "Damn fool was just sitting there, blocking traffic."

"Yeah," the first man continued. "But then the lady stepped off the curb to flag down this guy's taxi and the driver of the black car gunned it and aimed right for her."

"If this lady hadn't pulled her back he would've run over her for sure," still another witness claimed.

"I'll call an ambulance," the officer said.

"No, please. I'm fine, really," Elizabeth insisted. "It was just a glancing blow. I'm sure I'm just bruised." To prove her point she tried to stand again, only to catch her breath at the stab of pain that shot through her side.

"That may be, but if you're in that much pain you need to get checked out."

Within minutes Elizabeth was being loaded into an ambulance. On the way to the hospital, she worried about what Max was going to say. He wouldn't be happy to have his business here interrupted, she was certain.

In the hospital ER she was examined and X-rayed, and the superficial scrapes, one on the heel of her right hand and the other on her right knee, were cleaned and treated.

While she lay on a gurney waiting for the doctor on duty to come tell her the results of the X ray, a man in a dark suit twitched aside the curtains and stepped into the cubicle.

"Mrs. Riordan?"

"Yes?"

"I'm Detective Gertski with the NYPD. Sorry to bother you, but if you feel up to talking now I need to get a little information."

Detective Gertski appeared to be middle-aged, with thinning dishwater-blond hair and the beginnings of a potbelly. His manner was low-key, almost apologetic, but Elizabeth had a feeling that behind those calm brown eyes was a keen intelligence.

"Is it really necessary for the police to get involved?" Elizabeth asked. "This was probably just an accident."

"Not according to our witnesses. In New York it's unusual to get one witness who's willing to get involved. To have four, especially four who agree on what they saw, makes us sit up and take notice.

"Also, we take hit-and-run cases very seriously. In this particular case, since all the witnesses say the driver deliberately tried to run you down, we're classifying it as an attempted murder."

"Oh, my goodness," Elizabeth said in a shaken whisper.

"Can you tell us if there is anyone who would want to harm you?"

"No. No one. I don't even live here. I can't imagine anyone I know in Houston wanting to kill me, much less traveling all this way to do it. Besides, I saw the face of the man behind the wheel of the car. He wasn't anyone I know."

"Ever hear of a contract killer?"

Elizabeth gave a startled laugh. "That's...that's preposterous."

"Maybe. Maybe not," the detective murmured. "I see you're wearing a wedding ring. How about your husband? Would he have any reason to want you out of the picture?"

"I hardly think so. We're here on our honeymoon. We were married yesterday afternoon."

"Oh?" Detective Gertski looked around. "So where is he?"

"Oh, well, uh...Max had an important business meeting today."

"Hmm. Have you called him, or had one of the hospital staff notify him that you've been injured?"

"Well...no. I didn't want to worry him, since the injury isn't all that bad." In truth, her hip hurt like the very devil, but she didn't want to be an inconvenience or a burden. Max had married her for business reasons, not because he cared anything about her.

"What about money? Would Mr. Riordan profit from your death in any way?"

"No. Not at all. I can assure you of that. Max and I signed a prenuptial agreement."

"Really? What about insurance? Could he have taken out a policy on you before the wedding?"

"Detective, I assure you, you're headed in the wrong direction. My husband is a wealthy man. An extremely wealthy man. He would have no reason whatsoever to marry me one day and have me killed the next."

"I see," the detective said, scribbling in a notepad. "All the same, I'm going to need his name and a number where I can get in touch with him."

After the past week of calling back and forth, Elizabeth knew Max's cell phone number by heart, but she wasn't about to give it to the detective. She sighed. "Very well. My husband's name is Maxwell Riordan. We're staying at the Ritz-Carlton. You can probably reach him there sometime tomorrow." *And with any luck I'll intercept the call or we'll already be on our way home to Texas,* she thought.

"Tell me everything you remember," the detective probed in his deceptively easygoing way. Elizabeth had the feeling that beyond the almost-grandfatherly gentleness was a tough New York cop with the determination of a bulldog.

"There's not much I can tell you, Detective. It all happened so fast. I don't know what kind of car it was, just that it was dark and had dark-tinted windows."

"That jibes with the description that the four different witnesses gave," Detective Gertski said. "How about the driver? You said you got a look at him?"

Elizabeth shivered. "Yes. The side windows were tinted almost black, but not the windshield. I saw him for only a second, but I doubt that I'll ever forget that face. It was cold. As cold as a dead man's."

By the time Elizabeth returned to the hotel it was almost five o'clock, and the pain medication the ER doctor had given her was beginning to wear off.

The capsules had made her sleepy. Between the medicine

and the harrowing afternoon she'd had, she was almost out on her feet. As she let herself into the suite all she wanted to do was strip out of her clothes, take another painkiller and climb into bed. She hoped that Max hadn't been able to get tickets to a play. If he had, he and Troy would have to use them. She was exhausted.

It was getting dark outside, but there was no sign of Max. Elizabeth turned on a couple of lamps in the sitting room and limped into the bedroom. She hung up her coat, noticing as she did so that the camel-colored wool garment had a tear and a grimy stain along the right front side and two buttons were missing. Too weary to care, she peeled out of her clothes and boots.

She pulled a fresh nightgown from the dresser, retrieved from her purse the prescription bottle of painkillers the doctor had given her and headed for the bathroom dressed in only her ecru bikini panties.

In the bathroom she caught sight of her reflection in the mirror and grimaced. She was pale and her hair was disheveled, but worst of all, the bruising on her hip had begun to turn an angry purplish-black color. The size of a dinner plate, the livid mark wrapped around her right hip, spreading almost to her belly button in front and to her spine in the back.

Elizabeth groaned. She was never going to be able to hide this from Max, she thought, examining the injury closely. She would have to tell him about the incident.

She hated the thought of that. The last thing she wanted was to be a burden to him right off the bat. Maybe if she broached the subject at just the right moment, then glossed over the whole thing as nothing serious, he wouldn't be annoyed, she thought.

After taking another painkiller she brushed her teeth and washed her face. She was patting her face dry when the bathroom door opened.

Elizabeth gave a squeak and turned toward the doorway with the hand towel clutched to her breasts as Max strode in.

"There you are. Sorry I'm late. The meeting lasted—"

Max stopped in his tracks and stared at her hip. "What the hell!"

# *Seven*

Elizabeth caught her lower lip between her teeth and met Max's glare with a chagrined expression. "It, uh…it looks worse than it is," she said. "Really."

"I sure as hell hope so. Because it looks like you were run over by a tank."

"Not quite. It was a sedan," she said with a wan smile, but her attempt at humor made his frown deepen.

"What?"

"I, uh…I had a little accident."

"What kind of accident?"

"It wasn't anything you need to be concerned about. I stepped off the curb, and I guess I wasn't paying enough attention because a car grazed my hip."

"You were hit by a *car?*" His gaze dropped again to her hip, then jerked back up to meet hers. "And you don't think I should be *concerned?*"

Before she could answer he spied the medicine bottle sitting on the counter and snatched it up. "What's this?"

"Just a prescription for pain that the ER doctor gave me."

His eyes narrowed. She had thought he looked angry before, but that was nothing compared to his fury now. "You were hurt bad enough to be taken to the emergency room? Why the *hell* didn't you call me?"

"I...I didn't want to interrupt your meeting."

"Dammit, Elizabeth—"

The suite telephone rang, cutting him off. Still glaring at her, Max snatched the receiver off the bathroom wall telephone.

"Yes?" he barked.

Grateful for the interruption, Elizabeth turned her back, pulled on one of the hotel's cotton terry-cloth robes and cinched it tight around her waist, all the while trying to work through her confusion and think of something to say that would defuse the situation. She came up with nothing. She would have expected Max to be angry if she'd called him and interrupted his meeting, not the other way around.

"I see," Max said to the caller, still looking at Elizabeth as though he'd like to throttle her. "Yes. That will be fine. I'll be expecting you."

He hung up the receiver and fixed Elizabeth with a simmering stare. "That was Detective Gertski," he said in a chilling, soft voice. "He wants to talk to me about the hit-and-run accident in which my wife was nearly killed."

"Oh." Elizabeth blinked back the tears that were trying to well in her eyes and pressed her lips together to keep them from wobbling. Between her recent money woes, Max's blunt marriage proposal, the stresses of the past week, the wedding and now this, her emotions were bubbling just beneath the surface.

"That's all you have to say? Oh?" Max shook his head. "Great. This just keeps getting better and better. First you tell me that you had a minor accident. Then, under pressure, you admit that it was bad enough that you had to go to the ER.

Now this detective tells me that according to witnesses, the guy behind the wheel of the car was *trying* to kill you. Dammit, Elizabeth! What the *hell* is going on?"

"I don't *know!*" she wailed, losing it. She glared back at him, her chin quivering. "I'm tired, I'm in pa-pain and I've had a horrid day. So don't you dare yell at me!"

His image became blurry as her eyes filled. One tear, then another, spilled over her lower eyelids and raced down her cheeks. Max's expression changed from anger to horror.

"C'mon, don't do that. Ah, hell, don't cry," he pleaded.

"I'm not…cr-crying," Elizabeth sobbed between hitching breaths. "I…I never…never cry."

The ridiculous assertion brought a hint of a smile to his lips. "Yeah, you're right. What was I thinking? A tough cookie like you? Your eyes are just leaking, right?"

"That's not funny!" she stormed at him, and her face crumpled.

"Ah, hell, come here." Max stepped forward and pulled her into his embrace. Cradling the back of her head with one hand, he pressed her face to his chest and rocked her from side to side. "C'mon, Elizabeth, take it easy. I'm sorry. I shouldn't have yelled."

For Elizabeth, his awkward tenderness was the last straw. She had tried for so long to be strong and stoic, but she had reached the end of her tether. Collapsing against him, she grasped his shirtfront with both hands and let the sobs come.

They racked her slender frame. The sounds coming from her throat were agonized and heart-wrenching. Rubbing his hand over her back in a circular motion, Max said nothing.

To Elizabeth, his embrace felt like the last safe haven left in the world, and she reveled in it, absorbing the warmth and comfort, the feeling of security, like a starving man at a banquet.

"Oh, Max…it…it was so…so scary," she sobbed against his chest.

"I know, baby. I know. But you're safe now."

"The look in his eyes was…" She shivered, unable to continue, and more sobs overtook her.

Max grew still. "In whose eyes? You mean the man who almost ran you down? You got a look at him?"

Giving a watery sniff, Elizabeth nodded against his chest.

"Did you recognize him?"

"No. I'd never…never seen him before. I'm…I'm sure of that."

Max grew silent again, but Elizabeth could tell that he was dissecting every particle of information that she'd given him.

Gradually, her pent-up emotions spent, she quieted, and with calm came embarrassment. She stepped back out of his arms and reached for a tissue. "I'm sorry about that. I'm not usually a crybaby," she mumbled, dabbing at her eyes.

"That's okay. You had good reason." He waited while she blew her nose nosily, then asked, "Just tell me one thing. Why didn't you call me today?"

Elizabeth put her cool fingertips to her temples, then her forehead. She shook her head. "Do you mind if we continue this discussion in the bedroom? My hip is hurting terribly."

"Damn. Why didn't you say so before now? Do you need a pain pill?"

"No," she replied, shaking her head. "I took a couple just before you arrived."

"Then let's get you in bed."

Being careful not to touch her injured side, Max swooped her in his arms and carried her into the bedroom. There, as casually as though he'd performed the task a hundred times before, he stood her on her feet and stripped the robe off her before Elizabeth realized his intent.

"Oh!" she gasped. Instinctively she crossed her arms over her bare breasts. Heat flushed her entire body, from her toes to her hairline. She felt as though she was glowing.

A hint of a smile tugged at Max's mouth. "Hey, why so modest? I'm your husband, remember? You might as well get used to me seeing you naked. I intend for that to happen often." He trailed his forefinger along the top of her bikini underwear. "By the way, nice panties," he drawled, holding her gaze.

The gossamer touch left a trail of fire along her skin. His words and the look in his eyes deepened her flush several shades. Elizabeth was so befuddled and bombarded by so many different feelings she didn't know what to say. She stood there tongue-tied and feeling foolish, and watched him go to the bureau and get out a clean nightgown. He returned and dropped it over her head and bundled her into bed.

"There. Are you comfortable now?" he asked when he had her settled with the covers pulled up to her waist.

"Yes. Thank you," she mumbled. The painkiller was beginning to take effect and she was having difficulty keeping her eyes open.

Max sat down on the side of the bed beside her and hitched his bent knee up on the mattress. Her eyes popped open, the feeling of lethargy vanishing as she became aware of his heat along her left side where his leg pressed against her.

"Now then, tell me in detail everything that happened after you left here," Max ordered. "And don't leave anything out."

Striving to appear calm, Elizabeth folded her hands together atop the covers that lay across her waist. "Well, let's see. I took a cab to a little café that I know and had breakfast, then I walked the rest of the way to the museum…"

Step by step Elizabeth went through the sequence of events leading up to and immediately following the hit-and-run.

When she was done Max stared at her in silence for so long that she began to fidget.

"And not once, during all that time, did you think to call me?" he finally asked.

"I told you. I didn't want to bother you."

"Elizabeth, you're my wife. If something happens to you I want to know about it."

"But…I would have had to interrupt your meeting. I assumed if the deal was important enough for you to bring your assistant along on your honeymoon that you wouldn't appreciate being dragged away to see after me."

He gave her another long, level look. "Touché. I guess I deserve that."

"Oh, no! You misunderstood me." She reached out and touched his arm. Max had shed his suit coat and necktie before he'd surprised her in the bathroom, and beneath his shirtsleeve his arm was hard and warm to her touch, his big-boned frame in sharp contrast to her delicate build. "That wasn't a criticism, Max. I don't expect you to concern yourself with my welfare. I know we don't have that kind of marriage."

"What kind of marriage?"

"You know, a…a traditional, romantic one. The only reason you and I bothered with any semblance of a honeymoon trip was to keep up appearances."

Again, he stared at her in silence for a long time, the muscles in his jaw working. Elizabeth did not know him well, but she could tell that he was not pleased.

"You're wrong on all counts," he said finally. "I don't give a damn about appearances. We're here because I wanted us to have some time together to get to know each other better. I thought that was what a honeymoon was about."

"Well, yes. If you're in love."

Max looked up at the ceiling, as though striving for patience. "I thought we had all this settled. Look, we may not be in love—whatever that is—but so what? As far as I'm concerned that emotion is highly overrated. One I've never experienced, thank God. Mutual respect and admiration, loyalty, honesty—it seems to me that those are the things that are important, in a marriage as well as in a business deal."

Elizabeth stared at him, feeling absurdly like one of those characters in a cartoon where a light bulb suddenly flashes on over its head. "You think of our marriage as another one of your business deals, don't you?"

"Well, yeah. Sort of. Like any good merger, we joined forces for mutually beneficial reasons. Of course, a marriage has some enjoyable fringe benefits that you don't get in a corporate deal," he added with a seductive look. Reaching out, he ran his fingertips down her cheek to the corner of her mouth and continued in an even softer voice, "Like the one we sampled this morning. All day I've been looking forward to repeating the experience, but I guess now that'll have to wait until you're feeling better."

Elizabeth's face burned. In silence she stared down at her fingers, which were plucking at the covers.

Belatedly, it seemed to occur to Max that perhaps calling their marriage a business deal wasn't such a good idea. "There are other benefits, too," he hurried on. "Like companionship and having someone you can count on. That sort of thing."

She gazed at him in silence, and Max raked his hand through his hair. "Look, Elizabeth, I'm a businessman, and a damned good one. What I'm not good at is all the touchy-feely stuff. You know…discussing feelings and getting all emotional about things. But that doesn't mean that I don't care about you."

"I see. So what you're saying is you care about me in the

same way that you would care about any valuable business acquisition." She nodded. "I understand. You do have a sizable investment in me, after all."

Max frowned. "That's not what—"

"Don't worry. From now on I'll keep you informed of any changes in my condition or situation."

"Good. No, wait, that's not what I meant, either. Dammit, Elizabeth! You're twisting everything."

"But you just said—"

"Never mind that!" Max looked up at the ceiling again and sighed. "You're going to make me spell it out, aren't you? Okay, listen up. And listen good, because I'm only going to say this once." He looked straight into her eyes. "I married you for business *and* personal reasons. The business reasons you know. On a personal level, I married you because… well…because you please me."

Elizabeth blinked at him. "Excuse me?"

"I said, you please me. I like everything about you—your looks, your character, your intelligence, your soft voice, your grace, that beautiful thick hair." As though to emphasize his point, he reached out and touched his fingertips to the disheveled locks that lay against the pillow. "I also like the way you smell, all sweet and flowery and feminine."

Stunned, Elizabeth could only stare at him. It wasn't exactly a declaration of love, or even affection, but it was probably as close as a man like Max was likely to get.

In that moment she made up her mind that she would be the best wife to Max that she could possibly be. She would uphold her end of their bargain in every way that she could. He wanted to tap into resources of the "old-monied" crowd, so she would introduce him to them and coach him on which approach to take with which potential investor, how to deal with the myriad personalities and characters that made up Houston's high society.

Max almost had Elizabeth convinced that he did care about her when he added, "All that, added to the respect and admiration I have for you, seemed like a perfect foundation for marriage to me."

Elizabeth gave him a doubtful look. "You respect me?"

"Sure I do. I watched you this past year. You went through a tough time, what with Edward running off with Natalie Brussard and all the talk and speculation that was buzzing around. Then on top of everything else you found out that he'd robbed you blind. Yet you weathered all that with dignity and class."

Elizabeth shrugged. "What else could I do?"

Max's mouth twisted in a wry smile. "Plenty. You could have gone into seclusion, or reacted with bitterness and anger and sought revenge, or bad-mouthed Edward and his little chippy to anyone who would listen. But you didn't do any of those things. You held your head up like the lady you are and let the gossip and dirt swirl around you without once commenting. In my book, that's admirable."

Elizabeth shrugged again. "Don't give me too much credit. That's just my way of dealing with things. Sort of an instinctive reaction."

"That's precisely my point."

He waited a beat, watching her, as though expecting her to say something, but Elizabeth kept her gaze focused on her plucking fingers.

"Let's get back to the subject at hand. How badly were you hurt? I assume they X-rayed your hip at the hospital?"

"Yes, they did. The doctor said that I was lucky. Nothing is broken. I'm just badly bruised." Elizabeth shivered. "If it hadn't been for the little old lady who grabbed my coat and pulled me back, the car would have hit me a solid blow. Instead, the impact helped to knock me sideways. I landed on top of my rescuer."

"Did you get her name?" Max asked. "I'd like to reward her."

"No, but I'm certain the police have it."

"Good." Max fished his ever-present PDA out of his shirt pocket and made himself a note. "Now then," he said when done. "What were the doctor's instructions?"

"To stay off my feet as much as I can for a few days and let my hip heal. Maybe put cool compresses on the bruising if it bothers me too much and take the painkillers as needed."

A knock sounded at the hallway door to the sitting room.

"Damn. I almost forgot. That'll be Detective Gertski."

"He's coming here? Tonight?"

"Yeah."

Max stood up. Elizabeth started to do the same, but he stopped her with a hand on her shoulder. "Whoa. Where do you think you're going?"

"To talk to the detective," Elizabeth said.

"Oh, no, you're not. You're staying put, right here."

"But, Max—"

"Forget it, Elizabeth. The doc at the hospital told you to stay off your feet and that's what you're going to do," he said in a tone that brooked no argument. "If the detective needs to speak to you I'll bring him in here. Right now I want you to get some rest."

"But—"

To Elizabeth's surprise, Max bent over and gave her a soft kiss on the lips, cutting off her protest. Pulling back only partway, he looked into her eyes and whispered. "But, nothing. Now, go to sleep."

"All right," came her meek whisper. Actually, Elizabeth had neither the desire nor the strength to argue. Fatigue and medication were combining to make her so drowsy she could barely hold her eyes open, and her body longed for sleep.

"This shouldn't take long. After he leaves I'll order us dinner from room service." Max stopped in the doorway and looked back. "What would you like, by the way?"

"Oh, just something light. A salad or a bowl of soup."

"Gotcha."

Max closed the bedroom door behind him and strode through the sitting room to the suite entrance.

A check through the peephole revealed a balding, paunchy, middle-aged man standing in the hallway, looking all around at the opulent decor. Max opened the door. "You must be Detective Gertski."

"Yes. And you're Mr. Riordan?"

Max nodded. "Come in. My wife just finished telling me what happened."

"How's she doing?"

"She's banged up and bruised, but otherwise okay."

"Good, good. I'm glad to hear that. Your wife seems like a lovely lady."

"She is. Have a seat, Detective." Max gestured toward the sofa, and when they were both settled he added, "Now, tell me how I can be of help."

"First of all, in order to rule you out as a suspect, I'm going to have to ask a few routine questions of you, Mr. Riordan," the detective informed him. "I hope you won't take offense."

"No, go ahead. I don't have anything to hide."

"Where were you at one-twenty-five this afternoon?"

"In a meeting with my assistant, Troy Ellerbee, and a financier by the name of Lloyd Baxter. We met in Baxter's office in the Colfax building."

"I see. And if I ask Mr. Baxter and Mr. Ellerbee, they will verify that?"

"Absolutely."

"Did you hire someone to kill your wife?"

If the detective had hoped to rattle him with the blunt question, he failed. Max's expression did not alter one iota.

"No. I did not. For God's sake, man, we were married only yesterday."

"Yes, so your wife told me. Can you think of anyone who would want Mrs. Riordan dead?"

"Not at all. Everyone who knows her admires her."

"I see." Detective Gertski pursed his lips and ruminated for several moments.

"I'm curious, Detective. Do you always put this much effort into solving a case like this? I mean, what with all the gruesome crimes that occur every day in this city, how does a nonlethal hit-and-run merit so much attention?"

"To be honest, normally it wouldn't. The NYPD doesn't have the manpower to investigate every traffic mishap. Right now we're investigating the case as an accidental hit-and-run, but the more I talk to people, the more it's looking like a contract job."

Max frowned. "What makes you say that?"

"The driver of the cab that was behind the black sedan got the license number. We ran it through the system and found out that the plates had been stolen from a blue minivan in Queens this morning. By now the driver of the sedan has probably switched the plates back, so the car is untraceable. That's something a professional criminal would do."

"I see," Max murmured.

"We have four eyewitnesses. They all agree that the driver of the sedan seemed to be waiting for a chance to run over your wife. His car was sitting still with the engine running, blocking a lane of traffic and irritating a lot of other drivers. Their honking was what attracted the attention of the witnesses on the sidewalk. When Mrs. Riordan stepped off the curb the driver of the sedan punched the gas pedal and took aim at her."

Max shook his head. "This just doesn't make sense. Elizabeth is well-liked and respected. There's absolutely no reason for anyone to want her dead."

Detective Gertski mulled that over for a moment, then said, "Well, I suppose it's possible that this was a case of mistaken identity. All of the witnesses say that your wife was wearing a camel coat with a hood, which was covering her head and most of her face. Could be the driver of the car mistook her for someone else."

"That must be it," Max said with obvious relief. "There's just no other explanation."

"Your wife was the only one who got a look at the suspect. Would it be possible for you to bring her to the station house tomorrow? I'd like for her to go through some mug shots. Maybe she can pick him out."

"Sure. We can do that."

After Detective Gertski left, Max walked over to the window and looked out at the lights of New York. It had started to snow in earnest—big, fat, wet flakes that by morning would coat the city in white.

Knowing there was a lunatic out there who had tried to murder Elizabeth was worrisome. It had to be a case of mistaken identity. There was just no other logical answer.

Restless and uneasy, Max paced from one window to the next, staring out at the night skyline through a veil of falling snow without really appreciating the beauty before him or the almost pulsing life of the city. He felt on edge, torn.

Dammit, one of the reasons he'd asked Elizabeth to marry him was because she seemed so self-sufficient, he groused to himself. He'd figured that most of the time she would go her own way and not make too many demands on him, which was exactly what she'd done today.

Yet he had to admit, it irked him that she hadn't turned to

him for help and comfort after her close call. It bothered him even more that she'd felt that she *couldn't* turn to him.

Max shook his head. He'd had it all planned out. He and Elizabeth would have a pleasant, mutually beneficial marriage and with luck they would grow fond of each other as time went by. Now here they were, married one day and already he was feeling protective and definitely proprietorial. Go figure.

Impatient with his circling thoughts, Max strode into the bedroom. The only light was the soft glow from the base of the lamp on his side of the bed, but it was enough for him to see that Elizabeth was sound asleep. Standing beside the bed, Max watched her and grappled with the confusing coil of feelings that seemed to crowd his chest.

She looked incredibly beautiful and delicate. Almost like an angel come to earth. She was the kind of woman who could arouse in any man his most primitive, protective instincts. Apparently, he was no exception.

The very thought of anyone doing her harm made him feel almost murderous. Why in God's name would anyone want her dead? It didn't make sense.

The next morning Elizabeth awoke to the sound of raised male voices. Yawning, she sat up in bed, pushed her heavy mane of hair back out of her eyes with both hands and looked at the bedside clock. Good heavens. She'd slept for hours. It was past eight o'clock.

Tentatively, she pressed her hip. It was sore, but not as much as yesterday.

From the next room the murmur of voices reached another crescendo, drawing her sleepy gaze to the doorway. It sounded as though Max and his assistant were having an argument.

Too groggy to care, Elizabeth dismissed the men from her mind, fought her way from beneath the mounds of covers and climbed from the bed. Once on her feet she felt stiff and sore and so woozy she had to hold on to the bedpost for a moment to steady herself.

Wow, she thought, cupping her forehead. Whatever those pain pills were, they were potent. She could barely recollect her encounter with Max the night before, which had ended with Detective Gertski's arrival. After that everything was hazy. Vaguely she seemed to recall Max waking her up at some point and insisting that she eat a bowl of soup.

If they had talked at all during the meal she didn't remember their conversation. The moment she had finished her dinner she'd crawled back into bed and surrendered again to sleep.

Taking advantage of the solitude, Elizabeth limped into the bathroom. Showering and washing her hair helped to clear the cobwebs out of her mind. Afterward she blew her hair dry until it fell in a thick, shiny brown curtain around her shoulders. She then put on her makeup and dressed in brown tweed slacks and a cream-colored turtleneck sweater. Gold earrings, a gold rope chain and a gold bangle were her only jewelry.

Through the closed bedroom door she could still make out the men's voices, though they weren't as sharp as before. For a moment Elizabeth debated whether to stay in the bedroom or go out there and risk stepping into the middle of an argument. In the end she decided the heck with it. She wasn't going to remain cooped up in the bedroom all day.

The men's conversation stopped the instant she entered the sitting room. "Elizabeth. What're you doing out of bed?" Max demanded. "The doctor said for you to stay off your feet."

Troy's mouth thinned. He barely spared her a glance and a murmured, "Morning."

"Good morning," she returned as pleasantly as she could manage. Turning her attention to her husband, she replied. "The doctor said to stay off my feet as much as possible. He didn't say anything about complete bed rest. I can put my feet up in here."

"How is your hip?" Max watched her cross the room and frowned. "You're still limping."

"It's a bit sore and stiff, that's all." She sat down in an easy chair and swung her legs up on the matching plump hassock.

"Troy and I were about to leave for a quick meeting with Lloyd Baxter. I'll be back by noon."

Troy frowned. "Max, I don't think we'll be finished by then."

Max shot his assistant that steely-eyed look that Elizabeth was beginning to realize meant his anger was coming to a boil.

"I'll be back here by noon," he repeated, staring Troy down.

Troy didn't argue, but Elizabeth saw that the muscles along his jawline were clenched so tight it wouldn't surprise her if he cracked a tooth. In stony silence he started gathering up the papers and files that had been spread out on the table.

"When I get back we'll have lunch and then I'll take you to the police station," Max continued. "Detective Gertski wants you to look at some mug shots."

"Now, there's a productive use of time," Troy muttered under his breath, just loud enough for Elizabeth to hear.

"What?" Max asked.

"Nothing," his assistant replied, stuffing papers into his briefcase.

When the men were ready to leave Elizabeth started to rise, but Max stopped her with a hand on her shoulder. "No, don't get up," he insisted. "Just sit right there and take it easy." Bending over her chair, he gave her a lingering kiss and murmured, "Call room service if you need anything. Okay? I'll be back by noon," he repeated.

Still feeling a bit battered, Elizabeth was happy to oblige. The moment the door closed behind the men she leaned her head back against the soft upholstery and closed her eyes. After what seemed like only a minute there was a knock at the door.

Elizabeth groaned. What now? She hauled herself out of the chair and limped to the door. Going up on tiptoes, she looked through the peephole and gasped.

Her hand flew to her mouth and she jumped back, her eyes wide and horror-struck.

The person standing on the other side of the door was the driver of the black sedan!

He knocked again. Elizabeth stood perfectly still. Then, to her horror, the doorknob began to jiggle. Oh dear Lord! He was trying to jimmy the lock.

Elizabeth sucked in a sharp breath and backed away. She darted a look around. She had to hide. But where?

# *Eight*

Halfway to the lobby Max realized that he'd forgotten something. "Damn. I left the revised cost estimate in the fax machine after I sent it." The elevator reached the lobby and he motioned for Troy to get off. "Wait here for me while I run back up and get it. I won't be long."

"Sure," came Troy's clipped reply.

Watching him step off the elevator, Max sighed. Troy was still put out with him. Max had wanted to cancel today's meeting with Baxter and stay with Elizabeth, but Troy had hit the roof when he'd told him. Troy had been his assistant for more than ten years and this morning marked the first time that they had ever had a serious disagreement.

"Going up?" a man in the lobby called out.

Max nodded and held down the open button on the operating panel. The man and his wife stepped into the elevator and pushed the button for the fourth floor.

Max acknowledged their thanks with a nod, but his thoughts had already returned to his assistant. Troy had disapproved of the marriage from the get-go, but until this morning Max hadn't realized how strong his resentment was. He'd gone so far as to accuse Elizabeth of making up the story about being hit by a car, or at the very least, exaggerating what had happened.

"Can't you see that she's playing you?" Troy had shouted at him. "It's not enough that she married you for your money. It never is with women like her. She wants you to dote on her."

"What do you mean, 'women like her'?" Max had demanded, his own temper on the rise.

"Rich, pampered socialites," Troy had fired back. "From the time they're born they have everything handed to them on a platter and they grow up thinking the world revolves around them."

"Elizabeth isn't like that."

"Oh, yeah, right," Troy had sneered. "Look, Max, I don't have anything personal against Elizabeth, but a wife—any wife—is going to make demands on your time. And as you taught me years ago, time is money."

Having one's own words thrown back at you is never pleasant, Max thought. However, he could hardly get angry with Troy for learning a lesson well.

"That's true," he'd acknowledged. "However, since I have more money than I could go through in a lifetime, I think I can afford to spend some time with my wife."

"So you're willing to let this deal fall through for her sake?" Troy had demanded. "Even though the detective said it was probably a case of mistaken identity?"

The elevator stopped on the fourth floor and the couple got out. Still going over the argument in his mind, Max barely noticed.

In the end, he and Troy had compromised, and Max had telephoned Lloyd Baxter and rescheduled their meeting for ten o'clock.

The elevator stopped on Max's floor and he stepped off.

A few feet from the elevator he turned a corner and saw a tall, beefy man with a lumbering gait at the far end of the hall, walking toward him. The guy kept his head down and his overcoat collar turned.

Max frowned. Something about the guy bothered him, but he couldn't quite put his finger on what it was. They nodded to each other in passing, but the other man did not quite meet Max's gaze, and his uneasiness deepened. He didn't trust a man who wouldn't look you in the eye.

There was no sign of Elizabeth when Max let himself into the suite. Had she gone back to bed? he wondered. If so, her hip must be hurting her worse than she'd let on. He eased open one of the double doors that led into the bedroom. The first thing he saw was the empty bed.

"Elizabeth?"

He took a step into the room. Out of the corner of his eye he detected a movement. He turned in time to see his wife lunge out from behind the door, a crystal vase held high over her head in both hands. She brought the vase down with all her might. Max barely had time to raise his arm to fend off the blow.

"Ow!" he yelled as the heavy vase struck his forearm. "Dammit, Elizabeth! What the *hell* is the matter with you? You damn near broke my arm."

"Max?" She stopped in her tracks, her eyes wide, her face chalk white. Dropping the vase, she launched herself at him. "Max! Oh, Max, thank God!"

"Hey, take it easy." His arms closed around her as she burrowed against him and clutched his shirt with both hands. "Damn, you're trembling all over. What's wrong? What happened?"

"H-he was he-here. He…he…"

"Who was here?"

"That…that ma-man. Oh, Max!" she wailed, and started to sob against his chest.

"Okay, take it easy. Calm down. What man are you talking about?"

"Th-the man in th-the car."

Max tensed. "The one who tried to run over you?"

He felt her nod her head against his chest. "Are you sure it was him? Could it have been a hotel employee?"

"No. I'm positive it was the driver of that car. I'll never forget that face. He…he knocked on the door just a few minutes after you left. I looked through the peephole and saw him. Oh, God, I was so scared. You have to believe me! It was him!"

"I believe you. Shh. Take it easy, you're safe now."

"When I didn't answer he tried to pick the lock. So I grabbed a vase and hid behind the door. I didn't know what else to do."

Max remembered the man he'd passed in the hall. "Was he a big guy in a black leather overcoat? The swarthy type, built like a bull? Almost no neck?"

"Yes!" Elizabeth pulled back just enough to look up at Max. "You saw him?"

"Yeah, I passed him in the hall. It must have scared him off when he heard the elevator stop on this floor. Damn, I knew there was something that didn't sit quite right as soon as I saw him, but I just now figured out what it was. The corridor ends at the door to our suite. He had no business being this far down the hallway."

"How did he find me?" Elizabeth cried. "Why is he doing this?"

"I don't know, but I'm going to find out." Max grasped Elizabeth's upper arms to move her aside, but she clutched at him.

"Where are you going? Don't leave me!"

"Take it easy. I'm not going anywhere. I'm just going to make a few calls. The first one to Detective Gertski. Why don't you go back to bed and rest. I'll be right next door in the sitting room."

"No! I want to stay with you!"

Her paleness worried him. It would probably be best if she went to bed, but he could see the stark terror in her eyes. "All right. C'mon."

Swooping her up in his arms, he carried her into the sitting room and settled her on one of the sofas. To reassure her, he perched on the edge of the cushion beside her hip and held one of her hands. He could still feel her trembling.

One after another, Max made a series of telephone calls—to Detective Gertski, Troy, the hotel manager, his pilot and Lloyd Baxter. He had barely hung up from the last call when a knock sounded on the door. Elizabeth jumped as though she'd been shot.

"Take it easy. That's probably Troy." Max almost had to pry his hand from her grasp.

A quick look through the peephole proved him right.

"What the hell is the delay now?" his assistant demanded as he stormed inside through the door that Max held open. "If we don't get a move on we're going to be late."

"I've already phoned Baxter and postponed the meeting. You're going to meet with him at two."

"Me? You mean without you?" He shot Elizabeth a disgusted look. "I knew I shouldn't have let you come back up here alone. She talked you into this, didn't she? Dammit, Max—"

"Just shut up and listen." As succinctly as possible, Max explained what had happened, but when he finished Troy was still skeptical.

"Ah, c'mon. You don't actually believe that someone tried to break in here and kill her, do you?"

"Dammit, Troy, I saw the guy myself. I passed him on my way back to the suite."

"Just because you saw someone in the hall doesn't mean anything. It was probably another guest."

"Then what was he doing all the way down here? There's not another door within fifty feet of this one."

"Who knows? There could be any number of reasons. Hell, maybe he was lost. This deal is important. If we convince Baxter to invest we can get things rolling in Dallas next week."

"Look, I don't like this any more than you do, but Elizabeth is my wife now. I can't just let her fend for herself."

"Do you two mind?" Elizabeth said. "I'm sitting right here. Max, I don't want to be a burden to anyone." Troy snorted at that, but she ignored him and forged ahead, although she was trembling inside at what she was about to suggest. "If you'll just put me on a commercial flight home you can get on with your business here."

"No," Max replied.

"No? What do you mean, no?" Troy demanded. "That's the first sensible thing anybody has said since I walked into this suite. Send her home and let's get back to business."

Before Max could reply another knock sounded. He darted a look at Elizabeth and saw that her eyes were wide with fear. "Take it easy. That's probably the manager. I called and told him what happened and that we were leaving. He said he'd be right up with our bill and he'd bring a couple of maids with him to pack for us."

"You're checking out?" Troy looked outraged. "Ah, c'mon, Max. Don't you think you're overreacting?"

"No. I don't. And I'm counting on you to finish selling

Baxter on the deal. Be sure to get his commitment in writing. When you have the deal sewed up call me on my cell phone. If Elizabeth and I are still at the airport you can fly home with us. Otherwise, you'll have to catch a commercial flight back to Houston."

Troy opened his mouth to protest, but Max raised his hand and stopped him with a sharp "Not another word. I've made my decision." He went to answer the door, his gaze still locked on Troy. "You just be at Baxter's office at two o'clock."

The hotel manager was accompanied by two uniformed maids and a middle-aged man, whom he introduced as Lou Greer, the chief of hotel security. Without having to be told, the two women headed for the bedroom and began packing. Introductions had barely been made all around when Detective Gertski arrived.

While Max explained in detail what had happened, the detective took notes on a small pad.

"I don't understand why this man is doing this," Elizabeth said when Max had finished. "And how did he find me?"

"He probably followed you from the crime scene to the hospital, then from the hospital to the Ritz," the detective said. "A little bribe money under the table would have gotten him your suite number. *Why* he's after you is a mystery that we're still working to solve."

The first thing Detective Gertski did after he put away his notepad was to check the door lock. He squatted down on his haunches and examined the strike plate, the plunger and door frame around the lock. Then he stood up and shined a penlight down into the card slot. "Hey, come take a look at this," he said to the security man. Mr. Greer walked over to the door and he, too, peered down into the slot.

"Well, whaddaya know."

"What is it?" Max asked.

"Tool marks on the inner mechanism. Someone definitely tried to jimmy the lock."

"That does it," Max announced. "We're getting out of here."

"I understand how you feel, Mr. Riordan," Detective Gertski said. "If it were my wife this guy was after I'd probably do the same. But it might really help our case if you brought Mrs. Riordan by the station house to look at mug shots before you leave New York. As it stands right now, we have very little to go on."

"If Elizabeth did identify someone, would that be enough to arrest him?" Max inquired.

"Well…no. We'd need corroborating evidence before we could do th—"

"That's what I thought. Sorry, Detective. Weighed against the risk, it's just not worth it. I'm getting her out of this city. Now, before this nutcase succeeds."

The man in the black car watched the entrance to the Ritz-Carlton. A car-service limo pulled up and a phalanx of men, some in the hotel's uniform and others in plainclothes, hustled the target into the waiting vehicle. The man that he'd learned was the target's new husband climbed in after her. A shorter, balding man in an overcoat that had seen better days joined the pair inside the limo.

The sedan driver gave a disdainful snort. The shorter guy had *cop* written all over him.

The limo pulled away from the curb and the black sedan pulled out to follow, trailing about a block behind. Keeping visual contact with the limo, the driver picked up his cell phone and thumbed in a number.

"This is Angel," he said curtly to the party who answered.

"I've made two runs at the target, but she got lucky both times. I think she's spooked now, because it looks like she and her husband are leaving. I'm following her limo, but it looks like they're headed for the airport."

"What happened?" the other party demanded.

"I told you. The bitch got lucky."

"How?"

Angel's jaw set. An uncomfortable silence stretched out. He didn't like being questioned. The only man he answered to was the big boss, Tony Voltura. In the end he decided he'd make an exception, mainly because he was doing this job at the boss's request.

"I tried to run her over yesterday, but thanks to some busybody old lady who pulled her back out of the way, the car didn't strike her with a solid blow. She was banged up some, but nothing fatal. I was hoping she'd think it was an accident.

"Today I hid in the hotel stairwell outside her suite and waited for her husband to leave. When he finally did I knocked on their door a couple of times. The target didn't open up or say anything so I figured she was napping, and I went to work on the lock. I almost had the thing open when I heard the elevator stop on their floor. Within seconds, here came hubby, striding down the hall toward me. I had to haul ass outta there before he put two and two together and figured out what I was doing there.

"The target must have seen me through the peephole or heard me picking the lock, 'cause next thing I know the suite is crawling with people—the hotel manager, security, the cops. She and her husband have a cop in the car with them right now."

"Damn," his client spat. "So what's next?"

"She's got her guard up now, so I think we should back off for a month or so, let her think the danger is over. In the meantime I'll take care of the other jobs I've got hanging fire. Once she's back in her comfort zone and feeling relaxed, she's sure to make a mistake. When she does, I'll be there."

"That's it? That's the best you can do?"

A few beats of menacing silence ticked by. When the driver of the sedan finally replied, his voice had lowered to a threatening rumble. "You don't like the way I do things, then find yourself another man. Either way, I keep the money you've already given me."

"No, no," the client said in a rush. "I didn't mean that the way you took it. It's just that I wanted this over with as quickly as possible. Your way will work. You're right. After Elizabeth's been home in Houston for a few weeks and nothing happens, she'll let her guard down and make a mistake."

"Right," Angel said, and made a right at the next corner, aborting the tail on the limo. "I'll call you when I'm ready to fly to Houston."

The limo stopped in front of a nondescript apartment building.

"Where are we? Why are we stopping?" Elizabeth asked, looking around with alarm.

Max put his hand on her leg. "Take it easy. This won't take but a minute. Detective Gertski will stay with you while I run inside." He opened the limo door and climbed out, then bent and looked back inside at the detective. "Apartment 3B, right?"

"Yeah. Her name is Minnie Phelps."

"What is he doing?" Elizabeth asked, watching Max take the front stoop steps two at a time.

"The old lady who saved you yesterday lives here," the detective replied. "Your husband pulled me aside before we left the hotel and got her name and address. He wants to personally thank her and give her a reward."

Elizabeth's head snapped around. "Really?"

"Yeah."

"Oh, I'm so glad." Elizabeth looked back at the gray stone building, a warm feeling engulfing her. "She deserves to be rewarded. Everything happened so fast yesterday I don't remember much about her, but from the looks of this neighborhood I imagine she could use a financial windfall. I hope Max is generous."

Detective Gertski gave a snort of laughter. "Don't worry about that. I was standing beside him when he wrote out the check, not that I was trying to snoop or anything, so I couldn't help but notice the amount. I'd say Mrs. Phelps's money worries are over."

Max came out of the building with a stocky little woman wearing a print dress and apron and clutching a worn crocheted shawl around her shoulders against the biting cold. She was waving her hands and talking a mile a minute.

Max opened the rear door of the limo. "Get in, Mrs. Phelps. We'll talk inside where it's warmer."

The old lady scrambled into the vehicle, still talking nonstop. "Oh, my stars, would you look at this," she exclaimed. Her gaze darted around the roomy interior as her work-worn hands stroked the upholstery. "Why, this is genuine leather. And is that a bar? Oh, my stars. My friends are never going to believe this. Me, Minnie Phelps, sitting in a limo."

"Mrs. Phelps wanted to see for herself that you were all right," Max said to Elizabeth as he climbed in and resumed his seat.

"Yes, indeed I did," the chattering woman verified. "They bundled you off to the hospital so quick yesterday that I didn't get a chance to find out how you were doing, or even get your name. I figured I'd never hear from you again. Then, out of the blue, this handsome husband of yours rings my doorbell and gives me a check for more money than I've ever seen at one time."

Elizabeth leaned forward and took the old woman's hands in hers. "You deserve every penny. I don't know how I can ever thank you enough. If you hadn't pulled me back when you did I would probably have been killed. I'll be forever grateful."

Mrs. Phelps squeezed her hands. "I'm grateful to you, child. And to your husband. That reward money is a godsend for an old lady like me, living on a fixed income. Bless you both."

They talked for a while longer, then, after promising to call her the next time they were in New York, they drove away, leaving Mrs. Phelps standing on the sidewalk, beaming and waving.

Elizabeth put her hand on Max's arm. "That was a nice thing you did. Thank you."

"I take care of what's mine," he said with a shrug.

Tom Givens had the plane gassed up and ready when they arrived at the airport. Instead of going to the VIP lounge for people taking private planes, Max had the driver pull out onto the tarmac, up to the foot of the small jet's boarding stairs.

Elizabeth's nerves immediately tightened. Though she knew it was an illusion, she felt safer in the car.

"Sit still," Max told her as he and the detective climbed from the limo. Tom Givens emerged from the plane and loped down the stairs to greet Max. While he and the pilot talked, Max kept a wary eye out and Detective Gertski conducted a thorough, three-hundred-and-sixty degree visual sweep of the area. During his talk with Max, Tom's expression changed from smiling friendliness to grave concern, and he, too, began to check out their surroundings.

"It looks clear," Detective Gertski called to Max.

Max opened the rear door of the limo. "Okay, let's go," he said in a curt voice.

Quelling her fears, Elizabeth scooted to the edge of the seat and prepared to climb out, but Max swooped her up in his arms before her feet could touch the ground.

"Max, I can walk," she protested, but he ignored her and carried her up the aircraft steps with the ease and speed that he would a child. Following close behind Max, Detective Gertski continued to survey the area.

Inside the plane, Max carried Elizabeth straight through the cabin and into the small bedroom at the rear, then placed her on the bed.

From the doorway, the detective said, "I guess this is good-bye. I'll let you and your husband know if there are any new developments in the case. I'm real sorry your honeymoon trip was ruined, Mrs. Riordan, but you should be safe now."

# Nine

The moment Max stepped inside the plane with Elizabeth in his arms, she felt safer. That, however, was nothing compared to the relief that she felt a short while later when the plane hurtled down the runway, jet engines emitting a shrill, high-pitched whine, and attained liftoff. They climbed for several minutes, then banked and headed west-southwest.

"Goodbye, New York City, helloooo Houston," Tom Givens drawled over the intercom.

Out of the small window beside the bed, Elizabeth watched the city landscape fall away, growing ever smaller. She unzipped her high-heeled boots and tugged them off. With a huge sigh, she settled back into a pile of pillows mounded against the padded headboard and closed her eyes. Thank God. For the first time in almost two days, she felt completely safe.

Moments after the plane reached cruising altitude and leveled off, Max appeared in the doorway. "Are you okay?"

"I'm fine now," she said with a smile.

"Good. Get some rest. And holler if you need anything." He started to turn away, but she stopped him.

"Max, could we talk?"

"Yeah, sure. What's on your mind?"

"Several things, actually."

"Okay. What would you like to talk about first?"

Elizabeth smiled at his brusque, businesslike way of putting things in order of priority. She patted the mattress beside her. "Why don't you sit down and relax." She glanced beyond him into the main cabin. "Unless, of course, you have some important work to do."

"No, nothing that can't wait." He had already discarded his overcoat, suit coat and tie. Now he unfastened his gold cuff links and pocketed them. Hitching one bent knee up on the mattress, he sat down facing her and began to roll up his sleeves. "So? Shoot."

"Well, first of all, I was wondering what your schedule is like for the next week or so?"

"Why do you want to know?" he asked, with the reluctance of a man not accustomed to accounting for his time.

"Relax. I'm not trying to keep tabs on you. I simply want to start fulfilling my part of our bargain. To do that, I have to know when you will be available to attend social events or when we can entertain people in our home."

He looked at her for a long time without speaking. Finally he said, "By 'our home,' I assume you mean your River Oaks home or Mimosa Landing?"

"Oh, I'm sorry. I just assumed that you would move in with me. It never occurred to me that you might want us to live in your condo. I guess that's something we should have discussed before we got married."

"No, it's okay. Actually, I prefer your home."

"Oh, good," she said, making no attempt to hide her relief. "Because to tell you the truth, I couldn't sell the place. That would put Gladys and Dooley out of a job, and I couldn't do that to them."

Max cocked his head to one side, his gaze curious. "They've been with you a long time, haven't they?"

"Not just me. They started to work for my parents when they were a young, newly married couple." She wrinkled her nose and shot him a dry look. "I think in their hearts they consider the Houston house more theirs than mine."

"That's nice. And you're right, your homes are more suited to entertaining. As for my schedule, I've already telephoned my secretary and had her clear my calendar. For the next couple of weeks or so, Troy is going to have to take up the slack and handle whatever develops."

"Oh, dear. He's not going to like that."

"He'll probably have a stroke. But it won't make any difference. Troy and I have been good friends since we attended college together, but I pay him to do as I say, not to call the shots. No way am I going to leave you alone until we're certain you're out of danger."

A warm feeling of equal parts gratitude and relief washed through Elizabeth. "Thank you, Max. I appreciate that. I really am sorry to take you away from your business, but I have to admit, I do feel much safer when you're around."

"Yeah, well, I knew going into this arrangement that being a husband entails certain responsibilities and obligations. I always fulfill my obligations."

It was foolish of her to feel hurt, but she did. She should have known that he was acting out of duty. She stared down at her intertwined fingers resting against her abdomen. "Nevertheless, I appreciate what you did."

Silence stretched out. After a while she began to feel fidgety, and she cleared her throat. "Yes, well, uh…as you know, the day after tomorrow is Thanksgiving."

"It is? Hmm, I hadn't realized."

Elizabeth turned her head and blinked at him, her mouth

agape. "How could you not know that Thursday was Thanksgiving?"

Max shrugged. "I guess I had other things on my mind. Anyway, what's the big deal?"

"The big deal is it's a family holiday. One that the Stantons have always celebrated in a big way."

"Okay, then we'll celebrate."

"The trouble is, no one is expecting us to be back in time for the holiday, so we have nothing planned."

"So? Make some plans," Max said. "You've got two days."

Elizabeth shot him a pithy look.

"What? If you don't have plans you make some. What's so wrong with that?" Max asked, truly befuddled. "Call Gladys and tell her we're having Thanksgiving at home."

Elizabeth looked heavenward, as though seeking guidance from above. "Gladys and Dooley are on vacation this week. They're visiting one of their sons in Lubbock. I guess I could call Martha. She's a spinster lady with no close family. If she hasn't already made plans of her own maybe I could talk her into preparing a feast on short notice."

"There you go. Give her a call," Max said.

"You mean right now?"

"Yeah, sure." He reached into his shirt pocket and pulled out a cell phone and handed it to her. "Tell her and your aunt that we'll be there Thursday morning. Tomorrow we're going to be busy with legal matters."

"All right. I'll see what I can do," Elizabeth agreed. "What about your mother? Will she be home by Thursday?"

"No. Her cruise won't be over until the middle of January."

"And Troy?" Even though the man disliked her, she didn't feel right about leaving him out if he was at loose ends.

"He has family, sort of. His dad and a stepmother he despises. I'll have to insist that he take the long weekend off and go visit them. He's as big a workaholic as I am, so he'll argue with me, but in the end he'll go."

"I see. Well, then, I guess there will be just the two of us, Mimi and Aunt Talitha. Mimi is still at Mimosa Landing, by the way. She told me at the wedding that she would stay and keep Aunt Talitha company until we got back."

"Good." He gestured toward the cell phone. "So go ahead and set it up."

While Elizabeth made the call, Max kicked off his shoes and got comfortable, stretching out on his side next to her, his head propped in one hand. The entire time she talked she could feel his gaze on her profile, studying her.

"Martha, dear, I know this is short notice, but just do the best you can, okay? And you'll get a hefty bonus for this, I promise."

There was a short pause on Elizabeth's end and she grimaced as she listened to the other woman.

"Yes, yes, I know you don't expect to be paid extra, but I wouldn't feel right about asking you to work on a holiday otherwise."

The two women continued to argue for a few minutes, but finally the conversation ended.

"How'd it go?" Max asked when Elizabeth hung up.

Elizabeth gave a ladylike snort. "You heard. Martha always gets her nose out of joint when I offer her extra pay. She considers Aunt Talitha and me her family, yet she wouldn't hear of sitting down to Thanksgiving dinner with us.

"As for Aunt Talitha and Mimi, they're curious as to why we're coming home so soon, but I managed to put off explaining until we get there."

"Hmm. But we're set for Thanksgiving?"

"Yes. Martha is in a dither, of course. Which means she's in seventh heaven. She loves to cook and she's at her happiest in the midst of an uproar. I can picture her this very minute, flitting around the kitchen making a list and fretting.

"I almost feel duty-bound to call the manager of the supermarket in Brenham where she shops and warn them that she's about to descend on them like a tornado."

Max did not say anything for a moment, but when she turned her head and looked at him, her eyebrows rose.

"What? Why are you looking at me that way?"

"I'm just curious. Are you close with all your hired help?"

"I hadn't thought about it. I suppose I am. Why? Do you object?"

"No, not at all. I'm just surprised, is all. I seem to be learning new things about you day by day," he murmured.

"Is that right?" She raised her chin. "What's the matter, am I shooting holes in your preconceived notions?"

"Something like that," he admitted.

Elizabeth held his gaze as long as she could, but her huffy attitude did not faze him in the least. Finally she looked away and asked, "Will you be free a week from Saturday? Traditionally the Van Cleaves host a party at the country club on the first Saturday in December. Among Houston society that marks the unofficial start of the winter social season. I got my invitation a week or so ago."

"Really." Max's mouth twisted into a wry grin. "Gee, mine must have gotten lost in the mail."

"Yes, well, what can I say? The Van Cleaves are first-class snobs," Elizabeth declared with a dismissive wave of her hand. "They are mere second-generation Texans, but to hear them talk, you'd think their ancestors fought at the Alamo. Mimi swears that if they ever get caught out in the rain, they'd drown, their noses are so high in the air."

A wry smile tugged at Max's mouth. "The woman may be brash and unpredictable, but she sure tells it like she sees it."

"Anyway, by now news of our wedding is bound to be circulating," Elizabeth continued. "The Van Cleaves's party seems the perfect occasion for us to appear in public together as a couple for the first time."

"Do you think your hip will be healed enough by Saturday?"

"I'm sure it will."

"Then I'm game if you are."

"Good, that's settled, then." She fiddled with her wedding rings, turning them around and around on her finger. "You do realize that for the next few months we're going to be flooded with invitations, don't you? Not only is it the start of the social season, but people will be curious about us and want to see us together.

"Trust me, as we speak rumors are flying. Passing on juicy gossip is practically a major-league sport among the country club set. My friends and acquaintances are going to be looking for the tiniest sign of discord or coolness between us. Anything they can dish the dirt about."

"Hmm. No, I hadn't thought about that. Thanks for the heads-up, though." He mulled the matter over in his mind for a moment, then said, "We'll just have to appear the devoted couple in public."

"So…you're saying that you don't want the reasons for our marriage to become public knowledge?"

"That's nobody's business but our own."

At least she'd be spared that public humiliation, Elizabeth thought, exhaling a long, relieved sigh.

"As for the invitations we receive, I'll leave it up to you to decide which events we should attend," Max said. "I trust your judgment about social contacts. You know who in your set has the deepest pockets and who would be open to a good investment opportunity. Just let me know when to make myself available."

"Okay," Elizabeth said.

"So are we finished with our social talk?"

"I suppose so. For now, at least."

"Good. If you feel like it, I'd like to talk about your investment portfolio for a bit. I have some suggestions to run by you and your attorney regarding those."

"Such as?"

"Well, for one thing…"

For the next hour Elizabeth and Max lounged comfortably on the bed while they reviewed the performance of all her stocks. Before long they were relaxed and at ease with each other and exchanging ideas and opinions like old friends.

He had specific and sound reasons for advising her to dump certain stocks and several suggestions on how she could reinvest the money from those sales. One way was to invest in the venture that he and Troy were currently putting together.

The project involved buying up all the property in an eight-block-square area in a rundown section of downtown Dallas and renovating the entire thing to include luxury apartments, upscale shops, parks, jogging trails and professional offices.

"The aim is to attract young professionals—both singles and DINKS," he explained.

"DINKS? What is that?"

"It stands for Dual Income, No Kids couples. Typically these are young couples who have opted to postpone or forgo having a family. Hip people who want to live in the heart of the city near where they work. This will give them the option of walking almost everywhere—to work or to play—while still having a great home in a nice area. I've already started the process of buying up the property," he told her. "So far I've acquired about half of the area I have targeted. This project is a higher risk than others, but it's expected to bring in a high return on your money. Which is why I think it's right for you."

"It sounds good."

"Great. Why don't you go ahead and call Fossbinder and set up an appointment for us to meet with him tomorrow?"

"All right."

The call took only moments.

"We're all set for two o'clock," she said, handing the cell phone back to Max.

Another silence stretched out between then. Finally, giving in to curiosity, Elizabeth reached out and touched her fingertips to the scar that bisected Max's right eyebrow, tracing its trail over the bridge of his nose and left cheek. "Were you in a car accident?"

"No. That's a memento of my wild youth."

"Oh. I see."

"Why? Does it bother you?"

"No. Actually, it gives you a roguish look that I'm certain appeals to many women."

"Oh, yeah? Does that include you?"

Elizabeth smiled. "Let's just say that I'm still trying to decide. So are you going to tell me what happened or not?"

Max shrugged. "I'd just gotten out of the marines and was due to start college that fall. During that summer I was working as a roughneck on an offshore rig off the coast of Louisiana. I'd just come ashore from a two-week stint and I went to a local watering hole with a few of the other guys on the crew—one of those rowdy places where they play a little zydeco, a little country and a little rockabilly. We were looking to have a few beers and, if we were lucky, get laid."

Elizabeth's cheeks turned pink, but Max went on.

"I was twenty-two and feeling my oats. To make a long

story short, I flirted with a pretty little Cajun gal who was sitting alone at the bar. How was I to know that she and her boyfriend had just had a spat, and he had gone to the men's room to cool off? When he came back and saw me cutting a rug with his woman, he objected.

"I was bigger than he was so I figured I could take him easily. One or two punches and she and I could go back to dancing." Max slanted Elizabeth a sly look. "In case you're interested, I do a mean Texas two-step."

"Oh, really?" she replied, struggling not to grin. Try as she might, she simply could not imagine this intense, almost fierce-looking man taking a lighthearted twirl around a dance floor.

"Anyway, what I hadn't counted on was this hot-blooded Cajun coming after me with a beer bottle he'd broken against the edge of the bar. First swing, and he laid my face open. Made me mad as hell, and I got in a few good shots before my buddies stepped in. If they hadn't I would probably have bled to death."

"You mean you actually came to blows? Inside the bar?"

Max took in her shocked expression. "Let me guess, you've never been in a genuine redneck dance hall in your life, have you?"

"Well...no. I can't say that I have, but—"

"That's what I thought. Trust me, it's a different world from the cotillions and society events you grew up attending."

There didn't seem to be anything to say to that, and they both fell silent again.

"Speaking of accidents, how's your hip?" Max asked after a while.

"I think it's healing fine. It only hurts when I'm on my feet."

"Oh, yeah?"

He tipped his head up and looked into her eyes. In the

depths of his she could see the embers of desire heating up. Elizabeth sensed that what happened next was up to her.

With a few simple words she could douse that fire and turn away, and he would let her. If she had learned nothing else about this man she had married, she had learned that.

These past few days he had repeatedly demonstrated that her well-being was of concern to him. Whether or not that was because he considered her a rather costly business investment that needed safeguarding, or because he felt it was his husbandly duty, or because he was simply innately protective toward females, she had no idea. What she did know was that because of his concern for her, all it would take on her part was a claim of fatigue or discomfort and he would bank that fire for another time, with no recriminations.

Looking into those azure-blue eyes, Elizabeth realized that she did not want to turn him away. Maybe it was because he made her feel safe. Maybe it was a sense of wifely duty on her part. Or maybe, after all that had happened, she simply needed to experience the warmth of another's touch, needed to feel alive and wanted. Whatever the reason, she didn't question it. She simply smiled at him and murmured, "Mmm-hmm. In bed I don't hurt at all."

That was all the encouragement Max needed.

"Is that right?" he drawled, imbuing the question with so much sexual innuendo that it sent a shiver down Elizabeth's spine.

Elizabeth nodded, suddenly too shy to speak.

"I think I'd better have a fresh look at that bruise, just to be on the safe side."

Suiting actions to words, Max pried her fingers apart and trailed his fingertips along the top edge of her navy-blue trousers until he found the button. With a deft twist of his fingers and a downward zip, the pants loosened.

"Lift up your hips," he instructed, and Elizabeth obeyed.

Max pushed the trousers down to her knees, then stood up and moved to the end of the bed.

Before she realized his intent, he grabbed the bottom of both pant legs and snatched the dress trousers off her.

"Oh! Max, wha...?"

Ignoring her sputtering, he sat back down on the side of the bed, pulled her to a sitting position and peeled the cream sweater off over her head. He tossed the turtleneck over his shoulder and it landed on top of her trousers, which lay in a puddle on the floor.

Sitting in the middle of the bed, Elizabeth instinctively drew her knees up to her chest and wrapped her arms around them. She gave him an arched look. "You could have looked at my hip without taking off my sweater, you know."

"I know." He watched her with a sensual gleam in his eyes as he shed his own trousers and began to unbutton his shirt. Not in the least self-conscious, he stripped off his black briefs, again stretched out beside her on the bed, and pulled her back to a prone position.

"There's no point in hiding. I've seen all there is to see already," he drawled as, one by one, he brought her hands down to her sides. "Now, then. Let's have a look at that bruise."

Acutely embarrassed, Elizabeth lay still, trying to subdue the tremors fluttering inside her. She felt utterly vulnerable and exposed, but if Max noticed her discomfort he didn't let on.

He stared, his sensual expression changing to a frown as his gaze ran over the black-and-blue mark that covered half her abdomen and wrapped around to her spine in the back. "Damn. This looks worse than yesterday. Are you sure it doesn't hurt?"

"You know how bruises are. They always look worse the second or third day."

Max gently pressed his fingers to the discolored skin. "Does that hurt?"

Elizabeth shook her head. "It's just a bit sore, is all."

Taking her by surprise, Max scooted down in the bed, bent his head and placed a soft kiss to the center of the bruised flesh. The tender caress made her shiver, and he looked up at her and smiled.

Bending again, he strung a line of kisses along the edge of the bruise, following the arching curve to her navel, then downward, all the way to where the insulted flesh disappeared beneath her navy-blue bikini panties.

Encountering the tiny swath of silk and lace, Max raised his head, his sensual gaze meandering over the panties and matching bra. "Damn, woman, you wear the sexiest underwear. I would never have guessed that beneath that elegant, ladylike exterior you had on X-rated skivvies."

His brilliant blue eyes seemed to devour every inch of her, and Elizabeth felt her body flush from head to toe. "They are no such thing. They're perfectly decent undergarments. Just because they're pretty doesn't mean they're erotic."

"That depends on who's wearing them. Trust me, on you they're sexy as all get out." With a deft flick of his fingers he unfastened the front clasp on her bra and smiled with appreciation as the creamy orbs of her breasts burst free. "And even sexier off you," he added in a husky murmur, a second before his mouth closed over her engorged nipple.

Elizabeth made an inarticulate sound, her back arching up off the mattress as he drew on the sensitive bud. Without breaking off the kiss, Max took advantage of the opportunity and pushed her panties down to her ankles. In a frenzy of passion she kicked them off.

Without realizing what she was doing, Elizabeth sank her fingers into his hair and held his head to her breast. After a moment he abandoned the first nipple to seek out the other one. The air struck the wet, aroused flesh and made it pucker and harden all the more.

Max trailed his open mouth over the pearly mound to the tender valley between her breasts, his warm breath leaving a trail of moisture and goose bumps in its wake. The tip of his tongue traced small, wet circles on her skin, and Elizabeth shivered.

"Do you like that?" Max whispered.

"Y-yes."

He moved upward and strung nibbling kisses over her collarbone, the side of her neck. "And that?"

"Yes. Oh, yes."

He nipped her earlobe, and she felt him grin when the tiny pain elicited a groan from her. "Mmm, you like that, too, don't you?"

"Y-yes, I— Oh!"

In one motion, he grasped her waist with both hands and rolled to his back, holding her suspended above him. For a moment he held her there at arm's length, a slow smile curving his mouth at the confusion in Elizabeth's face.

"Max, wha…?"

"I'm just making certain we don't irritate that bruise," he murmured. Holding her gaze, he lowered her ever so slowly. Her eyes widened when she felt his sex nudging that most private part of her. Slowly, with exquisite torture, she felt him enter in tiny increments. Closing her eyes, she groaned and tried to complete the union quickly, but he wouldn't have it.

"No. Look at me. *Look* at me."

Elizabeth obeyed, and she watched his blue eyes darken and sizzle as, inch by inch, he lowered her onto him. She caught her breath as she felt him filling her, completing her.

When she was fully seated, he moved his hands downward and grasped her hips. With the gentlest of pressure he guided her movements. The rocking motion began slowly, but as the pleasure built, the rhythm grew, faster, harder.

Elizabeth braced her hands on his shoulders, her head back, eyes closed. Very quickly it was too much—too hot, too intense, too exquisite. Her climax came hard and fast, the pleasure beyond anything she'd ever experienced. Distantly she was aware of the high-pitched keening sound that tore from her throat, but she was powerless to silence it.

She collapsed on Max's chest, panting, spent, thoroughly sated. In the pulsing rhythm of her climax, her body continued to clench him tightly.

For several moments he lay quietly beneath her, his hands stroking her back with a hypnotic rhythm. "You okay?" he asked after a while.

"Mmm," The sound was all she could manage by way of a reply until he lifted his hips. Her eyes popped open. "Oh. You haven't…uh, you're…"

Max laughed. "Don't worry about me." Without breaking the intimate connection between them he rolled her onto her back. Braced above her on stiffened arms, he took in her flushed face and well-loved expression, and his mouth curved in a licentious smile. "That was just the preliminaries."

His hips began to move. Instinctively Elizabeth wrapped her legs around him.

"That'a girl," Max encouraged.

His mesmerizing gaze held hers as with every thrust his movements grew faster, harder.

After the shattering climax Elizabeth had just experienced, she would have sworn she could not be aroused again so soon, but to her amazement her body began to quicken and that gnawing, burning pleasure began to build again.

"C'mon. C'mon, baby, stay with me," he encouraged,

watching her face as the feverish pleasure built. "That's it. That's it. Now. Now! Aah, yes. *Yes!*"

With one last powerful thrust, Max sank deep inside her and went rigid, his back arched, his face contorted with pleasure.

In the same instant Elizabeth cried out as, once again, the world seemed to explode around her.

A hard shudder shook Max, and he collapsed onto his back beside her.

Neither he nor Elizabeth moved. Eyes closed, arms flung above their heads, they panted for air, hearts pounding.

After a while she felt him turn his head on the pillow next to hers. "I think we both just qualified for the Mile-High Club," he gasped.

Opening one eye, Elizabeth arched her eyebrow at him. "Both of us?"

"Yeah. Believe it or not, you're the first woman who's ever been on this plane with me. I can't swear that Troy has never entertained a woman when I wasn't on board with him, but it's a first for me."

"Tom! Oh, my goodness!" She bolted to a sitting position and crossed her arms over her bare breasts. She shot Max a horrified look over her shoulder. "I forgot all about him. Do you think he heard us? That he knows?"

Max laughed. "We weren't exactly quiet."

Groaning, Elizabeth flopped back down on her back. "Oh, dear. How will I ever face him again?"

Max rolled onto his side and pulled her hands away from her breasts. "Don't hide yourself from me," he ordered in a gentle murmur. "You're my wife and I like looking at you."

Pulling his gaze away from her breasts, he smiled. "And I was just teasing. Tom can't hear anything above the engine noise. Especially when he has earphones on."

"Are you sure?"

Max shrugged and made a so-so sign with one hand. "Pretty sure. But even if he did hear, so what? We're married."

Making an irritated sound, Elizabeth cuffed him hard on his bare shoulder and huffed, "Oh! If that isn't just like a man!"

If Tom Givens had any idea of the goings-on in the back of the plane, he had the good sense and good manners to pretend otherwise when Max carried Elizabeth off the plane and put her into his car.

By the time they arrived at her River Oaks home it was late, and the sight of the darkened house sent a shiver rippling over her neck, arms and shoulders.

"Where is everyone?" Max asked, flipping on the foyer chandelier.

"I told you, Gladys and Dooley have gone to visit their son in Lubbock."

"Oh, yeah, right." He looked down at the bags he was carrying. "Where shall I put these?"

"This way."

Elizabeth led him up the sweeping stairs. At the top she turned right and headed down a long corridor. Just before reaching the double-wide doors at the end of the hallway, she stopped.

"This is my room," she said, opening the door on her right.

Max took a few steps inside the room. "It's smaller than I expected for a master bedroom."

"Oh, this is not the master," she explained. "Edward didn't like to sleep with anyone. Right after we married he had this part of the house remodeled. This used to be the nanny's room. That closet over there was the nursery. It now connects to this room, the master bedroom on the other side and my bathroom."

Max crossed the room and poked his head into the closet.

"Damn, this space must be about twenty-five by twenty. That's bigger than a lot of bedrooms."

Elizabeth stood in the middle of the room, shifting her weight from one foot to another, not quite knowing how to navigate the subject of sleeping quarters.

"If, uh…if you want to take the master bedroom, feel free. I'm comfortable in here."

Max shot her a look and slowly shook his head. "Uh-uh. Not me. You're my wife. I sleep in your bed." He walked into the closet and through the door on the other side and stepped into the master bedroom. Elizabeth followed, wondering what was going on in his mind.

"Nice room," he commented. He walked across the bedroom, inspecting the hand-carved, twelve-foot-high Victorian four-poster bed and night tables, the pier mirror and the gentleman's chest.

He peeked into the sumptuous master bathroom and another enormous closet and a small sitting room. "Looks like Edward was nice to himself. This suite of rooms has obviously been remodeled with all the latest luxuries and creature comforts, and it covers the entire end of this wing of the house."

He looked again at Elizabeth. "You should be occupying this room."

"You…you mean you want us to move into here?"

"Not yet. First I'd like for you to completely redecorate this room. Make it ours."

# *Ten*

Elizabeth and Max arrived at Mimosa Landing just after noon on Thanksgiving Day. They no sooner stepped inside out of the cold than Aunt Talitha, Mimi and even quiet little Martha began to bombard them with questions.

"What happened?"

"Why are you back so soon?"

"Are you ill?"

"Oh, my, you do look a little peaked, child."

"I'm fine, Aunt Talitha. Just give us a minute to take our coats off," Elizabeth pleaded. "Then we'll explain everything."

With obvious impatience the women held their tongues until they were seated around the roaring fire in the front parlor, all except Martha, who lingered in the doorway.

The Mimosa Landing housekeeper was the exact opposite of her counterpart in Houston. Where Gladys was tall, raw-boned and a bit on the brusque side, Martha was a little dumpling of a woman, quiet and meek and unassuming.

Aunt Talitha gave Elizabeth an imperious look and thumped her cane against the floor. "Well? Out with it."

Elizabeth hated to upset her aunt, but she felt it best that she explain what had happened rather than risk her finding out later through a slip of the tongue.

Whitewashing the story as much as she could, she told them what had occurred. By the time she'd finished all three women were staring at her with shocked expressions.

"Oh, my word." Talitha put her age-spotted hand over her heart. "Why, that's awful. That…that monster actually tried to run you down in the street?"

"Yes. If it hadn't been for Mrs. Phelps I probably wouldn't be here."

"I do hope you got her address," her aunt said. "I must write to the dear lady and express my gratitude."

"That thug probably followed you to your hotel. He must've been watchin' your suite, waitin' for Max to leave." Mimi shivered and rubbed her goose-bumpy arms. "That's so creepy."

"I just don't understand this. Why on earth would anyone want Elizabeth dead?" her aunt asked.

Speaking up for the first time, Max said, "Detective Gertski thinks it's a case of mistaken identity. I'm inclined to agree, but after two attempts on Elizabeth's life, I decided to get her out of New York. I could have taken her somewhere else for the rest of our honeymoon, but she wanted to come home."

"Of course she did. You did the right thing, my boy. After that kind of fright the child needs to be with her family."

Aunt Talitha gave Max an approving look and reached over and patted his arm. "I'm so glad she has a real man like you to look after her now. Not some namby-pamby like that no-good Edward Culpepper. I never liked that man," she declared, thumping her cane against the Oriental rug for emphasis.

Mimi eyed Max and drawled, "All I can say, stud, is I sure as hell hope you're good in bed. 'Cause that was some cruddy honeymoon."

"Mimi, behave yourself," Talitha admonished in a weary tone that said she despaired of that ever happening.

"I think I hear the stove timer buzzing," Martha murmured, and hurried out of the room. Moments later she reappeared in the doorway and announced that dinner was ready.

Throughout the meal, speculation about the incidents in New York continued. Now that she was home, Elizabeth felt safe. The two scares seemed more like bad dreams than reality, and she wanted to put them out of her mind. By the time the meal was over she was sick of the subject.

Groaning and berating themselves for eating too much, the three women and Max adjourned to the den at the back of the house. The large room, built in 1950, was the newest addition to the rambling mid-nineteenth century farmhouse, and the one the family used most.

"Why don't you show me around the farm," Max suggested to Elizabeth before she had a chance to get comfortable. "I don't know about you, but I could use some exercise after that meal."

"Good idea," she replied, jumping at the chance to escape any more pointless speculation. Also, there was nothing she liked better than to show off her beloved farm.

"Mimi, would you like to come along while I show Max around?" Elizabeth asked her friend.

Mimi chuckled. "Are you kiddin' me, sugar? No way am I trompin' through the fields in these four-inch heels."

"You could change into a pair of sneakers."

That produced an unladylike snort. "Now, sugar, I ask you, do I look like a woman who would even *own* such a thing?"

With a dramatic sigh, Mimi plopped down onto one of the den's long sofas and stretched out. Talitha, as always, sat down in her padded rocker and hooked her cane over one arm.

"Go on, you two." With a bejeweled hand Mimi waved Elizabeth and Max on their way. "To tell the truth, Aunt Talitha and I are glad there won't be a male here to insist on watching a football game. While you two are tramping through the fields, steppin' in cow pies and freezing your arses off, we're gonna watch one of the shopping networks."

"Suit yourself," Elizabeth said with a laugh. She looked at Max. "Just give me a minute to run upstairs and change into my jeans and some walking shoes."

"Sure. Go ahead."

"Wait. I'll come with you." With languid movements, Mimi hauled herself off the sofa. "It'll give us a chance for a bit of private girl talk."

Arm in arm, the two women strolled out of the den. Over her shoulder Mimi sent Max a mischievous smile and winked.

Watching them go, he shook his head. "How in the hell did those two women ever become such close friends?"

"Yes, they do seem an unlikely pair, don't they." Aunt Talitha motioned toward the matching chair next to her own. "Come over here and sit down and I'll tell you the history behind their friendship."

For several moments after Max sat down the old woman stared off into space, as though mentally transporting herself back to another time.

"First of all, for you to understand, I'm going to have to give you a little family background," she finally said.

Max nodded. "Sure. Go ahead." He was an active player in today's fast-paced world. His instinct was to get to the point and get on with things. Had she been anyone else he would have tried to hurry her along, but Max was beginning to realize that it was futile to rush the old lady. Great-aunt Talitha did things at her own pace.

"Elizabeth's father, Ransom Patrick Stanton, was my brother Pierce's son. Pierce was much older than my twin sister, Mariah, and I. We were late-in-life babies for our parents, you see. So we were only five years old when Ransom was born, and he always seemed more like a brother to us than a nephew.

"Ah, he grew up to be a dashing, handsome young man," the old lady reminisced with a fond smile, her eyes growing misty. "The strong character and pioneering blood of the Stantons ran deep in him.

"The family was tickled pink when he married Victoria Trent. Such a lovely girl she was," Talitha said with a wistful sigh. "The very essence of genteel femininity.

"Mmm. Victoria and Ransom were the perfect couple. Everyone said so—he with his strength and confidence, his rugged good looks and winning personality, she with her softness, her compassion, her elegant beauty. Elizabeth inherited the best of both of them.

"And Lord, Lord, did that child adore her parents, especially her mother.

"Victoria died of breast cancer when Elizabeth was nine and the poor child was devastated," Talitha recalled with a sad note in her voice. "Not that she cried or carried on or anything, mind you. Truth be told, we were all praying that she would. Instead she grew even more somber and quiet and pulled back from everyone, holding all that grief and anguish inside her.

"Our next-door neighbor in Houston, Horace Whittington, had married Mimi just a few days before Victoria died. Mimi was barely nineteen at the time. Horace was a fifty-two-year-old widower."

"Ah, now I get it. The girl from the wrong side of the tracks snared herself a rich old man, and started living on easy street. I figured it was something like that. Despite the designer clothes and jewelry, she just doesn't have the polish of someone born to money." And he should know, Max thought privately. Neither did he.

Of course…Elizabeth had married *him* for his money, he thought with a frown. Yet he did not think of her as a gold digger, partly because the marriage had been his idea, and because theirs was a mutually beneficial deal, one they'd both entered into with their eyes wide open. He wondered if poor old Horace had known it was his deep pockets that had attracted Mimi.

Making a scornful sound, Max shook his head. "Ah, well. They say there's no fool like an old fool."

"I can understand why you would think that," Talitha murmured. "I'll admit, at first I thought much the same thing. We all did. But we soon learned better.

"Mimi had a hard childhood. After the deaths of her parents she was passed from relative to relative, but nobody wanted her. After about a year of that she went into foster care. That's where she stayed, bouncing from one home to another until, at sixteen, she decided that she'd had enough and ran away.

"When Horace met her she was a competitive ballroom dancer. I think he was the first person to show her genuine love, and Mimi loved him right back, with every fiber in her. For more than twenty years they were one of the happiest couples I've ever known. It just about killed her when she lost him.

"Horace, bless him, saw past the brash exterior to the innate goodness in Mimi—the big heart, the compassion, the honesty. And with the clear vision of a child, so did Elizabeth.

"For her part, Mimi understood the bottled-up pain and sense of loss in that motherless little girl's eyes and responded to it. Whenever the grief became too much for Elizabeth, quiet as a mouse she would squeeze through the hedge separating our Houston estate from the Whittingtons' and seek out Mimi. Elizabeth did not have to say a word. Mimi had only to look at that sad little face and she would drop whatever she was doing and open her arms to the child."

Talitha shook her head, her expression soft with the memory. "Whenever Elizabeth went missing I always knew where to find her. Many's the time I've walked into the Whittingtons' sunroom and found Mimi cuddling the child in her lap, quietly rocking her."

Shaking off the memory, Talitha turned her gaze on Max. "I will forever be grateful to Mimi for getting Elizabeth through that awful time. They've been close ever since.

"Of course, over the years, as Elizabeth matured, their relationship changed from one of mentor-child to a friendship between equals, but the tie is as strong as ever. It's a rare day that they don't spend some time together, if only dance hour."

"Dance hour?"

"Mimi started giving Elizabeth dancing lessons when she was nine. To this day, they spend an hour each morning dancing, either in the studio in the attic of the Whittington home, or the one here that Elizabeth had installed above the old carriage house. They dance to keep in shape, and because they both love it."

"Hmm. I'd like to watch that sometime."

"Good luck with that. Elizabeth doesn't like to have an audience. But the point of all this is that Mimi was a godsend when the child needed her, and she's Elizabeth's best friend now."

"Thanks for telling me," Max said. "Now things make more sense."

"Yes. It's interesting how a different perspective can alter your opinion of someone, isn't it?" Talitha held his gaze, and Max could see the shrewdness in her faded blue eyes.

"Yes. Yes, it is."

"May I offer you one piece of advice?"

"Sure." Max had the feeling she was going to, no matter what he said.

"A wise man would not try to break up that friendship."

He mulled that over for a moment then nodded. "I'm sure you're right."

The instant they were out of earshot, Mimi squeezed Elizabeth's arm and leaned in close. "I've been dyin' for hours to get you alone so I can ask this. How is he?" she whispered.

"How is who?"

"Max. You know…between the sheets."

"Mimi! What a thing to ask. Behave yourself."

"Don't be silly. That's no fun. Well?"

"Forget it. That topic isn't open for discussion."

They reached the top of the stairs, and Elizabeth pulled her arm free from her friend's grasp and hurried down the hallway to her bedroom. Mimi hurried after her, the soles of her backless stilettos slap-slapping against the bottoms of her heels with each step.

Inside the bedroom, Elizabeth headed for the enormous walk-in closet, but at the entrance she stopped and lifted up the back of her hair. Without having to be asked, Mimi pulled down the long zipper.

"Aw, c'mon, sugar. I'm your best friend. You can tell me. I won't say a word to anyone. I promise." She held up four fingers. "Girl Scout's honor."

Elizabeth paused in the act of stepping out of the long wool dress she'd worn for dinner and cocked a dubious eyebrow at her friend. "Oh, right."

She went into the closet and hung up her dress. Mimi followed close on her heels.

After stepping out of her pumps, Elizabeth hooked her thumbs underneath the waistband of her panty hose and peeled them off, as well, and tossed the gossamer garment into a satin-lined basket that held things to be hand-washed.

"And you were never a Girl Scout."

"Okay, okay. So maybe I would tell Doreen," Mimi admitted with a rueful pout. "But only because we have a bet goin'."

"You *what?*" Clutching the jeans she'd just pulled off the hanger in one hand, Elizabeth spun around. Wearing only the lacy light blue bikini panties and matching bra, she planted her fists on her hip bones. "You actually *bet* on my sex life. Honestly, Mimi, that's too much. Even for you."

"Now, before you get your nose out of joint, hear me out. I didn't mean for things to get out of hand—" Mimi sucked in a sharp breath, and Elizabeth saw that her horrified stare was fixed on her injured hip.

"Omigod! Oh, sugar, I thought you said that car just grazed you. That looks *awful.* It has to hurt like hell."

Looking down at the huge livid bruise, Elizabeth grimaced. The flesh was now a dark, almost greenish purple that faded at the edges to colorful shades of yellow, blood-red and blue.

"It's not so bad. You know how easily I bruise. It looks worse than it feels."

"Have you seen an orthopedic guy?" Mimi came closer, bent over for a better look and gently touched the insulted flesh with one crimson-tipped finger.

"No, I had an X-ray in New York. It'll be fine. She stepped

into the jeans, picked out a thick russet turtleneck from the stack of sweaters on the shelves at the back of the room-size closet and pulled it on over her head.

With Mimi dogging her heels again, she went back into the bedroom and sat down on the padded bench at the end of the bed to put on her socks and walking shoes. As she worked she aimed a narrow-eyed look at her friend. "And don't think you can distract me. Explain about this bet."

"Oh, you know how Doreen is," Mimi said with a dismissive wave of her hand. "She's between husbands and in the market for a lover. For the past year or so she's been trying to lure Max into her bed, with no success."

Elizabeth looked up in the midst of pulling on rust-colored socks. "Are you sure about that?"

"One hundred percent. You know Doreen. If she'd ever had Max as a lover, the whole world would know."

That was true, Elizabeth realized with an unexplainable sense of relief.

"When Doreen heard that you'd married Max she was pissed as all get out. She tried to save face by saying she'd only been kidding about him. And that he probably wasn't all that hot as a lover, anyway.

"I couldn't let her get by with that, now, could I? We argued and one thing led to another, and the next thing I knew, we had a bet going."

"I see. And just how were you going to find out?" Having finished dressing, Elizabeth ran a brush through her hair, then headed for the door.

"We agreed to accept your opinion," Mimi said, scrambling to keep up with her. "Everyone knows that you don't lie. So, c'mon, sugar. Tell me."

"No."

"Aw, don't be that way," Mimi pleaded.

"Sorry. I'm not going to discuss my sex life with you or anyone else."

In her comfy walking shoes, Elizabeth tripped easily down the stairs, but she couldn't lose her shadow. To keep up, Mimi kicked off her stilettos, sending them sailing over Elizabeth's head into the foyer below, and stuck to Elizabeth like a cocklebur on a sock.

"C'mon, sugar. If you can't tell me, who else can you tell."

"My point, exactly. My husband's prowess in bed is not fodder for gossip." At the bottom of the stairs, with one hand grasping the newelpost, she made a one-hundred-and-eighty-degree turn and headed for the back of the house.

"Ooh. That 'my husband' sounded very proprietorial. Is there something going on between you two that you've neglected to tell me?"

"No."

Mimi groaned. "C'mon, sugar," she said to Elizabeth's back, hurrying after her. "Look, if you don't want to get into details, I'll understand."

"My, that's big of you."

"Just tell me, on a scale of one to ten, where would you rank him? Ten being the best."

Elizabeth heaved a big sigh. "You're not going to let this go until I tell, are you?"

Mimi grinned. "You darn betcha I'm not."

They walked into the den and Max rose.

"Ready?"

"Yes. There are coats in the mudroom that we can use." Elizabeth bent and kissed her aunt's papery cheek. "We'll be back in an hour or so."

"Yes, yes. I know. Now, be off with you. And have a good time."

Elizabeth turned to leave, then stopped and looked at her friend. "Oh, by the way Mimi. That number you wanted?"

Mimi's face lit up. "Yes?"

Elizabeth's answering smile was smug. "It's twelve."

Her friend gasped and her eyes bugged. "Ooh. Be still, my heart," she murmured, fanning herself with her hand.

Max watched the exchange with a curious frown. "What was that all about?" he asked as he and Elizabeth bundled up in the mudroom.

"Nothing, really. That was just Mimi being Mimi."

They stepped outside into the cold. "She's a real character, isn't she?"

"Yes. Mimi is one of a kind," Elizabeth replied with affection. Another blast of frigid wind hit them and they both shivered and put up their coat collars. Though the temperature was only forty degrees, the humidity was high and it felt more like twenty outside. "Why don't we walk to the river?"

"Sure. Whatever you say. Lead the way."

Looking back over his shoulder, Max realized that the farmhouse sat atop a small hill, about a mile off a secondary country road. From the back of the house the land gradually sloped downward to the banks of the Brazos River.

"The farm is basically a long, irregular rectangle that stretches out from here equidistant to the north and the south along the east bank of the Brazos," Elizabeth explained. "That's probably a lot farther than you'd want to walk in one day. My foreman, Truman Sawyer, and the other hired hands ride four-wheelers to get around. We could use those if you'd like."

"No, I'd rather walk."

"Me, too."

In silence, they walked along a well-worn path toward the river, he with his hands in the pockets of the fleece-lined denim jacket that he purloined off a hook by the back door,

Elizabeth in a battered peacoat, her head up and a contented smile on her face. The wind blew her hair every which way, but she didn't fuss the way a lot of women would. She hardly seemed to notice.

"I can see why you love this place," Max said after a time, looking around at the gently rolling hills dotted here and there with stands of ancient oak, pecan, walnut and mimosa trees. "This is a beautiful spot."

"Mmm," she agreed absently.

They reached the river and stopped near a ramshackle structure made of hand-hewn logs and corrugated tin. Here the bank dropped off fifteen to twenty feet in a sheer cliff to the muddy waters of the Brazos below.

"That's the cotton gin that Asa built," Elizabeth said, pointing toward the aging log building. "In the old days farmers from miles around brought their cotton here to be ginned and baled and shipped to market.

"In the early 1800s paddle wheelers used to navigate up and down this river, selling goods and picking up crops. The first few years, while the settlers were getting established, their main cash crops were pecans and potash. Later, cotton and indigo and sugarcane products were their moneymakers. In more recent years we've started alternating the crops so as not to deplete the soil.

"Of course, that was long before the government dammed the river upstream near Mineral Wells. When the water level dropped, the big boats could no longer get through. Before that happened the Brazos was a deep, fast-running, clear river. In those days the banks on both sides were lined with mimosa trees along here, many of which survive to this day. That's how the farm came to be called Mimosa Landing."

She pointed downward. "Look down there, and you can see the remains of the old wharf."

Max leaned over and spotted a rickety wooden structure clinging to the steep bank about halfway to the water. "This place, and your family, have quite a history," he commented.

"Yes," she said with quiet pride.

"How many acres do you have all told?"

"A little over three thousand. Great-great-grampa Asa Pierce Stanton homesteaded the original plot of about six hundred acres shortly after he came to Texas with Stephen F. Austin in the early 1800s. Gradually he bought out other settlers up and down the river, people who couldn't make a go of it. By the time of the Texas Revolution against Mexico, he'd more than tripled his original grant.

"When he first arrived he built a two-room log cabin and got this place going, then sent back to Savannah for his sweetheart, Talitha Camille Brown."

Elizabeth walked over to an enormous mimosa tree and stood beneath the spreading limbs. "They were married in the spring of 1830 on this very spot by a roving preacher. The mimosas and wildflowers were in full bloom."

"Really?" Max said, looking around. "I'll bet this is a beautiful spot in the spring."

"Yes, it is," she agreed. Returning to his side, she gazed at the river, her hands tucked into her coat pockets. "From 1833 to April 1836, Asa served in the Texas Army. He was wounded at San Jacinto."

"The last battle in the war?" At Elizabeth's nod Max shook his head. "That's too bad."

"He survived, thank God. For his service, he was awarded an additional thousand acres of rich bottom land adjacent to his property."

Max let out a low whistle. "That's a lot of land. Is it all still intact?"

"Yes. No Stanton has ever sold so much as a teaspoon of this land."

"I guess you wouldn't, either, huh?"

"That's right," she vowed. "Not even if I have to take a job slinging hash at a greasy spoon."

Max almost laughed out loud, but he caught himself in time. She was deadly serious.

Turning his head, Max studied her determined profile. Including marrying me, he thought.

Why that thought bothered him, he didn't understand, but it did.

Without talking, they walked along the river bank for a ways, then turned back. Near the house, Elizabeth pointed out an old log structure. "That's the original cabin that Asa built, where he and Talitha Camille began their marriage. Out back of the cabin are the big cauldrons they used on wash day. In the fall they made soap and candles in them.

"That log building over there straddling the stream is the springhouse. That was the equivalent of a refrigerator in the old days. The flowing water inside keeps the temperature at a steady fifty degrees so the perishables all stay cool."

"What's that over there?" Max asked, pointing to a contraption set in the middle of a foot-deep rutted circle.

"That's the old sugarcane press. It was run by oxen or mule power. See the long bar that sticks out? That was hooked to the animal's harness, and as he walked in a circle, workers fed the sugarcanes into the hopper and the press squeezed out the juice. Years of the animals plodding created that rut in the ground."

"Fascinating," Max murmured, inspecting the machine at closer range.

"And that log structure over there beyond the springhouse is the smokehouse," Elizabeth went on.

"That structure over there must be the carriage house where you have your dance studio."

"Let me guess. Aunt Talitha told you about the dancing?"

"Yeah. I'd like to watch you and Mimi sometime."

Elizabeth started shaking her head before the words were out of his mouth. "Oh, no. The studios are off limits to everyone but us."

"We'll see," Max pronounced, and changed the subject.

Elizabeth gave Max a tour of the inside of both the animal barn and the equipment barn. In the latter Max looked over an enormous machine. "This looks new," he said, running his fingertips along the bright yellow paint. "What is it?"

"It's a combine for harvesting grain. And you're right about it being new. It was delivered just last Monday. Truman can hardly wait to put it to use. I swear, the man loves this machine almost as much as he does his kids," she said, chuckling.

Walking deeper into the barn, she pointed out a cotton picker, a disk, a hay baler and various other pieces of equipment that were foreign to him. Finally she climbed up into the enclosed cab of the biggest tractor that Max had ever seen. "This is another new piece of equipment," she said, bouncing on the seat. "You're seeing firsthand how your money is being spent."

He made a noncommittal sound and climbed up into the cab with her. "It looks like a first-class piece of equipment," he said. "That's good. I believe in buying quality."

"Oh, Truman's going to love you," Elizabeth said with a laugh.

"Oh, yeah? Do you suppose he'll let me drive this baby sometime?"

"I don't know," she teased, slanting him a dubious look. "Truman is verrry particular about his farm equipment."

"Hmm. I guess I'll have to get on his good side."

"That's no easy feat. A man has to prove himself to Truman, but once he accepts you, you've got a loyal friend for life."

"I kind of guessed that."

Outside the barn, they paused beside a corral to watch a feisty colt kick up his heels and run for the sheer pleasure of it. Elizabeth stepped up on the bottom rail of the wooden fence, bringing herself on eye level with Max.

"I can see why you love it here. I do, as well, but the trips back and forth from Houston are going to eat up time. Would you object to me having a helipad built here? That way I could switch to a helicopter at the airport and be here in minutes."

"I don't mind. But if I were you I'd get Truman's advice about where to put it."

"Good idea."

"Is Tom licensed to fly a helicopter as well as a jet?"

"No, but I am. I'll fly myself to and from the Houston airport."

"You? But…isn't that dangerous?"

"Relax. I flew helicopters when I was a marine. I've kept my license up to date."

"Okay. If that's what you want to do, go ahead. Just don't expect me to ride in it."

On the way back to the house, Max kept stealing glances at Elizabeth's profile. She was different here. Happier. More alive.

Her cheeks were pink from the cold, her hair mussed by the wind. But she wore contentment like an old soft coat. Her eyes gleamed with it. The hint of a smile around the corners of her mouth gave her a Mona Lisa look—as though she knew some basic truth about the meaning of life.

"You really love it here, don't you?"

"Mmm. I'd rather be here than any place on earth."

"Then why don't you sell the Houston place and live here all the time?"

"Several reasons. For the past few generations of Stantons, family business has required us to spend a lot of time in Houston. Over the years my family's roots have sunk almost as deep there as they are here. We've called the Houston house home number two ever since my great-grandfather's day. Another important point for me is it's next door to Mimi." She stooped and picked a long leaf off a plant and pulled it through her fingers. "And then there's Gladys and Dooley to think about."

Staring down at her delicate profile as they drew near the house, Max realized just how far off the mark his assessment of her had been.

He'd proposed because he'd known that she was in desperate financial straits. At the time he'd thought that her desire to hold on to Mimosa Landing was more a matter of saving face than anything else. He knew—hell, everyone in that part of the state knew—that this farm was and had always been the number-one symbol of her family's wealth and their place in society.

Not once had he doubted that she would accept his proposal. He had been certain that, being born to wealth, when push came to shove, she wouldn't be able to give up her privileged lifestyle and all the things that money could buy.

He'd been wrong. And that bothered him.

He could see by the passion in those blue-green eyes that the money meant little to her. What mattered to Elizabeth was this farm, this land. And the people she loved.

It seemed that, through plain dumb luck, he'd married himself one hell of a woman.

# *Eleven*

One of the first questions Aunt Talitha always asked whenever she met someone new was, did they play bridge? Not only was she a fanatical player, she felt the game was a social skill everyone should have. To her credit, she restrained herself the day of the wedding when she met Max for the first time. However, she put the question to him the moment that he and Elizabeth returned from their tour of the farm.

"Yes, I play. My parents taught me," he replied. "When you live in oil-field camps all over the world you have to make your own entertainment. I also played quite a bit in college."

"I knew it. I knew it," Talitha said with a gleeful thump of her cane. "Someone as smart as you just had to be a bridge player. It's a game of logic and strategy, a thinking-person's game. You'll be my partner," she informed him. "Elizabeth, dear, break out the cards."

"Are you sure you want to do that?" Max asked. "I haven't played in more than ten years. I'm really rusty."

"Nonsense. It's like riding a bicycle. Once you learn you never forget."

As always, Aunt Talitha was right.

They played until after ten that evening, and Max and Aunt Talitha trounced Elizabeth and Mimi every rubber.

Later, alone in the master bedroom, Elizabeth sat at her dressing table removing her makeup and watching Max in the mirror. "Thank you for indulging my aunt," she said to his reflection. "That was very nice of you."

"No problem." He picked up the shoes and socks he'd just removed and disappeared into the closet, which, like the master bedroom closet in Houston, was bigger than most bedrooms. When he returned to the doorway moments later he had shed his trousers and was working on the buttons on his shirt. "Anyway, I like your aunt. And I enjoyed myself. I'd forgotten how much fun playing bridge could be. These past ten or so years, I haven't taken much time for fun."

"You should. You know what they say about all work and no play. And you're very good at bridge."

"So are you and Mimi. Actually, I was surprised at how good she is. I didn't expect her to even know the game."

"Aunt Talitha taught her to play years ago, just as she taught me. Don't sell Mimi short. Behind all that sultry temptress stuff is a very sharp woman."

"So I'm beginning to realize." He slipped out of his shirt, wadded it up and tossed it into a satin-lined laundry basket just inside the closet. "Besides, I'm no dummy. I figured out within five minutes of meeting your aunt that I needed to keep on her good side if I was going to have a chance of keeping her niece happy."

"True," she admitted, meeting his gaze in the mirror. "But I thank you, anyway."

Max dismissed the subject with a shrug of his broad shoulders.

"I couldn't help but notice that there aren't separate master bedrooms in this house," he commented.

"No. It wasn't necessary to remodel here to suit Edward. He doesn't like the country and seldom came to Mimosa Landing," Elizabeth replied.

Max gave a disgusted snort and mumbled to no one in particular, "Edward is an idiot."

Elizabeth watched his reflection in the mirror as he walked toward her wearing only a minuscule pair of red briefs. Her heart gave a little skip and took off in a drum roll.

Lord, he was a magnificent-looking man, she thought, a bit dazed. Her gaze slid over his broad shoulders, muscled chest and washboard abdomen, the bands of long muscles in his legs that rippled when he walked.

Stopping just behind her, he put his hands on her shoulders and began to massage gently.

Exerting the slightest pressure, he urged her to stand, and when she did he turned her to face him and slipped his arms around her, holding their lower bodies together. The close contact left her in no doubt of his intentions. Neither did the gleam in his eyes.

Turning with her in slow circles, almost like dancing, he maneuvered them across the room toward the bed. She felt the mattress bump against the backs of her knees and let out a small cry as they tumbled together onto the soft surface.

"You want to thank me?" Max whispered against the side of her neck as he explored the soft skin with nibbling kisses.

"Mmm," Elizabeth replied, lost in the delicious sensations that were pulsing through her. Eyes closed, she gave herself up to the feelings that engulfed her.

"Then touch me," he commanded in a hoarse whisper. "I want to feel your hands on me."

She did as he instructed, and was rewarded when he

jerked. He seemed to catch his breath, then a hard shudder shook his whole body. "Ah, baby. Yes. Yes."

He returned the favor, and as his hands played over her, she recalled what she'd told Mimi and decided that she'd been wrong. As a lover, on a scale of one to ten, Max was at least a fifteen.

For the remainder of the holiday weekend, each evening after dinner they played bridge. And each evening after playing bridge, Max made love to Elizabeth. Her husband, she began to realize, had a healthy appetite for sex. And he had the skill and finesse in bed to arouse an equal hunger in her.

At first she had felt embarrassed, even a little guilty about responding to him, a man she barely knew, in such an uninhibited and wanton way, and for deriving such intense pleasure from their lovemaking.

After a while, however, she changed her mind and thought, Why not? Why the devil not? Shouldn't she get *something* out of this marriage? After all, she'd endured years of lackluster lovemaking with Edward. He had made that trek through the dressing room/closet from his bedroom to hers only occasionally, and even then his lovemaking had been mechanical. So why shouldn't she relax and embrace the intimate side of her marriage to Max?

"I wish you didn't have to go," Elizabeth said as she and Mimi hugged each other goodbye in the foyer on Monday morning.

"I know, but I've got tons of appointments this week. I need a manicure, a pedicure, a facial and a massage. Plus I need to get my roots done in time for the Van Cleaves's party."

"Do you want to ride to the country club with Max and me?"

"No. Dexter Campbell is escorting me. He's fresh off divorce number three and horny as a jackrabbit, so I'll probably have to threaten him with my gun when we get home, but at least I'll have an escort."

Elizabeth laughed. "Call us if he gives you any trouble."

The door opened and Truman stepped back inside, bringing a blast of cold air with him. Without a word and barely a glance toward the two women, the farm manager picked up the last of Mimi's suitcases and carried them out to her car.

Mimi grinned. "Don't you just love a quiet man?"

"Forget it. He's not your type."

Elizabeth and Mimi turned to see Troy step inside the foyer and close the front door behind him. Dressed in a natty suit and carrying a briefcase, he looked all business. His expression, particularly when he acknowledged Elizabeth with a curt, "Good morning" and a nod, was cool.

Never one to back away from a challenge, Mimi cocked one hip, planted her hand on it and looked him up and down. "And just what *is* my type, Mr. Ellerbee?"

"Rich and old."

Elizabeth sucked in a shocked breath, but Mimi didn't turn a hair. "I see. Well, that just shows how wrong you can be. Thanks to Big Daddy, I have all the money I'll ever need. Next time around I'll be looking for a young man with six-pack abs and the stamina to keep up with me."

She sauntered toward the door. As she passed Troy she gave his cheek a sharp little pat. "Careful, sugar-lump. I may just set my sights on you."

And with that she made her grand exit.

When the door closed behind her Elizabeth turned to Troy. "Mr. Ellerbee, you are entitled to your opinions, but when you're in my home, keep them to yourself. I will not tolerate you dishing out insults to my guests, particularly not to my best friend. Do I make myself clear?"

"Perfectly. Now, if you're finished with your 'lady of the manor' reprimand, I came to see Max."

"He must not be expecting you. He's out on the property somewhere." She motioned toward the parlor. "Have a seat and I'll send Truman to find him."

Without waiting to see if he followed her suggestion, Elizabeth marched down the wide central hallway, through the kitchen and mudroom and out onto the back porch. As she suspected, her farm manager was just coming around the side of the house. She stopped him and told him to tell Max that Troy was there to see him, then went back inside.

Aunt Talitha sat at the kitchen table in her nightgown and robe, drinking coffee and reading the newspaper, which was her daily morning ritual.

Halfway across the room Elizabeth paused and looked longingly at the backstairs, which opened into the kitchen. She was tempted to use them to go up to her room and leave the obnoxious man on his own, twiddling his thumbs, but a lifetime of ingrained good manners would not allow that.

Muttering to herself, slamming doors and banging china, she began to put together a tray of coffee and cookies.

Aunt Talitha lowered one corner of her newspaper and looked at her niece over the top of her reading glasses.

"Can I help you, Miss Elizabeth?" Martha asked.

"No, thank you, Martha. I can handle it."

The housekeeper looked at Talitha, who silently shook her head. Martha retreated into the utility room and busied herself sorting laundry.

When Elizabeth carried the tray into the parlor, Troy at least had the manners to stand.

"Truman is looking for Max. He should be here soon." She sat down on the sofa and Troy resumed his seat in one of the chairs opposite her. "How do you like your coffee?" she asked.

"Black. And you didn't need to bother making coffee."

"I know that." Elizabeth handed him the cup, then poured one for herself.

After a few moments of silence during which they tried not to look at each other, Elizabeth could keep quiet no longer. "You don't like me, do you, Troy?"

"No," he replied with no hesitation, no evasion, no attempt at diplomacy.

"Mmm." Elizabeth took a sip of coffee. "Why is that? I mean, you barely know me. What is it about me that you find so objectionable?"

"To start with, you married Max for his money. He deserves better than that."

"I see." Elizabeth pursed her lips and ran the tip of her forefinger around the rim of her coffee cup as she pondered that. "I'm sure you're right. But let me remind you, this marriage was Max's idea. And that he married me for my social contacts." She didn't mention the sex part. Some things were best kept to yourself. "And trust me, whether you believe it or not, I deserve better than that."

"Maybe. But you also take up too much of Max's time. I mean take now, for instance. He's probably out there mucking around in a barn. A *barn*, for God's sake! When he should be at his desk in Houston or meeting with investors somewhere. Until he married you, I doubt that Max had ever been in a barn before."

Elizabeth started to reply, but they heard footsteps coming down the hall, and a moment later Max walked in. His face was ruddy from the cold wind and there was an air of vitality and happiness about him. "Troy. This is a surprise. What brings you here?"

"I brought some papers for you to sign, and there are one or two things I need to go over with you."

"Fine. Let me grab a cup of coffee and we'll talk in the study." He poured himself a cup from the carafe on the coffee table and motioned for Troy to follow him. At the door he paused and looked back at Elizabeth. "One of the hands was using Truman's dog to herd the cattle into another pasture. It was quite a show. You ought to go out and watch."

Elizabeth had seen the dog work cattle hundreds of times, but she smiled at his enthusiasm. "I will."

For the better part of the morning the two men holed up in the study. Now and then Elizabeth and her aunt heard raised voices on the other side of the door, but it was impossible to understand what they were saying. When Troy and Max emerged, his assistant looked grim.

Out of politeness Elizabeth invited Troy to stay for lunch, but to her vast relief he refused.

Elizabeth and Max remained at Mimosa Landing for nine days, until the first Saturday in December when they left to return to Houston and attend the Van Cleaves's party.

Aunt Talitha had been invited, also, but she declined to attend, or to go to Houston for a few days. At eighty her energy level was not what it once had been, and she limited her socializing to only a few events each year.

"I'm not in the mood to stir these old bones. I'll stay here with Martha. We'll be just fine," she said when Elizabeth tried to persuade Talitha to go with her and Max. "Besides, I never could abide the Van Cleaves."

As Max drove down the half-mile drive, Elizabeth kept looking back over her shoulder.

"Are you worried about leaving her here alone?" he asked. "Or are you just going to miss her?"

"A bit of both, I guess," Elizabeth admitted, settling back

in her seat. "Most of the time, when I'm going to be gone for more than a day or two, she comes with me."

"Relax. She'll be okay. I made certain that Martha and Truman had all our phone numbers. If something does happen, they'll call."

"I know. You're right. It's just that she means so much to me. And she's getting frail as she gets up in years."

Max chuckled. "I wouldn't let her hear you say that if I were you."

She responded with a laugh, and a comfortable silence stretched out between them.

"Are you feeling safer now?" Max asked after a while, casting her a sidelong look. "We left New York ten days ago and there've been no more attempts to harm you."

"To tell you the truth, I haven't given the matter a thought since our first day at the farm. Now that you mention it, though, it is beginning to look as though Detective Gertski was right about it being a matter of mistaken identity."

Max nodded. "Yeah, so it appears."

"I just feel bad that somewhere in New York City there is some poor woman who resembles me who is in mortal danger, and she probably doesn't know it."

"Mmm. Maybe."

The drive from Mimosa Landing to the River Oaks house took a little over an hour. They were going through the little town of Hempstead, to the west of Houston, when the chirping of a cell phone interrupted their conversation.

"Is that mine or yours?" Max asked, casting her a quick look.

"I think it's mine." She dug into her purse, flipped open the phone and punched the talk button. "Yes?"

"Hi, sugar," Mimi said. "I don't mean to bother you, but I've got some news that couldn't wait until you got home."

It's Mimi, Elizabeth mouthed to Max. "Oh? What's that?"

"I just returned from having lunch with Bethany. Brace yourself, sugar. She told me that Natalie is back."

Elizabeth tensed. "What? Are you sure?"

"I'm afraid so, sugar. Bethany saw her in the flesh yesterday."

"Is she alone?"

"Yes. Seems that she and Edward have split. I thought I should warn you that Natalie is going to be at the Van Cleaves's shindig tonight. Just in case you changed your mind about attending."

"No. No, we'll be there."

"That's my girl," Mimi praised. "You walk in there tonight with your head high, on the arm of that sexy husband of yours, and act like she means no more to you than a cockroach."

Elizabeth laughed at the image. "I'll see you tonight."

"What was that about?" Max asked the instant she put her phone back into her bag.

"Mimi wanted to warn me. It seems that Natalie is back. Without Edward."

Out of the corner of her eye she saw Max's head whip around, his brows knit with a frown. She could feel his gaze boring into her. "Look, if you're not up to confronting her, we can turn around right now and go back to Mimosa Landing. My business can wait."

"No. No, we'll go. It's inevitable that our paths will cross at some time. Anyway, I'll be damned if I'm going to allow that woman to dictate my life," she said. Turning her head, she gazed out the window and tried to still the turmoil that raged inside her.

"Okay," Max said after a while. "It's your call."

Eight hours later at the Houston house Max walked out of the dressing room into the bedroom, muttering under his breath. "Damn. I never did like these freaking tuxedo ties."

Elizabeth looked in the mirror and saw that he had made a mess of tying the black tie. She stabbed another hairpin into her intricate, upswept hairdo and rose. "Here, let me help you," she volunteered.

Max watched her walk toward him, wearing a long form-fitting evening gown of midnight-blue silk crepe, and he caught his breath. The long skirt had a slit up one side that reached to mid-thigh and revealed the enticing curve of her leg with each step she took. Wide bands of material criss-crossed over her breasts, defining her tiny waist and the beautiful fullness of her bosom.

She stopped in front of him and undid the mess he'd made of the tie and started over. Max's big hands closed on each of her hip bones.

"Damn, but you look good," he murmured, gazing down at her as she nimbly knotted the tie. Her features were exquisite—her nose slender and ever so slightly tipped up on the end, those magnificent blue-green eyes fringed with dark lashes, high cheekbones and a delicate but firm jawline and chin. Her beauty was so elegant and classic, she took his breath away.

"Thank you," Elizabeth replied, not looking up.

"And you smell great, too." As always, her hair smelled of wildflowers. Added to that were the underlying clean scents of soap, toothpaste and the light, flowery perfume she always wore, which suited her so perfectly. He had yet to find out the name of the scent, he realized, and he made a mental note to himself to do so.

Her nearness pulled at him like some kind of powerful magnet that he couldn't resist. That he didn't want to resist. He bent and kissed the tender skin just behind her ear. "You know, we *could* skip the party and stay home," he murmured against her skin. "And have a little party of our own."

"Oh, no you don't. We're going to that party." She straightened the ends of the tie and adjusted his collar just so. When done, she looked up at him and admonished, "There are going to be several people there that you need to meet, so just get that amorous look off your face and behave yourself."

"Damn. I thought you'd say that. When we get back remind me where we left off."

Elizabeth walked back to her dressing table to finish her makeup and hair. Behind her, Max tipped his head to one side, his fascinated gaze fixed on her tight little rear end and the enticing flex of muscle beneath the blue silk. "Are you wearing underwear?" he asked.

"Max, for heaven's sake. What a thing to ask. Of course I am."

"It doesn't look like you are." Frowning, he looked closer. "Damn. Are you wearing a thong?"

Pink flooded Elizabeth's face, but she gamely tilted her chin at him. "With a clinging gown like this it's the only way to avoid having a visible panty line."

"I knew it! Let me see." Closing the space between them, Max reached out to pull up the gown, but she slapped his hands away.

"No. Stop that. Max, for heaven's sake. Now is no time to get sidetracked. We're running late already. Anyway, it's just underwear. You'll see it when we get home."

Max groaned. "How in hell am I supposed to discuss business? All I'm going to be able to think about all evening is that beneath that dress you've got on a thong."

Elizabeth sat down at her dressing table again and met his gaze in the mirror. "Poor baby. I'm sure you'll manage. Anyway, you're not going to be talking business tonight."

"What do you mean? I thought that was the reason we're attending this party."

"No. Tonight we're going to dangle the bait."

She sensed that his mood had changed instantly from playful and sexy to something bordering on anger.

"I thought we had a bargain?"

"We do." Elizabeth turned around on her dressing-table stool and looked him square in the eye. "Do you want my help in winning over these people?"

"You know I do, but—"

"Then you're going to have to trust me. I know that the object is to find investors for your Dallas project, but we have to do it in the right way, or it won't work. Believe me, I know these people.

"Tonight we need to stick together and circulate among the guests. As we do I'll drop some hints and make a few intriguing statements to people who are key players. I might even invite one or two couples to dinner, say…Tuesday evening. But tonight it's all about tantalizing them. Okay?"

"If you say so," Max conceded, though he still looked doubtful.

"Max, the main thing you have to realize is that these people don't take to hard sell," Elizabeth attempted to explain. "Try that on them and they'll respond with smiling Texas charm as they slam the door in your face."

A rueful grimace twisted his mouth. "Yeah, that's the treatment I've been getting for about a year now."

"For the most part, these people are the descendants of pioneering stock. Whether or not any of them has the business acumen or work ethic of their ancestors who accumulated their wealth is debatable, but, to a man, they like to think they do. Just as they like to think that any investment they make is their idea. And that it was a brilliant one, to boot."

"Hmm. I see your point." He thought for a moment, then nodded. "Okay, we'll try it your way."

Elizabeth turned back to the mirror and powdered her nose. She tucked in a stray curl, then rummaged through her jewelry box. "I don't know what I'm going to wear with this gown. I've sold all my good jewelry."

"Hold on a minute," Max said, and he disappeared into the dressing room. In a few seconds he returned with a flat box.

"I was going to give you these for Christmas, but I think you need them tonight."

"What is it?"

"Close your eyes."

She did as he asked, and Max looped the necklace around her neck. "Okay."

Elizabeth opened her eyes and sucked in a sharp breath, her jaw dropping. "Oh, my word. The Stanton diamonds!" she exclaimed in a breathless whisper. "Oh, Max, how… when…?"

"I put my man on finding the set the day you told me you'd had to sell them."

"They must have cost you a fortune to buy back."

He shrugged. "The important thing is, now they're back where they should be."

"Oh, Max." Tears welled in her eyes until his image in the mirror was a blur. Bounding up off the vanity stool, she flung her arms around his neck. "Thank you. Thank you. Thank you. Thank you so much. You don't know what this means to me."

"Hey, don't cry. C'mon, cut it out. You'll mess up your makeup, and we've got a party to go to."

# *Twelve*

Angelo Delvechio sat with his back to the wall at a table in the rear of the small neighborhood bar. He nursed a club soda, his icy stare fixed on the door.

He hadn't budged from his seat or uttered a word since he walked in and gave his drink order more than an hour ago, but everyone in the place gave him a wide berth. New Yorkers, especially ones in this borough, knew trouble when they saw it.

His cohorts and those who knew who he was called Angelo the Angel of Death. His size alone was enough to intimidate most people. At six foot three and over three hundred pounds, he was a mountain of a man. Blunt features, close-set "piggy" eyes and a face devoid of emotion combined to give him a menacing look that terrified most people.

Angelo had grown up in the neighborhood, and all of his life he'd been a bully and a troublemaker. No one had been surprised when he'd become an enforcer for the Voltura crime family.

Angelo glanced at the clock behind the bar. Dammit, where was Tony Minelli? His source had sworn to him that the man sneaked into this bar every night to pick up a fifth of whiskey.

A chilling half smile curved Angelo's mouth. Tony had never been much of a drinker before, but word on the street was he was hitting the juice hard these days. No doubt he'd heard about the contract out on him and was running scared. From what Angelo had heard, his target had gone to ground over a week ago, shortly after Angelo took out his running buddy, Lucky Lorenzo. Angelo's lips quirked again. Lucky's luck had run out.

Angelo's eyes narrowed, and the man at the next table picked up his drink and shuffled away. Dammit, he thought, gritting his teeth. It had taken him all this time and some persuasion to get a lead on Tony. He would make the little weasel pay for putting him to so much trouble.

The cold smile flickered again. Tony's other best pal, Leo Vittoli, had given him up. Funny how friendship faded when you had the barrel of a 9 mm Glock stuck in your mouth.

Angelo's gaze flickered to the clock again, then back to the entrance, just as his target slunk into the bar. He almost didn't recognize the man. Tony had always been a flashy dresser with a cocky attitude, but now his hair was long and scraggly, he had a week's worth of beard stubble and his clothes were filthy and looked as though he'd slept in them.

The scruffy-looking man hesitated just inside the doorway, his gaze darting around the room. Like one of those damned little ferrets, Angelo thought with disgust. Pretending to pay no attention to his surroundings, he bent over his drink as though he was soused, but he surreptitiously watched his target.

Casting fearful glances all around, Tony sidled up to the bar and signaled the bartender. Without speaking a word, the man took Tony's money and handed over a bottle. Clutching the brown bag to his chest, Minelli scurried out.

The instant the door closed behind the target, Angelo stood up and tossed some bills on the table. The other bar patrons fell silent. Most stared into their drinks or at the TV mounted behind the bar. Some covertly made the sign of the cross, but no one dared to look at the beefy, cold-eyed man making his way out of the bar.

Sticking to the shadows close to the buildings, Angelo kept his prey in sight and waited for the right opportunity. He knew it would come; he just had to be patient.

After a few blocks he realized that Tony was taking a roundabout route. He turned first one way, then the other, then cut over a couple of blocks to Times Square, where he tried to blend in with the theater crowd.

The ploy amused Angelo. Nice try, loser.

Following Tony was not difficult. He was easy to spot, even among the crowd. Clutching his bottle of liquid courage, he scuttled along like a rat trapped in a maze, his movements jerky and frantic. Even staying a half block or so behind, Angelo could smell the fear coming off him.

After a few blocks, Tony cast another desperate glance over his shoulder, then darted between two buildings. Angelo broke into a trot, which, at his massive size, was his top speed. Reaching the alleyway, he flattened himself against the building and peered around the corner. A few feet down the alley, a wino staggered out of the shadows and accosted Tony.

"Whatcha got there, man? Looks like a bottle. How 'bout sharin'?"

"Get away from me, asshole." Tony shoved the wino out of his way and hurried on.

Mumbling obscenities, the old bum staggered out onto the sidewalk, passing Angelo without seeing him.

Angelo slipped into the alley. Immediately the smell of rotting garbage, vomit and other human waste assailed his nose.

Silent as a ghost, he followed Tony into the darkness. Never taking his eyes from his target, he pulled his gun out of its holster with his right hand and a silencer from his pocket with his left. Inexorably closing the gap between him and his prey, he screwed the silencer onto the barrel of the weapon.

Angelo would have preferred not to use the Glock. He'd never been that good with a gun, and these days his eyesight was getting so bad he had trouble hitting anything unless it was at point-blank range, but he couldn't afford to let anyone know that. He'd no longer be of any use to Mr. Voltura, and he knew where too many bodies were buried.

Angelo's weapon of choice was a garrote. It was silent and untraceable. Plus he got a rush out of using brute strength to choke the life out of a target. But skittish as Tony was, he doubted he could get close enough to use the choking device that lay neatly coiled in his overcoat pocket.

With chilling calm, Angelo followed his target through the darkness, slowly gaining ground.

Tony must be close to the rat hole he'd been hiding in, he thought. He was getting careless, not checking over his shoulder as often. Or maybe he felt safe in the darkness of the alley.

With no more than twenty feet separating him from his target, Angelo stopped, raised the Glock at arm's length and took aim.

His finger had barely begun to squeeze the trigger when a shrill chirping sound broke the silence.

"Damn!" Angelo spat.

Tony darted a wild-eyed look over his shoulder and bolted.

Angelo got off two shots. The silencer reduced the Glock's reports to sharp *phttt, phttts.* Both shots missed.

Tony turned on more speed and disappeared around the rear corner of the building to his right, into the back alleyway.

Ignoring the incessant chirping phone in his pocket, Angelo lumbered after him, but his target was too fast. By the time he reached the intersecting alley, Tony was nowhere in sight.

Spewing a string of obscenities, Angelo kicked a garbage can and sent it clattering down the alley. Emitting hair-raising yowls, three startled cats streaked away and a rat scuttled along the foundation of the building, squeaking, whiskers twitching.

Bending from the waist, Angelo braced his hands against his knees and struggled to catch his breath.

"Damn, you're getting careless," he berated himself. He'd forgotten that the cell phone was in his overcoat pocket. He should have turned it off before he went out on this job. Hell, he should have left the damned thing at his apartment.

The annoying chirping continued unabated, finally penetrating his anger. Straightening, he fished the instrument out of his pocket and jabbed the on button. "Dammit! What the hell do you want?"

A moment of startled silence was followed by a throat-clearing sound, then, "It's been almost two weeks. I'm calling to find out when you're going to fulfill the Stanton contract."

"Dammit, I told you that I had two other jobs to take care of first. The first one is done and I was just about to complete the second one. If I had I'd be on a plane to Houston tomorrow, but thanks to you and this damned telephone, he got away. Now I'm going to have to hunt him down all over again."

"I just wanted—"

"I don't give a damn what you wanted. Don't call me again. When the job is done I'll call you."

The moment Elizabeth and Max entered the country club ballroom, their host and hostess, Carter and Helen Van Cleaves, rushed over to greet them.

"Elizabeth, darling, I'm so thrilled that you could make it."

Grabbing Elizabeth's hands, she pulled her closer and kissed the air on either side of her face. "And your husband, too, of course," she added, casting a speculative eye on Max. "When we heard that you two were married I wasn't sure you'd be back from your honeymoon in time."

"Actually, we cut our trip short for several reasons. One of which was to attend your party," Elizabeth assured her. "We couldn't miss the social event of the season."

Max watched with mild amusement as the older woman responded to the flattery, puffing up like a peacock. "Oh, you're such a dear sweet thing." Helen slanted Max a glance. "I do hope you realize what a terrific catch your wife is."

"I know. I'm a lucky man."

"Indeed, you are."

Another couple came in behind Elizabeth and Max, and the Van Cleaves excused themselves and began to work their way counter-clockwise around the room. All the while Elizabeth kept a sharp eye out for Natalie. Max stuck by her side and watched in silence as his wife worked her magic on each group.

That she'd been born to this way of life was evident. She was relaxed, friendly and warm and always seemed to know just what to say and what tone to take. At strategic points in their conversations she slanted him affectionate looks or squeezed his arm and dropped hints about how lucky she now felt to have Max to advise her on investments and money managing.

"He is a wizard when it comes to finance and investments," she said to a group that included two men who thought of themselves as investment gurus. With her arm slipped through Max's, she smiled at him with pride and added, "I feel so pleased and lucky to be in on the ground floor of his newest project."

"Oh? And what would that be?" one of the men asked, with obvious skepticism.

"Oh, dear!" Elizabeth clamped her hand over her mouth. This time she cast Max a contrite look. "Oh, I'm so sorry, darling. I wasn't supposed to mention that, was I."

"No. You weren't," he replied, playing along.

She turned back to the man with an apologetic look. "I'm sorry, Warren, but I'm not at liberty to discuss the project yet. Not until the preliminary business is finished."

"Come, come, my dear. You can't dangle a carrot like that, then change your mind. Tell us."

"No. I'm sorry. Really, I am. Ignore what I said. It was just a slip of the tongue. Now, if you'll excuse us, we really must go talk to the Martins."

"Damn, you're good," Max whispered in Elizabeth's ear as they headed for the next group.

She smiled up at him. "Only because I've known these people all of my life. I know their personalities and their strengths and weaknesses. It's just a matter of using the right approach with the particular person.

"For instance, Judge Felton and Blake Armour and a few others think of themselves as wise men, sages almost. You approach them by asking for their advice. On the other hand, as you just saw, neither Warren nor Simon can abide being left out. Getting in on the ground floor is almost as important to those two as the rate of return. Plus they're always competing with each other.

"I'm willing to bet that by no later than tomorrow Warren will have his wife call and invite us to dinner. I'll be surprised if Simon doesn't do the same."

"Do we accept?"

"We'll see," she said, slanting him a look of bland innocence. "But I think our calendar is going to be full for the next week. To make it up to them, we'll have them over for dinner the week afterward. Make Warren or Simon stew for a week and they'll be ready to sign on to the project the instant they step inside the house."

"Why, you clever little devil, you." Max threw his head back and laughed, a rich, robust sound of genuine amusement that drew curious looks from people all around them and sent a tiny frisson of pleasure down Elizabeth's spine.

When he regained his composure, he grinned at her and shook his head. "Dumb me, I assumed I was marrying a woman who could put me in contact with the right people, but that winning them over would be my problem. Who would have thought that behind that pretty face lurked a born negotiator."

He watched some of the pleasure drain out of her face, her expression turning polite but distant. "I'm sorry. My mistake. I've always felt that when you married someone you became their helpmate. I keep forgetting that ours isn't a normal marriage. I'll stop—"

"Hey, hey. That wasn't a criticism. Look, maybe I have a clumsy way of expressing myself. All I meant was, I'm beginning to realize how lucky I am. When I married you I got a lot more than I bargained for."

"Are you sure?"

"Absolutely. Don't change anything. You're doing great."

She looked deep into his eyes, searching for the truth. Finally she nodded.

They continued to work their way around the ballroom, greeting people, accepting congratulations and best wishes on their marriage and dropping hints and chitchatting. They had just finished a complete circuit of the room when they encountered Mimi standing alone at the edge of the dance floor, sipping champagne.

"Hi, you two." She gave Elizabeth a hug, then held her at

arm's length, her eyes widening. "The Stanton diamonds? I thought—"

"Max bought them back for me. They're my early Christmas gift."

"Good for him." She looked Max up and down. "Damn, stud, you do look great in a tux."

"Thanks," he replied in a dry tone. He snagged two glasses of champagne from the tray of a passing waiter and handed one to Elizabeth. "Man, I'm glad that's over."

Mimi laughed. "I know what you mean. It's kinda like running the gauntlet, isn't it. I've been having fun watching everyone else watching you two. They're all curious to see how you get along. But you can relax. Now that you've 'made nice' with everyone, it's time to enjoy the party."

"Where is your escort?" Elizabeth asked, looking around.

"Oh, I ditched Dexter hours ago," Mimi said with a dismissive flap of her hand. "He downed four martinis the first half hour and he shows no sign of slowing down. Which reminds me. I'll need to bum a ride home with you two after I pour Dex into a taxi."

"Sure. No problem," Max replied.

As she focused on something over Max's shoulder, Mimi's smile dissolved. "Uh-oh. Red alert. Slut at two o'clock, heading this way."

"What?" No sooner had Elizabeth asked the question than she spotted Natalie bearing down on them. All around them people stopped chatting to watch, and silence spread over the room like a wave.

"Great balls of fire. I can't believe that woman has the gall to come over here and speak to you," Mimi muttered.

"Hello, Elizabeth." Natalie's smile held cool challenge.

Elizabeth nodded. "Natalie. How was the Riviera?"

Surprise flashed across the other woman's face. Clearly

she hadn't expected a frontal attack by Elizabeth. "Well, well. I do believe that you've grown claws since we last met."

Ignoring the comment, Elizabeth merely stood her ground and stared at her.

After a few moments, Natalie began to fidget. "As to your question, the Riviera was fun at first. But after a while Edward can be a big pain. He's so persnickety about everything. But I don't have to tell you, do I?"

"What do you want, Natalie?" Elizabeth demanded. "I know you didn't come over here to exchange pleasantries or compare notes on Edward's idiosyncrasies."

"You're right. I wanted to get this first awkward encounter over with so that we can put this…unpleasantness behind us. After all, we're both adults. And we're going to run into each other fairly often."

"Not if I can help it," Elizabeth said baldly.

This time it was Natalie's turn to ignore her. "I was surprised to hear that you and Max were married." She turned her sultry gaze on him, giving him a thorough once-over. "I must say, your taste in men has improved."

Elizabeth did not bother to respond to that, but Natalie didn't seem to notice.

"You know, Max, if I'd known a year ago that you were in the market for a wife, I would have stuck around."

"It wouldn't have mattered. You're not my type."

"Ooh. Now, there's a challenge if I ever heard one." She glanced at Elizabeth. "You don't mind if I steal your husband, do you?"

Nearby several people gasped.

"Just for a dance," Natalie tacked on.

Elizabeth knew that the phrasing of the question had been deliberate. Natalie's smile was all innocence, but her eyes held pure malice.

"Gee, at least this time she had the manners to ask," Mimi drawled.

Natalie shot Mimi an annoyed look. "Must you always be so crass?"

"*I'm* crass?" Mimi chuckled. "Maybe so, but I'm not a home-wrecker."

"Ignore her," Natalie advised Max, tugging on his arm. "C'mon, dance with me."

"No," came his blunt response, no hemming and hawing, no attempt at tact or diplomacy.

Assuming his acquiescence, Natalie had already taken a step toward the dance floor before his one-word reply registered. She stopped and blinked at him, as though she hadn't understood. "What?"

"I said, no." He removed her hand from his arm for good measure. "That would be an insult to my wife."

"Oh, f-for goodness sake," Natalie stammered, casting an embarrassed glance around at the people watching the little tableau unfold. "All that stuff with Edward is water under the bridge now. Anyway, what's a little dance?"

"Sorry, my dance card is full." With deliberate movements he took Elizabeth's glass and set it and his own on a nearby table, then hooked his arm around his wife's waist. "C'mon, sweetheart. I think they're playing our song."

For Elizabeth, the few steps to the dance floor were like walking on air. Smooth as silk, Max folded her into his arms and picked up the beat.

"Thank you," she murmured, looking up at him with gratitude.

"You don't have to thank me, Elizabeth. You are my wife. I'll always protect you when I can."

"Oh. I see."

It had not been concern born out of affection that had

prompted him to take up for her, she realized. It had been simply that she was his responsibility, and Max took responsibility seriously.

Not that she *wanted* him to love her. That would be awkward, since she wasn't in love with him. But she had to admit, over the past few weeks she had come to respect and admire him. And yes, she was growing fond of him, despite his blunt, sometimes roughshod manner. He was someone on whom she could depend. Someone with whom she felt safe and secure. Someone she felt she could trust.

After what she'd been through with Edward, that alone made him special. She hadn't believed that she would ever completely trust anyone ever again. But for some odd reason, in just two short weeks of marriage, she'd come to trust Max.

Elizabeth sighed. It would be nice, and certainly make their life together more pleasant, if her feelings of fondness, friendship and trust were reciprocated.

"Good," Max pronounced. "As much as I hate to admit it, I think Mimi has the right idea. We've dangled the carrot enough. For the rest of the evening, what do you say we forget about business and Natalie Brussard and just enjoy ourselves. Okay?"

"Forget about business? What? Are you ill?" she teased, and felt his forehead with the back of her hand.

"Very funny," he retorted, and turned her in a series of dizzying circles. "You'll pay for that when we get home," he whispered in her ear. "Don't think I've forgotten about that thong."

Elizabeth laughed and laid her head against his chest. Anticipation and excitement bubbled through her. Count your blessings, she told herself as Max whirled her around the dance floor. You've married an honest, good man. Be happy with that.

To her surprise, she did enjoy the remainder of the evening. Max, it turned out, was a fabulous dancer. For a big man he was surprisingly graceful and light on his feet, and his sense of rhythm was impeccable. During the fast dances he led her through intricate maneuvers and twirled and dipped her. When the band played a slow song he wrapped both arms around her and held her close with her cheek against his chest, the side of his jaw against the top of her head, and they drifted to the music as though in a dream.

For Max's part, he was as surprised as Elizabeth. He'd made the suggestion to get her mind off her old nemesis, but as the evening wore on he discovered he was having a great time.

He and Elizabeth danced together as though they had been practicing for years, as though they were one. Had she not urged him to dance with Mimi he would have gladly partnered her exclusively.

"You know, stud, I owe you an apology," Mimi said the moment they began to move to the music.

"Oh? How's that?"

"I had my doubts about you at first. I'll admit, I tried my best to talk Elizabeth out of marrying you. But I've changed my mind."

"Oh? And what brought that about?"

"Oh, several things. The way you're all protective with her, the considerate things you do for her, like buying back the Stanton diamonds. You have no idea how much they mean to her and how difficult it was for her to part with them.

"But the real clincher was the way you handled Natalie. Stud, I could have kissed you when you turned her down." Mimi cocked her head and studied him through narrowed eyes. "I think you're going to be good for Elizabeth. And sure as shootin', she's going to be good for you."

The song came to an end, and as they started to walk off the dance floor the band struck up a lively jitterbug. Grinning, Mimi grabbed Max's hand. "C'mon, stud. Let's you and me show 'em how it's done. Let's burn up the floor."

"You're on."

On the sidelines, Elizabeth and the couple with whom she'd been talking turned to watch them. "Oh, my. Would you look at that. Trust Mimi to make a spectacle of herself," Nell Drexler murmured, grimacing as though she'd just smelled something revolting. Too late, she seemed to recall the close friendship between Mimi and Elizabeth. "Not that I'm criticizing, mind you," she rushed to add. "It's just that she's so…so exuberant. I must say, she and your new husband dance quite well, don't they?"

"Yes, they do," Elizabeth agreed, smiling at the pair. "When she was younger Mimi was a professional ballroom dancer."

Max and Mimi were in perfect sync, never missing a beat. After a few moments the other couples stopped dancing and cleared the floor for them. The pair then pulled out all the stops. Mimi danced with exuberance and sheer joy, her feet moving so fast they were almost a blur. With each hip-swiveling step the thigh-high slit in her gown revealed one gorgeous long leg.

"You might know she'd make an exhibition of herself."

The remark came from Elizabeth's right. She turned her head and discovered Wyatt Lassiter standing at her side. "Oh, don't be so stodgy, Wyatt. They're having fun. That's what a party is for, isn't it?"

He greeted Nell and Ethan Drexel, then took Elizabeth's elbow. "Excuse us, won't you. I need to have a word with Elizabeth."

"Certainly. We were just leaving, anyway," Ethan said.

"Phone me later in the week, Elizabeth," Nell called as her husband steered her toward the door.

Wyatt cast another sour look toward the dance floor. "Now, there's a perfect pair. She doesn't belong here any more than he does."

"I beg your pardon. That's my husband and my best friend you're talking about."

He looked at her then, his face stiff with anger. "Oh, please. We both know why you married Riordan. As for her…Edward should have put his foot down and insisted that you end that absurd friendship years ago. I certainly would have."

"Oh, really?"

"Never mind that. I didn't come over here to talk about Mimi Whittington." He glanced toward the dance floor again as the music stopped and the crowd around Mimi and Max applauded. "There's no time now. They're headed this way. But we have to talk, Elizabeth."

"Wyatt, I don't think—"

"I'll call you," he said, and walked away as Mimi and Max returned.

"Whewie! Can this man of yours dance!" Mimi exclaimed, fanning herself with one hand. "With a little practice and work you could compete in the pro circuit."

"Thanks. I'll remember that if I ever need a second job," Max drawled. "What did Lassiter want?" Max asked Elizabeth, watching the other man wend his way through the party-goers.

"Oh, nothing. He just stopped to say hi." She put her hand on his arm. "Before I forget, while you two were dancing the Drexels invited us to dinner next Friday. It seems he's heard a rumor that you've got an interesting project going and he'd like to discuss it with you."

"Hey, I thought we agreed, no more business tonight," Max growled, but the approval in his eyes warmed her.

"Looks like the crowd is beginning to thin," Mimi observed, looking around.

Max slipped his arm around Elizabeth's waist. "One last dance with my wife and we can leave whenever you ladies are ready."

It was funny, Elizabeth thought, how slipping into Max's arms had become so natural in just one evening. With her hands clasped together at the back of his neck, her cheek resting on his chest, eyes closed, she moved with him to the music as though floating in a dream. She did not have to concentrate on the dance. Her feet seemed to follow his of their own accord.

When the song ended and Elizabeth took a step back, Max bent and dropped a soft kiss on her lips. "Ready?"

A nod was all she could muster.

Ten minutes later, they said their goodbyes and climbed into Max's BMW.

"Mmm, I'm pooped," Elizabeth said, leaning back in her seat and stretching. "I can't remember when I've danced so much or had such a good time at a party."

"Yeah, that part was fun," Mimi said from the back seat. She leaned back against the plush upholstery. "But I'm glad that shindig is over. By the way, I don't know if you two realized it, but you make a dynamite couple. I mean it," she insisted. "You look stunning together."

Elizabeth sniffed, and Max held his tongue.

"Do you play golf, Max?" Elizabeth asked.

"Hell, no. I never could see how anyone could get enjoyment out of hitting a little ball into a hole."

"Mmm, that's too bad."

"Why?"

Elizabeth turned her head on the back of the seat rest and

looked at his profile through the semidarkness. "You'd be amazed at how many deals are made on the golf course."

"She's right," Mimi chimed in from the back seat. "I can think of at least three megamergers that were hammered out between the ninth and tenth holes."

"That's too bad. No way am I going to learn to play golf. The game is too slow for me. I'd go stark-raving mad by the third hole."

"I see." Elizabeth mulled that over. After a moment she said, "What about tennis? That's a fast game. It doesn't have the advantage of being able to talk while playing, like golf, but a lot of men, particularly the under-sixty ones, play tennis. After the game they discuss business over lunch in the club house."

"Hmm. That's more my speed. Except I don't know how to play."

"What sport *do* you play, stud?" Mimi asked.

"When I have time, I like racquetball."

"Figures," Mimi drawled. "A game where you can whomp the stuffin' outta the ball."

Without warning Elizabeth sat forward and yelled, "Stop! Max, stop!"

"What the—"

Max stomped on the brakes so hard Mimi catapulted forward. She would have slid off the rear seat had she not been wearing a seat belt.

"What is it? What's wrong?" Max demanded, but he was talking to her back.

Before the car came to a full halt Elizabeth had shed her fur coat and bailed out. Braving the icy rain, she ran toward the rear of the car.

"What the hell is she doing?" Max groused, trying to see through the car's rear window. "She's going to get soaked."

"If I had to guess, I'd say she's picking up a stray cat or dog."

"What?"

Mimi reached over the back of the seat and patted his shoulder. "Get used to it, stud. Elizabeth's got the softest heart of anyone west of the Mississippi."

Sure enough, an instant later Elizabeth jumped back into the car clutching something to her breasts. Something that was squirming and making a constant mewling sound.

"What the hell is that?" Max demanded, staring at the tiny, shivering lump of wet fur.

"It's a kitten."

"Told ya," Mimi drawled from the back seat.

"A kitten? It looks more like a drowned rat."

"Oh, poor little thing," Elizabeth crooned. "She's shaking, she's so cold and wet." She picked the kitten up and cuddled it against the side of her neck. "That's okay, little one. I'll take care of you. You're safe now."

"Oh, great." Max rolled his eyes. "That 'poor little thing' is ruining your gown."

"It doesn't matter. A gown can be replaced. This is a helpless, living thing."

"What're you going to do with it? The humane society isn't open until Monday."

Sucking in a sharp breath, Elizabeth glared at him. "I'm not going to take this baby to the humane society. They kill animals if they're not adopted in a couple of weeks."

"So you're planning on keeping it?"

"I may," she said with a defiant tilt of her chin. "If I can't find someone to adopt her."

"Uh-huh. Why am I not surprised." Max put the car into gear and drove on.

"There's an all-night pharmacy on San Felipe. Would you swing by there so I can get some supplies and kitten food?" Elizabeth requested.

"Sure. Why not?" Max agreed in a defeated drawl.

When he parked in front of the all-night drugstore, Elizabeth thrust the kitten at him. "Here. You hold her while I run in and get what she needs."

"Hey, wait—"

Elizabeth had already opened the door and bailed out.

"Damn." Max held the squirming, mewling kitten at arm's length in his right hand. "What am I suppose to do with this thing?"

"Pray it doesn't pee on your upholstery or your wife's fur coat." Mimi chuckled. "I warned you, stud. You married yourself a steel magnolia with a soft heart. But that's just part of her charm. I'd advise you to be patient."

Elizabeth came out of the store and scampered back to the car through the pouring rain, clutching a large sack.

The instant she climbed into the front passenger seat Max dropped the kitten in her lap.

"What is all that stuff?" he asked, with a nod toward the bulging sack.

"Just some food and kitty litter."

Resigned, Max headed the car toward home.

During the short ride, Elizabeth cuddled the kitten and murmured softly to her. After dropping Mimi off at her front door, Max drove back out onto the street, then up the long U-shaped drive at Elizabeth's house next door and under the shelter of the covered front portico.

She got out of the car and rushed into the house with her little bundle, unmindful of her sable coat or the bag of groceries. Shaking his head, Max gathered up her coat and the large sack and followed her.

He found her in the kitchen, drying the kitten with an old towel.

"Damn. That's about the ugliest cat I've ever seen," he observed, eyeing the bedraggled creature. He set the sack on the counter and took a closer look. "I've never seen a cat with markings like that. It's all black-and-white stripes like a zebra."

"Pay no attention to him, little one," Elizabeth crooned. "Once we get you fattened up and clean you'll be beautiful. Won't you?"

Max leaned his hips back against the granite countertop, crossed his arms over his chest and watched his wife cuddle the forlorn kitten. As he watched her, it occurred to him that Elizabeth would make a wonderful mother.

She stood and kicked off her shoes, then hurried around the kitchen, the kitten at her heels. In short order she set out food and water, the former of which the kitten pounced on as though she hadn't eaten in days.

"Oh, poor baby. You were hungry, weren't you," Elizabeth crooned.

"So…if you keep it, what are you going to call it?" Max inquired.

"Probably Bar Code."

Max laughed. "Damn, woman, you always surprise me. When I proposed this marriage it never occurred to me that you'd have a sense of humor."

Elizabeth shot him an annoyed look. "What did you think? That I was some cold, vacuous female who was too self-absorbed to see the humor in situations?"

"Something like that," he admitted.

Elizabeth's eyes narrowed, but by that time the kitten had scarfed down the food. She lined an old basket with towels for a bed and filled a shallow pan with litter, both of which she put in the utility room. The kitten was so full its tummy bulged and it wobbled after Elizabeth like a tiny drunk. She picked it up and placed it in the litter pan, and the kitten did what she was supposed to, then responded to Elizabeth's praise by winding itself around her ankles. Finally she put the bundle of black-and-white-striped fur into the basket. After scratching around a bit, getting the towels just so, the animal curled up in a ball and promptly fell asleep.

"Oh, look. Isn't it sweet," Elizabeth whispered.

Max strolled over to the utility room door and looked over her shoulder. "Yeah, sweet." He put both hands around her waist and murmured in her ear, "Now…about that thong…"

# *Thirteen*

"Elizabeth!" The front door slammed with a bang that rattled the entryway chandelier. "Elizabeth! Dammit, where are you?"

In the den Mimi looked at Elizabeth and raised her eyebrows. "Uh-oh. That doesn't sound good." She downed the remainder of her coffee and stood up. "I think you'd better go soothe the savage beast. Me, I'm outta here."

"Coward," Elizabeth teased.

"You betcha. Call me later, sugar," she said as she picked up her coat and scooted out the back door.

Elizabeth put down her coffee cup, moved the sleeping kitten out of her lap and headed for the front of the house. She nearly collided into Max when she stepped into the central hallway. His face looked like a thundercloud.

Behind him stood Troy, his expression a smug mix of delight and anger.

"You bellowed?" Elizabeth asked sweetly. She was not about to let herself be bullied, especially not with Max's assistant watching her with that self-satisfied smirk.

"This isn't funny, Elizabeth. I want to talk to you."

"Fine. Do you think we could do so someplace a little more private? Gladys and Dooley are in the kitchen."

Without waiting for an answer, she led the way into the study and sat down in one of the fireside chairs. Outwardly she was calm and composed, but inside she was unaccountably nervous, her stomach quivering. Which was silly. She hadn't done anything to rouse the kind of ire she could see in her husband's every move.

Neither man sat down. Troy took up a silent vigil beside the fireplace while Max paced.

"I just received word from my agent in Dallas that someone is trying to buy up the remainder of the property that I intended to include in my project."

"But…didn't you put down earnest money on all that property?"

"Yes. But that doesn't stop the owners from trying to squirm out of our deal and sell to a higher bidder. What's worse, I can't even let that property go and scale down my project to what I've already purchased. You want to know why?"

Elizabeth nodded.

"Because the property in question surrounds what I already own. According to the sellers, the people who are trying to outbid me intend to fill all the old buildings and warehouses with the most obnoxious and undesirable types of commercial enterprises imaginable—a millwork-and-cabinet shop that will have saws and woodworking tools running around the clock, a fertilizer warehouse, a lawnmower repair shop, a down-mattress-and-pillow company.

"At all hours of the day and night there will be the noise of air brakes and horns as trucks come and go, industrial clanking and banging and the stench of wet goose feathers and gasoline fumes. And as if that's not enough, the views out of the windows of what was going to become luxury apartments will be horrendous."

"That's…that's terrible," Elizabeth said. "Can't you hold the sellers to their contracts with you?"

"Maybe. Maybe not. It depends on how far the owners want to fight. They may have the new bidders backing them financially."

"Who are the new bidders? Maybe you can talk to them."

"A consortium of Houston businessmen," Max stated, scowling at her. "And don't you think I've tried to talk to them. Their spokesperson wouldn't give their names, only that they have no intention of backing off. After talking to him, I got the definite impression that the consortium's main goal is to harm me financially."

"Will it?"

"You bet. Best-case scenario, we're looking at months, maybe even years of court battles."

"Oh, that's awful. I'm really sorry, Max. Truly, I am. But why are you so angry with me?"

"Outside of myself and Troy, there are only four other people who know about this project—my secretary, who typed up all the papers, Lloyd Baxter, the man we met with in New York, and you and your attorney.

"Troy and Carly have been with me for many years and I trust them implicitly. Lloyd Baxter would have no reason to torpedo a project in which he has invested so heavily." Max paused, his hard-eyed stare drilling into Elizabeth. "That leaves you and John Fossbinder."

"John would never breech client-attorney privilege."

Max nodded. "That's the impression I got also."

Elizabeth's eyes widened. "You think *I* told someone? That *I'm* trying to ruin you?"

"You have to admit, it sure looks that way," Troy chimed in.

Elizabeth's head whipped around and her narrowed gaze fixed on his smug face. "I don't have to admit anything. Especially not to you. Or to you," she added, casting her husband a fulminating look. Head high, she rose and walked to the door with all the dignity she could muster.

"Where are you going?" Max demanded. "Come back here, Elizabeth. We're not through talking."

"Maybe you're not, but I certainly am." She jerked the door open and slammed it behind her.

Gladys poked her head out of the front parlor where she'd been dusting and muttered, "Land'o Goshen, I never heard such door-banging and yelling in all my born days."

Ignoring her, Elizabeth hurried up the stairs, but halfway to the landing she changed her mind and ran back down again. She grabbed a coat out of the entry closet. "I'll be over at Mimi's if you need me," she called to Gladys, and sailed out the front door.

"Humph. As if I couldn't have guessed that," Gladys muttered.

Elizabeth's cell phone chirped just as she was about to play her last three letters and end the game of Scrabble. She put down the letters *K, I,* and *V* perpendicular to the *A* already on the board and crowed. "Kiva."

"Kiva? What's a kiva?"

"A kiva is an underground ceremonial chamber that was used by the ancient Indians," Elizabeth informed her aunt. "So there. I win. I win, I win, I win!"

"All right, all right, you win. Now, will you please answer that telephone," the old woman snapped in her loving, crotchety way. "It's driving me batty."

"You're just a sore loser," Elizabeth teased, but she dug the instrument out of her purse and answered, "Hello."

"Mrs. Riordan?"

"Yes?"

"I'm sorry to disturb you at home. This is Carly, your husband's secretary. I was wondering if you'd heard from Max today?"

"No, I haven't."

Actually, she had neither seen nor heard from Max since she'd stormed out of the study of her Houston home the day before yesterday. She'd returned from Mimi's that evening to find him gone. He'd left word with Gladys that he was flying to Dallas to straighten out a business emergency and that he didn't know when he'd be back, which had made Elizabeth angry all over again.

How dare the man accuse her of being disloyal—*her* of all people. Then he makes matters worse by leaving without so much as a goodbye. Just when she had been starting to feel as though their marriage had a chance, he'd gone and pulled a stunt like that. Jerk.

"Oh, dear," Carly said. "I have a big problem. I received a call from the cruise-line this morning and they informed me that Max's mother fell and broke her leg on the cruise ship."

"Oh, no. How bad is it?" Elizabeth was immediately filled with concern, her anger at Max forgotten. The tone in her voice alerted her aunt that something was wrong, and the elderly woman listened intently.

"Apparently it's a bad break," Carly explained. "The ship's doctor put a temporary cast on her leg, but he thinks she should be seen by an orthopedic surgeon ASAP."

"Yes, of course she should."

"Oh, good, I'm so glad you agree," Carly exclaimed with relief. "As soon as I learned of the accident, I made arrangements for a private jet to fly her home. I just assumed that I'd be able to get in touch with Max and he would fly back in time to meet Iona at the airport, but I've been trying to contact him all morning, and neither he nor Troy are answering their phones," Carly continued.

"Don't worry about it. I'll pick her up and take her to an orthopedic surgeon, then bring her home with me. What time is she due to arrive?"

The instant Elizabeth hung up the telephone her aunt demanded to know what was going on.

"Oh, the poor dear," she said when Elizabeth explained.

"Apparently, it's a bad break. The cruise-ship line contacted Carly and she made arrangements to have her flown home in a private jet."

"That's good," her aunt said, nodding her approval. "She should be at home where her family can take care of her."

"Yes, well, Max is the only family she has left. I'm going to have to drive to Houston and pick her up. Her plane arrives in two hours."

Leaning on her cane, Talitha stood up. "I'm going with you. You may need help caring for her."

Between herself and Gladys and Dooley, Elizabeth doubted that, but she was glad for her aunt's company.

Elizabeth and Talitha arrived at the VIP lounge of the Houston airport just moments before the small jet touched down. Two male flight attendants carried Iona down the short flight of steps to where Elizabeth stood waiting with a rented wheelchair.

"Oh, my dear, I didn't expect you to meet me," Iona said, looking all around. "Where is my son?"

"He's away on business, and I haven't been able to reach him, so I came for you instead."

Iona spotted Talitha standing just inside the lounge. "Oh, dear, your aunt is here, too. I'm so sorry to be such a bother to both of you." Slowing down to accommodate her aunt's gait, Elizabeth steered the wheelchair through the lounge and out the door, where her car sat waiting.

"Mother Riordan, you're family now. Family is never a bother. We're happy to look after you."

"Yes, indeed," Talitha agreed, giving Iona's shoulder a squeeze. "Elizabeth has already made an appointment for you with Dr. Ron Watson. He's waiting for us at the hospital right now. He's a family friend, and one of the best orthopedic surgeons around. He did hip joint-surgery on me a few years ago, so I can personally vouch for him."

"That was very good of you. Still, I do so hate to be a burden."

"Nonsense," Talitha declared with a thump of her cane as they eased Iona into the back seat of the car. "Didn't we just say you weren't? Now, pull that cast into the car and let's be on our way."

As he'd promised, Dr. Watson was waiting for them. Leaving Elizabeth and her aunt in the visitors' lounge, he rolled his patient into a small examining room. From where the two women sat they could see various hospital staff going in and out of the curtained-off cubicle.

After a while the doctor came out and informed them that Iona was being prepped for surgery. "I'm going to have to reset the break and it's going to require some metal pins. After the surgery she'll be in recovery for a while, but if everything goes well, you can take her home once she's awake and lucid."

While they waited, Elizabeth called Max's cell phone several times, but there was no answer. Finally she gave up and called his secretary and asked that she continue to try to reach him.

It was after six when they finally arrived at the River Oaks house. With the help of Gladys and Dooley they carried Iona inside.

"You should've taken me to my apartment. We have an elevator there," the patient said in a slurred voice.

"We have an elevator here, too," Elizabeth assured her. "And we have one in the farmhouse at Mimosa Landing. So you're going to be just fine at either place. Now, no more apologizing and fretting, you hear? We are happy to take care of you."

They put her in one of the guest rooms that had its own TV. After a light dinner, Iona swore she wasn't sleepy, so Talitha sat by her bedside and they played gin rummy. Within twenty minutes, however, Elizabeth heard the clank of the elevator, and shortly afterward Talitha came into the den and announced, "She's out like a light. Fell asleep right in the middle of the game. I pulled the covers up over her and left her sleeping."

"Poor thing. It's been a rough day for her," Elizabeth murmured. She stood and stretched. "Speaking of rough days, I'm pooped. I think I'll have an early night myself."

"Me, too," her aunt said.

Normally Elizabeth used the stairs, but since her aunt always used the elevator she stepped into the cubicle with her.

On the second floor, she kissed her aunt's cheek and bade her good-night, then she tiptoed into Iona's room and peeked in at her to be sure that she was okay.

When satisfied, Elizabeth went back into her own bedroom, pulled on her nightgown and went to bed.

She was sound asleep when the shrill of the bedside telephone woke her.

Rising up on her elbows, Elizabeth cast a bleary-eyed look around. Finally she woke up enough to answer the phone.

"Yes?" she said sleepily.

"How is my mother? Where is she?" Max's voice snapped in her ear. "I just got back to the hotel and found a message from Carly saying that Mom had been injured and you were seeing after her."

A glance at the bedside clock told her it was past midnight. She wanted to ask where he'd been at that hour, but she held her tongue.

"She's okay." Sitting up, Elizabeth propped one elbow on her drawn-up knees and raked her other hand through her tumbled hair. "She broke her right leg onboard ship. The cruise-line flew her from the ship to St. Thomas, and Carly chartered a jet that flew her from St. Thomas to Houston. Aunt Talitha and I met her plane and took her straight to the hospital. Dr. Ron Watson had to put her leg back together with pins. He's an excellent surgeon and a personal friend of my family."

"Is she all right?"

"She is now."

"May I speak to her?"

"She's asleep," Elizabeth informed him. "I suspect that she's sleeping off the lingering effects of the anesthesia. It would be better if you called her in the morning."

"Should I come home?" Max asked.

"Only if you want to," Elizabeth informed him in the coolest tone she could manage. "Unless you don't trust me to take care of her, that is."

A long silence followed. "I trust you, Elizabeth."

"Oh, really? That's news to me."

"Look, I don't want to get into this over the phone."

"Fine. Do whatever you want."

"I just wanted to tell you that I'm grateful to you for looking after her. And I'm sorry you got saddled with this burden. If you'd like, I can send Carly to pick her up and take her back to her apartment and hire around the clock nursing for her."

Elizabeth ground her teeth. The man was maddening. In one breath he is polite, and in the next he goes and spoils his apology with a remark like that.

"Must you be so insulting? Do you really think that I would leave your mother's care to some stranger? Or that I would for one minute resent taking care of her? And for your information, Iona is *not* a burden. She's a dear, sweet lady, and my aunt and I are enjoying her company. She is welcome to stay as long as she'd like.

"Now, if you don't mind, I'd like to go back to sleep."

Without waiting for his answer, she replaced the receiver and plopped back down in the bed. As far as she was concerned, Maxwell Riordan could go butt a stump.

The next morning Iona was her old chipper self and getting around well on crutches. Elizabeth had just showered and was heading downstairs when she heard the telephone ring, and a few seconds later she heard Gladys inform Iona that the call was for her and it was her son.

Having no desire to speak to Max, Elizabeth slowed her steps. She could tell by Iona's voice how delighted she was to talk to him and how much the call had cheered her, and she was pleased for the old lady.

Elizabeth walked slowly down the hall and stopped outside the den. She knew Iona would expect her to talk to Max if she saw her.

As old people are wont to do, Iona told her son, in great detail, how she'd broken her leg, and how nice everyone had treated her. She also informed him that she had a follow-up appointment with Dr. Watson on Friday, and after that they planned to go to Mimosa Landing.

"So if you call and we're not here, that's where we'll be.

Your sweet dear wife is insisting that I stay with her while I'm on the mend," Elizabeth heard her tell him.

"When are you coming home?" Mrs. Riordan asked, then frowned. "I see. Can't you give me a guess? I understand. You're in the middle of tough negotiations. Well, I guess we'll see you when we see you."

After Iona hung up the phone, Elizabeth waited a beat or two, then walked into the den.

"Oh, my dear. You just missed talking to Max."

"Really? Well, don't worry. I spoke to him last night."

"He says he doesn't know when he'll be home. He's had some sort of problem crop up on his current project, and he said he couldn't leave until he's got everything under control."

"Mmm. Well, that's too bad, but I'm sure he'll work it all out."

"Oh, my, yes. My son is an excellent businessman," Iona said, beaming.

After a hearty breakfast Elizabeth and her aunt and mother-in-law retired to the den. Ensconced in their comfortable plush recliners, a game show on the TV, the two old ladies talked endlessly while Iona crocheted and Talitha worked on her latest needlepoint project.

Gradually their conversation faded away and each nodded off. Elizabeth looked from one to the other and smiled. Both ladies were sound asleep and snoring softly.

The doorbell rang and Elizabeth hurried to answer it before the chimes woke Talitha and Iona.

"Wyatt. What are you doing here? I thought you were going to call."

"I was driving by and I thought I'd take a chance that you were in."

"I see. Well…won't you come in." A bit uneasy, Elizabeth closed the front door and led the way into the parlor.

Wyatt looked around. "I assume that Gladys has gone to the grocery store, as she usually does on Wednesday?"

"Yes. Yes, she has." How, she wondered, had he known that? May I get you something to drink?" Elizabeth said, breaking the strained silence. "Coffee, perhaps. Mine isn't as good as Gladys's, but it's drinkable."

"No, thank you. I'm here because we need to talk, Elizabeth."

"Very well." She sat down in her favorite parlor chair and motioned for him to take a seat on the sofa, but he ignored her and began to pace. Finally he came to a halt and looked at her, his eyes seething. "How could you, Elizabeth?" he said between clenched teeth. "How *could* you marry that man?"

"Wyatt, I—"

"When I left you here, after my last visit, it was with the understanding that you would think over my proposal. Then the next thing I knew you had up and married that rough hooligan Max Riordan and the two of you were honeymooning in New York."

"Wyatt, I *did* think over your proposal, and it didn't suit me. I told you that before you left here that day. You just didn't want to hear it. I could never, under any circumstances, give over control of Mimosa Landing. Not to you or anyone. I'd think you'd understand that."

"You married Riordan for his money. You know it and I know it."

Elizabeth didn't know quite what to say to that. It was true, but somehow the idea of marrying for practical reasons seemed more acceptable with Max than with Wyatt. "Wyatt, please—"

"It infuriated me to see you with him at the Van Cleaves's party. To imagine you in bed with him. Dammit, Elizabeth, you were supposed to be mine."

"I…I'm sorry, Wyatt." She looked at him helplessly, wringing her hands. It was never her intention to hurt him. She didn't want to hurt anyone.

"It's clear now that I made a mistake in not marrying you on your terms." He made another pass around the room, both hands in his pockets, jiggling his change. "But it's not too late for us," he said, catching Elizabeth's gaze. "All we have to do is have an affair and that roughneck will drop you like a hot potato. Then you'll have Mimosa Landing and the trust he set up and be rid of him. And possibly, if we can get certain portions of the prenuptial agreement nullified, we'll get you a large chunk of his wealth."

Elizabeth stared at him, her mouth open, her mind zeroing in on the most pertinent part of his statement. "You read our prenuptial agreement, didn't you."

"Well…uh…"

"How else would you know about that clause?" She stared at his guilty expression. "Oh, my God, you read my entire file, didn't you?"

"Well…"

"*Didn't* you?"

"The prenup was right there in plain sight on John's desk. I'd gone into his office to see him about something and he wasn't there. Naturally when I spotted your name on the document I read it through. I was concerned, so I looked through your file as well."

"How *dare* you."

Though flustered at first, Wyatt seemed to shake off any embarrassment or guilt he felt. He shot her a challenging look.

"I make no apologies for what I did," he declared with a haughty look. "I was planning to make you my wife. Anything that concerned you *was* my business. Besides, I work for Fossbinder, Lassiter and Drummond. I have a right to look at the files. For Pete's sake, my father is a full partner in the firm."

"That's no excuse," Elizabeth snapped. "Neither you nor your father are *my* attorney, and I don't appreciate you snooping into my business. Your behavior was unethical and disreputable."

"Don't you get it? Everything I did, I did for you. For us," Wyatt yelled.

Elizabeth narrowed her eyes and studied his flustered face. "Oh…my…God! You're the one who's trying to ruin Max's Dallas project, aren't you."

"Yes."

She gasped. She had expected a hot denial, but he was so arrogant he admitted what he'd done as though proud of himself.

"I am part of a consortium. It wasn't difficult to get the others in the group to go after the property," Wyatt admitted. "To the others it was a business investment, but my plan was to hurt Riordan so badly financially that he'd go under. I did it for y—"

"Don't! Don't you dare say you did it for me," she ordered. "And furthermore, I don't believe for one moment that you love me. Why don't you admit it? The real reason you want to marry me is to get your hands on Mimosa Landing."

"So what?" he countered. "Mimosa Landing should have become part of the Lassiter holdings long ago."

"What?" Elizabeth was so taken aback by the statement she was stunned into silence. Before she could regain the use of her tongue, Wyatt grabbed both her upper arms, snatched her up out of the chair and covered her mouth with his.

Elizabeth's muffled screams were fruitless. She twisted and squirmed and pounded at his chest with both hands. The kiss was rough and unpleasant and made her queasy. She bucked and stomped on his immaculately polished shoes, trying with everything in her to break his hold, but she was no match for him. When he finally managed to pry her mouth open and plunged his tongue inside, she bit down, hard.

"Ow!"

Taking advantage of his distraction, Elizabeth pushed out of his arms and backed away, wiping her mouth with the back of her hand. "I told you to stop and I meant it," she said, panting.

"I'm bleeding. Why, you little bitch," he snarled. Closing the gap between them in two rapid steps, he dealt her a vicious back-handed blow. Pain exploded along the left side of her face, and the force of the blow sent her staggering backward. She bumped into an end table and sent a lamp crashing to the floor, then tumbled over the arm of the sofa onto the cushions.

Shock momentarily paralyzed her. She'd never been struck in her life. Then her face began to throb and the next thing she knew, Wyatt's furious face filled her line of vision. Kneeling over her, his knees on either side of her thighs, he inserted his hand in the V of her satin blouse and yanked. Cloth tore and buttons popped and went sailing around the room like bullets.

"No! Stop! Stop it!" Elizabeth cried out, slapping at him.

"You think you can play me along," Wyatt muttered, working at the waistband of her slacks. "Cheat me out of what should have been mine. When I'm through with you not even that oil-field roughneck will want you."

"Stop it! No! Noooo!" Elizabeth fought as hard as she could, but he easily overpowered her. In desperation she raked her fingernails down both sides of his face.

Wyatt yelled in pain. He touched his cheek with one hand,

and when he saw blood on his fingertips his expression turned crazed. "Why you—"

He drew back his hand to strike her again, but before he could deliver the blow something hard struck the top of his head.

"Ow! Wha…?"

"You get off her, you animal," Aunt Talitha raged.

"That's right," Iona added, delivering a blow with one of her crutches. "Git! Git your sorry carcass out of here. Right now, before we call the police."

The two old ladies pummeled him, Aunt Talitha with her cane and Iona with her crutch.

"All right, all right," Wyatt yelled, scrambling off the sofa. "I'm going. I'm going. Stop it. Ow! Ow! Knock it off, dammit," he ordered, but the blows kept coming as the two women followed him to the door, meting out punishment.

He scrambled out the front door, took the porch steps in one leap and jumped into his car.

"And don't you ever come back again," Talitha shouted, shaking her cane at him as he took off down the driveway, tires spinning.

The ladies shut the door and exchanged a triumphant look, but their victory was forgotten at the sound of a moan from the parlor.

As fast as they could, they hurried back into the room and found Elizabeth sitting up on the sofa, clutching the tattered remains of her blouse together with one hand and the other over the side of her face.

"Oh, my poor, sweet child, are you all right?" Talitha said, hovering over her. "There, there. Don't cry, sweetheart. He's gone. He won't hurt you anymore."

"If…if you and Iona, ha-hadn't been here—"

"Shush now," her aunt ordered, lovingly stroking the top

of her head. "Don't think about that. We were here, thank the Lord. And we gave him what for. Didn't we, Iona?"

"We certainly did. That monster. Who is he, anyway?"

"His name is Wyatt Lassiter, the scion of an old Houston family," Talitha said with a sniff. "And they're all no damned good. The men, at least. Like the worthless cur he is, Wyatt's been sniffing around after Elizabeth ever since her first husband ran off with another woman. I guess you could say he's a sore loser. Humph! I almost wish he'd come back so we could give him the thrashing he deserves."

"Me, too," Iona agreed. "Just you wait until my son hears about this. I wouldn't want to be in that young man's shoes when he does."

"Oh, no. I don't want Max to know," Elizabeth said.

"Nonsense. He's your husband. He should be told," her aunt declared. "I think we should call him right now and tell him to come home. You need his support, shaken as you are."

After their argument Sunday night, Elizabeth doubted that Max would care. He believed that she'd betrayed him. Why would he care what happened to her? In any case, they didn't have the close, supportive type of marriage that Talitha and Iona assumed. For the two dear old ladies to know that would hurt worse than any hurt Wyatt had dealt her.

"Talitha is right," her mother-in-law said. "Besides, how are you going to hide your injury from Max? Your face is already swelling. In a few hours you're going to have one beauty of a shiner."

"Here, let me have a look," her aunt ordered. Peering at the injury, she shook her head and tut-tutted. "I think you're right, Iona."

"Oh, dear." Elizabeth gingerly touched the area with her fingertips and winced. "I don't think anything is broken," she managed to say. "But my cheek hurts like the very devil."

Elizabeth closed her eyes. "I expected Wyatt to be upset that I chose Max over him, but I didn't expect this. He was like a madman. And some of the things he said didn't make sense. Twice he mentioned something to the effect that Mimosa Landing should have been in his family's hands long ago."

"Did he, now?" Aunt Talitha sighed. "I can answer that for you. I never told you before because I wanted to put the unpleasant episode behind me. Also because I was embarrassed that I'd let myself be hoodwinked in the first place. The reason for Wyatt's claim is, forty-something years ago I was engaged to his father, Henry, for a short time."

"What?" *Stunned* did not come close to what Elizabeth felt. She thought she knew all the family history.

"It was after my Martin was killed. I was fond of Henry Lassiter, but I didn't love him. Martin was lost to me, so I figured, what the heck. Possibly Henry could give me children to love.

"Lucky for me, I found out in time that Henry, like his father, was an abusive man, physically and emotionally."

"Really? Who told you?"

"Henry's own mother, Mary Beth Lassiter. She was a timid, cowed woman, almost ghostlike, the way she fluttered around in the shadows, as though she were trying to make herself invisible. You hardly ever saw her without some sort of injury—a bruise or a cut lip or broken bone.

"Poor soul. She lived her entire married life in fear of Clive Lassiter, Henry's father and Wyatt's grandfather. Mostly she tried to stay out of his way. When that wasn't possible, she tried desperately to please the man so he wouldn't strike her, but there's no pleasing a man like that, so she lived out a miserable life enduring beating after beating.

"Back in those days there weren't women's shelters like there are today, mind you, nor would the police get involved in domestic situations. Women were on their own."

Which explained why her aunt donated so heavily to women's shelters, Elizabeth realized.

"Poor thing," Iona said.

"Yes. But thank the Lord, she worked up enough gumption to pull me aside one day and warn me that her son's main reason for wanting to marry me was so that he could get his hands on Mimosa Landing, which, as you know, abuts property the Lassiters own. She told me that Clive Lassiter had married her for her property, and now her son was planning to do the same with me. She also said she didn't want me to suffer the life that she had.

"Naturally I broke off the engagement that very day," Aunt Talitha said. "Henry threw a walleyed fit. If your father hadn't been with me at the time, I'm sure he would have struck me. Ever since I've avoided him whenever I could, but he still blames me for denying him possession of Mimosa Landing. Evidently, he has infected his son with the same misguided notion."

"I see," Elizabeth murmured. The story explained a lot. For a long time she'd been aware that her aunt wasn't fond of any of the Lassiters, particularly Henry. Whenever they bumped into each other her aunt looked right through the man as though he didn't exist and refused to speak to him. Elizabeth had asked her aunt about it several times, but the only explanation she got was that Talitha couldn't abide the man. Now Elizabeth knew why.

She also now realized that the only reason her aunt had consented to having Henry's law partner handle the family's legal affairs was because, when it came to the law, John Fossbinder was the best.

Iona peered at Elizabeth's cheek. "Oh, dear. That's going to need some ice. Can you walk, dearest?"

"Maybe you should go to the hospital ER," her aunt suggested.

"No. No hospital," Elizabeth insisted. If she went to the hospital the doctor on call would question how she got the injury, and she was almost certain that by law he would be required to call the police. Elizabeth shuddered at the thought of the publicity that would cause.

"All right, then, let's get you into the kitchen. Gladys keeps a first aid kit under the sink."

On wobbly legs, flanked by the two older ladies, Elizabeth made her way into the kitchen. She was sitting at the kitchen table while her aunt and Iona quibbled about the correct way to treat the injury, when Gladys and Dooley came in through the mudroom, carrying sacks of groceries.

"What in the world has happened?" Gladys exclaimed when she saw Elizabeth's face. She quickly put the sacks down on the table and lifted Elizabeth's chin for a closer inspection.

"Wyatt Lassiter, that's what happened," Aunt Talitha said.

Gladys looked up, her face slack with shock. "Mr. Lassiter hit her?"

"He not only hit her, he tried to rape her. Right here in her own house," Elizabeth's aunt added with an indignant huff.

"That's right," Iona confirmed. "Talitha and I had to beat him off her."

"Oh, my. Dooley, come here and look at this," Gladys ordered, and her husband obeyed, frowning as he inspected the angry red, swollen flesh. "That ain't no slap. To make a mark like that a man would have to deliver a hard blow." He gave Elizabeth a stern look from under his bushy eyebrows. "You called the police yet?"

"I—"

"She won't let us," Iona explained.

"What's this?" Dooley gave her another stern look. "Now, that's just plain foolish, little girl. The man assaulted you and attempted to rape you. Those are both serious crimes."

"I just want to forget that it ever happened. I don't want the police or anyone else involved. Okay?"

"Hello? Anybody home?" Mimi called, and Elizabeth moaned. Here came one more person who would demand to know the whole story.

As always, Mimi had let herself in through the French doors in the study. "Where is everyone?" The tap-tap of her high heels sounded in the central hallway as she checked out the parlor, dining room, then the den. Finally the swinging door into the kitchen opened. "Oh, here you all are. What're you— Great balls of fire! What happened?" she gasped, staring at Elizabeth's face.

Before anyone could answer Mimi's shock turned to a scowl. "Did Max hit you?"

"No! It wasn't—"

"He most certainly did not!" Iona declared.

"Oops. Sorry, Mrs. Riordan. I didn't see you standing there."

Iona narrowed her eyes at Mimi. "I remember you. You were at the wedding. Mona…Minnie…Mamie?"

"It's Mimi. I was the matron of honor."

"Yes, well, I'll have you know, my son would never raise his hand to a woman. I brought him up better than that."

"Of course he wouldn't. I'm so sorry."

Iona sniffed. "As well you should be."

"It was Wyatt Lassiter who hit her," Aunt Talitha informed Mimi.

"What? That sorry, no-good son of a—"

Aunt Talitha cleared her throat and the two elderly women again launched into their story while Gladys cleaned Elizabeth's wound.

"Looks like there's a cut at the corner of your eye and the rest is abraded pretty bad," Gladys murmured, dabbing alcohol over the area and blowing when Elizabeth winced.

While all the women around him chattered, Dooley calmly pulled a camera from a cabinet and took a picture of Elizabeth.

"Dooley! What on earth are you doing?" she complained.

"Evidence." He took two more shots for good measure. "I got me a hunch that man of yours isn't going to be so quick to forgive and forget as you are."

"Good thinking, Dooley," Mimi said. "Max is going to wipe up the floor with Wyatt. I just hope he lets me come along to watch."

"He's going to do nothing of the kind. I want all of you to solemnly promise that you won't say a word to Max about what happened."

"Aw, c'mon, sugar. Wyatt needs to be horsewhipped, and you know it."

"And what good would that do? Max would just wind up in jail, charged with assault. Please. All of you. Promise you won't say anything to him about this."

"How're you going to keep it from him?" Gladys asked. "You're not going to be able to hide that shiner and bruised cheek with makeup."

"Not necessarily. Max is busy handling a crisis with one of his projects. I don't expect him back for at least a week." If then, she added to herself.

"Humph. You ask me, it's gonna take that cheek more than a week to heal," Dooley said. "But if you want us to keep quiet, so be it."

The others muttered their agreement, but it was clear they weren't happy about it.

"Okay, now that that's settled, I think Elizabeth should take some aspirin and lie down with this ice pack on her cheek," Gladys announced.

"I agree," Mimi said. "Better yet, let's give you one of the painkillers that doc in New York prescribed for you. You still have some, don't you?"

"Yes. I only took a few."

"There you go. C'mon, sugar," Mimi said, taking the ice pack from the housekeeper. "Let's get you upstairs and settled in bed."

In the master bedroom Elizabeth had barely kicked off her shoes when she had to run to the bathroom and be sick. Mimi held back her hair while she bent over the toilet and emptied her stomach of its contents.

"I was waiting for this," Mimi said as she wet a washcloth with cold water and handed it to Elizabeth. "Ever since I've known you, you've reacted to emotional trauma by losing your cookies."

"I know," Elizabeth said wearily. She took the washcloth and patted it over her hot face and neck, then rinsed her mouth with water. For good measure she gave her teeth a quick brushing as well.

"Now, where are those pain pills?" Mimi asked, already opening and closing drawers.

"Just give me a couple of aspirin. I…I don't think I should be taking anything stronger right now."

Mimi's head came up. "Why not?" She tipped her head to one side and gave her a keen look. "Is there something you're not telling me?" Her eyes narrowed more, then widened. "Oh, my Lord, are you pregnant?"

"No, uh…maybe…I don't know. That's just it. Until I know for certain, I don't want to take any chances."

"Are you late?"

"Yes, but you know how irregular I am. Being late this time could just be a reaction to all the changes in my life lately."

"Mmm. You mean like having a delicious stud in your bed most nights?"

"Mimi Whittington! You've got sex on the brain."

Mimi wrinkled her nose. "I know. Isn't it fun?"

Elizabeth chuckled, as she was sure was Mimi's aim, but the sound was weak at best.

"Okay, to err on the safe side, here's the aspirin." Mimi handed her the bottle, and when Elizabeth had taken two they traipsed back into the bedroom.

"I don't need that," Elizabeth protested weakly when Mimi retrieved a clean nightgown from the dresser drawer. "I'll just curl up on top of the bedspread with a chenille throw."

"Nonsense," Mimi insisted. "Trust me, you'll sleep better this way." She helped Elizabeth out of what remained of her blouse and her slacks. Too weary to argue, Elizabeth allowed her friend to unhook her bra and drop the plum-colored silk nightgown over her head.

"I don't see how I'm going to sleep at all, the way my face is throbbing."

"Don't worry, the aspirin will kick in pretty quick. They aren't potent enough to stop the pain, but they'll ease it."

Elizabeth held herself together until she was in bed. Mimi sat down on the mattress beside her and took her hand. "Do you want to talk about it, sugar?"

The tenderness in Mimi's voice and expression was her undoing. "Oh, Mimi. It was so awful," Elizabeth wailed. The floodgates opened and she began to weep uncontrollably.

"I know, sugar. I know." Mimi gathered her into her arms and rocked her, much as she had more than twenty years ago, when Elizabeth had been a bereft child. "Let it all out," she encouraged, rubbing her hand over Elizabeth's back in slow circles. "You have a right to cry. And you have a right to be angry. Just go with it. You'll feel better when you do."

Elizabeth wept until she could weep no more, great racking sobs from deep in her soul. They shook her entire body and hurt as they tore from her throat. Tears streamed from her eyes and dropped like warm rain on her friend's shoulder. Neither woman noticed nor cared.

If Mimi realized that Elizabeth's tears were not over just the attack by Wyatt, but Max's distrust and all the other things that had happened to her over the past year or so, particularly the past month, she didn't let on. She simply rocked her gently and let her cry it out.

After a while, Elizabeth's sobs turned to watery sniffles, then hitching breaths. When at last she quieted she pulled away. Silently, Mimi picked up the box of tissue from the bedside table and handed it to her.

"Thanks," Elizabeth murmured, and blew her nose. "I guess I needed that," she said, snuggling back down beneath the covers.

"I know you did." Mimi smoothed the heavy fall of hair away from Elizabeth's face. "You've been needing that for a long time."

"Tha-thanks for be-being here, Mimi," she said between sniffles.

"Now, where else would I be?"

Smiling, Mimi watched her friend's eyelids droop. She sat there for a few minutes longer, rubbing Elizabeth's arm in a slow, hypnotic up-and-down movement. When Elizabeth's breathing became deep and rhythmic, Mimi carefully stood, pulled the covers up to Elizabeth's chin and tiptoed out of the room.

# Fourteen

Max stepped inside his hotel suite and tossed his briefcase and overcoat on the first chair he passed. "I think we made progress today," he said. He shed his suit coat and added it to the pile before plopping down on the sofa, legs outstretched and crossed at the ankles, both arms resting along the sofa back on either side of him.

Behind him, Troy closed and bolted the door to the two-bedroom suite they were sharing. He looked at his boss's pleased expression and grinned. "Yeah, we did good. There's only one more property owner to bring into line, and we'll be all systems go on this deal."

After unloading his own personal belongings, Troy went to the bar and poured himself a drink. "You want one?" he asked Max.

"No, thanks."

"You know, I feel like doing a little celebrating," Troy said. "How about I phone a couple of lovely ladies, and we go out for an evening of dinner and dancing, and…well… we'll see where it leads? I happen to know a certain little blonde by the name of Monique who would drop everything for a chance to see you again."

Max gave him a long, under-the-brow look. "Aren't you forgetting something? I'm married now."

"Ah, c'mon. You're kidding, right? It's not as though your marriage to Elizabeth is the real thing. It's just a legal contract. A convenience."

"As I recall, we got blood tests, a license, we stood before witnesses and an ordained minister and exchanged vows and rings. In my book that's a real marriage."

"You know what I mean. It's not as though she means anything to you, or vice versa. I assumed you two would tie the knot, then pretty much go your own ways."

"Hmm." Max studied the mirror-polish shine on his black dress shoes. That's what he, himself, had assumed in the beginning. Even so, he still would not have cheated. An act like that went against everything in which he believed—honor, commitment and doing the right thing.

Still, he could hardly fault his friend for assuming otherwise. On the surface, his and Elizabeth's marriage did seem more of a matter of convenience than anything else.

But somehow, somewhere along the way, things had shifted and changed. He'd tried, but he couldn't pinpoint exactly how or why or when that had happened. And if he couldn't explain the whole thing to himself, he sure as hell couldn't explain it to Troy.

"Well, you're wrong," Max said. "Even if our marriage were nothing more than a formality, I'd still be a faithful husband. I don't break vows. Besides, in today's world, you're smart to limit your sexual contact to one person." He grinned at Troy. "Maybe you should give it a try."

"Are you kidding me? Knowing what I know? Uh-uh. No way, no how, no time." He shuddered. "I'd sooner remove my own kidney with a dull knife than be permanently tied to one woman."

Max laughed. *Permanent.* Strong word. And a strange one. Troy heard it and reacted with dread, but to Max it was the pinnacle, the brass ring.

He'd always wanted a permanent home. That was what his condo was supposed to have been when he purchased it—a comfortable, relaxing home base where he could recharge his batteries, a place that felt welcoming, a place where he felt at home. What it became, in reality, was a place to store his clothes and sleep occasionally.

Maybe that was because he didn't know how to go about creating a home. He'd grown up without a permanent base, moving from place to place, sometimes country to country, wherever his father's work took him.

As an adult he'd never felt any particular rush to return to his condo in Houston. There was nothing waiting there for him, or no one.

For the past ten years or so, at the end of a long day of business such as this one had been, all he had required was a shower and a comfortable bed. For that, one luxury hotel was much the same as another, whether it was in Paris, New York, Tokyo or any other city.

Since he married Elizabeth, however, he frequently found himself rushing to wrap up business so that he could hurry back to her, no matter how long it took to get there or how inconvenient.

Worse, sometimes in the middle of serious negotiating, he found his thoughts wandering to Elizabeth. Picturing those big blue-green eyes, her small, perfect nose, the elegant curve of her neck, her cheeks, that thick, shiny hair and how it felt to run his fingers through it.

Take today, for instance. While Troy had been pounding

home to the property owners that any additional monies they would make by breaking their contract with Riordan Enterprises and going with the new bidder would be gobbled up by attorney fees, Max's thoughts had drifted off to Elizabeth.

How was she doing? What was she wearing? Did she have trouble sleeping at night without him beside her, as he had trouble sleeping without her? The pull of that one small woman and the serenity and satisfaction he experienced when he was with her drew him like a powerful magnet.

Max studied Troy as he poured himself another drink. "What is your problem with Elizabeth, anyway?" he asked. "And don't tell me you don't have one. I'm not blind."

Troy took a sip of whiskey and shrugged. "It's not Elizabeth in particular, it's her kind in general."

"Her kind?"

"Society women, the kind who love you when you've got money, but let your family lose their fortune, and quicker than you can say Dow Jones they drop you for the next poor slob with a seven- or eight-figure bank account."

"I assume you're speaking from experience?" Max inquired, watching him.

He and Troy had been friends since their senior year of college when Troy transferred from Yale to Texas Tech. It had seemed strange to Max at the time that Troy had gone from living the frat-boy life at an Ivy League school to sharing a dorm room at a state-supported Texas college.

From Troy's terse comments and little things that he'd let drop, Max had figured out the reason for the chip that Troy carried around on his shoulder. The senior Ellerbee had not only gone bankrupt the previous year, he had committed suicide, leaving his wife and family to cope with the aftermath of his failure.

Max had earned everything he'd ever had—including his

education—by the sweat of his brow and the strength of his intellect, and he had no patience with a sniveling ex-rich boy's angst or anger. After only a week of sharing a dorm room, Troy had snarled at Max one time too many. In his usual blunt way, Max had told him he was sick of his complaints and his "poor me" attitude.

"You're not the first one life has kicked in the teeth and you won't be the last. So suck it up and move on, frat boy," he'd shouted at Troy in a nose-to-nose confrontation.

Surprisingly, Troy had, and he and Max had been the best of friends ever since.

"Yeah, I'm speaking from experience," Troy acknowledged.

"You want to talk about it?"

Again, Troy shrugged. "As you know, I used to have the lifestyle that your wife has always lived—old money, the best schools, all the perks those things brought. I was crazy in love with a girl back then. I'd known her since high school. I thought she loved me. But when the Ellerbee fortune went down the tubes, so did our relationship."

He turned from staring out the window and looked at Max. "That was when I decided to get serious about college. I swore that I would make as much money as I possibly could, as fast as I could."

"And then what?" Max asked.

"Then I would let her know what she passed up."

"Mmm. How's that working for you?"

Troy's mouth twisted. "It's not. I've made a lot of money, thanks to you, but whenever I think about contacting her, suddenly it doesn't seem like enough. I've got an uneasy feeling that it will never be enough. Anyway, I've never gotten up the nerve to confront her."

Max's cell phone rang and he got up and pulled it from the inside pocket of his suit coat. "Yeah."

"Mr. Riordan. This is Dooley."

Max stiffened, instantly alert. "What's wrong, Dooley? Why are you calling? Oh, damn, don't tell me that guy from New York is after Elizabeth again."

"No, sir. That's not it. I've been keeping a sharp eye out for him, like you asked. Don't you worry."

"Then what is it?"

"Well, sir, I can't rightly tell you that. I promised I wouldn't."

"You promised who, what?"

"Miss Elizabeth. She made us all promise not to tell you what has happened, and I won't break that promise, but I will say this much. If I were you, I'd get myself home. Now.

"That's all I can say. And when you do come home I'd appreciate it if you didn't let on that I called you at all."

"All right. You've got my word. And thanks for the heads-up, Dooley."

The throbbing in Elizabeth's cheek woke her. She glanced at the bedside clock and saw that it was almost six in the afternoon. She got out of bed and went into the bathroom, and groaned at the sight that greeted her in the mirror. She looked as though she'd gone ten rounds in a boxing ring. Her left eye was cut at the corner and the swelling in her cheek was grotesque. On top of that, both eyes were red and swollen from her crying jag.

After taking two more aspirin, she splashed her face with cold water and ran a comb through her hair. There wasn't much point in applying more makeup. No amount of makeup would compensate for the swelling nor cover the ghastly red-and-purple bruising.

She went into the large closet that connected both bedrooms and the bath and put on a bra and a simple, mid-calf-length jade wool dress, and stepped into a pair of strappy suede high heels. Her only jewelry was a pair of gold earrings and a twenty-inch gold chain.

"Hey, look who's here. Sleeping beauty," Mimi said when Elizabeth entered the den. "How do you feel, sugar?"

"Bruised and battered, but not down for the count yet."

"That's my girl," Aunt Talitha praised. "We Stanton women are made of stern stuff."

"I'll say," Mimi murmured, watching Elizabeth with concern.

"Oh, my dear, I still can't believe that horrible man hit you," Iona said, peering at Elizabeth's injury. "And he was angry because you chose my son over him? Humph. No small wonder, I say."

Gladys came to the doorway of the den and announced, "Dinner is ready. Oh, Miss Elizabeth, you're up. How do you feel?"

"Better. Thank you, Gladys."

They all, including Mimi, trooped into the dining room and sat down at the table, Elizabeth in her customary place at the end facing the large double doorway that led into the foyer. Gladys moved back and forth between the kitchen and dining room with serving dishes full of steaming food.

"I hope you don't mind, Iona," Elizabeth said to her mother-in-law. "We eat family style except for formal occasions."

"Mind? Goodness gracious, no. I prefer eating this way. I'm just a simple country girl, I'm afraid."

The housekeeper had just brought in the last dish when they heard a key in the front door lock. Elizabeth sucked in a sharp breath and cast a quick look around the table at the others. "That has to be Max. Remember. Not one word."

"But, how—"

"Just do it. Please."

"Max," Iona said, flashing her son a beaming smile.

"I'll go fetch another place setting," Gladys announced to no one in particular.

"Hello, Mom." Max put his garment bag down on the padded bench in the foyer and went straight to his mother's side and kissed her cheek. "Sorry your trip was cut short. How are you? How's your leg?"

"It's fine. Just fine. This sweet little wife of yours has taken excellent care of me."

For the first time since entering the house, Max looked at Elizabeth. "Thanks for seeing after her."

Elizabeth nodded, carefully keeping the unmarred side of her face turned toward him.

He said hello to Talitha and Mimi and dropped a perfunctory kiss on Elizabeth's upturned cheek. "Just give me a minute to wash up and I'll be right with you," he said, and disappeared down the hallway.

The instant they heard the powder-room door close, everyone started whispering at once.

"You see! I told you to call him," Aunt Talitha said, pointing at Elizabeth with the butter knife she held in her hand.

"Oh, dear," his mother fretted. "I know my son. Believe you me, he's going to be mad as a raging bull."

"What's your plan, sugar?"

"I know I have no choice but to explain to him what happened, but I hope to do that when we're alone. I'll try to keep my face turned throughout dinner. Then I'll tell him later when we're in our bedroom."

"Good idea," Iona agreed, nodding her head sagely. "With his father I always found it easier to break bad news if I got him all worked up with bedroom stuff first."

Mimi choked on the sip of water she was swallowing. Aunt Talitha cleared her throat and pretended an acute interest in the silverware pattern that she'd seen every day for more than seventy years.

Elizabeth felt heat rising in her neck and face like a mercury thermometer that has just been plunged in hot water.

"Okay, that's better." Max reentered the room and took his place at the opposite end of the table from Elizabeth.

"So. What's going on?" he asked.

"Nothing," all four women blurted out in unison, then quickly ducked their heads.

Max stopped in the act of spooning mashed potatoes onto his plate and looked around the table, his eyes narrowing when no one would meet his gaze.

"I see." He passed the potatoes to Mimi and picked up the platter of chicken-fried steak and helped himself to a large piece. What were these women up to? he wondered, ladling cream gravy over his meat and potatoes. They're all straining to act natural. Too much so.

Throughout the meal an uncomfortable silence hung in the room like fog, and when someone did venture to introduce a topic, the conversation was stilted. Even Mimi was quiet.

"Is something wrong with your neck, Elizabeth?" Max finally asked.

"My neck? Why, no."

"Then why are you holding your head that way?"

"What way? I don't know what you mean."

Max put down his knife and fork and stared down the length of the table at her. "Look at me, Elizabeth."

She slanted him a sidelong look. "I am looking at you."

Max scraped his chair back and stood up. Elizabeth's heart pounded as she watched him come around the table. Everyone else watched, not making a sound. When he reached her side he said, "Look at me, Elizabeth," and he took her chin between his thumb and forefinger and turned her face up to him.

Shock, then fury flashed across Max's face.

"What the bloody hell! Who did this to you?"

"What makes you think someone did it? I could have fallen."

"Uh-uh. I've been in enough barroom brawls to know a knuckle buster when I see one. Now, who did this? I want a name. Now."

"It was Wyatt Lassiter."

"Aunt Talitha!"

"The jig's up, child. He's seen the damage and he deserves to know who did it."

"Wyatt Lassiter did this? That son of a— Why in God's name would he attack my wife?"

Talking at once, Talitha and Iona jumped at the chance to retell the story, including the background of Talitha's broken engagement to Wyatt's father.

By the time they finished their tale Max was livid. Without a word, he strode back into the foyer and snatched up his overcoat.

"Max! Max, where are you going?"

"Where do you think? I'm going to find Wyatt Lassiter and give him a beating he won't soon forget."

"Max, no!" Elizabeth jumped up from the table and ran after him. She caught his forearm and clung to hold him back. "Max, please don't do this. The Lassiters are very influential people, particularly when it comes to the law. If you cross them you can kiss goodbye whatever hope you may have had of being accepted in Houston society."

"Dammit, Elizabeth, do you really think that means more to me than you do?" he snarled. His insides were roiling. He wanted—needed—to tear something apart with his bare hands.

Confused, she blinked at him and murmured low enough

for the others not to hear. "Yes. Of course I do. You married me for my social connections. Don't ruin things for yourself now."

Breathing hard, Max stared at her. He was tempted to tell her…? What? That she was important to him? That he'd come to like her more than he'd expected? He doubted that she wanted to hear that. She was obviously still operating under their original ground rules.

Besides, he wasn't certain exactly how he felt about her, or that he could put those feelings into words.

His mother and Talitha joined them in the foyer while Mimi watched from the doorway.

"My boy, Elizabeth is right," Aunt Talitha said. "The Lassiters are a mean bunch. Cross one of them and you have an enemy for life."

"Anyway, son, you're too angry to go over there right now," Iona added. "The temper you're in, you'll probably get yourself arrested."

"You think I'm just going to let this slide? This creep comes into our home and assaults my wife, and I'm supposed to do nothing?"

"On the contrary, I most certainly do think you should confront the man," his mother said. "I just think that you should cool off first."

"Your mother's right. Wyatt will still be there tomorrow. Give yourself time to come up with a plan," Talitha urged. "Oh, and here's something that will verify what happened." Reaching into her pocket, she pulled out an envelope. "Just in case Wyatt has the nerve to claim innocence."

"What's this?" Max asked.

"Polaroid pictures that Dooley made just after your mother and I walloped the tar out of Wyatt. We sent him packing, didn't we, Iona?"

"I'll say. That nasty young man took off like a scalded cat."

Max looked from one woman to the next, his anger abating somewhat at the thought of these two little old ladies beating the tar out of that stuffed shirt, Wyatt Lassiter.

"All right, you win," he reluctantly gave in. "I'll wait until tomorrow morning. But I am going to have this out with Lassiter, so don't any of you try your female wiles or pleas. Got it?"

The three women exchanged glances. They were clearly not happy with his ultimatum, but they decided to take what they could get.

"All right. I won't interfere," Elizabeth said.

"Me, neither, son."

"Nor will I," Aunt Talitha agreed. "To tell you the truth, I wouldn't mind being a fly on the wall when you catch up with him."

"Me, neither," Mimi spoke up. "I'd pay good money for a chance to see that. In fact, we could probably sell tickets. There are a lot of people who'd like to see Wyatt get his comeuppance."

"Now that that's settled, let's all sit down like civilized people and finish our dinner," Aunt Talitha ordered.

With somber faces, they all complied.

Max picked up his knife and fork and cut into his steak, but his gaze kept returning to Elizabeth's face. "You're going to have to call and cancel our dinner with the Drexels and any other social commitments we have," Max said after a while. "As swollen and bruised as your eye and cheek are, it'll be a while before you look normal again."

"I know," Elizabeth replied in a subdued voice. "I've already canceled everything."

"Good."

Later that evening, as soon as they were alone in their bedroom, Elizabeth broached the matter that had been eating away at her ever since she'd stormed out of the house the previous Sunday afternoon.

Taking off her gold earrings on the way, she walked to her dressing table. "Max, we have to talk."

"Okay," he said, disappearing into the closet.

Elizabeth unfastened the gold chain from around her neck, dropped it and the earrings into a cut-glass bowl on top of the dressing table, then went into the closet as well.

"We need to talk about your Dallas project."

"What about it?" Paying only scant attention, he pulled off his tie and hung it on the rack, then started unbuttoning his shirt.

"I did not leak information about it to anyone, nor did my attorney. It was Wyatt."

"Yeah, I know." He pulled his shirttails from beneath the waistband of his trousers and tossed the shirt into a satin-lined hamper.

Elizabeth stopped her contorting efforts to reach the long zipper down the back of her dress and turned her head to stare at him. "You know?"

"Yeah. You need some help with that?" he asked, and without waiting for her answer he walked over to stand behind her. "You've got some hair caught in the zipper."

"Since when?"

"Since when did you get your hair caught? Hell, I don't know."

"Very funny. I was talking about your project." The hair came free and Max unzipped the garment all the way to the bottom. Elizabeth stepped out of the dress. Wearing only skimpy lace panties, a matching bra and high-heeled strappy slides, she walked to the area in the closet where her dresses were and hung the garment on a padded hanger.

Damn, Max thought, staring at the three-inch swath of dark teal lace that miraculously clung to her lower hips and firm little tush. He'd thought the thong she'd worn the last night they'd made love was sexy, but looking at her in that little wisp of lace made his mouth go dry.

Though small, Elizabeth was perfectly proportioned, her body firm and curvaceous. And damn if she didn't have the most gorgeous pair of legs he'd ever seen—probably due to all that rigorous dancing that she and Mimi did.

"Max? Well?" She stood facing him with her hands on her hips and her feet planted. "How long have you known it was Wyatt who was trying to ruin your project?"

"Oh…uh, let's see. Since Monday, I think. Damn, woman, you have great taste in undies."

"Will you quit focusing on my underwear and talk to me," she snapped.

"Right. Um, since Monday." Max stepped out of his trousers and searched through his area of the closet for a pant hanger.

"Since *Monday?* You've known all that time that I didn't betray you? And you didn't bother to call and tell me?"

Standing there, wearing only his briefs, Max looked at her, thoroughly perplexed by the question. "Uh, I guess not. At the time it didn't seem like that big a deal."

"It didn't— Ooh. You…you *jerk!* You tactless, thick-headed oaf! You let me stew for three days. *Three* days," she emphasized. "All that time racking my brain trying to figure out who was attempting to undermine your project, and feeling guilty that maybe I'd inadvertently let something slip. And all along you knew I wasn't to blame!"

"Well, put that way, I guess I can see your point."

"Oh, you can see my point, can you?" she fired back.

Building steam, she stepped out of her high-heeled slides

and paced the length of the closet. "You accused me of being disloyal—"

"Hey, now. I never said you were disloyal."

"As good as."

Max crossed his arms over his bare chest and watched her stomp around the twenty-five-by-twenty-foot closet. During normal times she was serenely lovely, but damn, she was gorgeous in a full-blown temper. "Look, Sunday I'd just learned that someone was trying to wreck our project. I was blowing off a little steam. I didn't realize that I'd hurt your feelings."

"Hurt my feelings?" Elizabeth stopped pacing and stared at him as though he'd grown a second head. "*That's* what you think this is all about? I got my feelings hurt. For your information, I've never been so insulted in my life. You impugned my honesty, my loyalty."

Growing too angry to speak without crying, she picked up her shoes and turned away sharply to replace them on the shoe rack. "To have my own husband accuse me of that kind of dishonesty and disloyalty, without so much as hearing my side—"

Max walked up behind her and slipped his arms around her waist. "I know, sweetheart."

Elizabeth stiffened. "What are you doing?"

He snuggled his face into the side of her neck. "You're right. It was thoughtless of me. I'm sorry. But I didn't do it on purpose." He dragged his open mouth up the side of her neck and nipped her earlobe. His hands began to roam.

"Oh! You have to be *kidding!*" She jerked her head away from his marauding mouth. "If you think you're going to enjoy a session of makeup sex, you're out of your mind."

"Why not? Sounds like a plan to me," he murmured against her neck, not in the least deterred.

"How dare you! You think you can just mouth a lame, 'I'm sorry' and I'll melt in your arms! In a pig's eye!"

"C'mon, Elizabeth. We had a little misunderstanding. That's all."

"Ooh, you're hopeless!"

"You're right. You're absolutely right. I'm sorry. I should be horsewhipped," he vowed, but she heard the laughter in his voice.

"This is *not* funny! Oh, no, you don't," she snapped, slapping at his roving hands. "You can just cut that out right now. If you think for one minute that anything is going to happen between us tonight, you're an even bigger idiot than I thought."

She tried to squirm out of his arms, but Max merely chuckled and turned her around to face him. His sexy grin infuriated her all the more. "Wanna bet?" he challenged in that sexy rumble of his.

Elizabeth's eyes widened. "You…you wouldn't dare force me."

"Of course not." Max frowned at the thread of uncertainty in her voice. "There's no need for force, and we both know it. The chemistry between us is incendiary. We both know that, too."

"Oh!"

Max's attempt at defusing the situation seemed to infuriate Elizabeth and make matters worse. Ignoring her sputters, he lowered his head and began to string nibbling kisses along her neck and the tops of her shoulders, the underside of her jaw. "I missed you," he murmured against her skin between kisses.

He held her in his arms, but his grasp was not tight. If she'd put her mind to it she could have broken free. Instead she twisted and turned within his embrace and pushed against his bare chest. "Let me go," she demanded.

"In a minute," Max murmured, and kept up the gentle assault on her senses, stroking her breasts, pressing her close so that she could feel the evidence of his desire. With each hot caress of his lips and stroke of his hands, Elizabeth's resistance grew weaker. After only a few moments she winnowed her fingers through the mat of hair on his chest and kissed him back with burgeoning ardor.

Breathless, hungry for each other, they kissed and stroked and made desperate little sounds. Unable to bear the torment anymore, Max bent and swooped Elizabeth up in his arms and strode out of the closet, into the bedroom.

A while later, sated, Max lay on his back, staring at the ceiling, still breathing hard. Beside him, Elizabeth did the same. It was dark in the room, except for the light spilling out of the closet and the rose art-glass lamp on her dressing table.

"Max?"

Her soft murmur breached the deep silence.

"Hmm?"

"Sex doesn't change anything. I want you to know, I'm still angry with you."

He rolled onto his side and draped his forearm across her middle. "Elizabeth, listen to me. I'm not much good at apologizing, so pay attention. I'm sorry for being so obtuse. I'm especially sorry for doubting you. I knew before Troy and I ever took off for Dallas that you didn't leak the information to Wyatt."

"How did you know that?" she asked, her mouth still sulky. Absently she plucked at the short hairs on his arm.

"After I cooled off, I realized that you would never do such a thing. It's just not in you."

"Really?"

"Really." A rueful grimace twisted his mouth. "I guess I was just looking for someone to blame so I could vent. But I knew better." He captured her plucking fingers and brought them to his lips for a kiss. "Forgive me?" he asked, giving her a pleading look.

Though somewhat mollified, he could see that she didn't want to be. "I guess so," she said finally with a miffed air.

Sitting up, she reached for her robe that lay at the end of the bed and slipped it on.

"Where are you going?" Max asked.

"To brush my teeth and clean my face," she replied, and disappeared into the bathroom.

Lying back against the pillows, Max watched her go. He released a long sigh. He was happy, he realized. Genuinely, deeply happy. And totally satisfied with his life for the first time ever.

All because of one small woman.

How the devil could that be? From day one she'd been nothing but trouble. Yet...she made him happy. Go figure.

# *Fifteen*

"**I**'m here to see Wyatt Lassiter," Max told the receptionist.

The young girl looked confused. "Do you have an appointment, sir?"

"No."

"I'm afraid Mr. Lassiter is busy right now. He and Mr. Lassiter Senior are in conference with some clients."

Max looked around. He spotted a door at the end of the hall that bore a sign that read Conference Room and started that way.

"If you'd like to make an appoint— Wait! Sir! Sir, you can't go in there!"

Max's long stride ate up the distance from the receptionist's desk to the door in seconds. Without bothering to knock, he barged into the room. Instantly eight heads swiveled in his direction.

"What is this?" the elder Lassiter demanded. "We're in the middle of a meeting here. You can't just barge in."

"I already have." Without breaking stride, Max skirted around the table and walked to where Wyatt sat. Grabbing the lapels of his suit coat, Max hauled him up out of the chair, drew back his fist and punched him in the nose.

Wyatt yelled and blood spurted. He stumbled back two steps and crashed to the floor. "Oh, God! My nose. You broke my nose." Rolling in agony, he moaned, his hand cupping his broken nose.

Pandemonium broke out. Henry and his clients, two women and four men, jumped out of their seats and scrambled for safety.

"You...you barbarian!" Henry shouted. "Get out of here at once."

Ignoring him, Max hauled Wyatt up by the front of his shirt and shoved him up against the wall, holding him with his feet dangling about two inches above the carpeted floor. Nose to nose, Max snarled, "That was payback for what you did to Elizabeth."

"What...whatever she told you, it was a lie."

"Shut up, you weasel. I saw the bruise on her face. When it comes to slapping women around you're a big man, aren't you? But you're not so tough when you have to deal with an-other man. Now listen, and listen good. If you ever, *ever,* come near my wife again I will give you what you so richly deserve."

"I-is that a threat?"

"You bet your ass it is."

Unable to move his head, Wyatt rolled his eyes around at the other gaping people. "Did y'all hear that? He threatened me. You're all witnesses."

"I'm calling the cops," Henry threatened.

Shoving Wyatt away from him as though he could no longer bear to touch him, Max turned to Henry with a nar-row-eyed stare.

"You do that. I'd love to have this animal you call a son arrested for assaulting my wife."

"You...you can't prove that," Henry blustered.

"You think not? There are two respected, genteel old la-dies just itching to testify against Wyatt in court."

Henry put down the receiver.

"I thought you'd see it that way," Max said. "And in case you're entertaining any ideas about getting back at me by spreading rumors or trying to sabotage any more of my business deals, you should know that I took the precaution of taking a photograph of Elizabeth's face after your boy here got through knocking her around. I also have photos taken by her handyman immediately after the attack, and the witness statements on tape. Just imagine how convincing two sweet little old ladies will be on the witness stand."

Max pointed his finger at Wyatt, who stood hunched over, moaning into his bloodied handkerchief. "Count yourself lucky that all I did was bust your nose. I'm warning you, come near my wife again and I'll hurt you."

With that, he turned, stalked down the hallway and stormed into John Fossbinder's office. John looked up from the document he was reading.

"Hey, Max. How's it going? I didn't expect to see you today."

"This won't take long." After shaking hands, Max said, "I stopped by to tell you that I just broke Wyatt Lassiter's nose and knocked him on his ass."

"What? You did what?" John was so shocked he shot to his feet, sending the desk chair careening back into the credenza. "I assume you had a reason for doing so?"

"Damn right, I do." Max proceeded to tell him about Wyatt snooping into Elizabeth's file and using the information to try to undermine Max's project. The longer he talked, the more grave John's face became.

"As you can imagine, Elizabeth and I are giving serious consideration to getting another attorney. If you can't control your people any better than—"

"Don't worry. I'll fix this," John Fossbinder said with fire in his eyes. "You have my word on it."

* * *

Wearing dark glasses and a bandage over her injured cheek, Elizabeth spent the morning with Mimi, finishing their Christmas shopping. She tried not to think about the confrontation that was going on in the offices of Fossbinder, Drummond and Lassiter.

She and Mimi arrived home a little after two o'clock, but Max had not yet returned. Elizabeth imagined the worst, picturing him sitting in a jail cell, charged with assault. If he had been arrested, she hadn't the vaguest idea of how to go about posting bond for him.

"Has he called?" she asked her aunt and mother-in-law the instant she and Mimi walked into the den. At the sound of her voice the kitten came running, skidding on the hardwood floors until she crashed into Elizabeth's feet. Picking herself up, she twined around Elizabeth's ankles, meowing for attention. Elizabeth put her purchases down and picked up the mewling kitten, cuddling it absently.

"Yes. He said he had a few things to take care of at his office, then he'd be home," Iona said.

"Did he see Wyatt?"

"Apparently so. But he didn't go into details. All he said was he'd taken care of everything."

"Ooh. That man! I'm sorry, Iona, I know he's your son, but honestly, sometimes he can drive me crazy with his knack for understatement. Or no statement at all."

"Pshaw. Don't you worry, dearie. I understand. He's just like his father that way. Why, there were times when I wanted to whomp that man upside the head with a skillet he was so closemouthed."

"Who was closemouthed?" Max asked, striding into the den from the front of the house.

"Max," Elizabeth said with obvious relief. "You're home.

Thank goodness. Are you all right?" Her eyes conducted a quick visual inspection as she asked the question.

"I'm fine. Why wouldn't I be?"

"Why?" Planting her free hand on her hip, Elizabeth looked up at the ceiling and made a growling sound at the back of her throat. "Because you left here this morning with blood in your eye, ready to tear Wyatt limb from limb. All day I've been imagining all sorts of terrible things that could have happened to you, including you being shot by Wyatt or Henry, or ending up in jail. *That's* why."

Mimi looked from Elizabeth to Max, grinning. "Get her riled up and she's a feisty little thing, isn't she, stud?"

"So I'm learning. I usually don't care for temperamental women, but on her it's kinda cute."

"Do you two mind? I prefer that you not talk about me when I'm standing right here."

Max gave her an appraising once-over. "You were worried about me?" he asked with a hint of surprise in his voice, walking toward her. "That's nice." He gathered her to him, kitten and all. The playful animal immediately began to bat Max's necktie with one paw. Barely noticing, Max ran his gaze over her face. The other women fell silent, each watching with avid interest.

"Well…I, uh…of course I was concerned," Elizabeth replied. "You're my husband."

"That I am," he murmured, and lowered his head and kissed her.

His lips were soft and caressing, hers trembling and compliant. Under the tender assault her senses swirled. She was no longer aware of the three women watching them, or the kitten that lay on its back in the crook of her arm, purring. She was practically purring herself by the time Max ended the kiss.

She was a bit wobbly, and he kept his arms around her to steady her. With great tenderness, he touched her swollen, discolored cheek, and something lethal burned in his eyes. "And every time I look at what he did to you, I want to kill that animal."

"I should think so," his mother stated. "In the meantime, we're all waiting to hear what happened this morning."

"I can see that I'm not going to get any peace until I give you women a blow-by-blow account, am I?"

"You're darn right you're not," Aunt Talitha informed him.

"You came to blows? You actually came to blows? Ooh, this is getting good," Mimi exclaimed.

Max heaved a put-upon sigh and sat down on the sofa. "I found Wyatt and his father in the conference room with some clients. I walked in, jerked Wyatt up out of his chair and punched him in the face. I'm sure I broke his nose."

"Ooh, I would have loved to have seen that. Wyatt is so fussy about his pretty-boy looks."

"Hush up, Mimi, and let the man talk. Then what?" Aunt Talitha demanded, eagerly leaning forward, her hands stacked on the handle of her cane.

"Damn, you women are bloodthirsty," Max teased, but he finished the story, including his conversation with John Fossbinder after the altercation.

"After that I went to my office, spent a couple of hours briefing my people and came home."

"So you don't think that the Lassiters will file assault charges against you?" Elizabeth asked, still not convinced.

"No, I don't. First of all, we have the photos and Mom and your aunt for witnesses. Even if they were willing to go to court and have Wyatt's assault on you become public knowledge, I doubt that John, as head of the firm, would stand for it. For one thing, he thinks a great deal of you. For another, if Wyatt's assault on you and his unethical behavior were to be made public, it would reflect badly on the firm's good name and erode client trust."

Common sense told Elizabeth that Max was probably right. Still, Wyatt and Henry Lassiter made formidable enemies. Neither man ever forgot the slightest injustice, real or perceived. Max had humiliated Wyatt in front of witnesses. She could not believe that father or son would let the matter drop without seeking revenge in some way.

Expecting some sort of payback from the Lassiters, for the next few days Elizabeth jumped every time the telephone or the doorbell rang. She was so worried about what they might do that she had forgotten all about the man in New York who had tried to kill her. This is, until Detective Gertski telephoned on Friday morning.

He had asked to speak to Mr. or Mrs. Riordan. Max had taken his mother to see Dr. Watson for a follow-up check so Gladys handed the telephone to Elizabeth.

"Mrs. Riordan, I'm pleased to talk to you," he said. "I'm just following up. Have there been any more attempts on your life since you left New York?"

"No, none at all, Detective."

"I'm glad. Real glad. That sorta confirms our mistaken-identity theory."

"I agree," Elizabeth told him. "I'm sure Max does, also. We've been home for more than two weeks, and nothing has happened."

"That's good," the detective said. "However, to be on the safe side, I'd like to send you a photo array of men who fit the description you gave us. They all have prior arrests for crimes of this nature."

"You mean known hit men?" Elizabeth asked.

"Well...yes."

"You don't have to sugarcoat things for me, Detective. And yes, of course I'll look at the photos. I'll be glad to help in any way that I can to prevent him from harming someone else."

When she hung up the telephone, Elizabeth went upstairs to pack casual clothes for Max and his mother to take to the farm. She and her aunt, and Mimi as well, since she was such a frequent visitor, kept a country wardrobe at the farm and city attire at the Houston home, along with duplicates of makeup and toiletries. That way packing was never necessary when they moved from one home to the other.

The day before, while Max had been at his office, she and Mimi had gone shopping to build a wardrobe of country attire for him that he could leave at Mimosa Landing. At the same time Gladys had gone to Iona's apartment and gathered up most of her winter clothes.

Elizabeth had packed everything that Max would need and was in Iona's bedroom sorting through her clothes when Mimi poked her head in the door.

"Hi. Gladys said I'd find you here." Mimi plopped down on the edge of Iona's bed and bounced a few times, idly looking around at the blue-and-white decor. "I always did like this room."

"Mmm. Me, too." Elizabeth returned from the closet with an armload of long skirts and sweaters. "For Iona to wear pants over that cast, we have to slit them up the side, and there are only a couple of pairs that she's willing to sacrifice. She'll be able to wear these easier."

"You're sure packing a lot," Mimi noted.

Something in her friend's tone drew her attention, and Elizabeth looked up and saw that Mimi's usual ebullience was sorely missing. Her shoulders were slumped and her expression morose. "I'm only packing so much because Iona has nothing at the farm. Max has only a few things that he left there last week. I don't expect we'll be gone more than a week. Maybe not even that long."

"I know." Mimi sighed. "I just hate it when you're gone."

"Well, then, come with us."

"I don't know. I'm not sure if Max would appreciate me horning in on family time."

Before Elizabeth could reply Max called out, "Elizabeth? Where are you?"

She gave Mimi an apologetic look and answered, "In here. In your mother's room."

"Hey, here you are. Hi, Mimi." He walked into the bedroom and, as casually as if he'd been doing so for years, planted a sound kiss on Elizabeth's lips. "What're you doing?"

"Gladys picked up your mother's winter clothes from the retirement home and I'm packing the items that are appropriate for the farm. Your casual clothes are already packed and in the trunk of my car."

"What casual clothes? I took what little I had in the way of casual duds last time."

"Well, I purchased more for you. Shoes, socks and underwear, too. We'll leave all of it at the farm."

Max looked dumbfounded. "You bought clothes for me? How did you know sizes?"

"Yes, I purchased clothes for you. That's one of the things that wives do, Max. So get used to it. As for sizes, I got those from what you have in our closet."

"You see, stud. Wives are good for more than sex."

"Mimi!" Elizabeth groaned. To hide her red face she bent over the open suitcase and added the last few items.

"Yeah," he replied slowly. "I'm beginning to realize that."

Elizabeth closed the suitcase and snapped the locks closed. "There. Unless you want to change first, we're ready to go."

"Just give me ten minutes," Max said, heading for the door. He paused and looked over his shoulder at Mimi. "Are you coming with us?"

"I don't know. Are you asking me to come along?"

Max shrugged. "I guess I am. You're family, aren't you? It's up to you, but if you're going, shake a leg."

He disappeared through the door and Mimi stared thoughtfully after him. She slanted Elizabeth a look of surprise. "You know, sugar, I'll be damned if I'm not beginning to really like that man of yours."

Sunday evening Elizabeth hesitated outside the closed door of the study at Mimosa Landing. She could do this, she told herself. She had to do this. She raised her hand to knock, hesitated, then let it fall to her side again. Putting her ear to the solid panel of walnut she strained to hear, but the door was too thick. Maybe she should wait. The news would keep. Elizabeth shook her head. No. That was the coward's way out.

Before she could change her mind, she tapped on the door and opened it far enough to poke her head inside. Max looked up from the papers he had spread out on the desk. "Hi. What's up?" he asked.

"I, uh…I…there are a couple of things I need to discuss with you. When you have the time, of course." She made a weak gesture toward the papers on the desk. "I see you're busy now. I can come back later." She started to close the door, but Max stopped her.

"No, don't go. I'm never too busy to talk to you. Come on in. Have a seat," he said when she stepped into the room.

"I'd…I'd rather stand, thank you."

"Sounds ominous," he joked, stacking the papers together.

Elizabeth crossed the room and stood in front of the desk, her hands clasped in front of her to keep them from trembling.

"I have something to tell you. Actually, I have a couple of things to discuss with you."

"So shoot," he said, still rifling through the papers.

"I'm pregnant."

"Uh-huh" came his distracted reply. Then his head snapped up. *"What?"*

"I said—"

"I know what you said. I mean…I thought…that is…you said you couldn't have children."

"I said that the doctors said I'd probably never have children. It looks like they were wrong."

Max stared at her for so long that she began to fidget. "How do you feel about this?" he asked finally, his vivid blue eyes intent on her face.

"How do I feel? I'm deliriously happy. I'm thrilled. I'm walking on air," she said emphatically, unconsciously splaying one hand over her flat abdomen. "The question is, how do you feel about becoming a father?"

Max got up and came around the desk. He sat back on the front edge, captured her hands and pulled her to stand between his spread legs. Automatically, she rested her palms against his chest. "How do I feel? Right now, a bit stunned. Still taking it in. But if you're happy, I'm happy."

"Are you sure? That's a tepid reaction."

"I'm positive. If I seem uncertain it's just because you caught me off guard. I've never really given much thought to being a father, or what kind I would be if it happened."

Max tipped his head to one side. "Are you positive you're pregnant? We've been married only…what?" He twisted around and tried to see the desk calendar.

"Three weeks today," Elizabeth finished for him. "And yes, I'm sure. These days home-pregnancy kits are very accurate. Plus, I took the test three times. All three times it read Pregnant.

"At first I thought I was late because of all the things that have happened in the past month, but apparently I was wrong."

"I guess all you needed was the right husband."

"I guess," Elizabeth agreed, turning pink. "According to my calculations, I conceived either in the shower in New York, or somewhere about ten thousand feet over Tennessee."

A slow, self-satisfied grin curved Max's mouth. "You don't say."

She gave his shoulder a cuff. "Don't look so smug. I'm sure this isn't the first baby conceived in an airplane."

"It is for me. What the—"

"Meow," came Bar Code's plaintive cry.

They both looked down at the kitten rubbing against Elizabeth's legs. She had failed to shut the study door all the way, and Bar Code had squeezed through the opening to be with Elizabeth. The kitten had been her constant shadow ever since she had rescued her. At night, if Max didn't pick her up and put her out of their bedroom the kitten would happily sleep on their bed.

"Damn cat," Max grumbled, but it was a half-hearted complaint, and when he looked back at Elizabeth his expression was tolerant. "So…what was the other thing you wanted to ask?"

"Oh. That. It's really more of a favor."

"Whatever it is, the answer is yes. How could I refuse my pregnant wife?"

"All the same, you really should wait until you hear what the favor is before you say yes."

"That bad, is it? Okay. Shoot."

"Well…I was wondering if you would object to me asking your mother to come live with us."

Dumbfounded, Max stared at her with his mouth partially open.

"Well?" Elizabeth prodded.

"Are you serious? That's what you call me doing you a favor? You want my mother—your mother-in-law—to move in with us? On a permanent basis?"

"Yes. Unless you object. We have plenty of room, both here and in the Houston house."

"No, I don't have any objections," Max said, still dazed by the unexpected suggestion. "The only reason I haven't had her living with me is because I'm gone so much. I thought she'd be lonely all by herself in my condo. And I worried about her getting sick or something happening to her if she was on her own."

"Of course. You were right about that, but your situation has changed now. I'm sure the retirement complex where Iona lives is nice and there are other people her age around, but I think she would be happier with family, don't you?"

Max stared at Elizabeth again. He looked deep into her guileless blue-green eyes and felt something move and tighten in his chest. From the beginning he'd sensed that she was a nice person, but he hadn't realized just how big her heart truly was. Already she thought of his mother as family and opened her arms wide to her.

"There's no question that she'd be happier here. I'm just amazed that you want to do this. I always thought that wives and their mothers-in-law didn't get along."

"What nonsense. Your mother is a sweetheart. I'm very fond of her. Anyway, I grew up in a multigenerational home. It seems perfectly normal to me to keep your loved ones with you.

"Ever since Great-great-great grampa Asa built this place there have been three or four generations of family living here at any one time. That's why he built such a big house. Besides, your mother and Aunt Talitha are good for each other."

"Are you serious? Are we talking about the same two old

ladies? The ones who were arguing about a Scrabble word not half an hour ago? I thought they were going to come to blows."

Elizabeth laughed. "That was nothing. Don't you realize that they both get a kick out of their little spats?"

"No kidding? You could've fooled me." Max cocked one eyebrow in a skeptical look.

"They spend every waking moment together. Your mother is teaching Aunt Talitha how to make intricately pieced quilts and Aunt Talitha is teaching her to knit and needlepoint. They enjoy each other's company immensely.

"Another reason I'd like to have Iona here is so that I can look after her properly. She's not young, you know."

"I know." There had been few times in Max's experience that he had felt overwhelmed with emotions, but this was one. He was touched to his core by Elizabeth's generous spirit, that she thought of his mother as family and wanted her with them. And that she had every intention of looking after her as the years rolled by, just as she did her great-aunt.

He wanted to tell her or show her in some way how grateful he was, but he'd never been good at expressing his feelings, and he couldn't seem to find the words now. "Okay. If that's what you want, go for it," he said, and almost winced at his own abruptness and the flicker of disappointment in Elizabeth's eyes.

"Do you mind if I tell them about the baby?"

Max shrugged. "If that's what you want."

She pulled back out of his arms. "Good. I'll go do that right now. Do you want to come along?"

"Sure. Why not."

They found the two old ladies and Mimi in the den still playing Scrabble.

"When you finish that game, Max and I want to talk to all of you," Elizabeth said.

"Well, you're in luck," Iona replied, and plunked her last three tiles down on the board. *"Onus,"* she crowed. "I win."

"Uh. You got lucky on that last draw, is the only reason," Talitha grumbled.

Mimi started gathering up the tiles and racks to put the game away. "So, what did you want to talk to us about, sugar?"

Max stood in the doorway, arms crossed over his chest, one shoulder braced against the frame. Elizabeth pulled up a hassock in front of Iona's chair and took both of her hands.

"Iona, Max and I have talked it over, and we'd love to have you come live with us."

"What?" Looking flustered, Iona blinked her eyes several times, pulled one hand free of Elizabeth's grasp and placed it over her fluttering heart. "Oh, my. I wasn't expecting anything like this. That's so sweet of you, dear girl, but I can't impose like that."

"It's not an imposition, Iona. Truly, it's not. I love having you with us." Elizabeth slanted a quick glance at her great aunt and added, "I'm sure Aunt Talitha feels the same."

"Well, of course I do," the other old lady said, thumping her cane for emphasis. "I don't know why you're dragging your feet, Iona, unless it's just to be ornery."

"Ornery. I'm not the one who's ornery. Talitha Stanton, you know good and well—"

"Okay, okay. That's enough bickering." Elizabeth looked at her mother-in-law. "So? What do you think. Could you stand to live here and, at times, in Houston with us?"

"Well, of course, I love it here, and at your other house, too, but I don't want to be a bother."

"You won't be, Iona."

"Are you sure—"

"Oh, for Pete's sake, woman, say yes and let's get on with

things," Talitha commanded. "My favorite TV program is about to come on."

"Don't worry, Iona, you won't be a bother," Elizabeth assured her. "Actually, I expect you and Aunt Talitha will be a big help to me once the baby arrives."

For the space of two heartbeats the only sound in the room was the ponderous *tick-tick* of the grandfather clock. Then the other three women erupted at once.

"A baby!" Iona gasped.

"Oh, sugar, are you telling us you're pregnant?" Mimi looked at Max and grinned. "Way to go, stud!"

He bowed from the waist. "My pleasure."

"Huh. I bet," Mimi drawled.

"Oh, my stars. A baby. We're going to have a baby in the house again," Aunt Talitha said, then buried her face in her bony hands and burst into tears.

"Oh, don't cry, Auntie," Elizabeth crooned, moving over to give her aunt a hug.

"These are happy tears, child. I was beginning to think I would die without seeing the next generation of Stantons. And now…" She reached across the Scrabble table and squeezed Iona's hand. "Oh, Iona, we're going to have a baby to love and spoil. Isn't it wonderful?"

"Yes, yes indeed."

"That's right," Mimi said. "And Auntie Mimi is going to get in on that spoiling, too. I know the perfect baby gift. Just the other day I was in Neiman Marcus and I saw this one-of-a-kind, teeny-weeny little sable coat. It had a matching hat and muff, too."

"Mimi! Don't you dare."

"What? A girl is never too young for furs or diamonds."

"What if the baby is a boy?"

"Oh." She looked surprised, as though the thought had not

occurred to her. "Well, then I'll have an itty-bitty tux made for him. Oh! And a pair of Tony Lama boots. And when he's a little older, a little battery-operated pickup truck."

Elizabeth rolled her eyes. "You're impossible."

"Hey, it's not every day I get to be an aunt."

"Oh, Talitha, I just remembered," Iona said. "I have a crochet pattern for a darling baby blanket. I'm going to start it tomorrow."

"Good idea. And I'm going to knit some caps and booties. Oh, and I'll have to dig out the Stanton christening gown. It's in a trunk in the attic, I think."

Elizabeth watched the old ladies as they chattered away, her heart so filled with love that her chest ached and her eyes filled with tears.

She felt Mimi's hand on her shoulder. Her friend bent and whispered in her ear, "You've made them very happy tonight, sugar. Me, too, for that matter. Congratulations, little mama."

Elizabeth put her hand over Mimi's and looked up at her through the tears banked against her lower eyelids. "Thanks."

Her gaze sought Max's, and he gave her one of his rare, soft smiles and made a thumbs-up sign.

That night when they went to bed, Max made slow, sweet love to Elizabeth, his every movement tender and controlled. Elizabeth knew that he was exercising such extraordinary restraint because of the baby, and though there was no need, his consideration made her already full heart overflow with emotion.

# *Sixteen*

A few minutes after five the next morning Elizabeth experienced her first bout of morning sickness. She shot straight up in the bed, her stomach gave a lurch and she bolted for the bathroom.

Max came running right behind her. "What's the matter? Are you ill?"

She moaned, unable to answer, then bent over the bowl of the commode and retched, over and over.

"Damn." Max gathered her hair up and held it back with one hand and slipped the other arm around her waist to support her. "You must've picked up a virus. Do you have a fever? Or maybe it was something you ate."

Elizabeth threw up again and gagged and choked. Finally, wiping her mouth with some toilet tissue, she carefully straightened, leery of her uncertain stomach. She slanted him a wry look. "I don't have a virus, Max. This is morning sickness. It comes with pregnancy."

He looked appalled. "Are you serious? There has to be something a doctor can give you. Should I take you to the ER?"

"No. Absolutely not. This will pass."

He looked at the porcelain French clock on the counter. "When? Ten minutes? Thirty minutes? What?"

As awful as she felt, Elizabeth could not help but chuckle. "Oh, a bit longer than that. Three to four months is normal, I think."

"Months? You're going be like this for months?"

She bent over the sink and splashed cold water over her face and swished out her mouth. "It's different with every pregnancy, they tell me. Some women don't have any sickness, but from what I've heard and read, most do."

She put a dab of toothpaste on her brush and gave her teeth a quick cleaning, all the while watching Max's reflection in the mirror as his expression ran the gamut from concerned to disconcerted to outraged.

"There has to be something the medical profession can do. Dammit, we've put men on the moon. Surely we can find a remedy for morning sickness. It's a wonder that the human race doesn't die out, what with months of sickness and discomfort and then the pain of childbirth you have to go through to have a baby."

"It probably would, if the men had to go through pregnancy and child-bearing," she replied with a wry smile.

Elizabeth wet a washcloth with cold water, folded it longways and gingerly walked back into the bedroom, one hand splayed over her midsection. Max hovered over her as though she were an invalid.

Moaning with relief, she stretched out on her back, placed the cold, wet cloth on her forehead and closed her eyes.

Max pulled the covers up over her and tucked them in around her as though she were a child. "How do you feel? Any better?"

"Mmm. Some. My stomach still feels a bit queasy, but if I stay still it's not too bad."

"I'll be right back," he said, and hurried into the bathroom.

She heard some banging and rustling, then he returned with a glass of water, which he placed on the end table, and a small empty trash can from the bathroom.

"I'll put this waste can right beside you so you won't have to jump and run if the sickness hits you," he said.

She opened one eye and looked at him. "Thank you," she murmured, touched by his thoughtfulness.

Max went around to his side of the bed, climbed in and turned to lie on his side so that he could watch her. He smoothed his fingertips slowly up and down her arm.

Elizabeth smiled, drowsiness gradually overtaking her.

She awoke later that morning to find Max's side of the bed empty and something warm and incredibly soft against the back of her head. She rose up on her elbows and discovered the source of the warmth. Bar Code, who had been sleeping curled up against her neck, meowed in protest.

"What're you doing here, kitty?" she mumbled. She glanced at the door, but it was closed. Which meant that Max had let the kitten in. She turned a muzzy look on the clock on the bedside table and blinked several times to focus.

Good Lord! It was almost noon! She'd never slept that late in her life!

She threw back the covers and started to jump out of bed, then thought better of it. Moving with caution, ever mindful of her iffy stomach, she scooted to the side of the mattress, sat up and swung her feet to the floor. So far so good, she thought after a moment. Tentatively Elizabeth stood up and headed for the bathroom, with Bar Code doing her best to twine around her ankles.

Almost an hour later, showered, hair washed, teeth brushed and makeup applied, Elizabeth descended the stairs wearing her comfy jeans, a thick pink sweater and socks and loafers. The meowing kitten was at her heels.

Halfway down the steps she heard the other women talking in the front parlor and she headed that way.

Pausing in the arched entrance, Elizabeth experienced a moment of extreme happiness. A roaring fire danced in the hearth. Her aunt and mother-in-law were talking and drinking coffee as they busily went through a huge basket of patterns. Mimi sat curled up in a fireside chair with her feet tucked under her, reading the morning paper.

"Well, lookie here. As I live and breathe, if it isn't our little mommy-to-be," Mimi drawled when she spotted her. "Sleeping Beauty, herself."

"Good morning, sleepyhead," Talitha said, her sharp old eyes giving her great-niece a once-over.

"Good morning. I'm sorry I'm so late. Why didn't one of you come upstairs and wake me?"

"My son left us strict orders not to disturb you, that's why. He told us that you were up before dawn, sick as a horse. Max isn't inclined to exaggeration," Iona said with motherly pride. "So we knew you were probably exhausted. Now, you come over here and sit down."

Like a cricket, Iona grabbed her crutches, bounded up out of her chair and insisted that Elizabeth sit down in it. "You'll be more comfortable here, dearie, where you can put your feet up. Besides, I need to sit over here on the sofa by your aunt. We're picking out patterns for baby things," she explained.

Elizabeth was beginning to realize what an energetic person her mother-in-law was. She suspected that Iona was one of those women who had spent a lifetime waiting on others, and now, in her twilight years, she had difficulty sitting around doing nothing.

Iona popped up at the slightest excuse and flitted here and there, looking for some way to make someone's life easier.

Max's father had probably benefitted greatly from his wife's penchant for taking care of others, Elizabeth thought.

Folding down one corner of the newspaper, Mimi looked at Elizabeth over the top and murmured, "Just go with the flow, sugar. It's easier that way. These two are wound up like eight-day clocks."

Even had she been so inclined, Elizabeth did not have the energy or the heart to argue. She let herself be guided to the chair and obediently put her feet up as Iona slid a footstool under them. Bar Code jumped onto Elizabeth's lap before she could get completely settled.

Iona laughed. "I swear, you should've named that kitty Shadow. She never lets you out of her sight if she can help it."

"I know," Elizabeth agreed, stroking the purring kitten's head.

"As for you, Miss Mimi, Iona and I are not wound up," Aunt Talitha objected.

"Fiddle-dee-dee," Mimi shot back. "Why, I'll bet neither of you got so much as two hours' sleep last night, you were so excited about this baby."

"As well we should be," Talitha declared. "The last child born into this family was Elizabeth's younger brother, Ian, God rest his soul. Anyway, that baby will be here before we know it, and Iona and I intend to be prepared."

"That's right," her cohort agreed.

"Uh-oh, sugar. You better watch out. If these two join forces, your chances of getting your own way are about as good as Houston getting a snowstorm in August."

Talitha started to protest, but at that moment Martha came into the room bearing a tray with tea and coffee and crackers.

"I thought I heard you up, Miss Elizabeth," the housekeeper said. She placed the tray on the coffee table and straightened, her smile beaming as she turned to Elizabeth. "Your aunt told me the good news. Congratulations, miss. You are going to make a great mother. I'm so excited. It's going to be so wonderful to have a baby in the house again."

"Thank you, Martha," she said, accepting the woman's hug.

"The fresh coffee is for everyone else and the hot tea and saltine crackers are for you," the housekeeper informed her. "I have no personal experience, of course, being a maiden lady, but I've heard that if you sip hot tea and nibble on crackers, particularly if you do it before you get out of bed, you can control morning sickness."

"You know, I do believe that I've heard that myself," Talitha chimed in, nodding sagely.

"Oh, my, yes," Iona agreed. "And have you heard that…"

While the other ladies chattered away, Elizabeth took a sip of tea and exchanged an amused look with Mimi.

"Are any of you ladies expecting someone?" Martha asked.

The question brought a chorus of nos from the other women.

"Well, there's a strange car coming down the drive."

Uneasiness darted through Elizabeth, but she quickly suppressed it. It had been almost three weeks since they returned from New York, and in that time they had seen nothing of the man who'd tried to run over her.

"Now, who on earth…" Aunt Talitha squinted her eyes in an effort to better see through the lace panel between the long tie-back velvet draperies on either side of the window. "I wonder who that could be?"

"It's probably Max's assistant, Troy," Elizabeth said. "He's supposed to be here sometime today."

"No, that young man arrived over an hour ago. His car is still parked out front." With the help of her cane, Talitha stood up and headed for the window.

"Sit down, Auntie. I'll see who it is," Elizabeth said.

"You'll do no such thing." Talitha turned partway and pointed her cane at Elizabeth. "No jumping up and running around. Not when there are other ablebodied people around. Now, you sit right there and relax."

"I'm not an invalid, you know," Elizabeth objected, but she sank back in the soft upholstered chair, stroking the kitten and feeling like a chastised child.

Pretending not to hear that, Talitha stumped over to the window and twitched back the lace panel. "Why, I do believe… Yes! Yes, it is. It's Quinton and Camille. Oh, how wonderful."

Elizabeth and Mimi exchanged a look and groaned softly, so Talitha would not hear.

"Who are Quinton and Camille?" Iona asked.

"My late twin sister's grandchildren," Talitha said, "and Elizabeth's second cousins."

Martha's cherub face tightened. She quickly gathered up the used coffee cups and utensils and hurried back to the kitchen.

"Just what you need," Mimi murmured for Elizabeth's ears only. "A visit from Princess Camille. Quinton's fun to have around, but that sister of his is a self-absorbed, overbearing, snotty little bitch."

"Gee, Mimi, don't hold back," Elizabeth said with a weak chuckle. "But you're right. I have to keep reminding myself that Camille is Aunt Talitha's great-niece, too, just as I am, and she loves for her and Quinton to visit. I'd better go greet them. Camille will have her nose out of joint for a week if I don't."

With dread, Elizabeth stood up, dumping the kitten to the

floor again, and went into the foyer, arriving just as Talitha opened the door.

"Well, hello. This is a surprise. Come on in here out of the cold wind and give me a hug," Talitha ordered.

"Oh, my dearest auntie. You can't imagine the difficulty we had getting here. Our flight to Houston was detoured to Dallas, and we had to rent a car for the rest of the way. Thank goodness Quinton is a good driver because the highways are iced over in spots," Camille declared. "I swear, I think it's colder here than in New York."

"It probably is."

"Hi, Aunt Talitha." Quinton gave the old lady a hug and a sound kiss on the cheek. "How's my best girl?"

"Humph. You'd know if you called more often, now, wouldn't you?"

"Ah, you wound me, gorgeous." Clutching his chest with both hands, Quinton staggered back a few steps, then pretended to pull a dagger out of his heart. "But you're right. I do promise to call you more in the future."

"Humph. I won't hold my breath."

"Hello, Elizabeth," Camille said, her tone several degrees cooler than when she'd been talking to their great-aunt. She gave Elizabeth a perfunctory hug and an air kiss.

"Sorry about this, cuz," Quinton whispered in her ear when it was his turn to hug her. "I tried to talk Camille out of barging in on you, but you know how she is when she gets it into her head to do something. She was determined to swoop down on you, come hell or high water, so I thought I'd better tag along to act as a buffer."

"Thanks," she murmured. "I'm glad you did."

"Where is Leon?" Aunt Talitha asked, looking around Camille as though she expected to see her niece's husband come through the door at any second.

Right on cue, Camille's eyes filled with tears. "Oh, Auntie. Leon and I are through."

"Through? Don't tell me you're divorced again."

"Well…not officially. Not yet. I'm going to file after the holidays."

"Oh, for heaven's sake. You foolish, foolish child. If your marriage is in trouble, what are you doing here?"

Camille's chin quivered and tears started to roll down her cheeks. "Where else would I be at a time like this other than in the bosom of my family?"

Elizabeth stood back, marveling at how easily Camille could turn on the waterworks. She half expected her cousin to put the back of her hand to her forehead and faint like a Victorian maiden.

"Humph. I'll tell you where you should be, young lady. You should be at home with your husband, trying to work out your problems. You don't just throw away a marriage on a whim or because something didn't go your way."

"Oh. You are so mean and heartless," Camille wailed, dabbing at her eyes. "Just like Granny Mariah always said you were."

Oh, you're good, Elizabeth thought, watching her cousin's theatrics. Very good. Camille knew just what buttons to push with most people. Being compared unfavorably to her twin was guaranteed to soften Aunt Talitha's attitude.

"Oh, she said that, did she? Humph. A lot that feather-brained sister of mine knew." Talitha sighed. "You're here now so you might as well come on in.

"Well? What are you doing just standing here? Let's go into the parlor and get comfortable."

Camille dabbed her eyes again and batted her tear-drenched eyelashes at her aunt. "Then Quinton and I can stay?" Camille asked with a pitiful quaver in her voice.

"Of course you can stay, you silly girl. But you and I are going to have a serious talk before you leave. Understood?"

"Yes, Auntie," Camille replied in a meek voice.

"Here, let me take your coats," Elizabeth volunteered.

"Where is Martha?" Camille asked as she hung up the coats in the entryway closet. "That's a servant's job. I swear, Elizabeth, you are much too lax with your hired help. It's never wise to allow the line between employer and employee to blur."

"I'll keep that in mind. Now, come into the parlor and meet my mother-in-law."

"Oh, that's right. You're a new bride. I almost forgot."

"Don't you believe it," Quinton whispered in Elizabeth's ear. "Ever since she found out that you had remarried she's been straining at the bit to fly down here and get a look at your new husband. I only managed to talk her out of coming here that very day by pointing out that you were newlyweds and still on your honeymoon."

Elizabeth knew her cousins well, and it wasn't difficult for her to imagine Camille making such a snap decision, or for Quinton to rein her in. "Thanks again," she murmured back as they stepped into the parlor.

"Iona, dear, I'd like for you to meet my cousins, Camille Lawrence and her brother, Quinton Moseby."

They exchanged greetings and Elizabeth gestured to her best friend. "And of course, you both know Mimi."

"Oh. Mimi," Camille said as though she had just smelled something bad. "I didn't expect to find you here."

Unfazed, Mimi grinned. "Yep, it's me, all right. Just like the proverbial bad penny, I keep turning up."

Camille sniffed. "You said it, not me."

"All right, now. None of that," Aunt Talitha ordered with a thump of her cane. "You're barely inside the door and already spatting like children."

"You're right, Talitha, sugar. I'm sorry," Mimi said contritely.

The old woman's sharp gaze swung to her grand-niece, and Camille's pinched mouth.

"What? Why should I apologize?"

Her aunt's gaze did not waver.

"Oh, all right! I shouldn't have said that."

"Pay no attention to my sister." Quinton bent and bestowed a kiss on Mimi's lips. "Hiya, gorgeous. Looking good, as always," he said with a flirtatious wink.

Camille gave her brother a peeved look as she sat down on the sofa next to Iona.

Elizabeth returned to her chair. Almost before her rear end touched the seat, Bar Code nimbly jumped back into her lap and curled up.

"Eeeoow. You have a cat. Honestly, Elizabeth, you know how much I dislike cats," Camille said, grimacing. "You got this one on purpose to irritate me, didn't you?"

"Now, how could I do that when I had no idea that you and Quinton were coming for a visit?"

"Well, we're here now, so would you please put that animal outside where it belongs?"

"In this cold? Absolutely not. Bar Code is just a kitten. Anyway, she's a house cat."

Camille appealed to their aunt. "Aunt Talitha, can't you make her put that thing outside? It's your house, too."

"No, dear, I can't. Nor would I if I could. The kitten isn't hurting anyone and she's a good pet to have around."

"Well. I can see who has favored status around here."

"Don't be ridiculous, Camille," Talitha snapped. "You and Elizabeth and Quinton are all dear to me. I would never show favoritism. To imply that I would is insulting."

"I'm sorry, Auntie. It's just that I'm so upset now, with the divorce pending and all." Camille produced a lace-trimmed hankie and genteelly dabbed at her eyes.

Her aunt looked at her for a long time, then nodded. "Very well, child, you're forgiven. Now, back to this divorce of yours. Why on earth are you divorcing poor Leon? He has to be heartbroken."

"Oh, Auntie, you don't know what I put up with from that man." With a new audience to play to, her cousin laid it on thick as she listed her complaints against her fourth husband.

Once her litany of her poor Leon's shortcomings came to an end, Camille asked, "Speaking of husbands, where is this new husband of yours, by the way?"

"He and his assistant are out back," Talitha said. "He said something about showing Troy the new helicopter pad he had built."

"Oh, that's right," Elizabeth chimed in. "His new helicopter is supposed to be delivered sometime today."

"Humph. Men and their toys," Talitha muttered.

Camille's eyebrows rose. "He has his very own helicopter? My, my. He must be rolling in money."

"Don't be crass, young woman," their aunt ordered.

To change the subject, Elizabeth said the first thing that popped into her mind. "You know, Camille, as happy as Aunt Talitha and I are to see you and Quinton, I do wish you had called first."

"Why should I? This is my ancestral home as much as it is yours," she declared with a sniff.

"Wrong. This may be your ancestral home, but no part of this place belongs to you or Quinton. Two-thirds of Mimosa Landing and this house belong to me, period. The rest is Aunt Talitha's."

"Are you saying that I can't visit my aunt whenever I please?"

"Not at all. I'm merely suggesting that you do the polite thing and call first. If for no other reason than to give Martha time to get the guest rooms ready."

"Oh, pooh. Servants are there to do your bidding. It won't hurt her to hustle a bit. Besides, I happen to know that Martha keeps this entire house spotless all the time."

At that moment Martha returned to the parlor carrying a fresh tray of coffee and tea.

She place the tray on the coffee table and nodded to the newcomers. "Ms. Lawrence. Mr. Moseby. Nice to see you again."

"It's Ms. Moseby now, Martha."

"Oh. Pardon me, miss. I didn't know."

She started to leave, but Camille stopped her. "Oh, Martha, have Truman or one of the farmhands get our luggage out of the car. Tell him to put mine in the blue room. Mine is the purple-and-gray set."

"I'm afraid that room is occupied," Elizabeth said. "It's Iona's room now."

"But…I always stay in the blue room," Camille said with a huff. "Can't she move to another room?"

"If it's going to be a problem—"

"It's not a problem, Iona," Elizabeth assured her mother-in-law. "Camille, you don't seem to understand. Iona is not a guest. She lives here now. The blue room is hers. Permanently. And at the Houston house, she has the yellow-and-blue room."

"But…but I'm family."

"So is Iona. There are four other unoccupied guest rooms from which you may choose. I'm sure you'll find one to your liking."

"Oh, very well. The green room will do."

"Sorry, it's taken, as well," Mimi said with malicious glee.

"Of course, it does have twin beds, if you want to bunk with me."

"Oh, please." Camille gave an exaggerated shudder. "I'd sooner throw a mattress down on the sunporch. Oh, just put my things anywhere," she snapped.

From the back of the house came the sound of male voices, and a moment later Max and Troy entered the parlor. Max walked straight to Elizabeth and tipped her face up for his inspection. "Feeling better?" he asked, his gaze roaming over her pale face.

"Yes, thank you," she whispered back. His breath smelled of toothpaste and coffee. His cheeks were ruddy from the wind, and he'd brought with him the cold, sharp freshness of the outdoors. Combined with his own scent it was a heady combination.

Elizabeth introduced Max and Troy to her cousins, and as the men shook hands she could see Camille sizing Max up. Elizabeth bit the inside of her cheek to keep from laughing out loud. She saw the look of interest in her cousin's pale blue eyes and knew that if Max were free she'd go after him like a dog after a raccoon.

They had been talking for only a short while when Martha appeared in the arched doorway into the foyer and announced, "Lunch is ready, Miss Elizabeth."

Throughout the meal, as always, Camille made certain that she was the center of attention. She aimed most of her conversation toward Max and Troy. Most of her chatter was vapid gossip about the goings-on of the social set in New York and Europe. Every now and then she managed to sneak in nasty little barbs aimed at Elizabeth.

Elizabeth ignored her. She had long ago learned to let her cousin's envious remarks and veiled accusations roll off her like water off a duck's back.

"Tell me, Troy," Camille said in her best coquette voice. "Are you related to the Boston Ellerbees?"

Troy nodded and carefully spooned up a bit of Martha's delicious green chili chicken soup.

"Oh, I knew it. I just knew it," she crowed. "You look like your father. I've met your parents several times at social functions. Martin and Joan are their names, right?"

"Yes."

Camille's brow furrowed with puzzlement. "You know, I don't believe I've seen either of them in years. Did they move out of the country?"

"No. My father died several years ago. My mother remarried and she and her husband don't get out much these days."

"Oh. I see."

Troy did not reply, and when it became obvious to Camille that she wasn't going to drag any more conversation out of him, she fell back on her favorite pastime: taking digs at Elizabeth.

Casting a disapproving glance around the dining room, she gave a dramatic sigh. "Elizabeth, dear, I don't mean to criticize. You know that. But don't you think it's time to change the decor in here? In the rest of the house, too, for that matter. Tear down all this wallpaper and fancy woodwork. Modernize the place a bit."

"No, I don't. The kitchen and bathrooms have all the modern conveniences. They're just disguised to fit the Victorian era of the house. This place is a historic treasure. The house and everything in it is original, and that's how it's going to stay."

"Huh. Well, if it were up to me, I'd gut the place and make it ultramodern."

"Then isn't it lucky that the house didn't end up in your care."

"Now, see here—"

"Camille, hush up. Don't go picking at Elizabeth. She's in a delicate state as it is."

"What? Are you ill?" She cast Elizabeth a wary look and scooted her chair back a bit. "If it's something contagious I do wish you would have told me sooner."

Aunt Talitha laughed. "Camille, love, you're the spit out of your mama's mouth. She was the most self-absorbed person God ever put on this planet, and you're just like her. Elizabeth isn't ill. Not in the way you think, anyway. She's in a family way."

"A fam—" Camille sucked in a sharp breath, her gaze darting to Elizabeth. "Oh, my God, you're *pregnant?* At your age?"

It was Elizabeth's turn to laugh. "I'll be thirty the second of February, Camille. I'm not in my dotage yet."

"Well, better you than me. I, for one, wouldn't dream of ruining my figure that way."

"Ignore her, cuz. I think it's great," Quinton chimed in. "Congratulations. I'm happy for you. You'll make one terrific mother."

"Oh, shut up, Quinton," his sister snapped. "Don't you realize what this means to you and me?"

A look of puzzlement came over her brother's handsome face. "That we'll have a second cousin, once removed?"

"Not that. It means that our chances of ever inheriting from Elizabeth will be almost nil when this baby is born."

Quinton winced. "Camille, please."

"What is everyone getting so bent out of shape about? It's true. Aunt Talitha is old, and if Elizabeth never has a family of her own, we're next in line."

"Provided you outlive her," Max said in a low tone that Elizabeth had begun to recognize as a prelude to anger, like embers being stirred to life. "One could almost take that as a threat on my wife's life."

"Oh, don't be ridiculous! I didn't mean it that way," Camille quickly assured him. "We're blood kin. We spat and spar, but I would never do anything to cause Elizabeth harm."

Max narrowed his eyes. "How long are you going to be here?"

Another smile tugged at Elizabeth's mouth. As little as a month ago Max's bluntness would have made her cringe, but at that particular moment she was grateful for his hard-charger attitude. Here she'd been trying to think of a polite way to maneuver the conversation around to that very subject. Not Max. He wanted to know, so he asked.

Camille looked taken aback. For an instant, Quinton did as well, but he recovered quickly. "Actually, we haven't made any hard fast plans. Usually when we visit we stay a month or so."

"I see," Max said.

"If we're imposing—"

"No. I was just curious. Besides, this is Elizabeth's home. It's up to her to say who stays and who goes. Although, as her husband and the father of her child, I must insist that no one do anything to upset her. The next one who does will be out on his or her ear in a New York minute."

The statement did not agree with Camille at all. Her mouth tightened but she remained silent.

"I agree with Max," Aunt Talitha said, giving Camille a stern look. "And he's a man of his word, so you'd better toe the line, missy. Understood?"

"Oh, all right," her great-niece said, sulking.

"Good. Now that we're agreed on that, Elizabeth, Max and I would be happy to have you stay through the holidays." Talitha looked at Elizabeth, waiting for her agreement.

"Isn't that right, my dear?"

"What?" Elizabeth looked at her aunt and blinked. "Sorry. I'm afraid I was wool-gathering. What was the question?" Actually, she was marveling over Max's quick defense of her. Even though she knew that his concern was probably because of the baby, it nevertheless gave her a warm feeling.

"I said I insist that Camille and Quinton stay through the holidays. Don't you agree? It'll be so nice, having all the family here at once. Last year there was just Elizabeth and Mimi and me. And Martha, of course."

"Oh…why, uh…yes. Yes, of course. Please do stay."

# *Seventeen*

"Do you want to tell me what's going on between you and your cousin?" Max asked later that night as they were getting ready for bed.

Turning from hanging up the long black skirt that she'd changed into for dinner, Elizabeth gave a weak chuckle. "Is it that obvious?"

"Hey, I'm not the most sensitive guy around, but even I felt the daggers flying tonight. What's her problem?"

"It's a long story. Are you sure you want to hear it?"

"Shoot."

"Okay. But remember, you asked. If you'll recall, I told you about Mariah, Camille and Quinton's grandmother?"

On the other side of the closet, Max worked open the buttons on his shirt while watching her trade her lacy black bra for a jade-colored silk nightgown. Elizabeth felt his gaze on her. A few weeks ago she would have been self-conscious, but she was becoming accustomed to his nightly perusal. Max was so earthy and uninhibited that living with him was the equivalent of taking a crash course in human sexuality.

"Yeah, I remember. She was Talitha's twin, right?"

"Right." Elizabeth walked back into the bedroom. Max followed, turning off lights as they went, and climbed into the turned-down bed.

Elizabeth paused beside her dressing table to give her hair a vigorous brushing. "What I didn't tell you was that, according to Aunt Talitha and others, Mariah had been headstrong and willful. She was barely eighteen when she ran off with Owen Moseby, much to her father's disapproval.

"Don't misunderstand me. The Mosebys are a good family, but Owen had always been wild and shiftless. He was what in those days they called a 'rounder.'

"And back then eloping was something that young ladies of good breeding simply did not do."

"Judging from the way you reacted when I suggested we get married in Las Vegas, they still don't," Max drawled.

Elizabeth shot him an arch look. "Do you want to hear this or not?"

"Sorry. Go ahead," he replied, suppressing a grin.

"Despite his gruff exterior, Great-Grampa Charles still loved his daughter and missed her terribly. After about a year he could not bear the estrangement any longer, and as an olive branch he offered to give Owen a job—a very well-paying job—if they would just return home."

"So did they?"

Max watched Elizabeth walk barefoot toward him, massaging lotion over her hands and arms, that glorious mane of glossy brown hair tumbled around her face and shoulders. The voluminous nightgown hung on her body from two spaghetti straps over her shoulders and billowed out from there to swirl around her ankles, a cloud of soft jade silk that was in no way see-through or even clingy. Yet it was one of the sexiest nightgowns he'd ever seen on a woman—and he'd seen his share.

He enjoyed watching her, he realized. Every move she made, no matter how small, was poetry. The sway of her hips, her graceful walk, the subtle bob of her breasts with each step.

Elizabeth climbed into bed, adjusted her frothy nightgown, and lay down on her back next to him. Max drew in a deep breath, relishing the soft scent of jasmine and lily that surrounded her. Damn. Was there anything in the world better than the smell of a sweet, clean woman? he wondered. If so, he sure as hell hadn't found it.

Elizabeth's wistful gaze remained fixed on the ceiling. "Unfortunately, working for a living had never been on Owen Moseby's agenda. He declined the offer.

"That, it seemed, was the final straw. Aunt Talitha says that after that the breach between her father and sister grew wider. To this day she swears that he died of a broken heart. Whether or not that's the case, his health certainly started on a downward spiral about that time.

"Seven years later when his only son, my grampa Pierce, died of a sudden heart attack, all the fight just seemed to go out of Great-Grampa Charles. He passed away just nine days later."

"Hmm." Max lay on his side, his head propped up on one hand, admiring his wife's delicate profile. "I don't mean to disparage any of your family, but I'll bet Mariah hightailed it home then."

"Oh, yes. She and Owen were on the first jet out of Paris to Houston. They were certain that her father had cut her out of the will. They brought their attorney with them to the funeral, ready for another court battle. You can imagine how surprised she was when the will was read to learn that she, Talitha and my father, Ransom Patrick Stanton, were to receive equal shares in everything."

."Even a third of your families' fortune would have still been a whopping amount. By now it should be triple or more than it was back then. So what's Camille's gripe?"

Turning onto her side, Elizabeth bunched up her down pillow and lay back down to face Max. She smiled at him in that comfortable, confidential way that married couples do. He wondered if she was aware of doing so.

"I'm sure you could have done that, but Mariah and Owen demanded to receive her share of the estate in cash."

"Are you serious? That's the worse thing they could have done."

"I know. My father tried his best to make them see that, but he was only twenty-two at the time and fresh out of college, and they wouldn't listen. To them my dad was just a green kid who didn't know anything about money and finance."

"So what did your father do?"

"There wasn't much he could do. He liquidated a third of everything we owned, with one exception. Mimosa Landing. To pay Mariah for her share of the farm my father had to take out an enormous loan. It took him years to pay it off."

"Let me guess," Max said. "Mariah and Owen lived high and spent all her money."

"They were doing their best. They were both killed by an avalanche while skiing in Switzerland just a few years later. Colin Moseby, their only child, inherited what was left of his mother's money. He was Camille and Quinton's dad. Unfortunately for them, he was no better at managing money than his parents had been.

"I'll give him credit for one thing, though. Colin recognized that weakness in himself and was concerned enough about his children's future that, shortly before he passed away, he had everything, including the brownstone, put into a trust for them.

"They each receive a large sum every month. Most people would consider themselves wealthy if they had that much income. However, it's not enough to support the jet-set lifestyle that Camille had grown accustom to as a child and still demands."

"Okay, I can understand—sort of—why she might be ticked off at her grandparents, and maybe even her dad. But why does she take potshots at you?"

"She seems to think that she and Quinton were cheated because the amount their grandmother received all those years ago was so much less than it would be worth today."

"So? Everything is. Which just proves my point. If they'd invested Mariah's inheritance instead of spending it, they would still have their principal and much more."

"I know that and you know that, and so does everyone else on the planet except Camille. At one time or another we've all tried to explain it to her, even Quinton, but she's got it in her head that she and her brother got a raw deal, and she thinks that I should make it up to them by handing over the difference between what Mariah received and today's fair-market value."

"You're kidding me?" Elizabeth shook her head and Max rolled his eyes. "Damn. She may not know much about business, but I'll give her an A for nerve. That's crazy. With that kind of convoluted logic anyone who's ever made a deal runs the risk of the seller coming back years down the road demanding more money. Good grief. I've heard some cockamamy reasoning in my time, but that wins the prize."

"I agree. But she's stubborn. She thinks if she keeps on badgering, someday I might actually give in just to shut her up. In the meantime, her solution to the problem has been to marry money, divorce, then bleed her ex for alimony. Poor Leon, who is about to get the old heave-ho, is her fourth husband."

"Only an idiot would marry a woman with that track record."

"What can I say? Camille can have men panting in moments."

"How about Quinton? How does he feel about all this?"

"Quinton is a sweetheart. Underneath all that debonair charm, he's level-headed and intelligent, bless him. He knows that he and his sister have no claim on the Stanton fortune.

"Actually, he enjoys his life very much just as it is. He's in great demand among society matrons, being an unattached, handsome, heterosexual male from an old family. Bless him, he never gets upset, not even on those occasions between husbands when Camille moves back into the brownstone with him."

"Poor guy."

Elizabeth chuckled. "I guess he's used to her."

Max smoothed a tendril of hair off Elizabeth's cheek. "Will Camille succeed in wearing you down eventually?"

Her eyes narrowed. "Not a chance."

The determined glint in her eyes fascinated Max. Elizabeth was such a soft, elegant woman, it was easy to forget that she had a backbone of steel.

He smiled and leaned forward. "Good girl," he whispered against her lips as his mouth touched hers.

Angelo Delvechio had been in Houston less than two hours and already he hated the place. Texas was supposed to be hot and dry, like in all of those old John Wayne movies. Hot, hell. He was freezing his ass off. He glanced up at the temperature display above the car's rearview mirror. Crap. No wonder. It was twenty-three friggin' degrees. And a hundred percent humidity. And wouldn't you know it, the heater on this rental was on the fritz.

And what the hell was it with this friggin' rain? It was coming down so hard he could barely see the road ahead with the windshield wipers going full bore.

Another vehicle blew by him as if he was sitting still. "Bunch of damned cowboys," Angelo snarled. Since he'd left the airport, every third vehicle on the road was some sort of extended-cab, rocket-powered monster pickup truck with huge tires. Even men wearing suits and ties drove them for crissake. In New York the dark sedan he usually drove blended in with the rest of the vehicles on the street. Not here. Here in kicker country this black Caddy stood out like a hooker at a revival meeting.

Another pickup blew by him, and Angelo growled and gripped the steering wheel tighter. "You ever heard of a turn signal, moron?" he hollered at the other driver. "Or a seat belt?"

Angel was a careful driver. A *very* careful driver when he was on a job. The last thing he wanted was to draw the attention of a cop.

One thing good he could say for Texas: it had fantastic-looking broads. Plenty of T and A, with legs up to here.

And even they drove pickups!

This traffic was insane. These freaking cowboys were maniacs behind the wheel. They were outta their freakin' damn minds, for crissake! Certified suicidal. All he wanted to do was take care of this business for the boss and get the hell back to New York.

Following the onboard computer's directions, Angel maneuvered the jammed freeways and streets with extreme caution, finally turning into the covered driveway in front of his hotel.

With a sigh of relief, he heaved his three-hundred-and-ten-pound, six-foot-four body out of the rental and gladly handed over the keys and a tip to the valet. Even though he didn't need their assistance, he tipped the bell captain and the bellman also, not too much and not too little. Either extreme and they would remember him if questioned by cops later.

The garment bag he held slung over his shoulder by one crooked finger was his only luggage. He didn't plan to be here long.

At the front desk the good-looking broad behind the counter said, "May I help you, sir?"

"Yeah. I gotta reservation. Name is Petrie. John Petrie," he said, handing over the fake credit card and driver's license.

The woman barely glanced at the ID, swiped the credit card and handed it and the license back to Angel. All the while he enjoyed the view down the front of her blouse.

"How many days will you be staying with us, sir?"

"I'm not sure. Keep it open-ended. I flew in to have Christmas with family, but if something comes up, I may have to leave on short notice. You know how business is."

"No problem, Mr. Petrie. Here you are, sir," she said, handing him his copy of the paperwork. "You're in room 206. Is there anything else we can do for you?"

"No." He started to turn away, then pretended to remember something. "I almost forgot. Do you have some packages for me?"

"One moment, sir. I'll check."

The woman went into the room behind the counter and reappeared moments later with five small boxes. The brown parcel paper had torn on one corner of the largest package, revealing cheery red foil Christmas wrapping underneath.

"I'm so sorry about that," the desk clerk said. "But I don't think the package is harmed."

"No problem," Angel said. "It's for my five-year-old niece.

She'll have the whole thing ripped to shreds in minutes. That's why I had my gifts for my family sent here."

She laughed. "Smart move. If there is anything else we can do for you, sir, let us know. Enjoy your stay."

On the way to the elevator, Angel checked out the hotel restaurant and bar. It was only a little past six, and already a blonde with a surplus of cleavage sat at the bar. He might come back a little later and have a go at her, he thought.

Inside his second-floor room, Angel turned the dead bolt, attached the chain and hung his garment bag in the dinky closet. Then he removed the brown parcel wrapping on the five packages and set the colorful Christmas boxes on the bed.

Straightening, he smiled at the boxes and stretched and yawned.

Damn, he felt creaky. And randy as hell. Stripping as he went, he walked into the bathroom and turned on the hot water.

Twenty minutes later he came out of the steamy bathroom tying the sash on one of the hotel's terry-cloth robes.

He thought about the blonde downstairs in the bar. She was tempting, but now that he'd cleared his head he decided that the fewer people who got a good look at him, the better. A cold smile curved his mouth. Besides, he could slake that hunger on the target.

Tomorrow, maybe, if the weather cleared and luck was with him.

Angelo picked up the room service menu and ordered a salad, a baked potato and a twelve-ounce medium-rare steak for dinner.

An hour later, one hunger satisfied, Angelo rolled the dinner cart out into the hall, hung out the Do Not Disturb sign and locked and bolted the door.

With Jay Leno giving his monologue on the TV, Angelo

sat down on the bed and began to unwrap the boxes and re-move their contents. Five minutes later he had his Glock put together. He held the gun up at arm's length, aimed toward the window and dry-fired. The solid *click* brought another cold smile to his mouth. Perfect.

Angelo loaded the piece and slipped it beneath his pillow. Carefully, he gathered up and folded every scrap of the red foil wrapping paper and ribbons and stowed them in the bot-tom of his garment bag. The brown wrapping paper he stuffed into the trash can in the bathroom. After double-checking every window and lock, he turned off the TV and the lights, dropped the robe and lay down naked in the bed.

Lacing his fingers together at the back of his head, for a few seconds he relished stretching out his full length, feel-ing his tense muscles relax, one by one.

He stared up at the ceiling, studying the patterns made by the outside lights slanting in through the gap in the draperies. Tomorrow he would case the target's Houston home. From the information and the maps the client had given him, it was the best place to strike. The damned driveway at that godforsa-ken farm was a mile long and flanked by open fields. No way you could get from the road to the house without being seen.

No. Definitely, he'd have a much better chance here in Houston. And the Houston place was a helluva lot closer to the airport. With luck, he could do the job and be on a plane on his way back to New York before anyone knew she was dead.

Tomorrow he'd drive around, get the lay of the land, check out the comings and goings of the help and their employer.

Angel pictured Elizabeth Stanton and smiled to himself in the darkness.

Except for a few veiled barbs that Camille managed to slip by their aunt, the rest of the week was uneventful. On Tuesday morning Mimi left to keep an appointment in Houston and the day after that Max and Troy left to fly to Dallas.

By the time Friday morning rolled around Elizabeth was fed up with listening to Camille fuss and goad and whine. Though her stomach was feeling decidedly queasy, she could not abide another day with her cousin. She kissed her aunt and her mother-in-law a quick goodbye, waved to her cousins and Martha and practically ran out the front door with Bar Code in her travel kennel.

Normally Elizabeth would have left the kitten at Mimosa Landing, but she was afraid of what Camille might do to the poor animal while she was gone. At the very least, she wouldn't put it past her cousin to boot the kitten out into the cold before she got to the end of the drive.

An hour later when Elizabeth lugged the carrier into the Houston house, Gladys's only comment was "If you keep lugging that animal back and forth with you she isn't ever going to know which place is home."

"I know. But this is only temporary. I don't trust Camille not to take her and dump her somewhere if I'm not there."

"Humph." The housekeeper put fresh litter into the box in the utility room, then let the kitten out of the cage.

Elizabeth was primed with excitement, but before she could tell Gladys and Dooley her good news, Gladys demanded to know if she was sick. Sitting at the kitchen table, drinking coffee and reading the newspaper, Dooley folded down one corner of his newspaper and looked at her over the top of his reading glasses.

"No. Why do you ask?"

"Someone from Dr. Wright's office called yesterday to confirm your appointment this afternoon. Isn't he your gynecologist? Did they find something on your last mammo or pap smear? Something you're not telling us?"

"No. Of course not."

"Then why are you seeing a gynecologist?"

"Because Dr. Wright is also an obstetrician. I'm pregnant," Elizabeth said with a soft smile.

Astonishment, then joy flashed across the couple's faces. "A baby!" Gladys cried. "Oh, my goodness gracious! A baby!"

The older woman surged forward and enveloped Elizabeth in a hug. The combined scents of coffee, fresh-baked bread and vanilla that always seemed to cling to Gladys filled Elizabeth's nostrils, reminding her of those times as a child when she'd skinned a knee or received a slight or was hurt in any way and Gladys would comfort her. Smiling, she hugged Gladys back.

Gladys and Dooley had been yearning for grandchildren for years, but as of yet, neither of their sons had provided any.

"Oh, child, I'm so happy for you," the housekeeper said, wiping her wet cheeks and eyes with her apron as she released Elizabeth. "This is so wonderful. Oh, Dooley, did you hear? There's gonna be a baby in this house again!"

"Of course I heard her, woman. What do you think I am, deaf?" the crotchety old man snapped, but when he stood up and turned to Elizabeth, his face and tone softened.

"Yes indeed, it is wonderful," Dooley said, every line in his weather-wrinkled old face creasing deeper with his grin. He pulled her to him in a clumsy but tender embrace. Returning the hug, Elizabeth smiled and lay her cheek against his chest. Dooley, as always, smelled of the outdoors.

He released Elizabeth and shot his wife a look of exasperation. "Ever since that call yesterday, Gladys here has been driving herself and me and Miss Mimi crazy trying to figure out what could be wrong. It never occurred to us that you could be having a baby."

He reached out again and took Elizabeth's hand, holding it between his callused and scarred ones. "We're real happy for you, Miss Elizabeth. Real happy. Why, it seems like only yesterday that your mama, God rest her soul, sat right here at this very table and told Gladys and me that she was expecting you.

"We couldn't be happier about this child if you were our own daughter." Dooley paused, took off his glasses and knuckled his eyes as though they were tired, but both Elizabeth and Gladys saw the tears he'd tried to hide. He sniffed and snorted and added in a gruff voice, "Fact is, you've always seemed like our own daughter, anyway."

"Thanks, Dooley. I love you, too," was all that Elizabeth could manage, her throat was so tight with emotion.

"And speaking of babies, you'd better get a move on, girl, or you'll miss that appointment," Gladys ordered.

"Eek. I didn't notice the time." Elizabeth jumped up and grabbed her bag and started toward the door. "No, Bar Code, you can't go this time." She picked up the kitten and handed it to Gladys, then took off.

"And call Miss Mimi," the older woman added. "She said for you to call her as soon as you arrived."

"Okay. I will."

Elizabeth made the call as she drove out of the driveway. When her friend answered she put her on speaker phone so that she could drive with both hands.

"Hi, sugar. So? Did you tell them?" Mimi demanded.

"Yes, I told them. They're on top of the world, just like everyone at Mimosa Landing."

"Thank goodness. Now I can quit fibbing to them. You have no idea how difficult it's been for me to pretend that I didn't know that you had an appointment with Dr. Wright or what was wrong. Poor old things. All day yesterday Gladys was wringing her hands and imagining the worst. I gotta tell you, sugar, I almost cracked under the pressure."

Elizabeth laughed, and even to her own ears the sound was joyous, something she had not heard coming from herself in a very long time. Her euphoric laughter gentled into a warm, but no less deeply felt, happiness that filled her being. Emotions overflowed her heart, so exquisite they were almost pain. She splayed one hand over her flat tummy, awed by the miracle of it all.

A window curtain on the third story of the house across the street from Elizabeth's home twitched open an inch.

"Well, well, well," Angel murmured to himself. "Wouldya look who's here. Where you going now, pretty lady?"

Through his binoculars, he'd watched Elizabeth arrive only minutes ago, lugging a kitten in a cage into the house with her. That was a good sign that she was staying for a day or so. Women tended to take their furry little creatures with them.

Now, he observed, she practically skipped down the front steps, climbed into her car and zipped back down the long drive to the boulevard street in front of her property. There she stopped, turned on her left-turn signal and took off when it was clear to do so.

"Good girl," Angel praised. He approved of careful driving.

Lowering the binoculars, he decided it was safe to go somewhere and get a bite to eat and still get back here before his target returned.

He'd been lucky finding this place. In a hoity-toity neighborhood like this owners did not do anything so crass as put out a For Sale sign, so he'd just looked for a telltale Realtor's key box. Picking one of those was a piece of cake. So was breaking into the garage, where he'd hid his car, just in case a nosy cop came snooping around. And disarming that ancient home-alarm system was kid's play. These people were just asking to be burglarized.

He'd had a close call this morning, though, when a Realtor brought clients by to see the place. But Angel wasn't the best in the business for nothing. He knew his job. He never made a mess, never moved anything without returning it to its prior place. Nothing was amiss, no doors or windows were unlocked, the joke of an alarm system was on.

Every item that he'd brought into this house stayed with him. Most people buying a house this pricy didn't bother to look at the garage, but if they did, ninety-nine out of a hundred would think the car belonged to the home owner. It was a simple matter to tuck himself away in the attic while the Realtor showed the couple around.

It was early yet, only about a quarter till five, but Angel's stomach was still on New York time. He doubted that any Realtor would be showing the place at this hour. The utilities were off and it would be dark soon. Nevertheless, he policed the area to make certain he wasn't leaving anything to arouse suspicion.

When done, he loped down the grand stairway at the front of the house and made his way through the gathering gloom to the kitchen and out the back. He'd been careful to back the car into the garage, in case he needed to make tracks fast.

Lowering his bulk into the car's front seat, Angel sighed. He'd like to get a big Italian meal with all the trimmings, but he'd have to settle for fast food. He wanted to be back here watching when his target returned.

# Eighteen

Was it possible to be this happy? Elizabeth wondered, almost six hours later, looking at her reflection in the bathroom mirror. She leaned in closer and patted moisturizer onto her clean face and smiled at her glowing reflection.

Bar Code twined around her ankles, mewling pitifully, but Elizabeth didn't give in to the kitten's demand to be picked up. "Not now, Bar Code, I'm busy. But if you're good, just this one time, while Max is away, you can sleep in here with me."

As though she understood the promise, the kitten jumped up on the marble surrounding the soaking tub and prowled impatiently back and forth, as though saying, "Well? What are you waiting for? Let's get on with it."

Chuckling at the kitten's impudence, Elizabeth began to rummage through the plethora of little pots and potions and bottles that covered the top of her bathroom vanity when Bar Code made the strangest noise she'd ever heard come out of a cat. Looking down at the kitten, Elizabeth's eyes widened with astonishment. "What in the world?"

Back arched, teeth bared, tail straight up and big as a bush, the kitten made a noise somewhere between a hiss and a growl, its wild-eyed gaze fixed on something in the bedroom behind them. Every hair on the creature's body stood straight out, as though she'd stuck her paw into an electrical socket.

"Kitty, what—"

Then, in the mirror, she saw it—a shift in the shadows behind her, a movement so subtle she almost missed it. Elizabeth's heart began to pound. The only light she'd left on in the other room was the lamp on her side of the bed. The room was full of shadows, she tried to tell herself even as she pretended to search for something on the vanity top.

There it was again. That slow, stealthy movement. Oh, God! The closer it came, the clearer the outline of a man emerged. An extremely large man who carried a short length of heavy cord, the ends wrapped around his hands.

Oh, dear God! It was the man from New York! Panic and bile surged up inside Elizabeth. She had to get out of there. He was only a few yards from the bathroom door. Think. Think!

Still pretending she hadn't seen him, as casually as possible, she fluffed her hair. With no warning, she spun away from the mirror, slammed the door shut and pressed down the old-fashioned lever lock. The man rammed into the door a mere second after the lock clicked into place.

Then came an enraged sound and the big man's bulk hit the door again and again, but it held. All of the doors in this old house were solid wood, in this case solid mahogany, not those hollow-core, flimsy things that they put in houses these days.

In a panic, barefoot and dressed in only a long black silk nightgown, Elizabeth ran through the connecting door into the closet. The kitten streaked past her in a flash of black and white.

Elizabeth didn't dare turn on a light. He might see it under the door between the closet and her bedroom and know she was there. There were no locks on the closet doors.

The ferocious banging and cursing continued. With each thud Elizabeth jumped and tried to stifle her need to scream.

Feeling her way along the line of Max's suits, choking back the little sounds of desperation that clogged her throat, she finally located the door that led into Edward's old bedroom.

She opened the door so fast she nearly fell into the unused room. Straining to listen for the man, she hurried across the bedroom and cracked open the door into the hall. The thudding and cursing instantly seemed louder. The only lights on were the dim sconces on the wall that followed the curving stairs.

Elizabeth bit her lower lip. Did she risk running? He could come out of the bedroom at any second. Or should she try to hide?

A gunshot from inside her bedroom made the decision for her. Survival mode took control. Elizabeth exploded out of the room and flew down the stairs so fast her feet barely touched the treads.

Instead of running out the front door, she instinctively made a U-turn and raced down the central hallway. She made it to the study and reached for the door handle when another shot gouged into the door to the study, at about eye level, sending out a spray of splinters. One stung Elizabeth's right cheek, but she barely noticed the pain.

Glancing back the way she'd come, she saw the man leaning over the stair railing, aiming his gun at her. Oh, God. He was halfway down the stairs! She darted into the study and slammed the door and locked it. It was dark in the room, but she didn't bother to turn on a light.

Something brushed her leg, and she jumped and let out another shriek. Slapping her hand over her mouth, she backed up, straining to see in the dark.

Oh, God, did he have a partner? A pitiful mewling answered that question and her shoulders slumped. Until that instant she hadn't known that the kitten had followed her.

The big man's clumsy footsteps clumped down the hallway in her direction, and Elizabeth started to shake. Grabbing the wireless phone off the desk, she squeezed through the closed draperies, unlocked the terrace doors and burst out of the house into the freezing night.

She gave a brief thought to running to Dooley and Gladys's apartment over the garage. It was closer than Mimi's, but both Dooley and Gladys wore hearing aids. To wake them up when they were not wearing the devices was next to impossible. It would take a clap of thunder.

Elizabeth took the terrace steps in one leap and never broke stride, not even as she thumbed a number into the telephone.

"911. What is your emergency?"

"A man is trying to kill me," Elizabeth rasped out.

"Kill you?"

"Y-yes. He broke into my house. He's shooting…at me. Hurry." She gave her address and hung up, against the woman's orders. She had to concentrate on getting away from the man alive.

Ignoring the stepping-stones that Dooley had wound artistically around and through flower beds and a small stand of woods, Elizabeth made a beeline for the narrow archway in the hedge. Like an Olympic athlete in a track meet, she leaped over flower beds, short boxwood hedges and a trickling stream, and tore across Dooley's carefully tended lawn, the back of her silk nightgown fluttering out behind her like a black sail.

Please let her be awake, **God**, Elizabeth prayed silently. Please, please, please let her be still awake.

The frozen stubs of winter-dried St. Augustine grass prickled the soles of her feet like tiny needles. She was freezing cold, but whether the cause was the twenty-degree temperature or the killer coming after her was a toss-up.

Elizabeth shot through the narrow archway without breaking stride. The man fired again, and the bullet tore through the crepe myrtle branches just inches from Elizabeth's ear.

She screamed and ran for the French doors that opened from Mimi's den onto her back terrace. She could see her friend peeping out through the curtains to see what was causing the commotion.

Thank you, God! Elizabeth silently prayed. Thank you.

She had forgotten about the motion-sensitive lights that Mimi had installed after her husband died. One after another they began to come on as Elizabeth ran by, marking her path for the killer.

"Oh, God," Elizabeth groaned. Another bullet whizzed by and she screamed, a long, full-throated shrill of pure terror. "Mimi! Mimi, help me!"

Elizabeth's only advantage now was she could outrun the big man, and she poured on the steam until her heart felt as though it would burst. She ran so fast her feet barely touched the ground.

Shrieking every breath now, she leaped over the small hedge of azaleas that surrounded Mimi's stone terrace and negotiated its various levels. Reaching the top terrace, she crossed the cold stones and hit the door at almost full speed. She pounded with both fists. "Mimi! Mimi! Help! Help me!"

Her friend yanked the door open and her face slackened with astonishment. "Sugar, what in the world are you doing out at this hour in your nightie?" She glanced downward and her jaw dropped. "And no shoes? You'll catch your death."

"He's c-coming," Elizabeth gasped. "He broke into the house. He's try-trying to k-kill me."

"What? Who? Who's trying to kill you?"

"The man from New Y-York." She glanced over her shoulder toward the hedge in time to see her pursuer squeeze through the narrow arch. "See? See? Here he comes. Oh, God, I shouldn't have come here. Now he'll kill us both."

"The *hell* he will," Mimi declared, bristling like a mama bear with a cub. "Get in here, sugar," she ordered, and pulled Elizabeth inside.

"Mimi, we have to run. He'll break through this door. He's huge. I'm so sorry. I shouldn't have brought this down on you."

Elizabeth peeked around the edge of the door. The hulking man stalked across Mimi's lawn toward them with a determined gait. Whether that was because he had no doubt that he would catch her and kill her, or because he was too big and out of shape to run, she didn't know. But she *did* know that he was the most menacing creature she'd ever seen. "Oh, Lord, he's getting closer."

"Don't you worry, sugar. I've got me an equalizer."

If Mimi wasn't attending a formal or very dressy affair, she carried a large casual bag. Her current purse, a huge tapestry tote, sat on the hall tree by the door where she usually left it. She dug arm-deep into the bag. "Ah, there you are," she announced triumphantly, and pulled out an enormous revolver. "Now, I ask you, is that a thing of beauty or what?"

"Oh, my word," Elizabeth stared, awed.

"Yeah, I know what you mean. She's something, isn't she?" Gripping the weapon with both hands, Mimi pointed it at the ceiling. "This is a long-barrel .357 Magnum. It's the biggest, baddest gun around. If you don't believe me, just asked Dirty Harry.

"Now, step aside, sugar, and let me deal with this."

Elizabeth didn't know what else to do but obey.

Standing just inside the open doorway, Mimi braced the side of the gun barrel against the edge of the door frame. "Hey, fatso!"

The man was so startled that she was addressing him, he stopped.

"Yeah, I'm talking to you, you no-neck goon. Git! You hear me? Git off my property. Now!" Taking aim, she cocked the hammer and squeezed the trigger.

*Ka-boom!*

The revolver's recoil jerked Mimi's hands straight up and knocked her back a couple of steps.

The bullet hit a pine tree, and a small branch fell off onto the man's head. Letting out a startled yelp, he fought with the prickly branches and needles as though he thought he'd been jumped by a mountain lion.

"Oh, dear. You missed," Elizabeth cried.

"Miss, my fanny. Sugar, I hit what I aim at. I'm not trying to kill that big ugly slug. At least not yet. I was trying to scare him away. Don't you worry. Big Daddy taught me how to shoot. I can hit a freckle on a gnat's behind at a hundred yards with this baby," she drawled with pride.

Fortunately for Elizabeth and Mimi, the same couldn't be said for the man coming toward them. No-neck recovered from his shock and fired two more shots. One bullet dug into the door frame over Mimi's head and the other one shattered one of the two cobalt-blue enameled urns that flanked the door.

Lights came on in Gladys and Dooley's apartment above the garage. The houses in this neighborhood were all mansions, so far apart it was difficult to see or hear anything, but a few more lights began to blink on.

"Oh! *Ooooh*. Would you look at that!" Furious, Mimi stomped out onto the terrace and surveyed the damage. She whirled around and held her weapon at arm's length with both hands. "You shot my urn, you low-life creep! Big Daddy and I personally lugged those things through three airports and put up with a snooty French customs agent to get them here."

The man responded with another shot.

"Oh! Now you've gone and done it!" Incensed beyond reason, Mimi stomped to the edge of the terrace. "You got some nerve! Comin' onto *my* property, shootin' up *my* prized urn with some pansy-assed little ole peashooter of a gun."

Elizabeth darted out onto the terrace and grabbed Mimi's arm and began dragging her back. "Mimi, for heaven's sake. You're going to get yourself killed."

"Huh! Not by that goon. He couldn't hit the backside of an elephant with a shotgun at three paces."

"Mimi. Please, come inside."

She shook off Elizabeth's hold and stomped back to the edge of the terrace.

The man fired two more shots that whizzed right past her.

"All right, fatso, I gave you a chance to leave with that lard-ass of yours intact. But if you want a gunfight, you low-life piece of garbage, you've got one. Let me show you how a real gun works." She took aim, cocked the hammer back and squeezed off another shot.

*Ka-boom!*

The man yelped, grabbed his leg and started backpedaling. A siren wailed in the distance, drawing closer fast.

"Yeah, run, you good for nothin'!" Mimi yelled as the gunman hobbled back through the arch in the hedge.

"Hey! What's all the racket down there?" Dooley demanded from the top of the stairs that led to his and Gladys's apartment. "Hey! You there! What're you up to?"

"Get him, Dooley!" Mimi yelled.

Another pistol shot sounded.

*Boom!* The distinct sound of Dooley's shotgun reverberated through the night, and still more lights came on in the neighborhood.

The big man let out a shriek of pain.

Mimi whooped and pumped one fist in the air. "Way to go, Dooley! Give him the other barrel."

Keeping her gaze on the opening in the hedge, Mimi said, "Did you hear that, sugar? I think Dooley gave him a rumpful of bird shot. From fatso's pig squeal, some of the pellets probably broke his skin. It'll sting for days, but at that range it's not a lethal load. Of course, that's assuming that hulk is human. To me he looked more like a slug in a suit." Mimi laughed again and did a little victory dance in her stiletto heels. "I bet Dooley made a sieve outta his fancy leather overcoat."

Belatedly, it occurred to Mimi that Elizabeth had not said a word. "Sugar? Sugar, where— Oh, God, no! *Nooooo!*"

Elizabeth lay on her back, eyes closed, blood running from a gash in her left temple forming a puddle on the terrace stones. More blood blossomed from a hole in her right shoulder and spread over her bare skin and the black lace nightgown.

"What is it, Miss Mimi?" Gladys called, hurrying across the lawn toward her. "What's wrong? Who was that man? And what was all the shooting about?"

"Oh God, oh God, oh God," Mimi murmured over and over on her knees by Elizabeth's side. "It's okay, sugar. You're going to be okay. I promise. Just stay with me. You hear? You stay with me." She threw back her head and screamed, "Dooley! Gladys! Help! Help! Elizabeth's been shot."

"I'm here, Miss Mimi," Gladys said, huffing and puffing

from running. She dropped down on her knees by Elizabeth's other side. "Oh, my baby! My poor, poor baby."

Vaguely, Mimi heard tires squealing as a vehicle roared away. The shooter was getting away, but the only thing she cared about at that moment was her friend.

Dooley appeared through the darkness with his old blunderbuss double-barrel shotgun broken open and hooked over the crook of his arm.

"Merciful heavens," he murmured. "Is she alive? Does she have a pulse?"

Quickly, Mimi felt her friend's neck with her fingertips. "It's there, but it's getting weak. We have to stop this bleeding."

Gladys looked up at her husband and ordered, "Get me a couple of clean towels and one of those warm fleece throws off the couch."

"There are some in the dryer," Mimi called to his back.

Dooley returned in seconds with the items.

"I'm going out front to direct the cops and paramedics," he announced, and disappeared into the darkness.

Mimi spread the warm throw over Elizabeth, while Gladys folded one of the towels. She handed it to Mimi. "Here, press that tight against that head wound."

She folded the other towel and pressed it to the shoulder wound.

"Oh, Lord, Gladys," Mimi said in a quivering voice. "There's so much blood."

"I know. I know. Head wounds always bleed a lot," the older woman replied. Though her voice was more brusque than usual, Mimi could hear the fear there. "Just you hold on, Miss Elizabeth. Miss Mimi and me, we're with you, child. We're right here. And help is on the way. Hear 'em? You're going to be okay. Everything's going to be fine. Just hold on."

As if on cue, an ambulance came up Mimi's driveway and

three paramedics jumped out and ran over loaded down with
emergency equipment. A swarm of policemen and Dooley
were right behind.

The paramedics went to work on Elizabeth and a uniformed officer started asking questions.

"I'll tell you anything you want to know, but you'll have
to come along to the hospital with us," Mimi declared. "I'm
going with Elizabeth."

"But ma'am, I need to—"

"Save your breath, son," Dooley told him. "You heard
what she said. That goes for me and my wife, also."

"I'm going to get my coat and purse. Dooley, you and Gladys run and get whatever you need." She reached down and
swooped up the frightened kitten that was mewling around
her ankles and handed it to the housekeeper. "And do something with Bar Code."

Without waiting for an answer, Mimi darted into the house.
She emerged in less than a minute wearing her full-length
sable coat, which had been the first one she'd come to, and
clutching her purse, just as the paramedics were sliding the
gurney, with Elizabeth on it, into the ambulance.

Mimi stopped short and clamped her hand over her mouth
to keep from crying. Elizabeth had a bandage on her temple,
another on her shoulder, an oxygen tube up her nose and an
IV in her arm. She had no more color than the coarse white
hospital sheet on which she lay, still as death.

"C'mon, Miss Mimi," Dooley said, putting his hand on her
shoulder. "Don't fall apart on us now. Miss Elizabeth is going
to need your strength."

"He's right, miss," Gladys said. "C'mon along with us. I
put the kitten back inside and locked up all three places, so
we're all set. Let's go."

The elderly couple urged her to come with them, but Mimi

held back. She looked pleadingly at the paramedic. "Is…is she going to make it?"

The man gave her a look that turned her blood cold and said, "I can't say, ma'am. We've stabilized her. It's going to be up to the doctors to save her."

Urged by Dooley and Gladys, she stepped back and the young man hopped up into the back of the ambulance with another paramedic.

Moments later a caravan of police cars, the ambulance and Mimi's zippy little red sports car pulled out of the driveway. Police vehicles with flashing red lights on the top were parked up and down the street. Other police personnel were stringing yellow crime-scene tape across every entrance and exit to both Elizabeth's and Mimi's homes. Up and down the posh neighborhood, people in nightclothes had gathered and were standing around watching the spectacle.

Dooley, being the steadiest of the three of them, drove Mimi's car. Seated in the passenger seat, Mimi dug deep into her leather tote bag, cursing under her breath when she couldn't find what she was looking for.

"Great balls of fire, girl, what are you after in that bottomless pit?" Dooley asked.

"My cell phone. Why is it you can never find the damned thing when you need it."

"It's right there. In that outside pocket," Gladys said from the cramped back seat. "And can't we go any faster?"

"The police car up front has his siren on and so does the ambulance. You women calm down. Getting all bent out of shape isn't going to help Miss Elizabeth."

Mimi punched a speed-dial number on her phone and listened impatiently, counting the rings on the other end of the line.

"Yeah?" a sleepy voice answered on the other end.

"Max, it's Mimi."

# *Nineteen*

"**H**ow is she?" Max demanded the instant he stormed into the ICU waiting room.

In a glance, he took note that everyone was there, including Elizabeth's cousins and the household staff from both homes. All of them, even Camille, had red-rimmed eyes. Most terrifying of all, Gladys's and Mimi's clothes were smeared with blood. Elizabeth's blood.

Max's fear level skyrocketed. Dear God. She wasn't...? She couldn't be...? No. *No!*

"Dammit, can't any of you hear?" he shouted. "I want to know where and how my wife is. Someone had better start talking. Now."

Iona went to her son's side and tugged on his sleeve. "She's still alive, son. But..."

"But what?" he demanded.

"She's... She hasn't regained consciousness since she was shot."

"Oh, God." Max ran a trembling hand through his already tousled hair. "I need to see her."

"I know, son. I know. I'll show you where she is, but

first…" His mother tipped her head toward Talitha, her expression speaking volumes. "She's taking this hard," Iona whispered. "You know how she loves that girl."

"Right." Max wanted to see Elizabeth. Touch her. Luxuriate in the sweet, feminine scent of her. Feel her breath against his skin. Inhaling deeply, he reminded himself that she was important to other people, as well.

Talitha was so stricken she didn't seem to know he was there until he hunkered down in front of her chair.

"Max! Oh, thank the Lord, you're here," she said. Her bony old hands latched on to both of his as though he were a miracle worker.

He raised one age-spotted hand and kissed it. "How are you holding up?"

Elizabeth's aunt met his steady gaze, her faded old eyes filling with fresh tears. Talitha always looked as well groomed and regal as a queen, but at that moment she looked defeated, her red-rimmed eyes weary beyond measure. In the space of a few hours she seemed to have aged years; fear and the pain of uncertainty had deepened the wrinkles in her face and smudged dark circles beneath her lower eyelids.

That Talitha had been woken from a sound sleep was evident by the haphazard way her silver braids had been wound around into a coronet on top of her head. Wispy, curling tendrils had escaped her attention and floated around her face.

She clutched his hands. "Oh, Max. He shot her. Some strange man shot her in—" she broke off, her chin quivering "—in the head."

"What?" Max felt as though he'd been hit in the solar plexus by a battering ram. He'd been told that his wife had been shot, but not where or how seriously.

Talitha was so dazed by her own grief that she didn't notice Max's shock.

"Why, Max? *Why?* Who could have done this to our Elizabeth? I don't know what I'll do if—"

"No. Don't say it. That won't happen. It can't." Max straightened and looked around at the others. "Has the hospital given you a report of any kind?"

Talitha dabbed at her eyes, too overcome once more to speak.

Dooley looked around at the others, but no one seemed inclined to answer Max's question. Dooley cleared his throat. "Well, sir, the doc came out a while back. He said that they were...uh..." Scratching the back of his head, Dooley looked at his wife. "How'd he put that?"

"He said that they were cautiously optimistic," Gladys finished for her husband.

"What about the baby?"

"The same. Cautiously optimistic."

"That's not good enough. Where is she? I want to see her."

"She's right across the hall in the first cubicle, the one with all the blinds drawn. But wait, son," Iona begged, holding on to his arm. "Listen to me. This is ICU. Visitation is limited to one person at a time, for ten minutes, every four hours."

"To hell with that."

Max marched across the hall and into the ICU cubicle. The others hurried after him and crowded together around the open door.

The startled nurse standing beside Elizabeth's bed looked up and said, "I'm sorry, sir. You'll have to leave."

Max ignored her and went to Elizabeth's side.

"Sir? Did you hear me?" The nurse started around the bed, making a shooing motion with her hands, and in her most commanding manner said, "I'm sorry, sir, but you'll have to leave. Visitation isn't for another two hours yet. And then only one person at a time is allow—"

"Fine. You leave. Because I'm sure as hell not." Max grasped the woman's upper arm and hustled her out of the room. At the door, the others parted and made way for her.

The woman huffed and straightened her uniform when he released her. "Well. We'll just see about this."

Mimi saw her chance and slipped inside and opened the blinds on the glassed-in room so that the others could see.

Max had already dismissed the nurse from his mind and returned to Elizabeth's side.

"Elizabeth?" He bent over her and took her hand in his, being ultra careful not to hurt her. Shock rippled through him at how pale she was. She had a huge bandage on her right shoulder, and her head was swathed in gauze from her ear upward. How much of her beautiful hair they had shaved away he couldn't tell.

As usual, Max reacted to the fear that was eating him alive with gruffness.

"Elizabeth? Elizabeth, wake up. Do you hear me? It's Max. Wake up. Right now, dammit!" he roared.

In the doorway, the others exchanged uneasy glances.

"Excuse me, please. Excuse me. All you people are going to have to get out of here." A doctor, followed by the nurse who had tried to keep Max out of the room, squeezed through the cluster of people and into the cubicle.

Again, the family eyed one another, but no one moved.

"Sir, I'm Dr. Alexander. I'm afraid I must ask you to leave."

"Ask all you want. I'm not going anywhere."

"Sir, I must insist."

"No," Max replied without taking his eyes from Elizabeth. "This is my wife. I'm not leaving her."

"Ah, Mr. Riordan, is it? Sir, I know that you're worried about your wife, but I must ask you to leave," the doctor explained. "Visiting is restricted to specified times and—"

Max turned his head slightly and slanted the doctor a look

that stopped him in midsentence. "I don't give a tinker's damn about your rules. I'm not leaving this room until I know that my wife is going to be okay."

"Shall I call Security, Doctor?" the nurse asked.

Max narrowed his eyes at the woman. "Trust me, lady, you don't *have* enough security to kick me out of this room, but go ahead and call them if you want to start a melee." He turned his attention back to Elizabeth.

Standing in the doorway with the others, Aunt Talitha stiffened her back and thumped her cane on the tiled floor. The muffled sound failed to gain the attention of the nurse and doctor. Aggravated, she reached out with her cane and prodded the nurse in the back of one knee.

The nurse yelped when her leg buckled. "Oh! What...? Oh! How dare—"

"Oh, hush up. You're not hurt," Talitha snapped.

"Doctor," she said in her most patrician voice.

The sound of Talitha's voice caught Max's attention, and he glanced her way. She stood tall, her back almost ramrod straight, her chin up.

Max grinned.

"Are you familiar with the Stanton Wing of this hospital?"

"Yes, ma'am."

"And you, young woman?" she demanded of the outraged nurse.

"Yes. I am familiar with the Stanton Wing."

Talitha smiled her "Aha! Gotcha now!" smile.

"Good. And did you know that the Stanton family donated all the money to build the Stanton Wing? Or that your patient is the current head of the Stanton family?

"I thought not," Talitha continued when the nurse turned a sickly green. "Now, if her husband wants to stay by her side, he will. Do you understand?"

"Yes, ma'am."

"And you, Doctor?"

The doctor considered Talitha's stern expression and Max's dangerous one for only a moment. "It's all right, Nurse. Mr. Riordan can stay."

Max paid no attention to the doctor or the nurse or anyone else. No matter what they decided he was staying.

"Wake up, sweetheart," he said to Elizabeth. "Do you hear me? I said, wake up. Dammit, Elizabeth, don't you dare die on me!" he bellowed. "Don't you *dare* leave me alone. I couldn't bear to live without you." He waited a beat but got no response. "Dammit to hell, Elizabeth! I love you," he shouted. "Do you hear me? I love you."

Troy, who had been assigned by Max to deal with the police and the media, had joined the group only seconds before. He stood at the rear of the crowd in the open doorway, gaping. "Well, I'll be damned," he murmured to himself. "He's in love with her."

Iona shot him an exasperated look over her shoulder. "Of course he's in love with her. He married her, didn't he?"

"Listen to me, Elizabeth. You have to listen to me, dammit! I love you."

A tiny crease appeared between Elizabeth's eyebrows, and ever so slightly her head moved from side to side. "Don't…shout," she said in a barely audible whisper. "I… h-heard you."

"Did you hear that? Did you hear that?" Max exclaimed, looking around at the doctor.

"Well, now, let me have a look," the doctor said, stepping around to the other side of the bed. "Mrs. Riordan, can you hear me?"

"Y-yes," she whispered.

"Good. That's wonderful. I'm Dr. Alexander, by the way.

You are at Methodist Hospital in Houston. You've been shot."

"Sh-shot?"

"Uh-huh. You may not remember right away, but it'll all come back to you later. Probably when the pain eases." Pulling a penlight from the pocket of his lab coat, the doctor pried one, then the other eyelid open and shined the light briefly into each of her eyes. "How do you feel? Do you hurt anywhere?"

"H-head. And…sh-shoulder."

"Your head hurts, does it? Well, I can't say I'm surprised. And even though you probably don't think so right now, you're very lucky that your head hurts and that you're here to feel it. Now, just relax while I examine you a bit more and have a talk with your husband. Okay?"

Elizabeth started to nod, then thought better of it and made an umm-hmm sound.

After a bit of gentle poking and prodding and listening through his stethoscope, Dr. Alexander looked at Max and gestured for the two of them to move away from the bed.

Max complied and the group of people at the door crowded around them. "It's all right. They're all family," he said, answering the doctor's questioning look. Dr. Alexander shrugged and spoke in a low tone.

"I wasn't just trying to make your wife feel better, Mr. Riordan. It could have been a lot worse. The bullet struck her head here," he said, demonstrating on Max. "Just above and behind her left ear. My guess is, she probably turned at the instant of impact. Or, if the first bullet was the one that struck her right shoulder, it spun her around to the right just in time. Either way, she was extremely lucky.

"We believe that both bullets were fired from a considerable distance, which also worked in her favor. The bullet to the head struck at such an angle that it penetrated the flesh, but due to the distance it lacked the force to pierce the bone beneath. Instead it scraped along between the outside of the skull and the flesh for about an inch and a half before exiting out the back. Which accounts for that bodacious headache.

"As for the shoulder wound, she was lucky there, also. The bullet didn't hit any major arteries or organs. She may have to undergo some physical therapy to get full range of movement back in that arm and shoulder, but that's no big thing."

"I…was…really shot?" Elizabeth asked, drawing everyone back to her bedside. She tried to open her eyes, but it was too much of an effort and the light made her head hurt.

"Yes. Can you recall anything that happened last night?"

"I…oh." Her breathing grew rapid. "Y-yes. That m-man from New…York. He…he… Oh, God. H-have to get out… hurry…he's coming…" Becoming agitated, she made desperate little noises and tried to sit up. Several monitors above her bed began to beep.

"Whoa, now, take it easy," the doctor and Max said in unison. The doctor put his hand on Elizabeth's arm. "Calm down, Elizabeth. You're safe now. No one is going to get in here. Just relax."

"Max. I w-want Max."

"I'm here, Elizabeth. I'm here. You're safe with me."

"Wh-where…?"

"Here." He took her hand and held it between both of his. "I'm right here with you. I won't leave."

"Pr-promise?"

"Absolutely."

She sighed and slumped back against the pillow, only to tense again. "My baby? Oh, God, Max, the *baby*—"

"Your baby is just fine, Mrs. Riordan," the doctor answered for Max. "He or she has weathered this a lot easier than you. And I don't want you worrying about what happened. You're safe here. When you're feeling better and are more able to cope it'll all come back. For now, I'm going to give you something for the pain."

He turned away and murmured instructions to the nurse, and the woman hurried from the room.

"Is she going to be all right?" Max demanded.

"For the next forty-eight hours we're going to keep her under close observation. However, if she continues to improve, tomorrow we'll move her to a VIP suite for the remainder of her stay." The doctor glanced at Talitha and winked. "One in the Stanton Wing. Barring any adverse developments, I'm confident that she'll be well enough to go home for Christmas."

"Oh, praise be," Talitha murmured.

"And what about the baby?" Mimi asked.

"I wasn't whitewashing things for your peace of mind, Mrs. Whittington. The fetus is doing great. We can thank the quick arrival of the paramedics for that. They got Elizabeth's bleeding stopped, and her IV and oxygen going in just minutes. As I understand it, they were already on the way when your wife was shot."

"That's right," Mimi said, her chest swelling with pride. "She may look as though she's made of Dresden china, but our girl has a backbone of steel. One of the policemen who responded told me that the call had come in from Elizabeth herself. While she was tearing barefoot across the frozen grass in her nightie she still had the presence of mind to call 911 and give her name and address and report that a man had broken in and was shooting at her."

"Yeah." Dooley nodded his head. "One of 'em said he heard the gunfire before they even got to the house. Said it sounded like they were entering a war zone."

Max frowned. "How many people were shooting?"

"Well, sir." Dooley mulled that over, scratching the back of his head again. "There was that big guy who was chasing Miss Elizabeth. Miss Mimi, she nicked him with that .357 Magnum of hers. Plus she got off another couple of shots to scare him. And I got him in the rump with a barrel of bird shot from my old blunderbuss shotgun."

"Good grief." Max looked from Mimi to Dooley, then back. "Tomorrow I'm going to want a minute-by-minute account of everything that happened. And I mean everything. Not the abridged or sanitized version you gave the police."

Mimi gave him a "butter wouldn't melt in her mouth" smile. "Who me? Now, would I withhold information from our boys in blue?"

"In a heartbeat, if you thought it would help Elizabeth."

Mimi looked him in the eye. "Damn straight. But as it so happens, I told them the honest to God truth. And by the way, stud, expect a Detective Braddock to contact you soon. He's the one in charge of this case."

"Ah-hem," Dr. Alexander interrupted. "As I was saying, as long as our mother-to-be continues to regain strength and health, I see no reason why both of them shouldn't come through this just fine."

"Thank the Lord," Aunt Talitha murmured, one bony old hand over her heart.

The nurse returned with a syringe, but when she started to inject its contents into Elizabeth's IV, her patient became fearful and tried to draw away.

"It's okay, Elizabeth," the doctor said in a soothing tone. "We're just giving you some medication that should ease that headache," the doctor informed her. "You rest and let your body heal itself. The nurses will be in to check your vital signs every twenty minutes or so."

To Max he said, "She'll probably sleep once that pain medication kicks in. If you'd like, you can go home and get some rest. You look a bit frayed around the edges yourself."

"I'm staying," Max stated, his look daring the doctor to object.

Dr. Alexander merely smiled and shrugged. "Suit yourself. But the rest of you people are going to have to leave," he ordered, shooing out the family and friends.

As the crowd reluctantly shuffled out the door, Elizabeth's hand fluttered in Max's.

"M-Max?"

He bent over her, gently stroking what was left of her hair back from her face. "Yeah, baby. I'm here. What is it?"

"I...I...love you...too," she whispered, and drifted off to sleep.

Max gazed at her, his chest so tight he could barely breathe.

The first thing Elizabeth saw when she opened her eyes the next morning was Max. He sat beside the bed in a chair, bent forward, his head resting on his folded arms on the mattress beside her hips. He was sound asleep.

His face was turned toward her. Elizabeth took the opportunity to study him. His long lashes lay like fans on his craggy cheekbones. A hint of a smile curved her mouth. They were probably the only things about him that were remotely feminine.

The lower half of his face was dark with whisker stubble and his black hair was tousled. Fatigue and worry made the scar that cut diagonally across his face more prominent. At some time he had shed his suit coat and tie. His sleeves were rolled up, the top two buttons of his shirt open. He looked rumpled and strained, worry lines cutting deep into his tough face.

Elizabeth tried to move her right hand, but it hurt her shoulder too much. She stared at the top of her husband's head, his mussed black hair, the events of the previous evening coming back as her head cleared.

She glanced around at the glass walls and the door, both covered with blinds that were currently closed. She remembered the doctor telling her that she was safe. But was she? A shadow on the other side of the door moved and she caught her breath. Immediately a monitor above her head started beeping.

Max's head shot up off the mattress. "What? What is it?"

Two nurses came into the room at a run. "What's wrong, Mrs. Riordan? Are you hurting?"

"No. No, I just thought I saw…"

"What?" Max demanded.

"I thought I saw someone at the door, is all. I guess I imagined it."

"No, you didn't," Max said. He rubbed a weary hand over his eyes. "You probably saw the guards I hired. They're off-duty policemen." He went to the door and opened it. "Officers, would you step in here a moment? Honey, this is Officer Murphy and Officer Palowski."

Elizabeth traded polite greetings with the young uniformed policemen and thanked them for protecting her.

"They're doing the three-until-eleven shift," Max explained. "At eleven, two more officers will take their place and be here until seven, and two more will work from seven until three."

"So I'll have around-the-clock guards. For how long?"

"As long as you need them. Take a good long look at them, Elizabeth," her husband ordered. "I want you to know all of your guards on sight, so no one can sneak in here posing as a police officer."

Elizabeth's eyes widened. "Do you think he'll come here?"

"No. I don't think he'll be that brazen. Or that dumb. It's just a precaution."

"I see."

Shifting from one foot to the other, the two young policemen exchanged an uneasy glance. "Uh, Mr. Riordan, may we speak to you outside?" Officer Murphy asked.

"What is it?" Elizabeth demanded. "What's going on? Has something happened?"

"No, ma'am," Officer Palowski assured her with a sincere but guilty smile. "Just a little scheduling problem we need to go over with your husband."

Elizabeth started to say they could do that in front of her, but the three men stepped outside before she could.

Once the door closed behind them, Officer Murphy looked around and lowered his voice. "This may be nothing, Mr. Riordan, but I thought you should know."

"Yeah. Go on," Max said, impatient to get back to Elizabeth.

"Well, sir. About seven this morning, a man carrying a huge bouquet of flowers came to see your wife."

That caught Max's attention. A crease formed between his thick eyebrows. "A man? What man? Did he give his name?"

"He said he was Mrs. Riordan's uncle Melvin."

"My wife doesn't have an uncle. Melvin or otherwise."

"Damn. I knew there was something not right about that guy," Officer Murphy declared. "For starters, he looked like a mob guy. And he talked with a strange accent."

"What do you mean, strange accent? Was it Italian? French? Russian?"

"No, sir. Nothing like that. It was more like a Yankee trying to sound like a Texan."

That would have been funny, if Max hadn't been so worried. "What did he look like?"

"Big guy, around six-three, six-four. Must've weighed in at around two-seventy or eighty. Dark hair. Dark eyes. Cold as all hell, but dark. Wouldn't meet your gaze. Oh! And I thought he walked kinda funny. Greg here disagrees," Office Murphy said, nodding at the other officer.

"Funny? Define *funny.*"

"Well…it wasn't a limp, exactly, but I thought he was favoring one leg, and trying hard not to let it show."

"Yeah, maybe," Palowski agreed. "I wasn't watching the way he walked. I had my eye on that leather trench coat he wore. Real expensive-looking. At least from the front. From the back the coat looked like a sieve. It had at least a dozen or more tiny holes in it."

"Ah, damn!" Max grated through clenched teeth. "That was our shooter. The one who's tried three times to kill Elizabeth."

Max thought for a moment. "You two stay here. Don't let anyone inside. And I mean *anyone.* Not doctors, not nurses, not orderlies, not your best friend, not other police. Not anyone. I'm going to make arrangements to have Elizabeth moved. Now."

"Gee, we're sorry Mr. Riordan, we—"

"Don't beat yourselves up, guys. At least you kept him from making a fourth try." Max shook his head. "Damn, this guy's got nerve, coming here so soon after shooting my wife. Plus he's got to be hurting himself. Mrs. Whittington is sure that she shot him in the leg."

"Are you crazy? You can't make another attempt so soon."

"The hell I can't," Angel snarled into the cell phone that he held between his jawbone and shoulder. "And you're going to help me."

"Me! I can't be involved in this. Why do you think I hired you the first place? I can't be connected to this in any way."

"Too bad," Angel grunted. Sitting naked on the edge of the hotel bed, he squeezed antibiotic salve onto the gouge in his upper-right thigh. Damn nosy, interfering, sassy little blonde. If it wasn't for her he'd be home in New York by now, a hefty stack of thousand dollar bills in his pocket.

Damned broad. Came stomping out there in her ridiculous high-heels, banging away with that big, bad-ass six-shooter. The recoil alone should have knocked her on her butt. Who the hell did she think she was, Annie Oakley? Texans. Huh. Bunch of damned maniacs.

"I'll tell you what. I'll talk to your boss," his client said. "He'll understand why we need to delay. He's a reasonable man. Look how understanding he's been with me."

Angel stopped doctoring his wound, his eyes narrowing to dangerous slits, even though he was alone in the plush hotel room.

If Tony Voltura got wind of this foul-up, that his number-one enforcer couldn't take out one small woman, not even in three tries—four, if you counted his early-morning trip to the hospital this morning—he might start thinking Angel was getting too old for the job. If that happened, Angel knew that he might as well make out his will and have his best suit cleaned, because he was a goner. He knew where too many bodies were buried.

"Listen, and I mean listen good," Angel growled into the cell phone mouthpiece. "If you talk to Tony Voltura about this, if you visit him, send him an e-mail, if you so much as *think* of getting in touch with him—hell, if you send up a smoke signal—you'll be the one to die. You got that?"

"I...I..."

"*Yes* is the only sound I want to hear out of you."

"Y-yes."

Angel waited a few seconds. He could almost smell the fear coming through the cell phone. "Okay, then. And stop worrying. I've got it all worked out. Here's what we're going to do…"

It had taken Max less than five minutes to get approval for Elizabeth's immediate move to the Stanton Wing and any record of her stay in the hospital expunged from the regular records. Amazing how much a little money could grease the wheels of bureaucratic paperwork, Max thought, striding back to the cubicle.

"Well? What took so long? What was so important that the guards couldn't discuss it in front of me?" Elizabeth demanded the instant Max returned.

"We're moving you to a suite in the Stanton Wing. Remember? Dr. Alexander told us that last night."

"Why? I don't need a suite. I'm getting good care here."

"Yeah, but I'm not. There's not enough room in here for another bed."

"Oh, Max, I'm so sorry. How selfish of me not to think of that."

"No problem." Max suppressed a grin. It wasn't fair to use Elizabeth's thoughtful nature against her, but in this case it was for her own good. The fewer things she had to worry about the better.

"The fifth floor of the Stanton Wing is a locked wing and the door is four inches of solid steel. No one can get in without the consent of the patient or the patient's next of kin or guardian," Max said, scanning the ICU cubicle for anything of a personal nature belonging to Elizabeth and coming up empty. "What did they do with your belongings when they brought you here?"

"You mean my black silk nightgown that got shredded by rose thorns and my black bikini panties? That's all I had on when I went running and screaming from the house at almost midnight. As I recall, I didn't even have on any house slippers."

Max stopped his search and looked at her for a long time before he shuddered from head to toe. "I don't like to even think about that."

"Sit down, Max. Please," she begged, her eyelids at half mast. "You're giving me a headache, just watching you."

"Oh, right. They'll be here any minute to move you, anyway." He moved to the bedside and took her hand again. "By the way, do you by any chance have an uncle Marvin that you haven't told me about?"

"No. Why?"

"Not even on your mother's side?"

"No. Please, Max, tell me."

Max fixed her with a long hard look. "All right. I promised that I would be honest with you, so here goes. A large, dark-haired guy wearing a black leather coat came to see you about two hours ago. He was angry when he couldn't get past the door."

Elizabeth felt the blood drain from her face. "Oh, my Lord. He's not going to give up, is he? Not until he kills me."

"Or until we catch him." Max hitched up one leg and sat down on the side of the bed, hip to hip with her. "I'm not going to let him get to you again, Elizabeth. So don't worry."

She gave a mirthless little chuckle. "Easy for you to say. Sorry. I can't just shut my mind off. Okay, so maybe he won't get to me here. But what about when I go home? Or a week from now? A month? Six months? This man has proved that he's tenacious."

"First of all, I'm not leaving your side until this is over—

not for business deals, not for anything. Also, in addition to me, you'll have a personal bodyguard with you twenty-four-seven until we've got this guy, and the name of the person who hired him."

Max rubbed his fingers back and forth over the back of her hand and marveled at the difference between them. His hands were large, the skin dark and marred with scars from various nicks and cuts. Some were reminders of his days in the oil fields, but far too many were the result of youthful indiscretions. God knew he'd chugged his share of beer and rotgut whiskey and gotten into his share of brawls.

Elizabeth's hands were smooth and flawless, just like the rest of her. And they were so small, each movement as graceful as the flutter of a dove's wings.

He rubbed his thumb across the back of her hand, over and over. "Do you remember last night?" he asked, still gazing at his big, stroking fingers.

Elizabeth looked down as well. "Yes. I remember," she whispered.

"Do you remember what I said?"

"Yes," she replied in an even softer voice.

"I meant it. I'm in love with you." He tipped his head up to one side and tried to read her expression, to get her to look at him, but she demurred.

"I…I'm glad," she whispered.

"Good. Do you remember what you said?"

"Yes."

"Did you mean it?"

Elizabeth raised her head at that and looked him straight in the eye. "Yes. I meant it. Are you sure?"

"I've never been more sure or meant anything more in my life," he vowed, holding her gaze. "I will love you until the day that I take my last breath, and beyond, to the end of time."

"Oh, Max." Elizabeth gazed at him, overcome. Happy tears began to fill her eyes, and her bottom lip trembled. Her heart was so full she felt it would surely burst. She pulled her hand free of his grasp and touched the short hairs at his temple, ran her fingertips along his jaw, touched the corner of his mouth—that sharply carved, deliciously masculine mouth. "And I love you. With all my heart and soul. I always will."

Something flared in the beautiful blue depths of Max's eyes. He leaned forward and touched his lips to hers. It was a gentle kiss, an almost reverent kiss. Quivering lips touched quivering lips, breaths mingled, tongues touched ever so briefly, while hearts soared and bodies shuddered sweetly with desire held in check.

With excruciating slowness, their lips pulled away, almost to the point of parting, then pressed together again, and again and again.

When at last they reluctantly parted, Elizabeth cupped Max's face with her one free hand. "When did you know that you loved me?"

"I'm not sure. I think it came on me gradually. It started the first time we stayed at Mimosa Landing, a few days after the wedding, when you took me on a tour of the farm. The look in your eyes, the passionate love you have for that place, I found extremely appealing. It's your heritage, the place where generation after generation of Stantons have put their roots down deep in that soil.

"There were other things, too. I mean, I don't know any woman who would actually *want* her mother-in-law to live with her and her husband. Nor have I ever known one who would jump out into the pouring rain and ruin a several-thousand-dollar dress to rescue a scrawny, muddy stray kitten."

Elizabeth shrugged. "A dress is just a dress. An inanimate thing that can be replaced or repaired. A kitten is a living, breathing creature. Thank heavens I did rescue her. Bar Code saved my life last night."

"What do you mean?"

Elizabeth told him about the kitten's part in the frightful events of the night before.

"Thank God for Bar Code. From now on, that kitty is going to live the life of a queen," Max vowed.

"I thought you'd—"

A knock on the door made her jump and brought a look of unmitigated terror to her face.

"Take it easy, babe. I'm right here with you." Max went to the door and opened it a crack.

It was the hospital orderlies and a nurse, come to move Elizabeth.

The VIP suite actually consisted of one large room that could be turned into two—a bedroom and a sitting room—if the patient so desired. With her aunt and mother-in-law in mind, Elizabeth chose to leave the sliding dividing wall open, so that the two old ladies could visit in the comfort of soft recliners.

The room had the very latest in hospital equipment, but most was camouflaged to look as though it belonged in a home bedroom. What could not be camouflaged was hidden by silk-screen room dividers.

Long brocade draperies and ivory silk sheers covered the windows, and the style of the cherry-wood and walnut furnishings was Queen Anne, with a smattering of Chippendale. The colors of soft teal, pale peach and cream were soothing and the furnishings were elegant and comfortable.

"As I recall, Aunt Talitha had a hand in decorating all of the suites," Elizabeth said as the nurse and Max got her settled in the four-poster bed.

"Yeah. It looks like her," Max said, looking around.

The nurse had barely left the suite when someone knocked on the door. Max opened the door a crack. "What?"

"Sorry to disturb you, Mr. Riordan," Officer Palowski said. "But Detective Braddock is here to see you."

"Did you see his badge? You're sure he's police?"

"Yes, sir. I know him by sight."

Max told Elizabeth that he had to go to the lockout door at the wing's entrance and let in a detective. "He says he wants to talk to both of us, but if you're too tired I can talk to him on my own."

"No. I'd like to get this over with."

"That's my girl."

Max returned in less than a minute with the detective. He looked the man over as he greeted Elizabeth.

Detective Braddock was of medium height and build. He had salt-and-pepper medium brown hair and an ordinary face, not handsome, not ugly, either. Mr. Average Joe. Max guessed him to be about forty-three or four.

He looked exactly like what he was: a tough, smart cop with dogged determination. He also looked like the kind of cop—and man—that you could trust.

When the pleasantries were done, the detective wasted no time getting down to business.

"If you're feeling well enough, and you don't mind, I'd like to take your statements now."

"I don't mind at all. I was just about to tell my husband everything that I remember."

"Ah, good. We can kill two birds, so to speak. Do you mind if I record your statement? My penmanship is almost illegible, even to me."

"No. I don't mind."

The man pulled a small recorder out of his pocket, placed it on her pillow and punched the record button.

"This is Detective First Grade, Paul Braddock, Fourteenth Precinct." He named the date and time, the case number and the crime. Then he turned off the recorder momentarily.

"When I turn the machine back on I'd like for you to identify yourself, state the date and the time, as I did, then tell where you are and that you are giving the statement of your own free will."

"All right."

"And when I nod again and hold up two fingers, tell the entire story from start to finish, leaving nothing out, not the tiniest detail. Okay?"

"Yes. I'll do my best." Elizabeth cleared her throat, ready to begin.

"I may say something from time to time, for clarification, but you just pick up where you left off."

"All right."

Detective Braddock started the machine and Elizabeth did as he'd instructed.

"I had just returned to my Houston home after having dinner out with my best friend, Mimi Whittington, who lives next door to our Houston home. We were celebrating."

"What were you celebrating, Mrs. Riordan?" the detective asked.

"I had just received verification from my doctor that I am going to have a baby."

That brought the detective's head up, a look of surprise on his face. "I see. Congratulations." He looked back and forth between the couple, and could discern nothing but happiness and love in their faces.

"I had dropped Mimi off and gone home. Increasingly these days, my energy level nosedives around ten. Anyway, my housekeeper and her husband, who is our handyman, had gone home to their apartment above our garage, so I was alone in the house. I thought.

"After locking up and setting the alarm system I went upstairs to begin my nightly routine in preparation for bed—"

"Uh, excuse me, Mrs. Riordan, but are you certain that you set your alarm?" Detective Braddock questioned. "We all forget at some time or another."

"I am absolutely positive that all the doors and windows were locked. I'm an orderly person, Detective. Some things are so habitual—like brushing my teeth, cleaning and moisturizing my face, combing my hair—that I do them by rote. Locking up is one of them."

Elizabeth continued slowly, relaying every detail, right up to the time she ran out on the terrace to pull Mimi back inside.

"I guess that's when I was shot. Because the next thing I knew my husband was bending over me shouting at me to wake up. The rest of the story you'll have to get from Mimi and Dooley."

"We already have. And their statements gibe with yours. We also conducted a search of your home."

Max frowned. "Without a search warrant?"

"Didn't need one. Your house and the Whittington place are both crime scenes. Besides, Miss Talitha Stanton gave us permission."

"And?" Max prodded.

"The bathroom door received some damage. The perp tried to shoot off the lock, but those old woods are like iron and those old-fashioned locks, while they're easy to pick, don't give way easily to brute force. He never did get into the bathroom."

"He must have heard me when I ran down the stairs," Elizabeth said.

"Most likely. The only other damage was to the study door. We dug a bullet out of the pecan wood."

"Yes. That was the first shot. That must have been when he switched weapons from a garrote to a gun."

"You say you don't know this man?" the detective asked, aiming the question at Elizabeth.

"That's right. I'd never seen him before our trip to New York."

"Hmm. That's another thing we'll get to later. The reason I asked if you knew him is, there were no signs of forced entry. Not anywhere. Our man let himself in with a key and turned off the alarm system."

Detective Braddock had spoken carefully, keeping his tone neutral. He'd watched both of the Riordans for their reactions. They both seemed equally surprised.

"Are you positive?" Elizabeth asked. "I always set the alarm. It's the last thing I do before retiring for the night when I'm in Houston." She shook her head just a tiny bit. "I distinctly recall setting the system last night because I was still walking on air after seeing my doctor, and hoping that Max would come home soon so that I could share the good news with him."

"I see," the detective said. "Well, either someone supplied this guy with a key and the combination to the system or he's a pro at picking locks and disarming alarms. Can you give me the names of everyone who has keys and the alarm code?"

"Mmm, that's hard to say. I know for certain that, other than Max and myself, there are several people who have keys and who know how to turn off the alarm. There's Aunt Talitha, Mimi, Gladys and Dooley, but there are probably others. The locks haven't been changed in…oh…fifty or sixty years. I suppose there have been generations of family and employees who have keys to those old locks."

"I'd recommend that you change all the locks at both homes."

"It's being done right now. I'm also having state-of-the-art alarm systems installed at both places," Max supplied.

Surprise darted through Elizabeth. She spared her husband a look that said we need to talk later.

"Gladys and Dooley? They're the couple who work for you?"

At Elizabeth's nod Detective Braddock went on. "Could there be any resentment there? Any hard feelings? Maybe they don't think they make enough money, or have enough time off, that kind of thing?"

"Absolutely not," Elizabeth replied with a laugh. "Gladys and Dooley have worked for my family since before I was born. Gladys has doctored my skinned knees and spanked my fanny when I needed it. Never—not in a million years—would they hurt me."

"It was Dooley who filled that killer's backside full of bird shot," Max pointed out.

"Ah, I see." The detective scribbled something in his small notepad. "One thing of interest I found in your house was a fax. It was sitting in the tray on the machine. It's from a Detective Gertski in New York, telling you that he'd sent the photo array for a photographic lineup that the two of you had talked about.

"I was curious so I called New York and talked to Detective Gertski. He told me about the two attempts on your life while you were there. And, of course, you just confirmed them. Do you think the man who broke into your home last night is the same one who tried to kill you in New York?"

"Yes. I'm positive."

"And you, Mr. Riordan?"

"I wasn't here, so I didn't see the guy last night, but that would be my guess."

"Hmm. Mine, too," the detective agreed. "Do either of you have any idea who could be behind this? Or why?"

"No, that's the thing. I'm not perfect, but I don't know of anyone who dislikes me enough to have me killed."

"All right. Let's put our heads together. Give me names of people who just might have so much as the tiniest reason to wish you ill."

"Well…my ex-husband comes to mind. But since Edward took all my money and ran away with my worst enemy, I'd say he's already satisfied whatever vengeful feelings he ever had about me."

"You never know," Max said. "Guys like Edward seem to have a convoluted way of looking at things. And of course, they, themselves, are never to blame for anything."

The detective grinned. "I've run into a few of those myself."

"And there's Natalie Brussard. She ran off with Edward to get back at me for who knows what. I guess she thought I would shrivel up and die from a broken heart. She probably blames me that her affair with Edward didn't work out. When she returned to Houston and discovered that I was happily remarried she was livid."

"How about your cousins?" Max asked.

Elizabeth laughed. "Camille and Quinton? Oh, c'mon, Max. Camille is whiny and resentful, but I don't think she would harm me. Can you picture her hiring a hit man? She'd swoon at the sight of that man."

"Mmm. She is a ninny."

"As for Quinton, we've been close for most of our lives. All of his sister's complaining about their financial situation embarrasses him. He once told me in confidence that he and Camille each receive about five hundred thousand a year from their trust. When you have a beautiful, fully paid for, fully furnished five-story brownstone, you're hardly living an impoverished life.

"No." Elizabeth shook her head. "I can't fathom Quinton doing anything to hurt me. With him, what you see is pretty much what you get. He's charming and smart. If he wanted to, and if he applied himself, he could build an empire of his own."

"So why hasn't he?" Max asked.

Elizabeth chuckled. "He admits quite freely that he's never tried because he's too lazy.

"You can rule out Quinton. He's happy with his life just as it is. Jokingly, he claims that being a member of the impoverished branch of an old, revered family is in many ways preferable to being the heir to the riches.

"He's included in all the ritziest affairs, the most exclusive parties, gallery openings, wine tastings. At least once a week he's asked to attend a dinner or card party—usually as the unspoken partner of an unescorted young woman. That is, of course, if the hostess of the affair can find him at home.

"What with all the time spent on yachting trips, country weekends in New Port and often months spent at summer villas in the Caribbean and Tuscany and Greece, he probably spends more time away than he does at his New York brownstone. And all virtually free."

"Hmm. I'd go stark raving mad in a week," Max muttered. He eyed his wife and slipped in a question he'd been wanting to ask ever since the Mosebys had arrived. "Has Quinton ever had romantic feelings toward you?"

"Quinton? Are you kidding? We're cousins."

"Second cousins. There's no law against second cousins marrying. The so-called royals of the world do it all the time."

"Well, the Stantons don't," she said with a chuckle.

"Anyone else?" the detective asked.

"Well, I suppose Wyatt Lassiter might be angry enough to wish me harm. His father as well."

"Damn, woman," Max muttered. "For such a sweet-natured little woman, you sure have pissed off a lot of people."

Elizabeth lifted her chin. "I'd like to see your list."

"Detective Braddock would get writer's cramp."

"That's what I thought."

The detective scribbled some more, then looked up. "Anyone else?"

"Well…there is one other person." Elizabeth looked from the detective to Max. She caught her lower lip between her teeth. "There's Troy."

"Troy? Are you talking about Troy Ellerbee? My right-hand man?"

"Yes. Detective Braddock said name anyone who dislikes me. Troy doesn't like me."

"What makes you think that?"

"Because he told me so."

"What?"

"Max, you must have noticed how Troy gets all tight-jawed and surly whenever I'm around. He resents me and would like nothing better than if I vanished off the face of the earth."

"Maybe. But do you honestly think that Troy is the sort of man who would pay a professional hit man to eliminate you?"

Elizabeth looked at her husband for a long time without answering. "I don't know," she said finally. "And I don't think you do, either."

# Twenty

"There. How does that look, Mimi?" Talitha asked, stepping back to view her own handiwork.

"Mmm. Looks good to me. How 'bout you, sugar?"

"It looks lovely." Lying propped up on one of the sofas, Elizabeth supervised the decorating of the den at Mimosa Landing, happy to be home. And alive.

Normally by this time on Christmas Eve all their decorating—for the exterior and formal rooms—would have been done by professionals. The entire family always decorated the den at Mimosa Landing about a week before Christmas. This year, however, Aunt Talitha had insisted on waiting until Elizabeth was released from the hospital and came home to Mimosa Landing to enjoy the tradition.

"If you ask me, I think the problem is more the height of the tree rather than where the ornaments are placed."

"You know, Camille, I do believe you're right," Iona agreed.

"Oh, pooh on the both of you. This tree is perfect," Talitha declared.

As always, Elizabeth's aunt and Truman had argued about

the height of the tree she'd chosen. When the farm manager had dragged the spruce tree into the den earlier, he'd had to lop two feet off the bottom to make it fit.

"Damn fool woman," he had grumbled. "Says to me, 'We need a big tree. The den's a big room.' Humph. As if I don't know that. Been working here thirty-four years, ain't I?"

Max walked into the den and made a beeline for Elizabeth. "Pull your legs up a bit," he ordered after giving her a kiss. Elizabeth obliged, and he plopped down on the middle sofa cushion, picked up her legs and placed them across his lap.

She was covered with blankets and warm fleece throws. Burrowing through the pile, Max grumbled, "Where're your legs, dammit? You're covered up like a mummy."

"That's right. And don't you go uncovering her just so you can play touchy-feely," her aunt scolded. "She's barely been out of the hospital three hours."

"Would I do a thing like that?"

"Humph. In a New York second, if you got the chance, you rascal. And don't go wasting that tough-guy stare on me, Maxwell Riordan. I'm not impressed. And don't bother to switch to charm, either."

His mother laughed. "She's got you pegged, son."

"You're a bossy old harridan, Talitha Stanton," Max declared in a soft growl, his eyes narrowing.

"That's right. And don't you forget it, you scallywag."

His expression remained stern. Only the tiny twitch of one corner of his mouth gave him away.

He turned his attention back to his wife. "Troy'll be down in a few minutes."

"Mmm." She nodded and looked at the other women, trying not to purr as Max massaged her instep with his thumbs.

"I know we've discussed this before, but I hope you're okay with inviting him for the holidays? I think it'll be good for him to stay here for a while. He's been wound tight these last few weeks. I'm hoping that he'll see how special this place is, how much history it holds. Maybe he'll get bitten by the same bug that bit me."

Plus, Max told himself, on the remote chance that Troy was behind the attempts on Elizabeth's life, he wanted him there, where he could keep an eye on him.

"That would be nice, Max, but you have to accept that not everyone is going to like the country life. Mimi, for instance, likes it, but in short doses."

"I know. But you've got to try something to know whether or not you like it."

"Fine. Just don't be too disappointed if he doesn't share our enthusiasm. And don't you dare leave me alone with him."

Tipping his head to one side, Max studied her. "You really are afraid of him, aren't you?"

"At this point, with the exceptions of you, Dooley and Truman, I'm afraid of every man. Even Detective Gertski in New York. It occurred to me after we left that he stuck to me like glue. He even rode shotgun on our way to the airport. I'm sure that's not normal duty for a New York detective."

"Damn, Elizabeth, you're beginning to sound paranoid. So he went a little above and beyond. I, for one, was grateful for his help."

She waved her hand. "I know. I know. I'm jumping at shadows."

"Relax. You're safe here. To get to the house without using the road you'd first have to climb through several barbed-wire fences, then hike a half mile through a pasture dotted with cow patties and guarded by an unfriendly Texas longhorn bull and a herd of cows, which I can't see a New York hit man doing." Max grinned. "Especially not if he reads the signs Truman put up all around the place."

"What signs?"

"They read, 'No Trespassing unless you can cross this field in eight seconds or less. The bull can cross it in nine.'"

Elizabeth laughed. "You're kidding. Did he really put up signs like that?"

"You bet. I thought it was genius.

"The guards at the gates have the mugshot you picked out. But even if this guy is fool enough to try to get in through the fields, there's no cover. He'd be spotted as soon as he started. To use the driveway or any of the perimeter farm roads he'd have to get by the guards. There are two patrol cars with four cops blocking every gate, and we're in touch with them by walky-talky," Max said, nodding at the set on the coffee table. "Coming or going, no one gets past them without being patted down and their car searched. Well…almost no one." Max shot her aunt a stern look. "Aunt Talitha gave the deputies a tongue-lashing for even suggesting to touch her or her car."

"I should say so," the old woman huffed. "The very idea. Did they honestly think that *I* was going to smuggle in a killer to do away with my great-niece, whom I love as though she were my very own child? I've never been so insulted."

"After seeing her drive, I think they figured nobody would be fool enough to get into a car with her," Max whispered in Elizabeth's ear. "She intimidated the hell out of them.

"Until this morning, when I couldn't find my mother and Martha told me that she and your aunt had gone to the beauty shop to get spruced up for Christmas, I had no idea that Talitha still drove a car. Is that safe at her age?"

"Oh, dear. Don't ever let her hear you ask that," Elizabeth whispered back. "Anyway, she only drives around here—to the beauty shop, her card club, that sort of thing. And she always take the back roads."

"You're kidding me, right? I've seen your aunt on one of

those off-road vehicles that you use around here. Trust me, she's hell on wheels. This morning when she returned she ripped the back bumper right off one of the patrol cars at the gate. She never even stopped. I don't think she was aware of hitting the patrol car."

Max shuddered. "Damn, the thought of her behind the wheel of a car, with my mother riding shotgun, scares the living hell out of me. I can just hear the two of them bickering away about anything and everything while they're bouncing all over the countryside like a pair of geriatric barnstormers."

Through her giggles, Elizabeth managed to whisper, "I know. It's a problem. I just haven't gotten up the nerve to address it yet."

"Good evening, all."

They turned and saw Troy standing in the arched doorway. Elizabeth tensed. Beneath the throw, Max gave her leg a reassuring pat.

"Hey, Troy. Finished unpacking, huh? C'mon in and join us," Max invited.

Elizabeth pulled her legs off his lap and swung her feet to the floor. "Make yourself at home, Troy."

For Max's sake, she had tried to keep her voice polite, but her fear came through all the same. She couldn't help it. This man disliked her. Was it such a leap to hatred?

Troy had traded his suit coat for a navy cardigan over his dress shirt and tie, which Elizabeth supposed was his idea of casual attire. In his arms he carried a stack of gifts that came up to his chin.

"Just put those down on the floor somewhere, Troy," Iona instructed. "We'll arrange them under the tree when we've finished decorating."

Troy did as she instructed, then, to Elizabeth's dismay, he sat down in the chair next to the end of the sofa where she sat. Leaning toward her, he murmured, "Elizabeth, I'd like to talk to you alone—"

"No." She shook her head so sharply it began to throb, and she touched the bandage that wrapped from her temple around to the back. Out of the corner of her eye she saw Max look at her with a disquieting expression. "I…I mean, it's the holidays. No business."

"I phrased that wrong. I don't want to discuss business. This is a personal matter."

"Oh. I see. In that case…maybe later."

"Well, you handsome thing, you, if you're looking for someone to talk to I'm available," Camille said, giving Troy that look that Elizabeth had seen many times before when her cousin was on the prowl for a new man.

*It would serve you right if she caught you,* she thought with uncharacteristic ill will, then immediately felt ashamed of herself, whether for the insult to Troy or her cousin, she wasn't certain.

"You'll do no such thing," Aunt Talitha snapped, thumping her cane. "You get back over here, young lady. You volunteered to help with the decorating and for once in your life you are going to finish what you started, Camille Moseby.

"That's your trouble, young lady. You don't have the fortitude for the long haul. Least little thing comes along to distract you, or annoy you, or looks like greener pastures, or when things don't go exactly your way, you're ready to give up and throw in the towel."

"But, Auntie—"

Giving her great-niece an imperious look, Talitha pointed with her cane to the boxes of ornaments left to hang.

"Oh, all right." Sulking, Camille stomped over to the box and picked up another ornament, muttering under her breath, "I should have gone on that walk with Quinton."

Mimi backed up as though to view the ornament she'd just hung. Drawing even with Troy, she perched on the arm of his chair and whispered, "You look a little green around the gills, sugar lump. Say the word and I'll keep her away from you."

"Oh? How would you manage that?"

"Simple. I'll tell her you and I are an item."

"Huh. Talk about out of the frying pan and into the fire."

"Hmm," Mimi purred, and blinked slowly with almost feline satisfaction. She ran a crimson fingernail through the short, clipped hair at his nape. "Oh, but what a lovely way to burn."

"You should be so lucky," Elizabeth snapped at Troy. "And kindly remember that an invitation to spend the holidays with us does not give you license to insult my friend."

"Sorry. I didn't mean to offend."

"Sure you did," Mimi corrected before turning a concerned look on Elizabeth. "But it's okay, sugar. Don't you go getting yourself upset." She shot Troy a dismissive glance and shrugged one elegant shoulder left bared by the wide neckline of her oversize sweater. "Trust me. I can handle a pipsqueak like Mr. Ellerbee without taking a deep breath."

"Pip-squeak? Now, just a darned minute—"

"What about this one?" On the other side of the room, Camille held up an ornament that was a bit battered and tarnished.

"It looks to me like it's on its last leg," Max said. "Why don't you toss it out?"

"Oh, no! We can't do that," his wife cried. "That ornament has hung on our tree for over a hundred years. I think it should go near the top, where it won't get jostled and possibly broken."

"You're absolutely right," Max agreed.

"Well, then. What are you sitting there for? Get over here, young man, and make yourself useful."

Max narrowed his eyes. "Like I said. A bossy old harridan." Nevertheless, he did Talitha's bidding.

Perhaps to anyone else he looked his usual tough, intimidating self, Elizabeth mused. But she was learning to read Max, and the rare twinkle in his eyes told her that he loved being treated as one of the family.

In the past month he had changed tremendously. The harsh edge was gone, the almost myopic focus on business had broadened to include other aspects of life. He was learning to relax, to appreciate the gifts that he already had—his family and friends, the joy and security of being a part of something lasting like Mimosa Landing.

This land had been here for eons before the Stantons came and assumed stewardship. It would be here long after she and Max were gone. Hopefully their children and grandchildren and many generations beyond would continue that legacy and privilege. There was pride in working the land, a sense of accomplishment, and the sweet pleasure of having found your place in the world.

Max had also learned to open his heart and let love in. To return that love in full measure.

Elizabeth was certain that he had not foreseen that happening when he'd come to her with his bizarre proposal. Or that if he had, he would have gone through with the marriage. But what was done, was done and could not be undone.

Not that he'd want to now. He was truly happy. As was she.

"Now, back to what I was saying," he murmured when he settled back on the sofa with Elizabeth and again put her feet in his lap. "It seems to me that you're doing a lot of smiling for a woman who got out of the hospital just a few hours ago. What're you thinking about, Mrs. Riordan?"

"I was just thinking that, if it weren't for that man out there trying to kill me, this would be the happiest Christmas of my life. I have my family and loved ones with me, I'm head over heels in love with my husband. And I'm going to have my first child."

"First?"

"Yes. I know that I want more than one. Don't you?"

"With you as their mother? You bet." He gave her an intense look that would have scared her witless as little as six weeks ago, but now sent a shiver of delight trickling down her spine. "But let's get back to the other stuff. I particularly like that head-over-heels part."

"You would." As punishment, she pressed her foot against a sensitive part of his anatomy, and was rewarded when he sucked in a breath.

Hooking his hand around the back of her neck, he pulled her upper body closer and whispered while nuzzling her ear, "Oh, baby, you're going to pay for that later."

"How much later?"

Max drew back and read the mischief and desire in her eyes. "I've created a monster," he said, shaking his head. "And you know what the doctor said. No exertion for the next couple of weeks."

It was Elizabeth's turn to groan. "But, Ma-aax."

"Don't try those wiles on me. I'll—"

Martha appeared in the doorway. "Dinner will be ready soon. If Mr. Quinton isn't back from his walk by then, should I hold the meal?"

"Where *is* that boy?" Talitha put down the ornament she'd been about to hang and walked over to the window, twitching aside the sheer panel. "Ah, here he comes now. Goodness gracious, why is he running like that? Oh, my word! The barn is on fire! Smoke is pouring out of the doors!"

"What?"

"Oh, no!"

Talking at once, everyone rushed over to the row of windows across the back wall of the den.

Elizabeth grabbed her husband's hand as he bounded up off the sofa. "Max. Go help put it out. Please. Truman and the hands can't do it alone."

"I'd like to, babe, but I can't leave you here alone."

"Please, Max. Like you said, I'm safe here. Go. Please." She nodded toward Troy. "And take him with you."

He looked through the window at the barn. The smoke was billowing thicker. "All right. But you stay put, okay? Don't budge off this sofa."

"I'll be fine. Go."

"C'mon, Troy."

"*Me?* What can I do? I don't know anything about fighting fires."

"Neither do I, but we'll learn. C'mon!"

The men tore out of the den, grabbing coats off the hooks in the mudroom as they passed by. Max cleared the back porch steps in one leap and took off at a dead run for the barn, Troy following at a jog.

"Fire! The barn's on fire!" Elizabeth heard Quinton yell. "I was coming to get you! C'mon! I think we can save the barn if we hurry!"

The women crowded out onto the back porch, leaving the door open so that Elizabeth could hear. One of the many four-wheelers the farmhands used sat next to the steps. "Hey, hop on," she heard Mimi urge. "We can help, too."

"We can't leave Elizabeth," Talitha said, but her niece could hear the longing in the older woman's voice. Her aunt, bless her soul, dearly loved to be in the middle of things.

"Hold on." Mimi popped back into the house and stuck her head inside the den. "Will you be okay here with Martha for a few minutes?"

"Of course." She made a shooing motion with her hands. "Go. Go. They need all the help they can get."

For good measure, Mimi stuck her head into the kitchen, too. "Martha, sweetie, stay with our girl, will you?"

"Of course. Go on with you."

The four-wheeler started up. When the sound began to recede, Elizabeth disobeyed Max's order, leaving the sofa to totter over to the windows. She pulled back the curtain and caught her breath. "Oh, dear."

The barn itself wasn't on fire, she was somewhat relieved to see. The blaze had started in a haystack next to it. Probably by a carelessly flicked match or cigarette, she thought. The barn was in danger, however. Already flames were licking at one of the doors and smoke billowed against a spectacular sunset.

The barn was one of the oldest structures on the farm, and the thought of losing it made Elizabeth feel sick.

"Take a good look, lady. That's the last thing you're gonna see."

The brassy, New York-accented voice shot through Elizabeth like an arrow shaft. She spun around, then had to grasp the windowsill behind her to keep her balance. For a moment the room tilted slowly, then righted, and her gaze locked on the massive man in the black leather trench coat.

Illogically, it ran through Elizabeth's head that the man standing in the arched doorway fit Mimi's description of him to a T. *Loathsome-looking beast—like a slimy slug in a fancy suit.*

"You. How did you get in here?"

"You mean past those dumb-ass country cops? Easy. Having a copy of your aunt's keys helped, of course. It was cramped in that trunk, though."

"You hid in Aunt Talitha's trunk? How...how did you know they wouldn't search her car?"

"I have my sources. You've been one lucky broad. Fact is, you've become an embarrassment. But your luck has run out. I've had enough of Texas and crazy gun-toting women."

"Why? Why are you doing this to me?"

"It's what I do. People pay me to kill other people."

"Who is paying you? I'll pay you more. Please, don't do this. For God's sake, I'm going to have a baby."

"Is that right? Too bad. This is personal now. I don't like being made to look bad." He raised a gun with a silencer on the barrel. "Say your prayers quick."

*Phttt!*

Elizabeth screamed and made a dive for the floor behind a high-backed Queen Anne chair as a lamp exploded six inches from her hip.

*Phttt! Phttt!*

Tufts of cotton batting and upholstery material shot out of the back of the chair, just inches above Elizabeth's head, and she screamed again.

"Mercy sake's alive, what's all the racket in here—" Drying a coffee cup, Martha came around the corner from the kitchen.

The man swung the gun her way and squeezed off another shot.

*Phttt!*

"Martha, get down! Get down!"

The housekeeper threw the china cup straight up and began to dance around, hysterically flapping her hands and screaming every breath. "Aaah! Aaah!"

"Martha! Get down!"

"Shut the hell up!" the killer shouted, and punctuated the order with another shot. *Phttt!*

The volume of Martha's screams racheted up another notch.

Whether it was sheer dumb luck or the power of prayer, her hysterical dance took her out the door, through the mudroom and onto the back porch.

"Damn fool woman," the gunman grumbled.

Lying with her cheek pressed to the cold hardwood floor, head throbbing, heart pounding, her lungs working like a smithy's bellows and Martha's receding screams echoing in her ears, Elizabeth struggled to figure a way out. Think. Think, for God's sake. You have to *do* something. You can't just lie here like a lamb and wait to be slaughtered. *Think!*

She glanced toward the gunman. From beneath the chair she saw his mirror-polished shoes heading her way. Oh, God.

Then she saw it, right in front of her nose—Mimi's impossibly large tote bag, sitting on the floor beside the chair. Another glance at the approaching shoes told her she didn't have much time. Breathing hard, she worked her right arm out of its sling, grabbed the purse and yanked it to her.

*Phttt.*

"Whaddaya gonna do, huh? Hit me with your purse?" he said with a dry chuckle that sent a chill down Elizabeth's spine.

Ignoring the pain in her shoulder, she jammed both hands into the bag and made a whimpering sound of gratitude when they closed around the grip of the .357 Magnum and her forefingers found the trigger. In one desperate, continuous motion she rolled to her back and lifted her arms, leather purse and all, and as the black-clad figure came around the chair and loomed over her, she squeezed the trigger.

*Ka-boom!*

The bottom of Mimi's purse exploded and the recoil bucked Elizabeth's hands up over her head. If the purse had not been around the weapon it would probably have jumped right out of her hands.

The massive man gave an "oof" and stumbled backward several steps, clutching his abdomen, a stunned look on his face. He tumbled over a sofa, taking it over backward with him.

*Phttt! Phttt!*

On the way down he got off two wild shots before sprawling on his back, taking out a two-hundred-year-old vase on the fireplace mantel and gouging a hole in the original old pressed-tin ceiling of the den.

Sobbing, tears streaming down her face, Elizabeth climbed to her knees and held the gun out at arm's length again.

*Ka-boom!*

"Aaah! Don't shoot! Don't shoot! I give up. For crissake, lady, don't shoot me again."

From outside came shouts and screams. Max bellowed her name over and over. The sounds grew closer, but Elizabeth paid no attention. She clutched the arm of the mutilated Queen Anne chair and climbed to her feet. Unsteady but determined, she staggered across the room to the man, both arms stuffed into what was left of Mimi's purse, holding the Magnum in a two-handed grip. The gun's wobbling barrel protruded an inch or so from the gaping bottom.

She edged around the end of the sofa and the man lifted his gun, but his hand was so wobbly he could barely hold it.

"You're too...trusting, you stupid bitch," he said in his chilling flat voice. "This is a Glock. It holds...nine shots. I've...I've got one left."

"I've got more than one," Elizabeth said through gritted teeth. She was shaking and her tears streamed like an open faucet, but she didn't budge.

"You won't kill me. You don't have what it takes."

"Are you crazy? You tried to kill me and my unborn child. You so much as twitch and I'll blow your head off. I want to know who hired you."

He shook his head. "No." He groaned and pressed his free hand to his belly. "I'm...gut shot. For crissake, call 911."

"No. Not until you tell me who is paying you to kill me."

"C'mon, lady. I'm...in agony here."

"My sympathy is all used up. You can lie there and bleed to death, for all I care. I'm not calling for help until you give up the name. From the look of the puddle of blood, you'd better hurry."

The Glock slid out of his fingers and clattered to the hard-wood floor.

Elizabeth kicked it aside.

"All right. I'll...I'll tell...you," he whispered. "Be-bend down."

"Oh, no. This is as...close as I get. Just say it."

Unable to make a sound, he mouthed the name.

Elizabeth's eyes widened. "No. You're lying. You must be lying."

*"Elizabeth!"* Max yelled, and heavy footsteps hit the back porch.

The man made a feeble attempt to shake his head. "N-no. Not...ly...ing. Sw-swear. Please." His eyes began to roll back in his head.

*"Elizabeth!"*

Never taking her gaze from the gunman, she withdrew one hand from the purse, took the receiver off the phone sitting on a nearby table and punched in 911. At the same instant Max burst into the room.

His face was red, his eyes wild. "Elizabeth! Thank God!" He crossed the room in two long strides and snatched her into his arms. "Are you all right? Did he hurt you again?"

Sobbing, her knees buckling, Elizabeth sagged against Max and burrowed her face against his chest.

"This is 911. What is your emergency?" came a distant

voice from the telephone. "Ma'am? Ma'am, are you there? Please state your emergency."

Max picked up the receiver. "This is Max Riordan at Mimosa Landing. We have a man shot. Send an ambulance and the police."

"Did you say a man has been shot?" the operator asked.

"Just get somebody here. Fast."

"Sir, don't hang up. Don't hang—"

Max dropped the receiver and wrapped both arms around his wife.

More footsteps hammered across the back porch as the others began arriving. Soon everyone but Truman and the farmhands was crowded around, talking at once. They were making so much noise it took a few minutes for anyone to realize that the walkie-talkie sitting on the coffee table was squawking.

"This is Deputy Peters on the gate guard. Was that gunfire we heard?"

"Somebody answer that," Max barked. Holding on to Elizabeth with an iron grip, he could not stop running his hands over her body again and again, reassuring himself that she was, indeed, unharmed.

"Sir? Sir? Are you still there?"

Troy picked up the telephone receiver. On the verge of hysteria, Elizabeth almost laughed. Always a spiffy dresser who looked as though he'd just stepped from the pages of *GQ* magazine, Troy's face and clothing were covered with soot, as were Max's. "You heard the man. Get an ambulance and police to Mimosa Landing." He replaced the receiver, then calmly picked up the walkie-talkie. "Affirmative, Detective. We've had gunfire. A man is shot."

"We're on our way."

Quinton picked up the Glock. "I'll take this character into

another room away from the ladies and keep an eye on him until they get here."

*"No!"* Elizabeth turned within Max's embrace. "Put the gun down, Quinton," she sobbed, doing her level best to lift the Magnum again. "Now! Put it down or I'll shoot."

"Elizabeth! Have you lost your mind?" Camille demanded.

"No. It was Quinton who hired this man to kill me."

"Wha-what?"

"C'mon, cuz," Quinton coaxed. "You know me. I wouldn't do a thing like that. I love you. We've been buddies and pals since we were kids."

"It's too late, Quinton. You can't bluff or charm your way out of this. Before this…this creature lost consciousness, he told me who had hired him."

Quinton looked offended. "And you're going to take the word of a hired killer over mine?"

"Yes."

Cars screeched to a halt in the driveway and a second later the deputies banged on the door. "Police! Open up!"

A calmer but still shaken Martha started to go let them in, but Quinton pointed the gun at her.

"Stay where you are!"

"Oh, Quinton," his sister moaned. "You did hire him. Even after finding out she was pregnant, you didn't call him off."

Ignoring her, he swung the Glock from the housekeeper back to Elizabeth. "All of you stay where you are. I'm leaving."

"You're not going anywhere." Elizabeth tried again to raise the mutilated purse and gun. "I have a gun, too. And I have four shots left. Your hired gun has already fired all nine of his. Weren't you counting?"

Doubt flickered across Quinton's face for an instant, but

he decided to call her bluff. "I don't believe you. I don't think he'd be that stupid. Anyway, you won't shoot me. I doubt if you've got the strength even if you managed to muster the will."

"Open up! Open up in there!"

Surreptitiously, while Quinton had been watching Elizabeth, Max had slid his hands down her arms inside the purse. His hands closed over hers and steadied the wobbling gun. "If she won't, I sure as hell will," he growled, aiming the barrel at Quinton's heart. "And at this range, I can't miss."

Aunt Talitha stepped forward. The subtle move put her partway between her nephew and Elizabeth and Max. "Quinton Moseby, put down that gun this instant."

He swung the weapon toward the old woman. "Sorry, Aunt Talitha. I'm not a little boy anymore. That tone doesn't scare me now. I love you, Auntie. I truly do. Just as I love Elizabeth. I don't want to shoot either of you, but I will."

"You'll do no such thing," Camille declared, stepping between their aunt and her brother. "I'm not going to let you do something so despicable."

"Get out of the way, Camille. What are you being so protective for, anyway? You hate Elizabeth."

"For heaven's sake, Quinton. I don't hate Elizabeth. Oh, I admit I've always been envious of her. Who can blame me? She's beautiful and smart and always the perfect lady. Everyone likes her. Most of all I'm envious that she got to grow up here. But I still love her. She's family. I did all that grousing just to pull her chain a little.

"No matter what you all think, I'm not stupid. I know that Elizabeth hasn't and wouldn't cheat us. Our branch of the family has already received its share of the Stanton holdings. You and I just had the bad luck to have the flighty twin sister for our grandmother, is all.

"But I swear to you, I didn't mean any of that stuff I've been taunting Elizabeth with all these years."

"It doesn't matter. I had to. As you pointed out, if she has that child it will inherit everything. This way, with her and the child and Aunt Talitha gone, everything would have been ours. Now she's ruined it all."

"So I was to be next, was I?" their aunt snapped, her regal head held high.

"No. I figured I would step in and take Elizabeth's place running everything until you died. I swear, I never planned to kill you, Auntie."

"Humph. That's some comfort, I suppose."

"I don't understand, Quinton," Elizabeth said. "Why this sudden desperate need for money? You have what most people would consider a generous income and you've always seemed to enjoy your life as it is."

"True. But I'm in deep trouble, cuz. I owe a great deal of money to some very nasty, very dangerous people. The only reason they haven't nailed my knees to the floor already is because I told them I would inherit the Stanton fortune if I could get rid of you."

"Let me guess," Max inserted. "Gambling, right?"

"Right." He nodded toward the gunman. "He's the enforcer for the man to whom I owe the money."

"Oh, Quinton," his sister moaned. "Put the gun down and let's talk this over. We'll come up with a way to get the money."

"Don't you get it, Camille? It's too late for that. And I can't go to jail. I can't."

"Maybe it won't come to that." Camille turned to Elizabeth with a pleading expression. "Please, Elizabeth. Don't press charges. He's sick. Don't you see that? He has to be sick to have done such a thing. Pembrook Manor in upstate New

York is a lovely sanitarium, I'm told. He could go there and get some help, and get his head straight."

She turned back to her brother. "There won't be any stigma attached. Several of our friends have checked themselves in to Pembrook for treatment for stress. Why, it's almost the thing to do these days."

"Camille, child, I admire your love for your brother, but you don't always get to take the easy way out," Aunt Talitha said with uncharacteristic gentleness. "Don't you understand? This is out of Elizabeth's hands now. Even though Quinton's plan didn't succeed, he committed a serious crime by merely hiring this man to kill her."

"But, Auntie—"

"I'm sorry, child. For you and your brother. I truly am. However, in life there comes a time when you have to step up and take the consequences of your actions. That's something you and your brother have never had to do before.

"I blame most of this on my sister and your father. If Mariah hadn't spoiled him and the two of you, you wouldn't have grown up with this ridiculous sense of entitlement. Mariah always covered up for your father and you and Quinton whenever you got into mischief as teenagers. But this is a lot more serious than shooting up a few road signs or spraying graffiti on an overpass, or that time that Quinton got picked up for being drunk and disorderly. This time he's gone too far. Now he has to pay the piper.

"We will see to it that Quinton gets a good lawyer, but that's as far as family loyalty will stretch."

"No. No, that won't do." Quinton began to back away, shaking his head, the Glock held with the barrel pressed to his temple. His eyes were wild. "I can't take the chance of going to prison. I can't! I wouldn't survive a day in a place like that. I'd rather be dead."

"Quinton, no!" Camille took a step toward him, but he held his hand up, palm out to stop her, and transferred the barrel of the gun to his mouth.

While Quinton's gaze was focused on his aunt and sister, Max took the gun from Elizabeth and shifted her around behind him.

Her cousin kept backing up, his gaze swinging back and forth.

Truman appeared in the doorway behind him, his forefinger against his lips, signaling the others for silence. The old ranch foreman was several inches shorter than Quinton and probably fifty pounds lighter, but he was wiry and tough as a pine knot. Elizabeth had no doubt that he could overpower her cousin. Peeking around Max, she caught her breath as Truman stepped forward. In a blur of motion he knocked the gun out of Quinton's hand and wrapped his arms around him from behind.

For a few minutes all hell broke loose as the men tried to subdue Quinton. Martha rushed to the door to let in the deputies and paramedics, while the women all talked at once.

"Ma-Max…"

Elizabeth tugged on the back of her husband's sooty shirt and he turned just as her knees buckled.

"Elizabeth!" He scooped her up before she hit the floor. "Elizabeth! What's wrong? Did one of those shots hit you?" he demanded, his gaze fixing on the widening red stain on her sweater. "Ah, dammit! She's torn open her shoulder wound."

"There are a couple of ambulances outside," one of the paramedics told him. "I'll ride with you and do what I can to stop the bleeding."

"I've got a better idea. I'm flying her to Houston by helicopter. You're coming with us."

The paramedic glanced at Max's tough face. "Oh. Well, sir, I'd like to, but I'm with the Brenham Hospital. I'm afraid I'm not licensed to work in Harris County, and your wife needs quick attention."

"I don't give a damn about your license. You're coming with us. Now move! The rest of you sort everything out here with these officers," he bellowed on the way out. "When you're done, meet us at Methodist Hospital. Troy, you take care of things. Call and get me air clearance and permission to land at the medical center. Tell them I'm landing, no matter what. And look after these women."

"I'm on it, boss." Troy touched Elizabeth's arm and leaned in close. "You're one helluva woman, Elizabeth Stanton Riordan." His eyes met Max's. "Good luck."

Truman had run ahead to the helipad and was manning the gas pump when they arrived. "Thought you might want this thing topped off."

He replaced the gas cap and helped Max and the paramedic load Elizabeth into the chopper. "Thanks, Truman."

"Uh, Mr. Riordan? Two things before you go. Me 'n' the hands put the fire out. And I just thought you oughta know, I saw Mr. Quinton start that fire. It weren't no accident. I was coming inside to tell you that when I saw him holding a gun on y'all."

Max paused just an instant, his expression murderous. "Thanks, Truman. Thanks a lot."

He climbed into the cockpit, ran through a quick safety check and fired up the chopper. "You and the patient buckled in back there?" he shouted over the noise.

"Yessir."

"Then shut the damned door and put on these headsets so you can keep me informed."

"Oh. Yessir. Sorry." The man looked a little pale, but he twisted around and slammed the door. "Ready."

Max reached around behind him between the seats and touched his wife's foot. "Hang on, sweetheart. You hang on. You hear me?"

Elizabeth's foot wiggled, and Max took that as a yes. "Okay. Here we go!" he yelled, and with a steady *whomp, whomp, whomp, whomp, whomp* the gold-and-blue helicopter lifted into the blazing sunset, made an arching U-turn east and headed into the purple twilight over Houston.

# *Epilogue*

Max stood outside the door of the VIP hospital suite, watching Elizabeth through the glass window in the door. Happiness permeated every cell in his body. He'd never known that anyone could be this happy. That it was possible to love a woman the way he loved Elizabeth.

It had been almost eight months since he'd flown her to this very hospital, not knowing if he'd lose her, not knowing if he could go on without her. Eight months of happiness and contentment, of watching her grow and blossom with their child. He hadn't thought that he could love or admire her any more.

Then all day yesterday and through half the night he'd held her hand as she endured the pain and exhausting work of labor and childbirth, and his heart had filled with so much love he'd thought it would surely burst.

He shook his head slightly at his own arrogance. "You're one lucky bastard, Maxwell Riordan," he murmured to himself. He'd married himself a trophy wife as an entry into so-

ciety and their deep coffers, but the real prize had turned out
to be the woman herself.

"What are you doing out here in the hallway?" Aunt Talitha demanded.

Max turned his head and smiled at the entourage headed
toward him. Besides Elizabeth's aunt, his mother, Mimi, Martha, Truman, Gladys, Dooley and Troy came tromping down
the hallway, loaded down with huge stuffed animals, balloons, flowers, candy and magazines. They had all left here
around two in the morning, exhausted and walking on air.
Now that they were rested, they were all itching to get their
hands on the newest heir to the throne.

"Shh." Max placed his forefinger over his pursed lips.
"Before we go inside I want you all to see something."

He urged them to squeeze tight around the window and
look inside. "Isn't that the most beautiful sight you've ever
seen?"

Elizabeth sat up in the adjustable hospital bed, her baby
cradled in the crook of one arm, her gaze fixed on the sleeping infant's face. To Max, she was the essence of woman, loving, nurturing, strong and soft and so beautiful she took his
breath away. He knew that if he lived to be a hundred he'd
never forget this moment.

"Oh, my. Oh, she's so beautiful." Misty-eyed, Talitha
turned to Max and cupped his cheek with her hand. "Thank
you for sharing this with us. They look like the Madonna and
Child."

She and the other women dabbed at their eyes. Dooley and
Truman surreptitiously wiped at theirs as well.

"I know. I've already contacted a portrait painter. I want
them painted that way before the baby gets too big."

"You're a smart man." Talitha gave his arm a pat. "And a

good one. If I haven't told you so before now, we're all happy to have you in our family."

"Thanks. That means a lot." He looked around and grinned. "Now, who wants to hold Molly Elizabeth Stanton-Riordan? The most beautiful baby girl ever born."